FIRE AND I

Douglas Br... ...ncer, is now a Journe... ...g, more skills . . . and

Myrn, his bride... ...an Apprentice Aquamancer. Which means her powers of water will match Douglas's powers of fire.

Traveling into unknown lands to face an unknown evil, Douglas must put his skills to the test—without any help from his Master, Flarman. But the rules don't say anything about getting help from an Apprentice Aquamancer. Which Douglas needs when he's captured by a Coven of Witches . . .

AQUAMANCER

Praise for Don Callander's first novel, PYROMANCER:

"The Sorcerer's animated kitchen is a delight, as is his brassy Bronze Owl. I liked the revelation that the job of a fire-magician is to control fire as well as make it. That never occurred to me before. . . . There are nice original touches here."—PIERS ANTHONY

Ace Books by Don Callander

PYROMANCER
AQUAMANCER

AQUAMANCER

DON CALLANDER

ACE BOOKS, NEW YORK

This book is an Ace original edition
and has never been previously published.

AQUAMANCER

An Ace Book / published by arrangement with
the author

PRINTING HISTORY
Ace edition / January 1993

ISBN: 0-441-02816-0

Ace Books are published by The Berkley Publishing Group,
200 Madison Avenue, New York, New York 10016.
The name "ACE" and the "A" logo
are trademarks belonging to Charter Communications, Inc.

PRINTED IN THE UNITED STATES OF AMERICA

10 9 8 7 6 5 4 3 2 1

This book is for my own Myrn, Carol Ann, a daughter who has always had the kind of loving good nature and personal courage to prevail against all Ghouls, Ogres, Wicked Black Witches, Chimaeras, Banshees, Trolls, Barrow-Wights, Nightmares, Griffins, Gargoyles, Furies, Phantasms, Demons, Fiends, Gyres, Vampires, Bogies, Werewolves, Ghosts, Goblins and Hobgoblins, and all other dire things that go *bump* in the night.

—Don Callander
27 June 1991

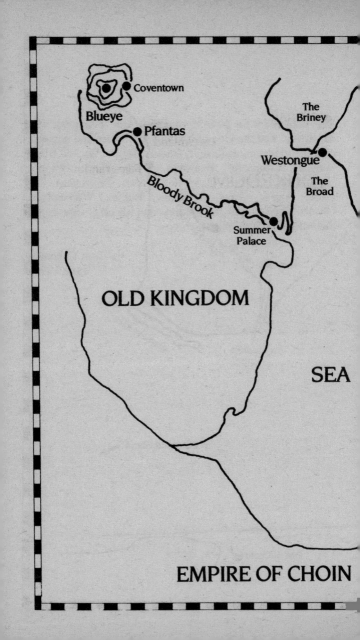

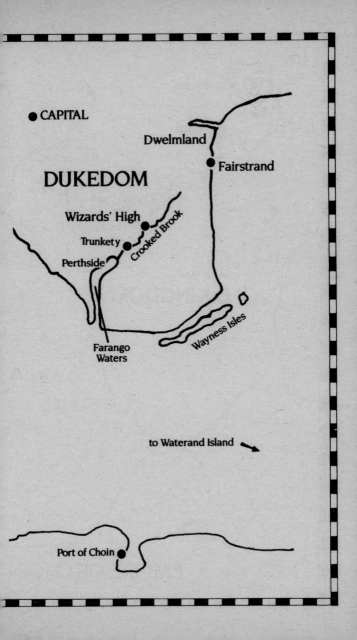

AQUAMANCER

Prologue

or, WHAT CAME BEFORE?

DOUGLAS Brightglade, son of a master shipbuilder lost at sea, apprenticed himself to a Fire Wizard, or Pyromancer, Flarman Flowerstalk, also called Firemaster, and lived at Flarman's home, Wizard's High, in Valley, in the land called Dukedom. After several years of intensive training, Douglas rose to the rank of Journeyman Pyromancer.

Douglas and his Master were called upon to assist a Water Adept, Aquamancer Augurian of Waterand Island, in battle against the very powerful and wicked Ice King, Frigeon.

Their ways parted, as Flarman undertook a mission of great danger to Frigeon's Ice Palace on the glacier Eternal Ice. Douglas was entrusted with the delivery of a magic Great Gray Pearl to Augurian.

While Flarman was matching wits with Frigeon, Douglas was lost overboard from a ship at Sea, was rescued by the Asrai, a Phosphorescence, and was cast ashore on Flowring Isle, where he met a pearl fisher's beautiful daughter, Myrn Manstar.

When Myrn was kidnapped by Duke Eunicet, one of Frigeon's evil minions, Douglas went to her rescue assisted by a Great Sea Tortoise named Oval.

Meanwhile, Flarman had escaped from Frigeon and sailed to Augurian's Waterand Island, where he and Douglas were reunited. The two Fire Wizards helped Augurian launch a fateful Sea Battle against Frigeon and his host of Goblins, Ghouls, Ogres, Banshees, and bloodthirsty renegade Men.

Under cover of this Battle of Sea, the Wizard and his Journeyman gained entrance to Frigeon's magic workshop deep inside the glacier under Ice Palace and destroyed the Pearl, a talisman that allowed the Ice King to be completely wicked.

Augurian enrolled Myrn as his own Apprentice, and she and Douglas planned to wed when she was far enough along in her studies. Meanwhile, the survivors gathered together to begin undoing the evil enchantments wrought by the Ice King. Frigeon himself was exiled to his glacier, which was rapidly melting away, creating a New Land.

Upon their triumphant return to Wizards' High, Flarman's cottage in Valley of Dukedom, Flarman gave a wonderful Homecoming Party for everybody who helped defeat the Ice King—and the Pyromancer assigned Journeyman Douglas Brightglade to Journey in his craft to Old Kingdom, to check on reports of a Coven of Black Witches there, and earn his full Mastery.

Here the story continues. . . .

PART ONE

Journeying

Chapter One

![decorative divider]

Leaving Home

JOURNEYMAN Wizard Douglas Brightglade, student of
the arcane and ancient magical arts and sciences, colleague of
Master Pyromancer Flarman Flowerstalk, fiancé of Apprentice Aquamancer Myrn Manstar of Flowring Isle, friend of
Dwarfs, Faeries, Dragons, Sea Creatures, Wraiths, and resident of Wizards' High in Valley of Dukedom, opened his
eyes to bright winter sunshine coming through his unshuttered
bedroom windows.

He stretched his arms wide and yawned, shook his close-
cropped brown locks, rubbed his Sea blue eyes, and slid his
bare feet out from under the counterpane.

In a furry flurry, Pert and Party, Wizards' High's resident
female cats, jumped from the foot of his bed to the broad-
planked floor and scurried to the window, mewing a greeting
to Douglas and to the morning.

"Breakfast!" said the Journeyman, aloud to himself, "but
a bath first. Then say good-bye and start my Journeying."

"Journeymen," said Bronze Owl, gliding through the open
window with a tremendous clatter of metal wings to perch
upon the bedstead, "are, by definition, travelers."

"I know! I know!" cried Douglas, pulling on his trousers.
This morning was the last of such homey comfort he could
expect for many a day. He was off on a mission for the
Fellowship of Wizards—at the moment consisting of himself, Flarman Flowerstalk, and the Water Adept, Augurian
of Waterand Island and Warm Seas—that very morning.

Bounding down the curving staircase, he found Blue Teakettle sputtering busily about her wide, slate-topped kitchen
worktable, herding pots and pans across the range, spouting
rapid-fire orders to Salt and Pepper, Butter Firkin and her

Wooden Molds, and to Toast Rack on the open hearth. Douglas greeted them all with a cheery wave and an appreciative sniff as he went through the kitchen door to the washstand, just outside in the courtyard between the cottage and the underhill barns and workshop.

The white porcelain ewer was filled with hot water, which sent clouds of steam into the winter-cold air. A fresh bar of soap rested in a slotted wooden soap stand near to hand. Clean, fluffy towels hung on bars under the washstand. Douglas's Razor, Shaving Brush and Mug, and brown leather Strop jumped into action at his appearance. Razor ran rapidly and smoothly up and down Strop, honing a keen edge for the young Wizard's fuzzy whiskers, while Brush jumped gleefully into Mug and whipped up a froth of fragrant lather.

The Journeyman Wizard washed and shaved, combed and dried, prancing from foot to foot on the chilly slates. He could have made them warm as toast at a magic word, but preferred to feel the tingle and pleasant pain of the cold on his bare toes.

Across the wide courtyard, through the door of the Wizard's workshop came a rumbling fuss. Firemaster Flarman Flowerstalk was having trouble with some experiment or other. A cloud of purple smoke poured through the open transom above the workshop's wide door, scattering the doves who were perched there arguing good-naturedly over the remnants of their breakfast.

The placid Ladies of the Byre paused to look back in bovine amusement. They were already on their way through the courtyard gate to the frost-whitened brookside meadow. Seven chickens paused a moment in their perpetual pecking, looked up in mild surprise, then went back to pursuing the last few insects of summer and spilled grains of wheat and barley in the cracks between the courtyard cobbles.

"Ding dang! Double fudge and saltwater taffy! Grumbles and mumbles!" came the Wizard's deep roar. *"Drat!!"*

Douglas grinned to himself. He quickly rinsed and carefully dried Razor before putting it in its leather traveling case along with Strop, rolled up tight, and Shaving Brush and a vial of fragrant, frothy liquid soap. He tied it all with an old leather thong.

"*Flagpant! Cryptomagler! Oh, Graddish!*" Flarman's vex-ation came flying from the workshop. The words seemed meaningless bluster . . . or perhaps they were enchantment words of some arcane spell Douglas had not yet learned. He indulged his large Bump of Curiosity by skipping across the courtyard to look in at the workshop's open door.

Pyromancer Flarman Flowerstalk stood on a tall, three-legged stepladder, furiously wielding a broom with one hand and a feather duster with the other. Clouds of bright dust swirled about him in a shaft of sunlight slanting through the transom. He sneezed explosively.

"*Oh, Graddish! Kerplunkt! Oh, Darnnat!*" he growled, attacking four years' accumulation of cobwebs and the con-densates of thousands of smoky alchemical procedures.

"What in World are you doing, Magister?" asked Douglas, laughing aloud in spite of himself at the sight.

"Spring cleaning!" replied the Wizard, giving in to a powerful sneeze. He floated gently down from the ladder top. "Cobwebs and dust balls, trash under the table, soot over the mantel, ashes beneath the grate! Once I had an Apprentice I could order to do this sort of thing but now I'm all alone and have to do it for myself, despite the fact that I am by far the oldest, most powerful, most highly respected Pyromancer in . . . in . . . Valley, anyway."

"I could help you," said Douglas, knowing this beloved blusterer very well, "or we could go in to break our fast and you could finish all this spring cleaning later—say *next* spring—although it should have been done months ago."

Things had been happening too fast and furiously ever since the Wizard and his Journeyman had gone off to subdue the Ice King, who had threatened to freeze World and enslave its various peoples. Flarman had been captured and taken to an Ice Palace on a glacier far to the north while Douglas had been lost at Sea, been rescued by a giant Sea Tortoise named Oval, and had fallen in love. Housekeeping had fallen by the wayside.

Along with a powerful Water Adept and a host of Faerie warriors, Dwarfs, Near Immortals, Sprites, Sea creatures and birds, fishermen and sailors, they had over-come wicked Frigeon in a great Sea Battle, destroyed his

dire enchantments—along with his Ice Palace—and rescued the Ice King's captives, including Douglas's own
father.

Like all momentous events, the Battle of Sea had been
followed by a great many important things to be done, like
the marvelous Homecoming Party at Wizards' High late
the last summer. Now, Douglas hoped, things were getting
back to normal—whatever normal was for a Journeyman
Pyromancer.

"I choose breaking my fast anytime," chuckled the old
Fire Wizard, throwing the broom and the duster into the
farthest corner of the workshop, where they got together
to continue the cleaning without supervision. "And if this
cleaning didn't get done *last* spring, what makes you think
I'll do it *next* spring? No, I'll do it after breakfast. After you
leave, that is."

This last he said with a touch of sadness, for Douglas's
new journey promised to be a long, dangerous one. Flarman
had once been content to be a solitary practitioner of Fire
Magic, almost a hermit, but that was before Douglas had
come to be his Apprentice. Soon they had grown to be the
fastest of friends, boon companions.

There had been nothing but company since they had helped
put an end to the wickednesses of the Ice King.

"This is the first time in months and months we've had
the place to ourselves for a few days," observed young
Douglas as they ate griddle cakes with fresh-churned butter
and maple syrup, flipped high and hot from Blue Kettle's
cast Iron Griddle. "The Homecoming Party and the visitors
since we returned to the High . . ."

". . . and a Wedding scheduled for the next Midwinter's
Day after this one," added Bronze Owl, who never hungered
nor ate, being solid cast metal. He was the guardian of the
front door to the cottage, and Douglas's wise teacher in all
matters of animal and fairy worlds. He came to the breakfast
table just for the conversation.

"And a Wedding, which is a tremendously long way off!
Does anyone miss Myrn as much as I do?" wondered Douglas,
wistfully. He stared mournfully at his latest forkful of pancake,
then popped it into his mouth and sighed at the same time.

"Hardly!" laughed Flarman, spearing his own fourth, fifth, and sixth of the fluffy, golden brown pecan pancakes from Griddle. "But then, none of the rest of *us* plan to marry the lass."

"Perhaps not," said Owl, "but the place seems emptier without Myrn Manstar blithely about and around. She brings her own kind of sunshine, doesn't she?"

"I'd groan with agony," said Douglas, "except it isn't becoming for a Journeyman Wizard to display such emotion."

"Ha!" snorted Flarman. "Bawl your head off if you like! No one will notice!"

"But even you must admit that Wizards' High just isn't the same without pretty Myrn," said the Owl, "or is it my imagination?"

"Not at all!" said Flarman. "Myrn Manstar, soon to be Brightglade, is already a part of me and mine, I'm happy to say. Has she written us this week yet, m'boy?"

Douglas pulled a carefully rolled piece of parchment from his left sleeve—he had long ago taken to carrying important things in the deep, wide sleeves of his Wizard's robe, as did his Master—and held it out to Flarman.

"No, no!" said the Wizard, shaking his head vigorously. "Read the parts you want us to share. I know all about lovers' letters."

Douglas was a bit startled at this revelation. He'd never imagined Flarman as a love-struck youngster.

"Come to think of it, I don't see why not," he said, although Flarman thought he referred to reading the letter aloud.

Douglas read (in part):

" '*My Dearest Douglas,*
    I have a few moments now to write, between day's work and night's sleep, both of which I anticipate with much joy, as they bring me closer to the things I am most eager for—and I hardly need tell you what those are! The lessons are hard but fascinating, and my Master says I am learning them well, and fast!
    " '*All goes smoothly for a Flowring Isle lass whose ambitions a scant year ago were simply to own and sail*

*her very own fishing smack, get married, and have at
least four or five sons and daughters to be pearl fishers
after her.*

*" 'At the moment I am just beginning to learn the
making of tea. Yes, this is a very important aspect
of Aquamancy, my Master tells me. The powers of
prognostication come, he says, from the water. The
tea leaves are only a catalyst. I actually managed,
yesterday, to predict the exact hour of our daily rain-
storm . . . no great feat when you know it comes each
afternoon at the same hour.*

*" 'But I don't want to spend these precious few minutes
with you talking shop. Suffice to say, I brew and pour very
good teas, which would surprise my good mother!*

*" 'Living on Waterand is luxury compared to life on
Flowring, although I often wish I were home, sailing on
Father's boat or diving for pearls, as I did before I met a
certain young Fire Wizard, whom I miss even more than
sailing. . . .*

*" 'Augurian just knocked on my door to tell me that
the Mail Porpoise is about to leave for the Mainland,
and can carry this letter to you although not as quickly
as our old friend Deka, but the good Wraith is very busy
these days. So I'll close. My Master says to say that he
is well and very busy, or he would bring me by for one
of Blue Teakettle's wonderful dinners.*

*" 'As for me, if I had time I would pine for your
touch and your smile . . . and Flarman's and Owl's and
everyone's there at the High. As it is, I must close
and send with this all my love, husband-to-be! Write
to me soon!*

" 'I am, then, yours . . . entirely! Myrn' "

"I'll be with Augurian in a week or so," murmured the
Wizard. "Have you answered her letter?"

"I've written a short note only, telling her about my
departure and reminding that I will probably not be able
to write regularly for some time," said Douglas, handing
him another piece of parchment. "I expect you will keep
her informed, too?"

"As well as you keep *me* informed. She'd rather have it direct from you, of course. You can perhaps find some messengers where you're going, to carry your letters to her—and to Augurian and me on Waterand, too. And there is always Deka the Wraith."

This friend, an ephemeral interdimensional Emanation, could carry written or memorized messages great distances in a wink.

"I'll save Deka for emergencies, as when I can't stand being alone any more," the Journeyman said softly, pushing away from the table. "It's time I started."

His farewells at the big double front door were affectionate but brief. Flarman shook his hand, then gave him a loving great bear hug. Bronze Owl clapped his brazen wings together so hard nobody could hear for a moment. Blue Teakettle stayed in the kitchen and scolded Scouring Pad for doing a perfect job on Griddle. She dribbled hot tears on Stove, making a rather mournful sizzle.

Black Flame, the older Wizard's Familiar, came and rubbed against the Journeyman's legs, purring loudly, and his two wives jumped to Douglas's shoulders and tickled his ears with their whiskers.

The Ladies of the Byre mooed farewell from the meadow, turning their heads together in the direction of the cottage. In the thatched roof above, the Mouse family cheered and waved bits of red flannel to their friend and provider of bits of cheese and soda crackers on cold winter nights.

Douglas quickly said his farewells to one and all, then strode off down the cottage walk, through a rickety wooden gate, down to the River Road, and on to the bridge. He paused to wave once again to the rather forlorn group on the door-stoop of the Wizards' cottage.

Flarman would love to go along. Douglas thought to himself as he crossed Crooked Brook. *And I'm surprised that Bronze Owl didn't decide to come along, too. Black Flame would never leave Flarman, of course, but he wishes he were on the road again, I'm sure.*

He stopped to say good-bye to Precious and Lilac, the High's nearest neighbors. They were winter-pruning their apple trees. This elderly couple were like fond grandparents to the young Pyromancer.

"Is the Lady Myrn in good spirits and health?" asked Lilac. She was already at work sewing Myrn's wedding gown. "She must be beside herself, being so far away from you."

"As we would be, if we were separated," said her husband, smiling fondly at her. "Take a pocketful of these late-autumn keepers with you, my boy. Nothing like apples to keep you in good health. . . . An apple a day keeps the bedbugs away! . . . Or something like that," he added, quite seriously. "Keeping bedbugs under control is important for travelers, I should think."

"Old Man," his wife gently chided, digging a sharp elbow into his ribs, "what do you know of traveling? You've never been farther than the Oak 'n' Bucket in Trunkety!"

"I did, too, travel in me youth," protested Precious. "Before I got good sense and married you, that is."

"I wish I had time to listen to your travel stories," said Douglas with genuine regret, for the old man was a very good tale spinner and well worth the listening. "But I want to be down at least to Farango Waters by nightfall."

"To visit your Lady Mother and your father," Lilac said, nodding in approval.

"That's my plan, but I must start now to get there before dark."

"Go on, then," said she, drawing him into her arms and giving him a warm kiss on each cheek. Precious started to shake his hand but turned the handshake into a grandfatherly hug, instead.

"Go in good health, and don't forget to eat those apples each day," called the orchardman after him.

With the warm feeling that comes from being loved, Douglas walked briskly down the southern bank of Crooked Brook, past the high-arcing Victory Fountain in midstream, installed by the Water Adept, Augurian, to commemorate the defeat of Frigeon. He recrossed Crooked Brook at Trunkety Bridge, following the Trunkety Road into the center of Valley's largest—and only—town.

On the broad, oak-shaded Green, he looked in first at the Oak 'n' Bucket but found no one there except the red-cheeked Innkeeper, who was busy sweeping out the debris of the night before: pipe dottles and chestnut shells and occasionally a broken glass. Douglas loved the tobaccoey, winey, beery smell of the taproom, but he didn't linger longer than to tell the Innkeeper that he was on his way and to send any messages he might receive on to the High.

Crossing the Green, he met the town's Schoolmaster amid a chattering, leaping, laughing, excited crowd of Valley youngsters. They clustered about him like a swarm of happy honeybees, all dressed in their very best, faces scrubbed to a shine and hands scoured spotless.

"Hello, Frackett!" greeted Douglas. "Good morning, children!"

"On your way again?" said the onetime Wizard. "A Journeyman must journey, they say. Well I remember . . ."

"We're on our way to visit Wizards' High!" interrupted several of the children, forestalling one distraction, as children do, by creating another.

"Yes, the Wizard Flarman has kindly invited us to spend the afternoon with him," said Frackett. He was no longer the morose, low-bent, and lonely old man Douglas first had met many months before. Frackett had spent two centuries as an outlooker in the wilderness of Landsend, far to the northeast, marking the comings, goings, and nefarious doings of Frigeon on his glacier. With the fall of Frigeon, he had returned to civilization and a happier, more sociable life, as Trunkety's Schoolmaster.

"Well, now, little friends," Douglas said to the class, "you'll truly love every minute at Wizards' High, I know, but take my best advice and don't put your fingers or noses into places where they don't belong. Some things at the High are extremely dangerous, if you don't know what they are!"

"We won't, we promise!" cried the children, and they trooped off after Schoolmaster Frackett while Douglas strolled into Dicksey's Store to purchase a few last items to bring to his mother.

Dicksey himself, looking plump and prosperous once again after the severe trials of Dead Winter and Dry Summer, was

waiting upon two Trunkety housewives. He nodded to the
newcomer and the ladies curtsied gracefully with broad smiles
and a few words of affectionate teasing, mostly concerning the
year-off midwinter wedding.

"We're getting ready already," said one. "Embroidering
and sewing, preserving jams and jellies, and pickling and
planning the banquets. We can hardly wait!"

"Nor can I," agreed the Journeyman Wizard, much to their
delight. Douglas was a complete favorite with everyone in
Valley, but especially the housewives and farm wives. As
Apprentice he had done all of the shopping for Wizard's
High at the Trunkety Tuesday Market and he knew them all
well by name and reputation.

The ladies wandered off to examine some of the many
wondrous new goods Dicksey had on sale. Increased ease
and safety of travel on Dukedom's highroads since the end
of the war had returned prosperity to Valley. The proprietor
bustled about collecting the baking chocolate, sewing needles,
and silk thread that Douglas's mother required.

"And next week, please, send a sturdy, reliable boy up
to the High to get Blue Teakettle's shopping list," Douglas
reminded him. "Left to himself, Flarman would forget to buy
food when he's hard at work."

Dicksey made a note of it on his slate and shortly saw the
young Wizard off at his door.

"Fair journeying!" Dicksey called after Douglas. The
housewives came to add their farewells. Squire Frenstil, just
arrived on horseback from his farm outside town, stopped to
say hello and good-bye.

"Sure you don't want to borrow a mount?" he asked.

"No, but many, many thanks," said Douglas. "I'll be
going by packet from Perthside to Westongue and it
would be much too long before you got your horse
back."

"Ye must enjoy tramping in winter," observed the gentleman farmer, who had once been the Master of Horse of the
late Thorowood Duke, sire of the present Duke, Thornwood.
"Well, I don't blame you! If I were younger, I'd beg to go
along with ye."

"And you'd be welcome," said Douglas.

He waved and set out again, determined not to be delayed further by the many friends who seemed to have made it a point to be along his road just by accident this morning.

Three thousand miles or so to the east and south, on Waterand Island in Warm Seas, Apprentice Aquamancer Myrn Manstar prepared for bed in her pleasant tower-top apartment above the magnificent Palace of Augurian.

Myrn was a slim, raven-haired young lady. She had sparkling hazel-green eyes and the strong, self-confident movements of an experienced sailor, which she most certainly was.

After rereading Douglas's latest letter her thoughts were of Douglas and his journey.

Journeying was a very important part of a Journeyman's training for Mastery—in any craft, she knew. Someday soon, she hoped, she would be setting out alone on a journey of her own, leading to promotion to Journeyman Water Adept in Augurian's footsteps.

She imagined Douglas striding along the road from Trunkety to Perthside, in the bright winter afternoon, whistling cheerfully as he went. She knew instinctively that he would stop to say good-bye to Precious and Lilac, and to look in at the Oak 'n' Bucket and Dicksey's store before he took to the road.

"Douglas, take care!" she said aloud as she plumped her pillow and composed herself for sleep. "You're going farther away than ever now."

Chapter Two

Perthside to Westongue

SOME time before his journeying began, Douglas had been told by the Fire Wizard of the message from Cribblon. It disturbed Flarman greatly.

"Cribblon I remember as an Apprentice to a certain Aeromancer once, but his Master . . . ah . . . was not able to finish his education after Last Battle of Kingdom. The lad evidently still practices magic enough to recognize other magicks and magickers when he meets them.

"He reports to me a Coven of Black Witches in the mountains of the Far West, on the western border of Old Kingdom. He says they are rapidly expanding their evil influence, gaining control of surrounding towns and peoples. It's what Witches sometimes do, when they decide to band together in a Coven. If they think they can get away with it, that is!"

"Even Witches deserve to be left alone if they haven't done anything harmful to others," Douglas maintained.

"That's so, but you must remember that just *being* a Black Witch is pretty good evidence that some wickedness is being done or contemplated," Flarman responded. "It's many long years since I knew Cribblon, to tell you the truth. He may be misreading the situation entirely. There are good Witches just as there are bad Wizards. Some of my best friends are White Witches," he added, a touch wistfully, Douglas thought.

"This bunch needs looking into, at and over," Flarman continued quickly, before Douglas could ask about that wistfulness. "Good or bad, we must know about them, and they about us. If their intentions are benign, all to the well and good! It's their right, even if we don't approve of their methods.

"But we can't tell from this long a distance. Witches of either color are very private persons and their strongest magicks are hiding and confusing hexes, you may recall."

Douglas would go and look them over, Flarman decided, determining, if possible, if these Witches were using their magic wickedly, making trouble for other, less gifted people.

"I don't expect they'll be as much trouble as Frigeon was, however. I would go with you but Augurian and I have to get to work sorting out Frigeon's—Serenit's, that is—tangled web of selfish, evil enchantments."

Stripped of his awesome powers, Frigeon had changed his name to Serenit and had been exiled to a distant land. His spells remained, matters of primary importance to the Fellowship. The Ice King had put many people and places under deep, dire spells to suit his ambitious ends. It would take all three Wizards and eventually Myrn, too, years to right all of the Ice King's wrongs, even with the reformed sorcerer's help— those that could still be righted.

"You're more than a match for a whole Coven," claimed Bronze Owl. "Besides, the experience is necessary for you as you prepare for your Master's examination."

Douglas was eager to go for two other, very personal reasons: he was eager to test his growing Powers of Wizardry on a difficult professional task after his many years of training.

And he wanted some such task to absorb him over the time he had to wait for Myrn to reach the stage in her own schooling in the art of Aquamancy to allow them to be together without constant and prolonged separations.

His way was west, but the fastest way was to go south and west first, to the scenes of his childhood on Farango Waters; to bustling, shipbuilding Perthside at the mouth of Crooked Brook.

On the road he still met people who just happened to be there in order to say good-bye and good luck. One such was the Valley farmer, Possumtail, who still divided his time between his land and captaining the Valley Patrol, formed to keep the peace and assist the hundreds of dispossessed wanderers of Dead Winter and Dry Summer.

He sat now, slouched in his worn saddle, looking weary but quite alert, armed with sword and dagger and the authority of his friends in Valley.

"Things are quiet, now that winter has taken its grip," he said. "I'm for home and some winter's rest. I've sent the Patrol on ahead of me."

"They'll have scattered to their cottages and crofts," Douglas said with a nod. "I saw none of them on the road."

Possumtail dismounted on the pretext of checking his mare's cinch buckle, but really to share a moment with the Journeyman Wizard. They had worked very closely in the terrible days of the Dead Winter Frigeon had sent to keep them busy while he began his conquest.

"I'm that surprised ye're afoot," the Patrol Captain said. "Didn't ye ask Frenstil for a mount?"

"I wanted to walk," claimed Douglas. "Frenstil offered several times, but I refused. I need time and a closeness to the land. I'm on a very special Journey, you see. It'll determine whether I'll become more than just a Journeyman in my craft. Many never go beyond Journeyman, you know."

"I've no doubt at all about your Mastery," said Possumtail, preparing to remount. "Best to ye, young Wizard! Keep your feet warm, is my best advice. And your wits about you, too. The roads are not always safe, even now."

Douglas thanked him and they parted, the farmer toward his warm but lonely cottage and Douglas toward his parents' home on Farango Waters at Perthside.

He arrived just at dusk at the comfortable, two-storied beam-built house in which he'd been born. It overlooked the busy shipyards beside upper Farango Waters. His father had long ago built a captain's walk on its roof, the better to survey his yards and the shipways on the fjord that stretched all the way to open Sea to the southwest.

The shipwright father and quietly lovely mother were more than just delighted to have their famous son in their home once again, and they were full of news of their own lives.

"Glothersome Nunnery prospers under a new rule," said Gloriana, Douglas's mother. "The old rule of silence now applies only within the walls of the convent itself. It's a wonderfully peaceful place to rest or spend a few days, away from this constant pounding, sawing, shouting of workers and screeching of machinery, the comings and goings of the shipyards. The Glothersome Sisters are much more involved in World, now. They teach school and crafts, care for the poor and the sick, cultivate their wonderful gardens to feed wayfarers and strangers, and make a bit of profit besides. I help as much as I can."

"She's as near to being a saint as I know herself," insisted the senior Douglas, smiling at his wife's modesty. "If anything, I'm more proud of her than I am of you, my dear son."

"You're building Thornwood Duke a navy?"

" 'Tis a *merchant* fleet we're building for His Grace," protested his father, "although, truth to tell, each capital keel we lay down is fully capable of becoming a warship, should the need ever arise again."

"Surely there will not be war again!" cried his wife. She had lost her husband for many years and nearly lost her only child, thanks to Frigeon's ambitious war making.

"I truly don't know of any wars brewing, these days," said Douglas to reassure her, "and Flarman or Augurian would be the first to hear if there was one."

"Where are you off to, then?" asked his mother.

"I've a Journey to undertake to the Far West of Old Kingdom, where there are some Black Witches concerting, we are told. Witches have the potential for making mischief, especially if they're banded together. Flarman wants to know who they are and what they intend."

"Won't it be dangerous?" asked Gloriana.

"Travel in Old Kingdom is always dangerous," observed the elder Douglas. "You'll be careful, son?"

"Of course! And I'm rather better prepared than most for any such dangers," Douglas pointed out.

"Of course!" echoed his father. "It's just that we're your father and your mother and we will worry about you, no matter what."

The next day he went with his father to inspect the three great merchant ships on the Perthside ways, and to arrange for his passage on the next vessel to leave for Westongue, on Dukedom's northwest coast.

The workmen downed their tools and came to clap the young Wizard on his back and wring his hand. Many of them had been captives of the Ice King, as Frigeon had wished to deny their shipbuilding talents to his enemies. Those who had remained behind had been forced to work for the usurping Duke Eunicet, Frigeon's tool. They all wanted a full accounting from Douglas of the former Duke's trial and punishment.

"It'll be a long, long time before anyone sees or hears of Eunicet again," Douglas told them. "He and that general of his, an ill-favored, slovenly and sly man named Bladder, are marooned together on a desert island far to the south of Waterand Island in the loneliest part of Warm Seas."

The ship workers cheered his words and insisted that he stay and share with them their hearty working man's lunches.

"Have you doubts about your coming marriage?" Gloriana said that evening, mentioning the subject for the first time. "Are you truly ready to marry? Some young men rush into marriage, I have seen, when they still need to look further afield for a life's companion."

Douglas nibbled on a piece of chocolate cake as he considered her question.

"When you ask me directly, I can only answer just as directly, Mother," he said at last. "I have no doubts about Myrn or about marriage with her. It feels perfectly right. To both of us. We've talked of it many times this past summer."

"Good!" said Gloriana. She was knitting as they talked, in yarns of blue and white—a baby's shawl or sweater. Douglas couldn't decide which. "No one can be entirely sure in such matters, but I must tell you that I also feel perfectly at ease with your decision. Your father and I are unworried—beyond the normal concerns of parents, of course. And I hope you can live with those worries."

"I see them as signs of your love for me and for Myrn, too," said Douglas, feeling rather humble and yet very happy at his mother's words.

Said Gloriana, "Here's your papa, fresh from the toils of profit-and-loss and engineering drawings! Shipwright, do you think you could make us some popcorn?"

Douglas sailed on the newest Perthside ship for Westongue. The splendid square-rigger would be taken into the Ducal service on arrival there. In Westongue Douglas hoped to find a ship that would be going—or could be chartered to take him—across the wide, shallow bight of Sea called the Broad—to some point on the east coast of the land still known as Old Kingdom, although there had been neither king nor kingdom in that place for more than two hundred years.

Douglas had Sea in his blood from his heritage of shipbuilding, reinforced by his adventures the year before. He loved to sail and was fascinated by everything connected with ships.

The good ship *Ramrod* carried him without incident down the long fjord of Farango Waters, around Cape Fioddle, the southwesternmost tip of Dukedom, and up its long, low, sandy west coast to busy Westongue. This port served Capital, the seat of Thornwood's government and, other than distant and more isolated Wayness Isles on the south coast, was Dukedom's only deepwater port.

When they moored Douglas recognized a familiar figure on the dock and waved, gleefully.

"Ahoy! Ahoy, Thornwood! Here's a Journeyman Wizard most pleased to see you once more!"

The young and handsome Duke of Dukedom waved back, grinned broadly, and gave the younger man a strong embrace and a buffet on the shoulder when Douglas stepped ashore.

"I came down from Capital to look over *Ramrod*," he explained. "I hadn't known that you were aboard her."

Douglas asked after Thornwood's mother, the Duchess Mother Marigold, whom Douglas and Flarman had rescued from Frigeon's frozen workshop under Eternal Ice. Thornwood urged him to come upriver to Capital to visit her and see how things were going, now that a proper Duke had taken the helm, as he put it. His training as a Seaman showed in many of his mannerisms and phrases.

But Douglas begged his pardon, explaining his mission was too important to delay, much as he'd like to have seen Capital. He'd never been there.

"I never interfere with Wizard's work," said Thornwood, seriously. He had spent some months hiding from his enemies at Wizard's High as a boy and had learned a lot about Wizards' ways and means.

"But at least spend a few days with me here, while we find you a ship going west. There're some people here who perhaps can give you good advice on that score. They may be able to tell you something of your destination, too. No one should go to a far land totally unprepared."

He would have said more but just then the sailors who were to take over *Ramrod* from the Perthside builders' crew arrived in an untidy and laughing marching body. There were things to which Thornwood had to attend.

"Go up to my brand-new Sea House, just finished," Thornwood said. "You can walk there from here, when you're ready. There it is . . . there, with the tallest roof and the long captain's walk."

He turned to his business. Douglas shouldered his luggage, a stout leather knapsack, and walked up the sloping shingle beach to the imposing building the Duke had pointed out. Painted a bright white with black trim, it already served as a beacon and landmark for sailors approaching Westongue from open Sea.

Somehow the Ducal staff at Sea House had already been told he was coming. He was greeted by name, most warmly, and shown to a comfortable suite next to Thornwood's own. Its windows overlooked the busy roadstead and waterfront, and it had a brass bedstead, a brass-framed mirror, and a brass-bound telescope mounted on a tripod in the bay window to watch the ships come and go.

He was doing just this later when Thornwood knocked at the door and brought in with him a gnarled, weather-beaten elderly seaman he introduced as Captain Mallet.

"So, ye're headed for Old Kingdom, eh?" said Mallet over lunch. "I won't ask why, for 'tis none of me business, but I've got to say you may be foolhardy, lad! Friend of the Duke or not, I must be honest with ye. There's a load of wickedness, evil and other bad doings yet in Old Kay. Old Kay is as we call it and not many Men goes there these days!"

"I must go. I can take care of myself," said Douglas, a bit miffed at the other's obvious doubt. "I am a Fire Wizard."

"Pupil of Flarman Flowerstalk," put in Thornwood, with a twinkle in his eye.

"Old Flarman! Well, why di'n't ye say so, laddie? If ye're a mate of that old fire-spitter, you'll do better over on the other side than any ordinary Man, I 'spect. But make no mistake! 'Twill be dangerous, and I be a Man who has rubbed noses with danger all over Sea and much of World, so to speak. I admit I only knows of Old Kay what lies quite near the coast. I never goes far inland meself! When folks I meet ashore asks me what an anchor is, I know I'm too far from salt water."

He laughed at his own joke. Thornwood chuckled and Douglas was appeased.

"I've heard tales, however," Mallet went on, shaking his finger in caution. "Wish I could give ye more details, lad . . . er, Wizard! But, no, I would just be saying hearsay to ye, and that'd not be much help."

"There's this problem of getting someone to put me ashore somewhere useful," Douglas prompted.

"I can help ye there. My poor dead daughter's husband, a good and brave young 'un much your own age, is in port and looking for cargo or charter. Mayhap he'll take ye, as far as Summer Palace."

"Summer Palace?" Douglas pricked up his ears at a new name.

"Aye, 'tis a town on the east coast of Old Kay, near the mouth of the large river they call Bloody Brook."

"That river was scene of terrible fighting in the Last Battle of Kingdom," put in Thornwood. "I recall my great-grandfather speaking of it, although he was not there."

"Me own great-great-grandfather *was,* and never come home," said Mallet. "Lucky for me, he left behind a young bride and several stout lads, one of which was me own great-grandfather."

"And beyond Summer Palace, what?" asked Douglas, making notes as the older man talked.

"'Tis a mystery to me, and to most others I know of, this side the Broad. Not many goes deep into Old Kay, as I say. Of them that do go, not many come back. The stories . . . well, they dwell on Goblin hordes and armies of Unburied Dead! No more o' that!"

"From Summer Palace, then, you're on your own, young Wizard," said Thornwood. "For the life of me, I wish I were able to go along."

"You've much to do, rebuilding and repairing your land and rescuing your people after Eunicet's misrule," declared Douglas, stoutly. He knew, better than most, the damage Frigeon's wily, self-serving puppet had done to Thornwood's Dukedom.

"Beside that, this journey I must make alone. It's part of my preparation for professional Mastery," he explained. "I can't accept undue assistance in this."

They visited the saucy fore-and-aft rigged schooner *Pitch-fork,* belonging to Mallet's bereaved son-in-law, a youthful Seacaptain named Pargeot. Douglas liked him from the first.

The Journeyman Wizard knew enough about ships and sailing to see that *Pitchfork,* despite her unusual name, boasted a tight, streamlined hull, taut rigging, and was served by a well-trained crew. Her sails were clean white and unpatched, of the best Westongue canvas. Her decks were obviously holystoned and washed clean at least once each day, a good sign of a well-mastered vessel.

"We'll try our best to get you all the way to Pfantas," Pargeot said when they met later at Sea House to sign Douglas's hire charter. "Bloody Brook is wide enough almost all the way, according to the old charts I've seen. Is it deep enough, is the question? Can it be an awesome, fearsome opponent in spring flood? And there are said to be mischievous Sprites everywhere and wicked Goblins, never to be taken lightly."

"Sounds daunting," agreed Douglas, "but I must try, and your father-in-law tells me Pfantas is the farthest inland I can hope to get by water, saving me a lot of hiking through rough country."

"So 'tis!" agreed the Captain. "We'll sail at tide's turn tomorrow afternoon, young sir. The crossing should be easy at this time of year, and should take no more than four days to sight land on the other side."

"I'll be ready," said Douglas. "Is there anything I can do to help, once we're at Sea?"

"Stand a few watches on deck," suggested the other, getting up to leave. "I've a good crew, but I'm short of experienced officers—due to most of them still being off on Eunicet's ships at Sea somewhere, and not returned yet."

"I can do that," said Douglas. "I learned a little of Seamanship under Caspar Marlin. Have you heard of him?"

"I knew Caspar before he first sailed to Choin," said Pargeot with a pleased grin. "Him and me were better than friends; shipmates! When we're away, I'll ask you to tell me of Caspar and where you met him. But for now, tell me if he is well."

"Caspar is very well, and in my own service as Captain of *Donation,* my flagship," put in Thornwood Duke. "If I'd known you two were friends, I would have told you long since."

"Good news to hear at any time, Your Grace! I thank you both and now must see to my ship, if you'll excuse me."

Douglas went to bed early that night. He was tired and had found that unless you were a sailor or a roustabout and enjoyed the noisy pleasures provided behind the Westongue waterfront, there was not much else to do after dark.

His dreams were uneasy with uncanny visions of Trolls, Goblins, Undead Warriors, and Witches flying, screaming, through dark air over a roiled and roaring river. At last he put them out of his mind with a conscious effort and fell into a deeper, most restful sleep.

Chapter Three

![decorative]

Storm on the Broad!

"I DON'T like the looks of that black sky," said Captain
Pargeot to Douglas when they met on *Pitchfork*'s quarterdeck
the morning of the fourth day of the voyage.

"I'm not much of a weather prophet, but I see what you
mean," said Douglas. "Look at those birds, will you!"

A huge flock of white Seabirds flashed overhead, speeding
downwind for the distant shore of Old Kay, not yet visible
from *Pitchfork*'s deck. The raucous flock flew as fast as
Douglas had ever seen birds fly, mewling with urgency and
letting nothing turn them aside from their headlong course.

"If Bronze Owl were here," thought Douglas aloud, "he'd
go question them about why they are fleeing."

"No mystery about that! That's a storm upwind and it's
coming fast! The birds are heading for shelter, probably
some bay on Kingdom's coast," said the Captain with a
wry grimace. "We may wish we could do the same, quite
soon!"

Douglas watched for a while from the deck. Impressive
black banks of rolling, lightning-shot clouds fast approached
from the northeast. The crewmen, going about their tasks
on deck, paused frequently to cast apprehensive glances
sternward. Orders were shouted in rapid sequence and sails
came down, flapping wildly, to be manhandled to quiet and
tightly furled about their yards or brought entirely to the deck
and stowed away.

The very air was heavy with menace, tasting on the young
Wizard's tongue like some of Flarman's more violent fire
spells. When the weather turned dirty and Sea rough, he'd
have trouble getting a meal, let alone a hot one, he knew. At
last he went below to find himself breakfast. Even while he

ate he was aware how *Pitchfork* pitched, rolled, and tossed about, more each minute that passed. Her timbers groaned, and cordage snapped, screeched, squealed, and twanged as the wind force steadily rose. The waters beyond *Pitchfork*'s thick bulkheads roared and tumbled, whipped into higher and higher foam-capped peaks by the unceasing gale.

"If I didn't know better," said Douglas to Pargeot when the captain came below to grab a bite of lunch, "I'd guess that this was a storm sent by Frigeon."

"No, storms are usual in these latitudes, although not at this time of the year. The Broad is quite shallow, you know, which makes any storm that much worse. However, I've been in stronger! We've turned into the wind now. We'll ride it out under stays'ls. It shouldn't last more than . . ."

A shout from above stopped his words. He spun about to rush back on deck, saying, "Stay below, Douglas Brightglade! It'll be safer. Until this blow passes."

Douglas tried to make himself comfortable on a settle in the saloon, reading a book on spontaneous combustion Flarman had slipped into his pack for just such occasions.

It became more and more difficult to remain, even stretched out on his back on the settle. The deck sloped first stemward, then sternward, with rolls, twists, and unexpected pitches in between. The motion became so violent the Journeyman finally tucked his book under a cushion in order to devote both hands to hanging on, so as not to end up pitched to the deck.

Water, forced into the cabin under the usually tight doors and windows, sloshed back and forth alarmingly, even though the Journeyman realized the seepage didn't mean the ship was floundering.

"Pity the poor sailor on a day like this," he misquoted. He had regained his sea legs a few hours after sailing, but this sort of wild gyrating was making him wish he hadn't eaten so hearty a breakfast.

Conditions must be, he thought to himself, very rough on deck, judging by the ship's sounds as well as motions. He could hear, faintly, shouts of her officers through the thick oaken deck, but couldn't make out what was being said.

There came a terrific crash, a flurry of louder cries just over his head, the sound of rapid chopping, and another crack, as if a piece of wood had been split in twain under great stress. A yard or perhaps even a whole mast must have been torn from its moorings and dropped over the side, Douglas guessed, and the crew was frantically cutting away the trailing rigging.

There were powers in World that even a Master Pyromancer could not resist. A full-blowing storm on the Broad was definitely one. The immense strength of the raging waters and the howling wind combined to overwhelm his fire powers, alone. For the first time since his adventure under the ice of Frigeon's fracturing glacier, he felt real fear.

Soon there was a moderation of the storm wind, although Sea continued to toss the ship about angrily. Douglas rose carefully and made his unsteady way to the saloon's door and down the companionway to *Pitchfork*'s waist. Clinging to a hatch combing for balance, he stuck his head out into driving rain just as *Pitchfork*'s first mate staggered into sight, head bent and shoulders thrusting into the downpour.

"Captain went overboard when the mizzen was carried away!" wailed the mate, his eyes wide with apprehension and sorrow. "We couldn't go about to reach him before he was lost to sight!"

Douglas gasped in horror. He'd known the young Sea-captain for but four days, but liked and trusted him. Now he was gone—into a Sea no man could long survive. There was nothing the young Wizard could do for him, except . . .

"Asrai! Sea Fire! Save a poor sailor overboard!" he shouted into the raging wind. If the Phosphorescence heard . . . the mate had not stayed to hear Douglas's call.

Shivering in wet horror and sorrow, Douglas turned about to retrace his steps down the passageway toward the main cabin.

A second, even greater crash and a wild shudder ran through the ship's length, shaking the vessel as a dog shakes a squirrel. The shock threw the Journeyman to his knees and then onto his face, banging him with great force against a bulkhead.

Cold, salt-bitter water shattered the companionway door

behind him and poured through, pinning him to the deck with its weight. At the last possible moment Douglas instinctively took a great gulp of air.

In complete darkness he was plucked up bodily by the in-rushing water and hurled toward the aft end of the passageway. He was smashed through the thin partition that separated passageway from saloon.

"Hang on just a few minutes," he told himself, unable to tell whether he was moving or still, deep or shallow, or . . . what? His lungs began to ache for air.

I've been through this before, he remembered, striking out in an attempt to swim to the surface. *I must drop my boots or they'll drag me. . . .*

Before he could bend to push the heavy seaboots off against the pressure of the water, he surfaced, just in time to feel himself swept by the raging torrent through a gaping, jagged hole in *Pitchfork*'s high-tossed stern . . . a hole big enough to drive a coach-and-four through, he thought, foggily. Once again, he gulped a desperate breath of air.

The water had carried him from the passageway, through the saloon, and out the saloon portholes into open Sea. As he passed through the windows he was dashed against the foot-square timber that supported the sloop's massive rudder. He spun out and down into thundering darkness, stunned.

"What was that!" cried Myrn Manstar. She started from her bed atop the Waterand tower, terror gripping her heart in an iron hand and squeezing out a second scream. "Douglas! Where are you?"

She listened, shaking with sudden fear, but all she could hear was the soft rustle of the great fountain in the palace forecourt. A gentle, warm breeze came through the seaward windows, and a crescent moon sailed placidly across the Warm Seas sky.

"*Something* happened!" gasped Myrn, regaining her composure quickly. "This is terrible—knowing something has happened, but not knowing what!"

She shrugged into a light robe and went to look from her window, then walked barefoot to the door, stopping to listen once more. Hearing nothing, she opened the door.

Turning right, she went to knock softly on Augurian's study door, knowing somehow the Water Adept was yet there, not in his bed.

"Myrn!" said Augurian when he saw her. "Come in, please! What has wakened you?"

She explained as best she could. The Water Wizard nodded in understanding and led her to a seat beside his broad worktable, piled high with papers, scrolls, and books.

"You've formed an unusually strong bond with young Brightglade, I see," he said.

"Do you think something has happened to Douglas?" she cried in increased concern.

"Probably, Apprentice. Probably. Not unusual at all, I believe. Wait a short while."

He went to another, smaller table on which rested a tangle of glass tubing, flasks, beakers, retorts, and all the paraphernalia of his craft. He mixed three colorless liquids from stoppered bottles and swirled them in a bulbous flask. The liquid turned deep indigo almost at once.

Augurian placed the graduate on the windowsill and gazed at it for several minutes while his Apprentice waited, holding her breath.

"Well, my dear, do you still feel that Douglas is in great danger?" he asked at last.

Myrn took a deep breath and closed her eyes. Her shoulders relaxed in relief.

"No, Magister. I feel he is, if not safe, at least not in the great peril that awakened me."

"In sudden and dire straits," said the Water Adept, gesturing at the graduate where the liquid was now clear again, "a heart in danger cries out, involuntarily, and his close loved ones hear the cry. Your training here for the past year has sharpened your awareness of these phenomena, you see."

He emptied the glass cylinder into a sink and washed it carefully while she watched in silence.

"In time you may even be able to speak to Douglas over long distances, when you most need to. Not at all unusual. Happens all the time."

"I wish I could now," said Myrn, smiling weakly.

"You probably could if you tried hard enough. But I advise against it, as it might distract him at what he is doing to save himself. And it would be extremely tiring to you, and you have lessons to learn and tasks to do tomorrow, young Apprentice. Best that you get back to bed! I am about to retire myself."

As the young lady rose to leave, he smiled warmly and patted her hand reassuringly.

"Try not to let it concern you, Myrn, although I know it probably will. The rapport you felt is, if nothing else, a sign of your rapid progress in Wizardry."

She thanked him and left. The Water Adept watched her go, saying to himself, "Remarkably rapid progress!"

Douglas regained his wits when he hit the foaming surface of Sea beyond the ship's stern. He opened his mouth to shout for help, and a gallon of salt water hit him in the face. He spent several moments coughing and retching to rid himself of it, struggling to keep his head above the surging waves.

Riding the top of an upsweeping wave, Douglas saw no sign of *Pitchfork* in that fleeting moment, only towering, hurtling ranks upon ranks of dark green waves all about him.

Unlike his previous involuntary swim in the middle of Warm Seas, these waters were winter cold. The wind whipped with maniacal fury about and over him. Sharp, painful raindrops needled his face and neck, churning the waves about him into amber froth.

The wind suddenly fell off as he slid down into the trough between waves. A new, hard-driving rain torrent beat down the chop, slowly calming even the great breakers.

He trod water, hampered greatly by his waterlogged clothing and boots. His hand struck and clutched at a thick piece of timber, the very rudder post that had stunned him a moment before, torn from its bolts. He clung to it with both hands and found that, if he relaxed a bit, it was enough to keep him afloat.

How long could he hang on, thus? Already his reserves of strength were being sorely tried. Douglas clung to the wallowing sternpost, concentrating on breathing regularly and keeping his grip with cold-numbed fingers. He had lost all track of time. The low sun was blinding him. The waves, while much less steep, were still too high for him to see far as he vainly searched for *Pitchfork* or for her lifeboats—or her sailors, like himself, cast adrift.

The wind that remained drove him onward. He wasn't aware of it, too bemused from the sharp blow on the head and the suddenness of the catastrophe to do more than breathe and cling.

It didn't at first occur to him to call again on the Asrai, for his own sake, although the Phosphorescence, the Cold Sea Fire, had saved him once before from drowning.

"The sun's too bright now. If I don't get some help by night-fall," he promised himself aloud, "I'll call Asrai, then."

He drifted down the wind, now in almost a dreamlike state.

Douglas came to himself in sudden panic when his feet hit something underwater and he lost his grip on the timber.

Is it Oval once again rescuing me? he wondered, fuzzily. But a moment later his feet hit the shifting sand bottom again and a lesser breaker pushed him to his hands and knees.

Blinded by salt foam, he crawled gratefully up the slope of the beach, then stopped to rest and get his bearings against a towering black rock. The sun was setting behind it. After a few moments he half rose and staggered around into the lee of the pinnacle, to sit with the last of the storm tide washing about his legs, allowing the level rays to warm him and begin to dry his clothing. He still wore his heavy seaboots. He'd forgotten to drop them.

The sun plunged behind a distant, flat horizon and evening cold came at once with a brisk offshore breeze. The waves had retreated with the falling wind—or perhaps the tide had turned, he thought. The sodden Journeyman Wizard stood, a bit more sure of his quaking legs now, gathering an armload of driftwood as he walked away from the surge.

With deft touches of his fingers and short, magic words, he set the damp wood afire. Its light would be a beacon to others, as well as warming himself. Other survivors were out there, perhaps, struggling to make the beach.

Fire made him feel master of his fate, once more. He pushed up handfuls of damp sand as a backstop and gathered more wood to feed the fire through the rest of the night. Eventually he fell into exhausted sleep, against his will.

This is the dawn of the fifth day and Pargeot was right, it took four days' sailing to make landfall, he thought as he woke the next morning. *Poor Pargeot! I do hope Asrai reached him in time. Well, maybe if I survived, he did, too.*

He felt rather fine, despite the knot on his forehead and aching muscles everywhere, but ravenously hungry all at once. Nothing was broken; he still had on his heavy Westongue pea jacket, with its high collar and anchor buttons. And damp but serviceable seaboots. The winter air was bitingly cold but the rising sun was pleasantly warming.

He patrolled up and down the broad beach for several miles in each direction to warm himself further, and to search for stranded shipmates, or at least their bodies, or anything washed ashore that might be useful.

He found a heavy wooden cask of dried beef from *Pitchfork*'s galley stores, and pried it open to feast on good, although very salty, Valley beef. He shoved several handfuls of the wood-hard meat into his wide Wizard's sleeves against future need.

About to turn back from his beachcombing, he sighted a huddled lump, half-covered with sand, just above the high-water mark. A half-buried body, he thought, from its shape. When he investigated, it was his knapsack, its contents still safe and dry!

"Myrn's Waterproofing Spell really works!" Douglas laughed, his first since before the storm. In the knapsack he found his supply of Fairy Waybread and munched hungrily on a bit of it as he retraced his steps to his fire. The magically baked traveling food had saved him many hungry miles before and saved him from a diet solely of salted beef now.

His spirits rose and his sense of adventure came to the fore, as it always did when old troubles were behind him and new problems challenged him from ahead.

Chapter Four

Marbleheart

DOUGLAS'S investigations showed that he'd been cast up on a narrow, along-shore sandy barrier island separated from the mainland by a mile-wide shallow lagoon.

Nothing for it but to swim, Douglas decided, although he didn't relish the idea of getting wet all over again. He stripped off his clothes and his seaboots and stuffed them into his watertight knapsack, then waded out into the water until he was forced to swim, pushing the sealed knapsack before him, and using it as a float.

"I'm getting pretty good at this," he said to himself. "For a Fire Adept, I seem to be spending a lot of time in water. Myrn would be more at ease here, I would think!"

He chuckled to himself fondly, remembering the pretty Apprentice. "Well, I can hear her now. 'Fire Wizard! Why didn't you levitate over the water as Flarman taught you, long ago?' "

The water was warm, compared to the Broad, however, and he shortly found, to his surprise, that it was almost fresh, with only a slightly brackish taste. It served to wash the dried salt from his body and hair, making him much more comfortable.

"A river's mouth?" he wondered, aloud. Talking to himself was another habit he had acquired from Flarman, who kept up running conversations with himself while he worked. "And, if so, is the river nearby?"

"Not far away," said a cheerful voice, startling him by its nearness. He missed a stroke and submerged completely for a moment. He hadn't seen the long, brown, sleek-bodied animal floating on its back in the water ahead of him, forelegs folded on its chest.

"Sorry!" said the animal, waving one forepaw. "I didn't mean to startle you."

Douglas trod water and examined the creature apprehensively. It had a narrow, streamlined body covered with luxuriant fur. Including tail and whiskers, it stretched at least five feet long in the water. Its narrow, pointed face was pleasantly rodent, with a pert and upturned black nose and wide-set, intelligent eyes above flaring gray whiskers and sharp, white teeth.

Its front paws grasped a cracked and battered mollusk shell. It balanced a round, smooth, flat stone precariously on its furry chest.

"Good morning, Otter," spluttered the Journeyman, regaining his grip on the floating knapsack. "I recognize your kind. I've met your species before, but not so large!"

"Why, actually, I'm of the Sea Otter family. I call myself Marbleheart—after this beautiful pounding rock I found, you see."

The Sea Otter indicated the disk of stone on his chest.

"It's for breaking things open," Marbleheart explained when Douglas showed cautious curiosity. "Otters are among the few animals who use tools, you know."

"I seem to have read that, yes. The Otters I knew in Crooked Brook didn't, but they are considerably smaller than you, as I said."

"Us Sea Otters grow pretty big. I think it's due to a vastly better diet. Do you mind if I finish off this clam? I like my breakfast fresh."

Douglas shook his head.

"I'm swimming to the mainland shore, over there. Delighted to make your acquaintance."

The Otter nodded politely. "Maybe I'll join you. I sense there's more to you than just an ordinary shipwrecked sailor."

"Come if you wish," said Douglas, striking out once more for the mainland. Twenty minutes later he waded out of the lagoon and found a grassy spot at the top of a sand dune to dry himself with a blast of hot air—a handy bit of Fire Wizardry.

He'd pulled on his clothes and was munching a bit of dried beef when the Sea Otter came out of the water a short way

away, shaking his long, thin body as a dog would do, to rid
himself of excess water. He trotted close and sniffed at the
food, more curious than hungry.

Better to be polite, thought the Journeyman. He's big
enough and has teeth sharp enough to be dangerous if he
wants to be.

"Here, try some," he invited, handing the Otter a chunk of
the beef. "My name, by the bye, is Douglas Brightglade."

The aquatic mammal sniffed the morsel suspiciously, then
gulped it down in one bite.

"Not bad! I could learn to like it, although I much prefer
the taste of fresh seafood," decided Marbleheart.

"Where I'm headed, fish may be hard to find," said
Douglas.

"That," said Marbleheart, beginning to groom his drying
fur, "prompts me to ask, where are you headed, Douglas
Brightglade?"

Douglas hesitated. There was no reason why he shouldn't
tell a stranger of his journey, he decided.

"I am going west to the far border of Old Kingdom, looking
for a man named Cribblon in a town called Pfantas."

"I've heard of it. Never been there, though."

"Do you know the geography of Old Kingdom, then?"
asked the Journeyman, hoping for more information on his
destination.

"Oh, no," replied the Otter. He stretched on his stomach
in the warm sand and began to sun himself. "No, I know
the shore here quite well, but I admit I've got only curiosity
about the hinterlands."

"And what is this place called?"

"Men call it Summer Palace," said the animal, sleepily.
"Why? I don't really know. It always seemed a curious name
for such a forlorn, lonely marsh. There's a pretty fair-sized
human burrow, what you'd call a city, not far that way. It's
on the main river channel."

"I suppose I can reach this city by going inland for a while
and looking for the river?"

"Sure. But the way is pretty swampy for a dry-land person
like you. It's easy to get lost among the bayous, lagoons, and
creeks and such, if you don't swim too well. There's a dry

pathway, however, now that I think of it," the Sea Otter said, sitting up.

"Where can I find it?"

"Be easier to show you."

"I don't want to take you away from home. . . ."

"Nonsense! Home is anywhere there's water . . . and food. And where there is water there is almost always food."

Marbleheart evidently had made up his mind to be Douglas's guide so the young man accepted his assistance, despite his misgivings about strangers in this strange land. When he rose to resume his journey, Marbleheart asked him politely to carry his marble disk—he didn't want to leave it behind, he said, and it slowed him down to walk on only three legs—then fell into step beside the Wizard, showing the way.

The Otter walked with a curious *gallumping* stride, arching his long back high and then running out from under it on his short, web-footed legs. The effect was more than a little comic and Douglas could be forgiven for laughing at the sight. Marbleheart didn't seem to mind.

Whenever their way lay beside water, the Otter chose to swim instead of walking, and that was at least half of the time. In the water he reminded Douglas of the Porpoises of Warm Seas, swift, streamlined, and graceful.

As they went they chatted in a friendly manner. Douglas told the Sea Otter of Flarman and their adventures defeating the evil Ice King. Then he explained his interest in the Witches' Coven in the west.

By the time they passed through a dense screen of ten-foot reeds with feathery tops and found themselves on the bank of a broad, slow river, he had learned the Otter's history, also.

"I was born in a cozy burrow on the south shore of the Briney," Marbleheart told him. "It was a hard life, but a good one. The Briney is full of tasty cod and scrumptious sole. Mama and Papa taught us to swim fast and fish well and have a marvelous time, in the water and out. By the time I was old enough to strike out on my own, I was larger and stronger than any of the other kits of my litter. I was the first to leave home."

"How large a litter?" asked Douglas, thinking of Pert and Party, the cats of Wizards' High, who regularly bore four or five kittens to Black Flame.

"Only seven in all. We were a pawful. Mama always said! I made my way south over the sand spit to the Broad, wanting to see World on my own. Since then I've wandered almost everywhere there is to be, along the coast of Dukedom, even to the top of your Farango Waters. Delightful place, if a bit too noisy with shipbuilding and dangerous with net fishing. The fishermen were rather unfriendly. They were jealous that I caught the biggest and best Sea Trout that swam the Waters."

The fishermen had chased him away from their nets, throwing stones and sometimes shooting arrows, but Marbleheart considered it all a great lark.

"Oh, I knew they were trying to kill me at times, but I understood. Life isn't all games, even for a Sea Otter. Fishermen have a living to make, too."

Douglas found himself warming to the animal. Marbleheart was jolly, self-confident, and a bit of a clown at times.

"I swam all the way across the Broad on a wager," the Otter boasted, "with a disreputable old cormorant I met. More or less settled down here. It's much quieter, no shipyards or fish nets. Loads of loud, muddy-footed birds, however. They always think I'm after their eggs or chicks. I'd have to be nearly starved to eat a loon's egg, let alone a chick. Ugh! All feathers and bones!"

They came in late afternoon to a shallow harbor in a graceful river bend. Breasting a last dune, they stopped to look down on a strange sight.

As far as eye could see, the flat sandy land was covered with the ruins of a vast city. Walls, columns, pavements, broken towers, and weed-grown plazas reached to the horizon, all laid out in straight lines and graceful curves, colonnaded squares and ornamental oval patches that once had been gardens, Douglas decided.

Most of the walls were broken down, stones and brick lay scattered everywhere, columns lay where they had fallen ages before, and the paving was cracked or tilted or buried in drifting sand.

Few of the buildings had upper stories or even roofs, and only a huddled handful had doors or windows covered with sun-bleached cloth. And yet, faint threads of smoke from supper fires showed that someone lived, still, in Summer Palace.

A half dozen long, narrow boats, once gaily painted but now chipped and weathered to bare, gray wood, were tied to the downstream side of a crumbling stone pier jutting out from the riverbank. Nets had been stretched to dry across rows of broken-off columns.

Everything seemed to have lost color to the sun, turned white as old bones. There was an air of desolation and depression about the whole huge, ruined place.

"Summer Palace," murmured Marbleheart. He pointed to a low rise on the distant horizon where there stood a gaunt pile, glinting in the leveling sunlight, a tangle of tumbled but once-ornate stonework. "They tell me that was once a magnificent burrow with golden roofs and a hundred crystal gables and tall arched doorways. You can still see some of the arches, I think."

"You've been in the city?" asked Douglas, studying the ruins.

"Oh, yes, any number of times. The people are pretty pathetic, for my taste. No sense of play at all. They'll watch you steal their fish stew right off their tables and then sit around and argue about it for hours instead of giving proper chase. Not much fun! I found my breaking stone here, however, and thus my name, so I'm sort of fond of the place."

He led the Journeyman down into the dilapidated city, through streets littered with blocks of stone fallen from buildings and dried sea-grape leaves and faded flowers blown from weed-choked gardens.

The broad avenues had originally been carefully paved with pink and gray granite cobbles set in swirling patterns, Douglas noted. The sides of the streets were choked with blown sand and debris, overgrown with thorny wild rose bushes and drooping bunches of roughly serrated yellow dune grass. The only sound he could hear was of the grass rustling mournfully in the evening breeze.

The Otter took Douglas to a side street just a bit less cluttered than the others, where the houses were, at least, roofed with musty reed thatching. Gray smoke made smudges in the air as it escaped through chinks and cracks where once there had been elaborate decorations and fenestrations. Coughing and low, monotonous murmuring came from behind each door, draped with weathered, ancient tapestries, but no one was abroad at this twilight hour.

"Here's the house of the one they call Majordomo," announced Marbleheart. "I'll leave you here. I find Majordomo a fool leading fools, quite hard to suffer—and besides, I want to catch the ebbtide. Good-bye!"

He scampered off without another word, not waiting for Douglas to say thank you for his guidance.

Douglas knocked politely on the rickety doorframe of the Majordomo's house. It was opened after a long pause by a tall, dry-looking individual in a ratty, once-white periwig and a rusty red long-tailed coat over stained white breeches so patched and mended that it was hard to tell what was repair and what original cloth.

"Ah, sir!" the man said in a polite but haughtily affected drawl. "How may I serve you?"

"You must be the Majordomo," said Douglas. "I'm Douglas Brightglade, Journeyman Fire Wizard, pupil of Flarman Flowerstalk, also called Firemaster. . . ."

"Welcome to Summer Palace, Master Journeyman Wizard!" interrupted the man. "Please to come in out of the night's airs."

He held the door curtain wide and allowed Douglas to precede him into a lofty, dim, and dusty entryway. Through arched doorways on either hand were two outsized, bare rooms that took up most of the ground level of the building. A winding stair led up to a boarded-up second-story landing.

"I am familiar with the rank, reputation, and accomplishments of the Great Wizard Flarman," said the Majordomo when Douglas turned from his inspection of the interior. "As his colleague, you are most welcome at Summer Palace. Unfortunately," he added with exaggerated sadness, "His Majesty King Grummist is not in residence just now. But you are undoubtedly most weary from your travels. May I suggest dinner, at once, while I have a suitable room prepared for your rest?"

He led the way through the left-hand archway to a scarred, most ancient table almost as long and wide as the kitchen table at Wizards' High. A small, smoking fire of damp driftwood in a vastly ornate fireplace provided some warmth. Douglas was puzzled by the servant's extreme and cold formality but he let it go unnoticed as the functionary seated him at the top of the table and clapped his hands imperiously for dinner to be served. He had something much more important to worry about.

King Grummist, who had been the lord of Summer Palace, had perished over two hundred years earlier in the terrible carnage of Last Battle of Kingdom!

Chapter Five

The Waiters

DOUGLAS found that evening most strange, to say the least.

The Majordomo was scrupulously polite, but overly subservient. The dinner, served on fine old porcelain with gold service, was adequate but extremely bland, without salt or spices at all. Douglas asked for salt to go with the roast fish put before him by a timid and entirely silent serving maid who obeyed Majordomo's summons. It was produced at once—without comment or apology.

The Journeyman dined alone in the huge, dim room. The Majordomo hovered behind his chair, filling his glass with a watery, too-sweet wine when it was only a third empty and silently removing the empty dishes as each new course was brought from a kitchen somewhere outside the house.

No one came to see the visitor. The street outside remained empty, although occasionally Douglas could hear distant voices, a door closing, or slow footsteps echoing in a bare passage somewhere.

He ate dessert, a particularly tasteless egg custard, and was offered coffee and brandy; he accepted the first, refused the second. Hardly more than four sentences had been spoken during the entire meal.

"You will wish to retire," said the man, drawing back Douglas's chair smoothly and at precisely the proper time. "If you will be pleased to have a seat in the drawing room across the hall, I will see that your quarters are properly prepared. It will take just a moment or two, Sir Wizard. May I recommend a book from our extensive library? His

Majesty has eclectic tastes in literature or you may find the technical books of greatest interest."

"Do you have an atlas of Kingdom?" Douglas asked, and a thick, musty old volume was brought to him by the silent maid in the cold drawing room. He spent the next quarter hour studying the shape, names, and extent of ancient Kingdom, alone and in complete silence except for the dry rustle of turning pages.

At least I can find out something about where I'm headed, he thought, and soon located Pfantas, mentioned by Captain Mallet back in Westongue. The town lay two hundred miles upstream of Summer Palace on what the atlas identified as the Ferngreen River. Douglas remembered it had been renamed Bloody Brook because of the infamous Last Battle, fought on its banks. The book must have been compiled long before the Fall of Kingdom.

He calculated distances and estimated the length of the journey ahead.

At best, if I can average, say, twenty miles a day, that's a hundred and twenty miles in a week, saving one day for rest and washing clothes and such things. I expect it'll take almost a fortnight to reach Pfantas, and find this man Cribblon.

The Majordomo appeared silently at his elbow. Douglas put his finger on the spot marked Pfantas and looked up at him.

"I intend to go here, Majordomo. Can you tell me how long it will take me to get there?"

The other seemed taken aback.

"I am not at all sure, Sir Wizard. I have never traveled to Pfantas myself. I recall someone saying that on horseback it takes five days, with relays every fifty miles along the River Road. That was some years ago."

"Yes, something like two hundred years ago," said Douglas dryly. "You have no idea how things have changed over the intervening years?"

"No, I am afraid not, Sir Wizard. We are very isolated here on this coast. We don't get many visitors or much news."

"When was the last time you heard from the . . . His Majesty, the King?" Douglas was almost afraid to ask.

"I cannot tell you exactly," said the servant, uneasy at the question, "but it has been quite some time. . . ."

"Well, then, I'll just have to start out tomorrow and find out for myself, Majordomo. By the way, do you have a name?"

"Er, yes, Sir Wizard. I am called Delond."

"Delond, my name is Douglas Brightglade and as I am neither ennobled nor even knighted, I prefer to be called that name, especially by a gentleman who is undoubtedly three centuries older than am I."

The words made Majordomo even less comfortable and he changed the subject, avoiding the use of either Douglas's title or his name.

"Your bedchamber is prepared, sir. May I show you the way?"

"Oh, good," sighed Douglas, unenthusiastically. "I might as well get a good night's sleep."

But sleep was difficult to come by.

The storm and the shipwreck had exhausted him physically, but not mentally. The apartment to which Delond showed him was spacious, fairly clean, but rather damp and musty, with windows open to Sea breezes, now rather warmer than the night before. The young Wizard paced restlessly for some time before sliding between patched sheets.

"What's wrong here, I wonder," Douglas asked himself as he hovered just short of the edge of sleep. "I smell enchantment; that's it! These people don't know or want to know what World has done outside of Summer Palace for two centuries. I wonder . . . ?"

He fell asleep and dreamed of Flarman, Bronze Owl, and Myrn Manstar. His friends, in the dream, talked of Douglas as if he were nearby and would soon arrive at Wizards' High when they should have known he was two hundred leagues away to the west.

Over breakfast he realized that he had to do something about the enchantment he knew surrounded the ruined city and its inhabitants. Perhaps these people were happy the way they were, but he doubted it. It was unhealthy, to say the least. They were doing barely enough to keep alive, no more.

"Delond?"

"Sir, er . . . Douglas?"

"Better! Come around in front of me, Delond, and let me look at your face for a change."

"It is hardly fitting," the other objected, but he obeyed a direct order and stood at stiff attention before Douglas across the long table, his eyes unfocused, staring straight ahead.

"No, that's not good enough!" cried Douglas, thumping the table for emphasis. He kicked the nearest chair, spinning it about to face his.

"Sit down!" he commanded sharply.

Delond moved as if sleepwalking, around the long table to the chair. Douglas waited until he had perched stiffly on its edge, still looking straight ahead over the Journeyman's shoulder.

"I suppose that's as good as I'll get for the moment," Douglas sighed. "Look at me when I talk to you, Delond!"

The servant turned his head as if it were on gimbals and stared directly at and through Douglas. The scene made the young Wizard chuckle, and his soft laugh disturbed the man servant so that he dropped his eyes to the tabletop for a brief moment. Douglas gestured slowly with both his hands.

"Do you have something you wish to tell me?"

Delond looked suddenly pale and frightened, opened his mouth, closed it, dropped his eyes again, then looked for the first time directly at the young Wizard.

"What do you want to tell me?" encouraged the Journeyman, as though the man had answered his first question.

"The . . . the . . ."

"Yes, Delond? Come, you can tell me. I am a friend and pupil of a powerful Wizard, and a Wizard in my own right. I can help you."

"The King . . . ," began Delond, and Douglas was almost surprised, but not quite, to see drops of perspiration forming on the Man's pale brow.

"We are . . . Waiters," Delond ground out, at last. He had an expression of miserable pleading in his eyes. Douglas saw the maidservant enter the room with his breakfast, but halt uncertainly when she saw the Majordomo actually seated at the table.

"Come here, miss," ordered Douglas. "Be seated here, on my other side. Put the tray down, please."

The girl, for she seemed hardly older than Douglas, obeyed, as silently as ever.

"You are Waiters?" prompted Douglas, turning to Delond again. "Waiting for what? No, waiting . . . ah, I see! . . . For King Grummist to return?"

"Yes, that's it," gasped Delond, sighing raggedly in relief. "We were . . . ordered . . . to await the return of His Majesty the King."

"The King has not come in a long time, but you are loyal servants, so you wait, eh?"

"Exactly, sir!" Delond said.

The maid nodded, solemnly, her eyes huge in her ashen face.

Douglas thought about this for the time it took to eat his dry toast and tasteless jam and sip half his coffee (heavy with slightly sour cream, oversweetened and weak). He turned to the maid.

"Your name is?"

"Antia, sir, if it pleases you, sir."

"And if it did not, you'd change it?" chided Douglas, gently.

"Of course, Sir Wizard!"

"Great Greasy Goblins!" swore Douglas. "This is the sort of nonsense that went on at Frigeon's court! Not even under Eunicet was it known in Dukedom!"

The two servants looked extremely ill at ease and, moreover, baffled.

"Now, Delond, who told you to wait for the King?"

There was another long, queasy silence. Douglas calmly finished his breakfast. He thought, *Two hundred years will have weakened the third-class spell I sense, which makes these people behave so utterly irrational.*

At last, when Douglas glanced up at the Majordomo again, Delond cleared his throat and gulped.

" 'Twas the Magister, really, who spoke *for* the King," spoke up Antia, suddenly. "I wasn't there, but I heard of it."

"Yes," blurted Delond, leaning forward. "I *was* there. The Magister . . ."

"Did this Magister have a name?"

"His name is . . . was . . . Farlance," recalled Delond, and the maid Antia nodded.

"Farlance? Seems to me I've heard of him," said Douglas, and indeed he had. The Wizard Farlance had once been a member of the Fellowship of Wizards, a colleague of Flarman's and Augurian's, long ago. "I believe Farlance perished in Last Battle," Douglas mused aloud.

"Perished!" shrieked the girl, biting her knuckles, eyes wide in horror.

"Someone will have to tell you this eventually or you will live and die with no choices of your own," Douglas said firmly. "Delond, do you want to know why King Grummist has not returned?"

"No, Sir Wizard, I mean . . . Douglas."

"Listen to my words and watch my hands. . . ." He made a flowing, convoluted gesture where neither could avoid seeing it clearly.

"The King will *never* return!" he said loudly, for he sensed others were listening. The air took on a sulfurous and lightning-like smell, moving fitfully about them and stirring the drapes that closed the windows to the morning light.

Delond screamed softly, like a sorely wounded bird. The maid Antia began to weep great wracking sobs, burying her face in her apron. From beyond the curtained door of Delond's house came cries and shrieks of grief and disbelief and then the sounds of many feet rushing toward the house.

The Waiters were learning they need no longer wait.

It took several hours to calm them down and tell them, as best Douglas knew, the truth about Grummist's tragic end and the story of the Last Battle of Kingdom. He kindly avoided dwelling on the King's foolish, last-minute attempts to bargain with the Dark Powers for his own life. It had led only to greater disaster and a more agonized death . . . and the breakup of Flarman's beloved Fellowship as well, despite a hard-won victory.

At last the fifty remaining Waiters stopped weeping and gathered around Douglas in Delond's dining hall to listen to the unheard news of the last two centuries, silently but slowly recovering their wits and common sense.

An elderly footman asked, "We exist to serve the King! Without the King, what are we?"

"Free men, for one thing," replied Douglas. "Responsible men and women, who can take care of themselves."

"But who can we serve? We are trained to serve!" came fearful cries from all sides.

Douglas shook his head. He was unsure how much help he should give these poor, forlorn souls. Too much would be as fatal as too little, he suspected.

"But we *must* serve!" wailed a laundress. "Or we are nothing!"

"Nonsense," Douglas said angrily. "You're free men. Who should you serve? I'll tell you. *Serve each other.*"

"*Each other?*" they cried out, some in abject fear . . . but others repeated the words in wonder. They fell at once into a furious discussion of this novel idea.

"How can this be? Who will rule? Make the decisions? Give the orders?"

"Figure it out for yourselves!" said Douglas, shaking his head.

They were positively dumbfounded. At last young Antia spoke up.

"It is *sensible* that we *serve* each other, isn't it? And if we *serve* each other, why can't we also *rule* each other!"

Their logjam was at last broken. Douglas saw it would take them weeks, months, perhaps years to reason it out, feel out the details, but they were on the right track at last.

"Rule and serve!" cried an excited Delond. "Serve and rule! Sir . . . Douglas . . . Wizard?"

"Yes, Delond?"

"We owe you an extremely deep debt of gratitude."

"I don't think so. I just told you the plain harsh truth."

"The truth, to show us the way," said Antia. "We will long remember you, Douglas Brightglade!"

"Douglas Brightglade!" they shouted. "Make a speech, Wizard!"

The Journeyman Wizard stood and bowed to the assemblage.

"It's close to noontime. I must be getting on my way and you have a lot of things to decide and do," he told them. "It isn't going to be easy, you know. I can't help you any more than I have. You must clean out and fix up your ruined city, mend your ruined houses, and rebuild your neglected lives. Learn how to be served rather than just to serve, how to rule justly and mercifully, and be ruled in turn by common sense and humane, open minds."

The Waiters listened, their faces aglow, yet very serious.

"Now, let's all have a good, sustaining lunch, with lots of pepper and salt, marjoram and rosemary, and . . . well, all the things you've neglected to use for too long. Ale and cakes, if you like. Together!"

A sturdy old table was enthusiastically hauled from the dust of a long-empty house, wiped clean, and spread with age-yellowed linen. In a few minutes it was loaded with porcelain dishes and gold-ware fit for any king. The serving dishes were heaped to overflowing with all manner of good, spicy, savory things to eat. Glasses were filled with truly well aged and heady wines.

"Are you going to stay here forever?" asked a voice at Douglas's elbow. Marbleheart was daintily sampling a spiced wing of chicken from a vast platter on the table.

"No, no!" whispered Douglas. "They might want to make me king, and Wizards make the very worst sort of kings! Let's leave while they're still arguing. They'll be just fine! People get exactly the government they deserve, Flarman Flowerstalk says."

"I've decided to go with you," announced the Sea Otter, licking his paws appreciatively. "Say, the food here has vastly improved all of a sudden!"

He selected a drumstick from the platter. Douglas laughed aloud.

"Well, I've gotten quite curious about what's to be seen beyond Wide Marsh. Beside that, you might need me. If you'll take me with you, that is."

"Curiosity is a very useful quality," said Douglas, remembering the day he first encountered the Fire Wizard who advertised for an Apprentice with a Large Bump of Curiosity. "Very necessary for anyone, even an Otter."

"Otters have the most curiosity of anyone," claimed Marbleheart, stoutly. "I wonder where we'll sleep tonight?"

"Let's find out," said Douglas, and after they'd retrieved his knapsack and topped it off with some choice foods from the Waiters' gala table, the new-made friends slipped quietly away, down a cracked and sand-clogged boulevard to the river.

"It wouldn't be such a hard trip if we both could swim," observed the Otter, dabbling his forepaws impatiently in Bloody Brook. "But I guess we'll just have to walk, unless Wizards can become fishes."

Douglas was examining one of the long, narrow, high-prowed gondolas tied to Summer Palace's crumbling stone pier. The Waiters had been using them for fishing, he decided, for they were worn, smudged, and smelled strongly of fish. They'd once been graceful, heavily gilded vessels for carrying noblemen and their ladies up and down the river.

"How do you think these things are propelled?" he asked. "Ah, here's an oar."

"That's disappointing. I thought it might go by magic," said Marbleheart, poking his inquisitive nose into the nearest boat.

"No, servants rowed them."

Battered and stained as it had become, something about the slim grace of the gondola reminded him of a pearl fisher he knew. Myrn, island born and bred to ships and sailing, would have appreciated the beautiful craft, if she could see it. A memory returned to him as he thought of her.

"There's something a friend of mine told me, not long ago. 'What good is being a Wizard if you can't make a boat go without sail or oars?' she asked me, and she taught me just the Propelling Spell we need."

"I was wondering when you were going to do some magic," cried Marbleheart eagerly. "Let's go!"

He leaped nimbly into the gondola, followed more carefully by the Journeyman. When Douglas spoke Myrn's spell and made a pushing motion with his left hand, the gondola slid gently backward into the river . . . but came to a stop with a sharp jerk that tumbled the Otter to the floorboards in a furry heap.

"Some sailors we are!" he chortled. "Wait, I'll untie the mooring rope!"

Once freed, the beautifully proportioned craft slid with increasing speed into the slowly moving current. Douglas described a tight circle with his left hand and the boat turned sharply, pointing upstream. The Wizard gestured away upstream and the boat reversed itself and accelerated smoothly in that direction.

"Better than swimming, almost," laughed the Otter in pure delight. He trailed a paw in the water over the side and watched the V-shaped ripple it made. "We should make Pfantas by tomorrow, at this rate!"

Douglas doubted it. "Lots of things might happen on an adventure like this," he warned his new companion. "And probably will."

"Water is the most powerful element, by far," Augurian was saying. They were seated on the battlements above crashing surf stirred by a Sea storm so far away they weren't aware of it otherwise. The tall walls of this wing of Augurian's Palace stood with their stone feet right in the surf.

Below them, cadet Porpoises played excitedly in the foaming breakers, gliding swiftly down the wave-fronts and darting off to the side or leaping joyously into the air just before the crests curled over and hurled themselves onto the black and green rocks.

"There's certainly a lot of it," said the Apprentice Aquamancer.

"It's not just a matter of *quantity*. It's also *quality*," said her Master sternly, sensing that her mind was not entirely on his lecture.

"Let's see; water is solvent, mover, life giver, mountain breaker, pathway . . ."

She went on at some length, mollifying her dignified Magister with what she remembered of earlier lessons. He sat back, his eyes half-closed, as if listening to poetry in the wind. When she fell silent at last, he shook himself slightly and rose. Myrn followed him toward the broad stair down to the Palace forecourt, with its enormous, four-story-tall fountain. Augurian paused.

"You seem distracted these days, young Apprentice. Even so, you're very quick to learn."

Myrn let the spray from the great fountain dampen and cool her face. It was winter on Waterand but the tropical heat was still intense at midday.

"I . . . I'm sorry, Magister! At the oddest times I have thoughts of . . ."

"Of Douglas Brightglade, I suppose," chuckled the Water Adept. "Well, I don't complain about that. Douglas is like a son to me, also. Think of him all you wish, but remember . . . the sooner you learn your basic Aquamancy, the sooner you can rejoin your young fire-eater."

"I know," said Myrn with a bright smile. "We'll make some steam, I think, together!"

Augurian laughed outright. The girl was a delight to him, strong yet flexible, earthy yet innocent. Wise and yet ever eager to learn. She could make sail and steer, reef and tack with the best sailors. She knew Sea's moods, sudden swings, and color changes better than any Mortal he knew, himself not excluded.

She had great courage, great self-confidence, yet she was gentle, polite, and pleasant to everyone. Even Grand Dragon, who now came often to visit and tended to be a bit haughty with everyone else, laughed with Myrn and played games with her he had forgotten ten thousand years before. Like water itself, she flowed to the occasion.

"Flarman will be here soon." Augurian resumed his way down the marble steps. "Will you see to preparing his rooms? I'll make plans for our dining. Flarman loves a good table better than I, but I enjoy having him enjoy our hospitality."

Myrn took the last nine steps three at a time, waved her hand at the Water Adept, and disappeared in the direction of the Palace's guest quarters.

"Makes me wish I had taken time to have a family," Augurian said to his Familiar, the silently swift, patient

Stormy Petrel, who just then swooped down to perch on the fountain curbing.

The seabird, as usual, said nothing, but Augurian thought he nodded his great head in agreement—and friendly amusement, too.

Chapter Six

The Savannah Horses

MARBLEHEART spent most of his time in the water swimming from boat to shore and shore to boat, finding all sorts of interesting things to investigate and delicious— he said—things to munch.

At first Douglas propelled the Summer Palace gondola by Myrn's magic. Then, becoming bored with doing and seeing practically nothing—except blue sky, brown river, and yellow reeds all the same height on either side—he stood on the after-deck and fitted the long oar into its rest. Swinging it back and forth in the rowlock to push and pull the curved blade through the water, he found he could drive the gondola easily, breasting the slowly flowing river current. It was welcome exercise, once he got the hang of it, and something useful to be doing.

At Summer Palace the river had been broad and the current lazily looping right and left, syrup slow. As they moved upstream, however, its course became choked with densely tangled floating mats of hyacinths, water lilies, and low-lying mud aits built up around snags of branches and sometimes full trees, swept down by past floods.

Between the islets, the stream flowed so slowly that its direction was barely perceptible. Choosing the passages that appeared deepest and widest, Douglas rowed steadily on.

By late afternoon, open water had all but disappeared. Douglas navigated by the lowering sun, alone. Even this failed when he ran the gondola's sharp prow against an unusually thick and tangled snag that blocked the stream course, disturbing a nest of newly hatched alligators, who swam quickly away, squeaking furiously.

Backing water to free the bow from the snag, he tried another channel, only to find their way impeded by a vast floating mass of sweet-smelling purple hyacinths. Even Myrn's strong propulsion spell was unable to push them through the intertwined stems and bulbous leaves.

After retreating and trying several other paths, he realized he was becoming confused, especially as the sun was now below the horizon.

"Can you tell which way the current is flowing?" he called to the Otter, who was sitting on another hyacinth mat, fluffing his fur.

"Better turn back! We'll never get the boat through here."

Douglas shipped his oar and sat down to ponder the situation in Wizardly fashion. The Sea Otter jumped aboard from the hyacinths.

"Actually there are several dozen channels," he said. "You just keep picking the wrong one, I guess."

"You're a big help," Douglas sniffed sarcastically. "Got any better ideas?"

"Hoy! I'm a Sea Otter, not a riverine one," Marbleheart protested. "I don't know anything about rivers except that they get shallower and smaller as you go away from Sea. As I said at the beginning, if we could swim . . ."

"I *could* change myself into a fish. No, not a fish! A certain Otter around here has too big an appetite," mused Douglas. "Beside, shape changing is a very uncertain business. There's always the danger of not being able to change back. If I changed into an Otter, I might have to stay an Otter forever!"

"Not what I'd call a fate worse than death," chuckled the Sea Otter.

Douglas stared at the wall of reeds on all sides, each reed as thick as a man's thumb and standing eight feet out of the water.

"I could fly out of here, but then I couldn't take the boat—or the Otter, for that matter, over that distance. Too tiring. No. Instead, I'll loft myself above the reeds with Flarman's Levitation Spell," he decided. "Maybe I can see our way to a clear channel."

"Worth a try," said Marbleheart, excited by the prospect of seeing more magic. "What should I do?"

"Stay put! Don't wander off and don't let the boat get in among the reeds where I can't see it," Douglas ordered.

He performed the appropriate incantation and gestured to lift himself gently into the air, slowly rising until he was looking down at the hundreds of square miles of marshland around them. From this vantage he could just see the broken towers of Summer Palace in the distance and a ragged line of mountains to the west, but little in between but the occasional glimpse of open stretches of water rapidly growing dark as the sun fell.

"We've twisted and turned so often," he called in disgust to the Otter, "I can't even see the way to backtrack. I'll have to check all possible channels by sight, first, then move the boat. It'll take days!"

He took a long time, sitting cross-legged atop nothing, much to the Otter's amazed delight, turning slowly about clockwise to study the lay of the wetlands in all directions.

"That way, I think," he decided, at last. He produced a brass pocket compass from his right sleeve and carefully noted the direction of the most promising channel. Once he dropped back into the boat there were no landmarks to tell which way to go.

"Please, Marbleheart, swim on ahead and check the depth of the way I chose, so the boat won't get stuck in the mud. What are the tides hereabouts, anyway?"

"Not large," said Marbleheart, splashing eagerly into the water. "That, a Sea Otter can tell you. It's second nature to notice such things for us. The tide turned two hours ago and is ebbing now."

"Which means it'll get shallower and shallower around here unless we find a deep channel," sighed Douglas. He checked his compass once more and pointed out to the Otter the way to go.

It went well but slowly for an hour while twilight stayed in the sky. At times the reeds, sand, and mud banks closed in on the narrow boat so that the Journeyman could touch the stalks at either side by spreading his arms wide. Then they would suddenly emerge from the narrows into wide, still lagoons, completely clear of vegetation. The next problem was choosing a suitable exit through the reeds on the far side of each pool.

The Sea Otter made sure they had enough water under the gondola's keel to remain afloat and clear of subsurface obstructions, but seeing soon became difficult even for the Otter's night-sharp eyes.

"It isn't getting any deeper," panted Marbleheart, pausing to rest a moment on a great green lily pad with upturned edges like an enormous pie plate. "On the other hand it isn't getting any shallower, either. We can go on for another half hour or so, but could you see well enough to steer?"

"Not really," admitted Douglas. He allowed the gondola to coast to a standstill in the middle of one of the open pools. "Better stop for the night."

"There'll be a moon later on. Maybe we can go on under moonlight," the Otter told him.

He went off in search of his supper while Douglas contented himself with a meat pasty and a rather wilted salad taken from the Waiters' luncheon at Summer Palace.

Wide Marsh came to life as full night fell. Choruses of chirps and croaks filled the air, punctuated by alligators booming, warning everyone away from their personal banks and ponds. The air hummed with the wings of hungry insects homing in on Douglas's tender skin and warm blood.

After some thought, Douglas conjured an insect-repellant envelope about the gondola and listened to the angry comments of tens of thousands of mosquitoes until they gave up in disgust and went whining off to find their suppers elsewhere.

"I'll take a short nap," he decided when the Otter returned, smacking his lips over some undisclosed wetland delicacy.

"I'll just snuggle close and benefit from your bug spell," agreed the other, and in short time they were both sound asleep in the bottom of the gondola, gently rocked by tiny wavelets.

A thirty-foot alligator with a wickedly sharp grin glided silently into the lagoon. He nosed curiously against the mosquito shield, suspiciously eyed the frail-seeming gondola for a long moment, but moved off again, wary of the invisible blockade he had felt but couldn't see.

The sleepers didn't even wake when a fight broke out between several night birds over a fish carcass floating on the glassy surface at the other end of the lagoon.

"Pad Foot!" said a husky voice near Douglas's right ear. "Pad Foot, come look at what I've found!"

The Journeyman awoke without starting, opening his eyes just a slit to see who had spoken. He felt the Otter stir ever so slightly, then lie very still as well.

The rising moon was silvery bright just above the tall reeds edging the pool; bright enough for one to see very well, Douglas discovered.

The gondola rocked slightly. Glancing over the side, he caught sight of a pair of gnarled and spindly arms and twisted, webbed fingers grasping the side of the boat.

A moment later a pair of huge, luminous yellow-green eyes peered cautiously into the boat. They blinked slowly.

"Gangoner, what are you going on about?" called a new voice from some distance away. "I'm coming. . . ."

Slowly sitting up, Douglas saw a swift-moving chevron of ripples pointed in their direction on the glassy surface. The disturbance slapped softly at the side of the gondola and a second, even more grotesque pair of hands and two wide-set, gold-glowing eyes appeared over the side near where Douglas lay. The first impression Douglas had of the night visitors was that they were giant frogs, mottled green and black with wide, toothless mouths.

"Hello, there!" said the one called Gangoner cheerfully, if a bit hoarsely. "Welcome to Wide Marsh!"

"Thank you," said Douglas. "I'm afraid I fell asleep!"

"For some, nighttime is for sleeping," observed the creature. "But for us, it's time to look to our tummies, you know."

"Not fond of Otter, are you?" asked Marbleheart, also sitting up and watching the visitors warily.

"No, no! Fishes are best, oysters are even better, if we can find 'em and clams. Then a salad of water-lily root and lotus buds for roughage. This night we've already dined, anyway."

The frog-creature named Gangoner introduced himself and his companion, Pad Foot, quite politely. Whatever unease their appearance initially caused, Douglas quickly put aside. Despite their lumpy ugliness and guttural voices, they seemed gentle, friendly beasts.

He told the marsh dwellers his own name and Marbleheart's and invited them to come aboard.

"We're a bit lost here, not being able to find the main river course," he explained. "Perhaps you could help?"

Pad Foot, the smaller and more talkative of the two, nodded his understanding as he climbed wetly aboard the gondola and perched on the forward thwart. He was, indeed, a huge amphibian, green with three yellow stripes down his flanks.

"We're never quite sure of the currents here ourselves. I think the tide is just beginning to rise, but 'tis too early to show."

"If you're heading upriver we probably can't help," considered Gangoner, scratching his belly as he joined his companion. "We've lived all our lives here in Backwater, you see. No desire to brave the turbulent currents and salty tides."

"I've never seen creatures quite like you before," said Douglas, offering them bits of waybread.

"Ummm, good!" cried Pad Foot. "We are of the race of Goblins—"

"Goblins!" exclaimed Marbleheart. "I expect Goblins to have no interest in strangers, except as dinners."

"No! No! We are *Hob*goblins!" Gangoner said quickly. "We're only distantly related to those wicked flesh-eating Great Goblins you've heard about. We're true water *Hob*goblins, rather. Goblins are ever so much larger and ever so much nastier."

"We're hardly nasty, at all," added Pad Foot, earnestly. "Not the least bit, in fact. No, no. We like the retired, quiet life, although it is nice to meet strangers from solid ground once in a while, you know. This bread is really quite delicious!"

Douglas gave them both a bit more of the fairy food. Waybread is very difficult to use up. It tends to run out only when you fail to share it with every hungry thing that comes along.

The froglike Hobgoblins chatted for a few moments longer about their reclusive lives in Backwater of Wide Marsh.

Douglas wasn't surprised to find they knew little of World, beyond the reed beds and hyacinth rafts. They had only a hazy knowledge of the long-ago Last Battle of Kingdom, part of which had been fought not far inland.

"My great-granddaddy told me that as many died when they fled in panic into Wide Marsh as died by sharp sword, swift arrow, and heavy battle-ax," shuddered the gentle Pad Foot. "This place can be dangerous to those too big and burdened with cold iron to tread lightly in mud or swim the waters. On moonless nights you can still hear the warriors calling out in dread."

"Indeed!" exclaimed Gangoner, wrapping his long, thin arms about his shoulders and shivering. "Even boatmen are easily lost hereabouts, without a guide."

"That's our problem, isn't it?" interrupted Marbleheart. "I could perhaps swim my way out in time, but Douglas here will have a hard, wet time of it, I think, unless someone helps us."

The Hobgoblins munched Waybread thoughtfully for a moment before Gangoner raised a skinny, webbed finger.

"Aha! Jenny Greenteeth!"

"Just the person!" agreed Pad Foot, nodding vigorously. "Where do you think she is these days?"

"And who is she?" asked Douglas.

"She's a Water Sprite who came here a century or more ago looking for her young husband," Pad Foot explained. "He'd perished in Last Battle. She found his body in a common grave and reburied him under a willow tussock, here in Wide Marsh. She stays nearby to tend his grave."

"Rather sad little lady, but I suppose friendly enough, all the same," Gangoner added, pulling a long face.

"She goes as far as the Savannah country, upriver, I think. She's told us of it, on occasion," said Pad Foot.

"Could you possibly find her to ask her to guide us to the main channel so we can go on up Bloody Brook?" asked the Journeyman Wizard.

"We'll try. That's all we can do, can we, Gangoner? Jenny Greenteeth is hard to find if she doesn't want to be found," said Pad Foot. "Certainly we'll try, won't we, Gang?"

"Of course," said the other Hobgoblin. "But we'll have to begin at once, for it's a bit of a distance away and I assume you don't wish to be lost much longer, young Wizard."

"As quickly as you can, please. We would appreciate it greatly."

"Well, we've enjoyed talking to you and sharing your delicious, scrumptious bread. Ummm, a little more would be most welcome, eh? To see us on our way," suggested Pad Foot, and Douglas broke off two generous chunks of Waybread and handed them over.

The Wizard and the Sea Otter sat in the gondola, talking quietly, unable to go back to sleep. The quarter moon sailed calmly to the top of the sky and started down the other side, making Wide Marsh a strangely beautiful nightscape, the stillness filled with distant calls and nearby murmurs.

Toward false dawn the water beside them erupted, and there, perched on the upturned prow, appeared a green-glowing Water Sprite with long, lustrous green hair, sad green eyes, and, yes, green teeth!

"Jenny Greenteeth, I presume," said Douglas, with a courteous bow.

"Too right!" sighed the green-toothed Sprite with a shy smile. "My friends Gangoner and Pad Foot have asked me to guide you to the mainstream through this marshy maze. Is this so?"

"Yes, we asked Pad Foot and Gangoner to seek you out," said Douglas, gravely. "Can—and will—you help us find our way?"

The Sprite leaned into the boat and stroked Marbleheart's sleek sides and back languidly.

"I'll not help the enemies of my dear, dead Casimar," she said flatly. "If you are of the Last King's party or of the Dark Powers, I am not available."

"No, I wasn't born by about two hundred summers when Kingdom fought its Last Battle," Douglas assured her. "I am Douglas Brightglade, a Journeyman Wizard. My master, Flarman Flowerstalk, did fight in Last Battle, though, as a member of the Fellowship of Wizards."

"Ah, yes," said the tiny Sprite, nodding her head. "I remember hearing of that Fellowship. They did all that was mortally possible to win the day for the Confederation of Light. I have little love for Faerie, however, if you are one of that kind of Being."

"I count Faerie Queen Marget and her consort, Prince Aedh, among my friends," Douglas replied, honestly. "They were, more recently, very active in defeating the wicked Ice King, Frigeon. You have no reason to distrust them, I think, Mistress Greenteeth."

"Perhaps not, if a Wizard says so," begrudged the green girl, shaking her head. "I was told they turned and ran away during Last Battle, causing many deaths among Men and Sprites, especially."

"As I was told the story by Flarman Flowerstalk, it was an honest mistake, such as often happens in confusion of battle," said Douglas. "They have more than made up for any error they may have made, in the Battle of Sea, two years ago."

"I hadn't heard of that fight. It makes no difference," said the maiden with a shrug. "I'll guide you, young Wizard, for your sake and for the sake of your brave Master. Although I can't understand why anyone would willingly to go *up* Bloody Brook."

Douglas told her of the Witches' Coven in the Far West. The little Sprite listened in absorbed silence until he had finished.

"Well, then, let's begin," was her only comment. "The way isn't short or easy, I'm afraid. You've got yourselves into a tangled, twisted reach called Backwater. But I can put you on the open river above the marsh in three or four hours, if all goes well."

The Sprite was as good as she was gloomy. By midmorning the gondola floated freely on rippling, open river once again. They were still surrounded by tall reeds and papyrus flowers, but there was a clear watercourse ahead leading toward rising ground and tree-clad, low hills.

"Douglas Brightglade," sighed the green Water Sprite, not the least bit tired by her long swim, "I'll leave you here and return to my love's grave side. Fresh flowers, purple hyacinths, and yellow lotus, I place there every morningtide, and in the evening we sit and talk, my love and I, until the moon rises or rain comes down."

"Are you happy here?" Douglas asked in sympathy.

"Happy? Not at all! Content? I suppose so. The spirits of both the good and of the wicked who fought here are often held captive in this existence by the violence and terror of their destructions. You'll see many signs of them as you pass through Old Kingdom. I do what I can to ease the ages-long suffering of my brave Casimar, whose true wife I am. Our clan was drummed to war and he must go, you know. I hope that he will pass to his final rest someday. And then I will follow him there." She sighed even more deeply.

"Jenny, is there anything a Wizard can do for you?"

The Sprite shook her head, but managed a wan smile.

"No, I really suppose I am happiest, after all, to be here. If you have loved, you will know what I mean."

"I . . . I see," responded the Journeyman, softly. "I might do the same, were my love lost to me in such a manner."

"Then you understand," said Jenny Greenteeth, and without further ado she slipped gracefully back into the river. "Have care on your voyage, Douglas Brightglade. This land is haunted by its past. Many evil and troubled spirits are still abroad."

She was gone without a ripple.

Marbleheart broke the wistful mood of their parting, crying cheerfully, "Well, what to do now, Wizard? Rest? Or move on, now that we can see our way clear?"

Douglas shook off the sadness of the little green wife's plight. Taking up the long sweep, he fitted it into its rowlock and began to swing it side to side, driving the slender gondola swiftly up the mile-wide, slowly flowing river.

"If you fear Witches and Sprites, Goblins and Ghosts, all wicked and fierce things that go about in the night," he said to the Sea Otter, "then I will understand if you decide to return to your home."

"My goodness, no!" exclaimed the Otter, flipping himself over the side of the boat into Bloody Brook. "It's getting more and more interesting all the time. I wonder what's next?"

"Some rowing, a swim, perhaps, and a couple of hours' sleep," decided Douglas, swaying rhythmically and sending the gondola knifing up the middle of the stream. "And after that . . . who knows?"

By midafternoon they had passed the last of the Wide Marsh reed beds and meandering water mazes. The banks here were gently upsloping grasslands dotted with groves of wide-spreading trees making pools of deep, blue shadow in the green-gold landscape.

The weather, which had been chilly and wet since Douglas had left Valley, now turned warm. A pleasant springlike breeze blew the scent of opening wildflowers and new-sprouted mead grasses across the broad savannahs.

"There are some pretty weird-looking beasts swimming in the shallows ahead there," reported Marbleheart, reappearing beside the gondola after an hour of exploring the riverbanks. "They're watching us."

Douglas, who had given over rowing for a rest, stood on his thwart and shaded his eyes with his hand.

A herd of white and chestnut brown horses, standing belly deep in the stream, turned to face the approaching gondola, unmoving but alert.

He made a hand signal to the right and the boat veered slightly to bring them closer to the grassy north bank. A great dappled gray stallion moved toward deeper water but the other horses—his mares, Douglas presumed—waded ashore and disappeared under overhanging willows.

"Ahoy!" called Douglas, waving. "We're harmless travelers going upstream to Pfantas. No need to fear us!"

The stallion continued to move toward them, swimming easily with his proud head arched high out of the water. Douglas stopped the gondola, not wishing to alarm the beautiful animal. The dappled gray halted about twenty feet off.

"I must be forgiven," he said in cultured accents, "for doubting the innocent purposes of anyone going toward Pfantas. It seems to me that only Black Witches and other evil-looking beings go that way these days. We avoid contact with them as much as possible."

"I am a Fire Wizard," admitted Douglas, introducing himself and his companion. "We're on a mission upriver for the Fellowship of Wizards, you see. Any Black Witches we meet would probably consider us their enemies."

"Not all Witches are wicked, I'm told," said the horse. "But you are wise not to believe any Witch friendly or filled with good intentions, at first meeting."

"We don't mean to bother you, sir Horse," said Marbleheart. "We'll just pass on our way up the stream, if that's what you prefer."

He was uneasy at the size of the animal, it was obvious, and he moved close to Douglas for support.

"Not at all!" objected the stallion, tossing his long mane. "My wives will never forgive me if I don't make you welcome and offer our hospitality. Hospitality is everywhere a hallmark of good breeding."

They accepted his invitation—out of curiosity, mostly—and followed him out of the water and into the willow grove, where his mares awaited their arrival with nervous but keen interest.

"We live peacefully on these lush grasslands," the stallion explained as they drew near. "We come to the river to bathe and drink, of course. There is not much traffic on the Brook and none at all on old Greenfern River Road. As you can imagine, we're always eager to hear the latest news, if strangers seem well disposed to us."

He gracefully introduced his ladies in order of age as they crowded around, eager to greet the Man and the Otter.

"Mocking, Stocking, Truelove, Rachael, Rusty, and her twin Misty. This is Gerda, and this is my youngest wife, Winnie. And I am Finnerty," he said. "We are Savannah Horses now, but our ancestors carried Warriors of Light and the Fellowship of Wizards into Battle."

Douglas told them of his own background. Finnerty nodded vigorously, and exclaimed, "The names you mention, Flarman and Augurian and even Frigeon, are well known to us, although the last of us who remembered Last Battle is long since gone to the grave. These names are the stuff of legends among us, and now we'll add Brightglade and Manstar, Bronze Owl and Marbleheart

the Sea Otter, and even Bryarmote the Dwarf—although
we warhorses have never been very fond of Dwarfs, I
must admit. As for the Faerie folk, we love them best
of all."

"How we would love to see Queen Marget of Faerie!"
cried the mare Rachael. "She, we revere most among all
Near Immortals from the old tales and our own long history."

"I know and love Marget well," Douglas told her. "When
I see her again, I'll ask her to drop by some time and greet
you, for you are all so beautiful—and loyal as well, I see."

The younger mares squealed with excitement and wanted to
know as much as Douglas could tell them of the Faerie Queen,
but the elder ladies calmed them down with a few gentle
words, and shortly the herd and their visitors moved inland
a way so the horses could graze on the fresh spring grass.

Douglas spent the rest of the afternoon and evening telling
the Stallion of the recent war against Frigeon, which was news
to the Horses of Savannah as it had been to the Waiters and
Jenny Greenteeth, too. When night fell, Douglas retired to
the cushioned thwarts of the gondola and there slept soundly,
while the Horses and the Otter went to play in the river by gib-
bous moonlight, leaping and sliding and diving until it set.

"What lies upstream?" Douglas asked Finnerty after breakfast.

"Black Witches and their Warlocks, that's for certain!
We've watched from hiding as a half dozen or more went
up the river in recent years, flying low on their haddocks—
their broomsticks, you know. We've heard rumors from the
waterfowl that they are up to dire mischief, somewhere in the
west. Nothing you could put a fore-hoof on; just gossip and
rumors."

"We had report of it from a former Wizard's Apprentice
named Cribblon," Douglas said. "Have you heard of him?"

"No, that name means nothing to me," said the horse,
shaking his head and mane. "In fact the only name we've
heard from the water birds is that of the Witches' leader.
Her name is said to be Emaldar. She's titled both Witch
Queen and the Beautiful. I heard those names also from a

dirty, disreputable old Warlock on whom we took pity some months back. He said he was off to join something he called a 'coven'. If you know what that is, I don't."

"I know what it might be," admitted the Journeyman. "What was his name, this tramp Warlock?"

"He never said, which didn't surprise me. We harried him out of the Savannahs when he tried to catch and ride poor Rusty. We sent that rustler hustling, I can tell you!"

"Good for you!" cried Marbleheart. "Do either of you want some of these freshwater oysters? They're delicious!"

The Journeyman and the Stallion said, "No, thanks."

Marbleheart fell to pounding the oyster shells furiously on his pink marble disk, making such a racket that Finnerty nudged Douglas with his muzzle and they walked slowly up the bank to a slight rise where they could see the river for some miles in both directions.

"We don't usually care to be ridden, now, you see. I guess we have become somewhat feral over the years. But I feel that we, once servants of the Light in a small way, should offer to help you on your mission. I would be willing to carry you on my back—"

"No, no, thank you, and I really do appreciate it, Finnerty. There are several reasons why I refuse your very kind offer. Our gondola, not being a live thing, can be sacrificed to circumstances if the need arises. It's quite fast and comfortable, and never gets hoof weary or needs fodder. Besides, I should think your mares and the new foals, when they come—I notice several of your ladies are expecting—will need the freedom of the Savannahs and your protection."

"There *is* that," agreed the horse, with some relief. "But if you had needed us, we would be willing and happy to oblige."

"Thank you," repeated the Journeyman sincerely. "Stay here and keep an eye on any other travelers going up Bloody Brook. Is there a way you could send word to me if, say, more Black Witches come along?"

The horse considered this for a moment, then nodded.

"Yes, we are on friendly terms with the Whooping Cranes and the Teals, who make their summer homes in Wide Marsh.

They would be pleased to carry word to you, anywhere you might be in Old Kingdom."

Marbleheart, having had his breakfast of oysters, was waiting when they returned to the boat, and Douglas prepared at once to shove off.

"Have a safe and fruitful voyage," called the Savannah Horses. "Come to visit us again!"

"I wouldn't want to go against *them* in a fight," said the Otter, settling down on the middle thwart while the Wizard plied the long sweep. "Such great, frightening beasts! Only the Walruses of the Briney are more imposing and fierce looking."

"But the Horses were most kind and hospitable," objected Douglas, setting the gondola into midstream. Their speed left a foaming wake behind them.

"So are the Walruses, generally," said the other, sleepily. "It's just that they *look* rather intimidating."

Douglas scanned the river as far ahead as he could see. It remained very wide, still rather slow and deep, but straight running across the grassy plain. Far ahead these grasslands ended at a line of dark forest which came down to the water's edge on both banks. Its dark band marched to the horizons both to the north and south.

"We'll spend tonight in the forest, I think," he told the dozing Otter. "Looks like an oak wood, mostly."

"I wouldn't know an oak from an acorn," murmured Marbleheart.

"You'll learn soon enough," said Douglas. "I wonder what Myrn is doing this beautiful morning."

In the sunny stone-flagged courtyard of Augurian's Waterand Palace that afternoontide, Myrn struggled with a very difficult spell. If performed properly, it allowed her to lift, move about, and balance in midair a great, crystalline globe of water. Augurian had set her the task and left her to practice the required skills by herself.

"Concentration is most important," he had reminded her before he hastily left for other, drier parts.

She began the spell carefully enough but, as she was thinking of Douglas and of being at Wizards' High, her concentration was not as deep as it should have been. The globe of water wobbled and distorted erratically, bulging from side to side, then flew apart into sparkling droplets and doused her with sun-warmed water.

"*Bother!*" sputtered the drenched Apprentice. "*Drat and sturm!*"

"Ah, ah, ah!" cautioned a laughter-filled voice behind her. Spinning about angrily, she beheld Flarman Flowerstalk in brown traveling robes brushing water drops from his beard.

"Magister!" cried the Flowring lass, delightedly. "You're here at last! I'm so sorry about the wetting!"

"It's just harmless water. Now, if it had been fire . . . Well, I'm glad to find you immersed in your studies," said Flarman, trying to look very serious about it all and failing completely. "Mooning over a certain runaway Journeyman, too, I surmise."

"Douglas is not a runaway!" Myrn insisted, snatching up a towel from a nearby bench and rubbing her long, black hair vigorously.

"Joshing only, my wet, pet Apprentice!" Flarman said with a deep roar of a laugh. "No, perhaps not, but I haven't heard a word from him since he left Westongue myself, and I wonder if you've done better."

"The last letter he wrote from Thornwood's Sea House in Westongue," said Myrn, giving the Fire Wizard a loving hug and a kiss and a dry corner of her towel. "Shouldn't we ask Deka the Wraith to check up on him? He may need help, even now!"

Augurian, hearing their voices in the fountain court, hurried down from his Water Tower workroom, smiling broadly, to welcome his oldest and best friend and fellow Wizard.

"I have to keep her under tight rein or she would go dashing off to 'check on' that Journeyman of yours," he told Flarman. "And her studies . . ."

"Am I that bad?" wailed Myrn, looking truly downcast. "I try so very hard!"

"No, no, you're really very good and a remarkably apt pupil of magic. You just let your thoughts wander once in a while, like a moment ago."

"Oh, dear, did you see that? I almost had it."

"Good! Good, better, and best! How about some lunch, friends?" said Flarman. "Magically transporting so much mass is conducive to a large appetite."

He plucked three handfuls of water from the fountain and sent them spinning in slow orbits about his head. Augurian applauded mockingly—the two Wizards constantly teased and tested each other about the relative merits of each one's specialty—and Myrn giggled in spite of herself.

"After lunch we'll get to work on Frigeon's foul enchant-ment of the Busibodies of Blowheart, or whatever they're called," said the Fire Wizard, making the water balls change colors rapidly in turn, azure blue and magenta and bright green, and fly about him in three different directions at once.

"Always thinking of your stomach!" admonished Augurian. "Fortunately, Myrn had no hand in preparing lunch."

"I can cook rings around our Wateranders!" exclaimed Myrn. "They think all great cuisine consists of coconuts, sweet potatoes, fish and pork roasted whole, wrapped in savory leaves and buried under a bonfire in wet sand!"

"Flarman may test you on that one day soon," warned her Master. "Come now! I must admit seeing Flarman's ample girth makes me think of food also."

Flarman swirled the three bright globules of water high over their heads and let them arc down into the fountain basin to the sound of a minor-key musical chord, instead of dull plops.

They strolled arm in arm across the courtyard to enter the Grand Reception Hall. On the terrace beyond, sarong-clad servants were swiftly setting a table for three in the shade of a mauve-and-blue-striped awning.

"I think we'll hear report from Douglas when he reaches Pfantas and finds our friend Cribblon, no sooner," said Flarman to soothe Myrn and reassure Augurian. "Until then, he has just to behave himself and enjoy his travels through interesting new lands."

"I somehow doubt it will be all that easy," said the Apprentice Water Adept. "I looked it up and asked some questions of the few people who know about Kingdom since the end of Last Battle. Bloody Brook can be treacherous in more ways than one, they all agreed. And since Last Battle, strange things have happened to the people and their land."

"Then you won't be surprised if we don't hear from the Journeyman today?" teased Flarman.

"No, not surprised. Furious! We'd better hear from him by month's end," Myrn said, seriously. "Journeyman's journeying or not, I'm not going to let anything happen to that man!"

"Nor are we, pretty Apprentice," said Augurian. "Pass the salt, please."

Chapter Seven

Faerie Forest and Battleground

NIGHT and the outliers of the great oak forest came abeam at about the same moment. The river plunged in under the ancient oak trees, which arched over it like a black roof to a lightless tunnel.

The forest has an air of watchfulness, neither menacing nor benevolent, Douglas felt in his bones.

"It were best," recommended Marbleheart, who also felt the watchfulness of the forest, "if we put off going into the woods until daylight. It'll be deep-Sea dark, even at noontide in there."

"You're right, of course," said the Journeyman Wizard, swinging the bow of their boat over to the right bank. "I could easily light our way, but why call anyone's attention to ourselves? It's time to get some sleep and have a bite to eat, anyway."

"I've already eaten," Marbleheart said. "Crayfish cocktail and watercress salad! Yummm!"

Douglas was content with Waybread and the last bit of *Pitchfork*'s dried Valley beef. He built a small, hidden fire, mostly for company as the night air was warm, and turned his pocket handkerchief into a soft, woolly-warm blanket with the familiar, old spell remembered from his first journeyings with Flarman.

"No need for a tent in this weather," he told the Otter, who was standing by, wide eyed as always at the young Wizard's everyday magicking.

They sat in companionable silence, listening to the night bird calls and the croaking of frogs on the river marge. After a while, the Otter turned to Douglas.

"How does this forest feel to you, Douglas?"

The young man sat very still and breathed deeply.

"There is a presence here, I deem," he said at last. "What do *you* feel, Marbleheart? Animals are supposed to be more sensitive to such things."

The Otter trotted to the edge of the circle of light about their fire and stared off into the dark toward the great, spreading trees.

"A presence, definitely. A watcher, I'd say."

"Not especially hostile, but definitely watchful," agreed the Wizard. "Maybe I should . . ."

He drew a leather case from his right sleeve, opened it, and studied its contents. Looking over his shoulder, the Otter saw the case was sectioned with loops of colored silk tape. In each loop nested a glass vial the size of a man's little finger. Some were filled with powders: white or colored, fine or coarse. Others held clear or cloudy liquids, in many muted or bright colors. Some glowed faintly in the dark and others seemed to bubble or swirl slowly around and around in their vials.

After studying their cryptic labels, Douglas carefully selected two of them; one of coarse white crystals, the other half-filled with an oily, greenish liquid.

"These should do it," he decided. Placing the vials on a flat place on the ground, he carefully unstoppered each, and allowed a drop of the liquid to fall on his palm and even more carefully dusted the greenish droplet with three tiny crystals.

"Exactly a scant smidgen," he explained to the Otter. "Too much will ruin the spell."

"Oh?" asked Marbleheart in awe. "What next?"

"This," said Douglas.

He extended his hand over the middle of the fire and allowed the green globule, which had hardened into a tiny pebble of green with white striations, to drop into the hottest part of the fire.

The pebble grew larger at once, floating in the smoke and heat of the fire like a toy balloon, until it suddenly burst with a musical *ping*.

"I understand you are looking for information?" said a tiny Firefly, its tail flashing green, settling on Douglas's left hand, where the chemicals had been mixed.

"Yes, please, if you will be so kind," Douglas replied, unsurprised.

"Hoy!" exclaimed Marbleheart. He peered curiously at Firefly, who in return blinked his light in polite interest.

"Fire creatures are always at a Fire Wizard's beck and call," said the Firefly. "I'm proud to be of assistance to the pupil of Flarman Firemaster."

"We travel up Bloody Brook," explained Douglas. "Through the dark oak forest and far beyond. Is there something we should know about this forest before we enter it?"

"You're right, of course," said Firefly, beaming brightly. "This is the Forest of Forgetfulness, or *Craylor Wendys* in the Faerie tongue. My family has lived here since long before there was the Kingdom War. We lighted the way for those who went out each night of Last Battle to recover dead and wounded and those driven out of sanity during the dreadful fighting."

"Forest of Forgetfulness? I don't seem to have run across that in my lessons," said Douglas.

"It's one of the oldest forests of Faerie that were planted in the Very Beginning," said the tiny fly, solemnly. "You've never heard anything about them because no one who goes into one, uninvited, can remember being there when he comes out. If he comes out, that is."

"Is there a way to go through and not lose your memory?" Marbleheart asked.

"Oh, yes, it's very simple! Go and politely ask permission to enter, and it's almost always given."

"And if we don't?" asked Marbleheart with morbid curiosity.

"You'll forget you ever were here, along with most of everything else you really care to remember."

"The danger is very great, you see," Douglas explained to his companion. "You might forget how to swim or that you like to eat."

"That's terrible! Who do we ask permission of, friend Firefly?"

"At the near edge of the forest, on this side of the river, stands a hollow Sentinel Oak, a dozen yards apart from all the others. It's extremely old, and inside lives a family of Woodland Elves who serve Faerie as wardens. Knock at the opening and when the Elf warden answers, politely ask him to obtain for you permission to pass through the Forest of Forgetfulness. Faeries are real sticklers for protocol."

"Thank you, Firefly," said Douglas. "Can we offer you anything to eat or drink? How can we repay your enlightenment?"

"Nothing, thank you, I've dined and was on my way to a fire dance rehearsal when I heard your call. Thank you just the same. It's been a pleasure. Glad I could shed some light."

"We won't keep you, then," said Douglas, and they watched his tiny green tail light weave off between the dark trunks of the trees.

"Handy, traveling with a Wizard," commented Marbleheart as he snuggled down to sleep against Douglas's hip.

"Handy is what Wizards are all about," yawned the Journeyman. "G'night, Otter!"

But the Otter was already asleep.

Douglas found the ancient, wildly twisted Sentinel Oak a few dozen steps beyond their campsite. He knocked against the bark beside a hole at shoulder height.

An Elf, eight inches tall, dressed in brown mouse-skin breeches, a red felt jerkin, and wearing a floppy green cloth cap that came down over his ears, appeared at once. There was a pale green poplar leaf tucked as a napkin under his chin, and he clutched a fork in one hand and a knife in the other.

"Sorry to interrupt your fast breaking, Watch Elf," said Douglas, bowing. "Good morning, however!"

"As good as you care to make it," replied the watchman, politely. "What can I do for you while my griddle cakes are cooling?"

"Simply that my companion and I beg permission to pass through this forest by way of the river."

The Elf swallowed the mouthful of pancake stuck on his fork and waved his knife at them while he chewed.

"I'll have to check with the Guardians," he said, swallowing at last. "With all these here Witches and Warlocks coming along the river, they're getting especially strict. 'Twill take an hour or so."

"There's no hurry. Tell the Faerie Guardians I am Douglas Brightglade, Journeyman Pyromancer, student of Flarman Flowerstalk of Wizards' High. They will have heard of him."

"Even I've heard of the Fire Wizard," said the Elf, visibly impressed. "And of you, too, Douglas Brightglade."

"Word does seem to get around," mused Douglas. "But I suppose the doings of the Faerie Queen are as interesting to ordinary fairies as the doings of Thornwood Duke and Prince Bryarmote are to their own peoples."

"Precisely," agreed the Watch Elf with a nod. "I'll ride at once to Faerie Hill in the forest."

"Oh, please! Finish your breakfast first," Douglas urged him. "I can wait an hour or two."

"Absolutely not!" cried the Elf, pulling his leaf napkin from around his neck. "Ertalla! Ertalla!" he called over his shoulder. "I'm off to the Hill! Be right back! Entertain Lord Douglas while I'm away!"

"That's me wife, Ertalla," he explained to Douglas. "She'll be right up," and he leaped on the back of a Bluebird who came to his whistle, and made a beeline for the center of the Forest.

The Watch Elf returned in less than half an hour, accompanied by five Faerie warriors in full regalia, crimson and gold coats and tall bumblebee-fur shakoes held in place with golden chains. They rode unusually large, ruby-throated hummingbirds. The soldiers saluted Douglas crisply with long, thin lances as their mounts thrummed to a hovering halt before him.

"Lord Douglas, Brightwing's friend, we greet you!" cried their Officer. "We fought in Battle of Sea under Prince Aedh and remember you well. It's a pleasure and an honor to welcome you to Craylor Wendys, the Royal Forest of Remembrance"

"Thank you!" responded Douglas with a deep bow. "I thought it was called the Forest of Forgetfulness."

"It is—by our enemies," explained the Faerie warrior, relaxing his stiff posture. "Friends remember. We invite you to join us at our morning parade, which is about to begin. We're here guarding one of the four Great Gateways to Faerie. The Gate lies within this hallowed Forest. Few Mortals have ever seen it, and fewer have passed through it."

"I would be honored, but unfortunately I'm on urgent business for the Fellowship of Wizards," replied Douglas, shaking his head with regret. "And I suspect it's best if even I don't know where your Gateway is. It would be a secret shared, and, as Queen Marget once told me, a secret shared is no longer secret."

"Her wisdom is only surpassed by her graciousness," said the guardian. "We truly regret that you are not able to stay awhile with us. As it is your wish, you have our full permission to pass through the Forest upon Bloody Brook. Nothing will stay your course. However, it were best if you and your companion did not set foot on dry ground beyond here until you emerge on the lea on the far side. There are certain pitfalls and snares set for the unwary intruder, you see. Perhaps we should send an escort with you. . . ."

"How far is it to the other edge of the forest?"

"In Man-miles, exactly twenty-eight, by the river," said the Faerie Guardian.

"Then we should be beyond the upper edge before noon-time," decided Douglas, "and will have no need for escort nor reason to stop on our way, if the Brook is clear of obstructions."

"Bloody Brook is highly revered," said the other. "It is kept free of snags here, natural or otherwise."

"Then I thank you and apologize again for not staying to visit," said Douglas with another deep bow. "Give my best wishes to Her Majesty the Queen when you see her next, and to the Prince Consort. Her time of birthing must be very close."

"We expect word daily," acknowledged the soldier.

"And we must be on our way, unfortunately," Douglas said. "I wish we could linger until you have heard."

The Faerie Guardians saluted with their sharp lances again and, executing a neat about-face aboard their metallic-green-and-red hummingbirds, disappeared into the forest's daytime gloom.

"And thank you, too, for your courtesy," said Douglas to the Watch Elf. "May you and your wife have a quiet day."

"Every day is quiet here," said the Elf wife, who had enjoyed talking to Douglas and the Otter and serving them griddle cakes the size of small coins, delicious and rich with clover honey and milkweed butter. "It's the way we like it. In the olden, terrible days, we had enough excitement for six Elf lifetimes hereabouts."

Although they would have liked to stay and chat with the kindly couple, the travelers returned to their boat and shortly pushed off, heading in under the first of the overarching oaks.

"We might have stopped long enough to see their morning parade," complained the Otter. "I confess to being very curious about these Near Immortals."

"A Bump of Curiosity is a good thing to soothe, but there is at least one drawback to accepting Fairy hospitality," lectured Douglas, spelling the boat swiftly forward against a current much stronger than it had been in the two days before. The river here had grown narrower and the heavily wooded banks steeper. "Fairy Time runs differently from ours."

"How do you mean?" Marbleheart wriggled his nose in perplexity. "A day is a day, isn't it?"

"We might go with the Guardians, watch their parade, and have lunch with them and take a quick look at the Great Gateway, which I understand is quite a splendid and memorable sight to see, but when we resumed our journey, we might find that not a single day but a hundred days, perhaps even a hundred years, had passed."

"Great Groupers! Let's get through this place," cried the Otter. "I don't even intend to swim these waters!"

Douglas grinned and stepped up their speed. There was really no reason not to speed. The river was, as the Faerie Guard officer had said, unobstructed, deep, and straight as an arrow.

Under the trees it was dim, cool, and still—rather restful, in fact. After three hours of steady skimming they sighted a bright light ahead, the last arching of the Forest oaks at the western verge.

Beyond, the noontime sun shone on treeless, emerald green meadowlands rolling gently to the horizon. At the farthest reach of sight rose low purple hills and, dimly in haze beyond them, a dark blue north-south range of mountains capped with snow.

The river in front of them now wound lazily from side to side, sliding rapidly around an occasional ait or rippling over rock-bedded shallows.

As they ate their noontime meal on the move, the travelers heard singing and, rounding a sharp bend, came upon a crowd of twenty or so diminutive men and women seated on smooth rocks along the shore, harmonizing beautifully in song.

At the approach of strangers the singers were startled into silence and seemed about to bolt into the brush beside the stream, but Douglas called out to them in Faerie, and the Nixies—for that was what they were—skipped lightly out upon the water to meet the gondola, greeting the travelers shyly but courteously and asking for news.

"You've heard about the Battle of Sea against Frigeon?" asked Douglas, and they shook their heads. The Wizard moored the gondola to a sapling among the rocks and brought the dainty people up to the present. He was getting quite good at it by now.

"So, Frigeon is a changed man since he regained his conscience," Douglas finished. "He'd locked it away in a Great Gray Pearl, which allowed him to do all sorts of wicked things without feeling remorse. He has even changed his name and is now called Serenit. As punishment, he's having to help undo all his evil spells and other harms, and is held a virtual prisoner in the land once known as Eternal Ice, although it hasn't got much ice left these days."

The Nixies laughed with glee at the news and cavorted on the river in such a merry way that Marbleheart, who loved nothing better than a romp in water, joined them—the first time he had been in the river since they had entered the Forest of Remembrance.

"We were especially terrified of Frigeon-that-was," explained the Nixie Choirmaster. "Long ago we lived far to the north of here, and when Frigeon came to live nearby, his icy magic froze our pretty streams, so we left our elder home and fled southward."

"You were not here during Last Battle of Kingdom, then?"

"No, we came a bit later. Fortunately so, for these now-peaceful meadows were the scene of the worst fighting in the Battle. Two hundred years ago or more, that was. Tens of thousands of Men and thousands of Near Immortals fought here for seven dreadful days and fearful nights. Thousands were destroyed, including an amazing number of Faeries, who are very difficult to destroy."

"I've heard the story from one who was there," said Douglas, nodding sadly. "So this is Last Battleground? It doesn't look so grim now, though. I've rarely seen a more peaceful-looking place. It reminds me of my home Valley."

"We're proud of our work clearing the devastations of war we found everywhere when we first came here," said the Choirmaster. "The whole plain was littered with broken weapons and horribly ravaged bodies of Men and beasts."

"It must have been truly horrible!" gasped the Otter.

The Choirmaster bobbed his head solemnly. "We buried the dead in long barrows on the western edge of Battleground. By then they were but rotting rags, rusted armor, and bare bones! We managed to separate the enemy from the companions by the remains of their armor, so they didn't have to share the same grave mounds, at least. We did whatever we could, but I fear many have been uneasy between death and life ever since."

"Where are these barrows? I would have thought you'd put them in the center of the field, or perhaps here by the streamside."

"Our elders consulted with the Queen of Faerie and she advised us to keep the barrows as far from the habitations of Men and Near Immortals as possible—especially far from the Faerie Forest—yet still within the Field of Chaos, so we interred their bones in the far west, under the foothills of the Tiger's Teeth Mountains. You can just see their peaks there," he said, and pointed off to the west.

"That's where we're headed," said Marbleheart. "The place we're looking for—Pfantas. It's in the foothills, I understand."

"You're correct," said the Choirmaster. "None of us has been that far west, but rumors come to us . . . not a pleasant land to visit, I fear."

He called his singers to attention with a rap of his baton and they sang a farewell-and-safe-journeying song as the sleek gondola surged forward once more, breasting the swift current.

Bloody Brook shortly began whirling madly about sharp, half-sunken rocks and foaming as the calm waters turned to rapids, but even so, Myrn's reliable pushing magic was strong enough to move the boat against the current at great speed.

Marbleheart dived in and swam ahead. He reported the water was still many feet deep if they avoided the shallows on the outside of curves. Both travelers kept close watch from then on so as not to run afoul of snags or damage the gondola's thin hull on unseen ledges beneath the surface.

That night they slept aboard the boat and in the morning pushed on as quickly as they could safely go. The Choirmaster's words had infected Douglas with a sense of urgency. The air had turned cooler again, and they were slowed by morning mists that hung over the water and didn't lift until well into midmorning. Otherwise, the day passed without incident.

By late afternoon they were close under the barren foothills of the Western Mountains. The densest fog yet suddenly lowered about them, cutting off all distance and shrouding everything in an eerie white silence.

Douglas made landing and, picking a red maple leaf from the ground enlarged and altered it into a tent snug against the damp night air. He also started a fire which, despite his best magical efforts, burned with only a feeble light and meager heat.

It turned quite cold after an unseen sunset. A mournful breeze blew fitfully out of the north. It carried to them an acrid, musty smell, something like last year's moldering leaves, Douglas thought, with just a hint of something else, something unpleasant and ill intentioned, in the swirling mist.

He shuddered from the chill and moved his blanket closer to the fire. When he looked about for his companion, Marbleheart was nowhere to be seen. The Otter often went off in the evening to seek his preferred food and to explore the riverbank out of Otterly curiosity.

"He'll be back when he gets cold and wet," Douglas reassured himself, and he went to sleep almost at once.

Marbleheart followed the river for a few hundred yards, looking for something to eat. A tiny, hesitant trickle fed in from the north, between clay banks only dimly visible when the fog shifted for a moment.

He followed the streamlet but lost it when it disappeared into the ground in a low and damp place.

"A spring, I guess," he said aloud to himself. "Wonder what *that* is?"

"That" was a spark of bluish light that flashed once and disappeared, as if someone had opened a door late at night and light from a room had spilled out for just a moment before the door was quickly slammed to.

A relative of the Firefly we talked to on the other side of the forest, Marbleheart decided. *I'd like to ask him a few questions about the way ahead, if I can find him.*

He hunkered along, Otter fashion, covering considerable ground quickly despite his ungainly land gait. The steady trot, if that is what you'd want to call it, lulled his mind until he was almost asleep on his feet.

He was barely aware when he passed between two low, steep-sided hills covered with dry grass that rustled uneasily. He thought it rather queer that the grass here was sere and bleached almost white. Everywhere else about, things had been green and new budding with early spring. There was no wind at all now.

He came upon a low, wide-open, timber-framed doorway in the side of the hill on his right. A dim light—a bluish flickering only—showed from deep within. The air seemed to vibrate with . . . ?

"Uh, time to go back, I think," Marbleheart thought aloud, shivering despite his warm coat.

A harsh, whispering voice from inside the door said, "No, come in, Sea Otter! You are to be King of the Hill here, very shortly. Let me prepare you for your coronation!"

The Otter shook his head groggily and tried to turn away,

but an unseen hand, rough and hard as horn, reached out and plucked him from his feet by the scruff of his neck.

"Oh, I say, now!" protested Marbleheart, trying to twist about to sink his sharp teeth into the unseen fingers. His jaws snapped closed on nothing!

The blue light crackled angrily and went out, plunging the doorway into ebony blackness. Another invisible hand clutched the Otter's snout, choking off his air supply. Almost at once, the blackness became even darker. Marbleheart lost consciousness.

Somewhere a nightjar rasped into the thickening fog. Somewhere there was brief, evil laughter, softly, slightly un-sane. But there was no one to hear it.

Chapter Eight

Barrow Wights

DOUGLAS was awakened by the distant pound of hoofbeats.

When he sat up and looked cautiously about he found the fog was thicker than ever, an impenetrable wall all about him. The sounds rang clear but somehow changed, magnified and carried by the mist. The hoofbeats were coming rapidly nearer.

A chill of fear touched his spine when he remembered where he was and the terrible things that had been done two centuries past on this very spot.

He shook himself, much as did Black Flame, straightened his posture, and rose to his feet, facing the approaching horsemen—if that was what they were—coming at a muffled gallop along the grassy bank of Bloody Brook. He could now hear the soft jingling of harnesses and the occasional creak of saddles under the weight of a rider, or a soft strike of metal against metal.

Out of the fog a dark figure on a tall, pale horse loomed before him and reined suddenly to a halt. Douglas recognized him as a Faerie Rider, although he'd never seen one before that moment.

"I thought you ought to know," the Rider said in a fair, polite baritone, speaking in Faerie tongue, "that the Otter Marbleheart has been trapped in one of the barrows. He will be reft of soul at midnight, if not sooner rescued."

"Marbleheart!" cried Douglas, for the first time realizing the Otter was still nowhere to be seen. "Where?"

"The first group of barrows to the north of here," said the Rider, pointing with the lance he carried in his right hand. "I can tell you no more, Fire Wizard."

"So the rascal's curiosity has gotten him into trouble, eh?" said Douglas somewhat grimly. "Thank you! I'll rescue him. Who is it holds a friend of Brightglade in thrall?"

"Goblins—who have profaned these ancient and sacred places," said the Faerie knight. "Barrow-Wights, Men call their sort. Will you ask for our assistance? We know you to be a Faerie friend, beloved by Brightwing, and under our protection, if you seek it."

"Where are you bound in the night, and at whose behest?"

The knight considered this question briefly before he answered.

"We are Wanderers, a Faerie Rade," the knight said, somewhat sadly. "Marget and Aedh have called us home. We ride to the Great Gate in Craylor Wendys. I cannot say what their purpose is but we consider it imperative that we answer the call at greatest haste. We have ridden day and night from where we were camped in Emptylands."

Douglas was aware of dozens more Faerie riders as shapes just beyond his vision in the fog.

"If Marget of Faerie calls, you must go as quickly as possible, of course," he said. "I'll not detain you. I'll take care of friend Otter. Give my best wishes to your Queen, Sir Knight. Go in peace as well as in haste!"

"Thank you, Douglas Brightglade. You are a gentleman as well as a Wizard," said the Knight, turning his horse away. The sounds of hooves, galloping again, quickly faded away.

"Goblins, this time!" sighed Douglas. "Not Hobgoblins! And if they have taken over an Enemy barrow, they'll have acquired much evil power, the books say, drawn from the unease of the anciently dead warriors of the Dark Enemy!"

He sat beside his fire for a few minutes, thinking before acting as Flarman had taught him, and then held up his right hand, forefinger extended, and spoke a Word of Power.

A bright orange glow sprang up above his head, piercing the mist to a hundred or more feet. By the light he began searching the ground nearby on his knees, crawling in the wet grass along the top of the riverbank. After a short while he found what he sought and, plucking it up, stowed it in his wide left sleeve.

Next, I'll need a special kind of light to find my way in evil places, he thought. "Ah, here!"

He picked an orange globe-shaped seed pod from a vine that grew among the thorny bushes bordering the river. Placing the pod on his left palm, he made a simple gesture with his right hand, starting with his fingers clenched, lifting his hand and spreading the fingers wide at the same time.

The papery pod rapidly swelled until it was the size of a man's head, then even larger. Taking out his jackknife, Douglas carved large, round, cheerful eyes, a triangular nose, and a wide, smiling mouth into the dry pod skin, now as thick as a pumpkin's rind.

The bright flame over his head flowed down to rest within the pod and shine steadily through the carved eyes, nose, and mouth and glow softly through translucent skin.

"A good, old jack-o'-lantern!" Douglas exclaimed with satisfaction. "Fit to frighten away even the most horrific haunts. Now to find their borrowed barrow."

Trusting his instincts as much as reason, he found a tiny rill not far upstream and recognized at once the marks of the Otter's webbed feet in the soft clay beside it. The marks led away from the river.

Following swiftly, he came in a few minutes to the oozing spring. From there his lantern showed him the loom of the first pair of burial mounds. The fog was still thick, but the jack-o'-lantern's gleam, golden yellow and cheerful, cut through the worst of it, revealing everything almost as if it were day.

Circling the right-hand mound, then the one on the left, Douglas searched for signs of the Otter's passage. At length he found the place where Marbleheart's footprints ended abruptly at a steeper-than-usual hillside.

"There's a door here," he murmured to himself. "And Marbleheart must be within."

"And," he added, "I'd better hurry. It's almost midnight!"

He stepped forward, placing his left hand against what seemed to be a steep slope of rough gravel and sere, matted grass. His hand passed right through, followed by the rest of his body. The entry had been hidden by a simple illusion.

He was in a straight, roughly paved, dirt-walled passage angling down into the very heart of the mound. The tunnel was empty, except for a spear, a ten-foot shaft from which hung a moldered gray pennant, caught in a rusty bracket on one wall. No way to tell what color it had once been. It fell to dry shreds and dust when he reached out to touch it.

"That style of spear was used by the Enemy. And I doubt a Light pennant would disintegrate like that, even after two centuries," he told himself. "Our flags were woven of noble metals. This is one of the Nixies' mounds for *Enemy* dead!"

The jack-o'-lantern lighted his way down into a great, low-ceilinged, oval room perhaps sixty feet long, twenty feet wide, and six feet high in the center. It was empty except for a single flat block of jet black stone, roughly rectangular and three feet high, at the far end.

On its rough surface lay the unconscious Sea Otter!

"No time for being dainty," said Douglas aloud, awakening tumbled echoes. He heard the distant sound of footsteps approaching from outside the barrow, shuffling in the dry grass. The jack-o'-lantern flickered wildly for a moment.

"Marbleheart! Marbleheart!" Douglas called out sharply. "Forsake those wretched dreams! Awake and follow me out of here. It's in your own tomb you are sleeping."

The sleek water mammal stirred, muttered something Douglas didn't catch, then rolled on his back and put his four feet in the air, obviously intending to continue his deep slumber.

The footsteps paused at the barrow doorway, as if listening—or sniffing. Douglas reached out to pull the Otter's left front foot. Marbleheart shook the foot irritably and opened his eyes to glare at his friend in the flickering light of the orange jack-o'-lantern.

"Come on! Get up, Marbleheart. If you ever want to swim again in Sea, or chase a tasty trout for your dinner, or crack a clam on your marble disk, now you must arise and follow!"

The sound of Douglas's voice—and the words he chose as well—roused the groggy Otter. Marbleheart rolled over the edge of the altar stone and landed on his feet.

"W-what is this place?" he asked in sudden horror, fully awake.

"A Goblin brought you to this barrow to take your life."

"G-g-g-goblin?" asked Marbleheart, shuddering. "Let's g-g-g-go!"

Before they could reach the tunnel ramp, it was filled with a vast, misshapen hulk of a black-furred beast with saucer-huge eyes and a gore-stained, knobby club in one fist. It stopped in the room's entrance and threw up its other hand to protect its large eyes from the lantern's bright rays.

"Who s-s-s-s-sneaks into our unholy place?" hissed the Goblin in a rasping, barrel-deep, echoing voice. "Who dares to waken the new King of Barrow Wights?"

But it hesitated to rush forward, bothered by the lantern's now-steady gleam, which appeared to burn his eyes painfully.

"Is that it?" Marbleheart whispered hoarsely. "If I stayed, I'd be their King?"

"You want the job?" snapped Douglas, facing the monster in the doorway. "Stay behind if it beckons to you, but I'm leaving."

"I'm with you! I don't want to be King of anything, anywhere, especially if it doesn't have deep running water. What do we do?"

"Follow me! Stay out of my way but stay close!" ordered the Journeyman Wizard. He stared the Goblin in the eye.

"*I* entered your stolen barrow mound, and *I* rescued the innocent creature you would enslave to be King of the Undead," he announced boldly.

"And who, in the name of the ever-hating, blazing-eyed beasts of blackest Hades, are *you*?" the Goblin bellowed, amplifying his voice several times over so that it would be even more daunting.

"I am called Douglas Brightglade," began Douglas. The Goblin roared with hysteric, maniacal laughter.

"Ha-ha-ho! A name like that! How can you bear it?"

"It's my true and natural name," insisted Douglas calmly. "And my title is Journeyman Wizard."

"Oh, I am so *impressed*!" sneered the beast. "I've eaten a few Wizards in my time, and you are the puniest of them all.

Most of them were at least a hundred years old and tough as old crows."

"I greatly doubt that you could handle even an Apprentice," scoffed Douglas, maneuvering himself into a position for a dash through the arch and up the ramp.

"Oh, no, you don't!" screamed the Goblin, gnashing long, shark-sharp teeth and pushing his bloodstained club forward to block the way. "We aim to make the slippery little one Goblin King Underhill. We intend to make of *you* a foggy dawn breakfast! Hark! My beautiful, dutiful, flesh-hungry, bloodthirsty fellow fiends are coming for the rites and the meal!"

There was the sound of mumbling and harsh, derisive laughter from a distance outside the barrow.

"Oh, very well," said Douglas, "if you don't choose to behave properly, I'll have to take *drastic* action!"

The black Goblin threw back his head and laughed even more loudly at this, but Douglas set down the lantern and reached into his sleeve for what he had picked in the grass near the river.

He held it aloft between forefinger and thumb for the Goblin to plainly see. The jack-o'-lantern's light fell full upon it.

"*F-f-f-f-four-leafed clover!*" screeched the filthy beast in sudden falsetto, flinging his overlong arms about his head. "*Put it away, put it away, put it—*"

"No, too late for that," Douglas shouted, so that the Goblins above could hear every word. "I call upon you all to return to your former haunts! Go at once! By the power of this sweet clover with four leaves, I *demand* your obedience! Away! Away!"

The Goblin in the doorway squealed like ten pigs caught in a fence, and the shouts from above stopped abruptly and changed to cries of terror. Footsteps rapidly retreated. The Goblin before him swung his mace high, intending to strike at the Wizard blindly.

"No *you* don't!" yelled Douglas, waving the clover. "Time for you all to depart this World!"

With a gesture of revulsion he hurled the four-leaf clover full in his adversary's ugly face. It burst on the creature's forehead in a great bloom of terrible flame, which in seconds consumed the entire wailing Goblin. Where it had stood only a small pile of dry, evil-smelling ordure remained. Then even that burst into flame when Douglas pointed his finger at it, and burned to a fine wisp of gray ash.

"You've killed him!" gulped the Otter, peering fearfully under Douglas's left arm.

"No, just sent him where he can't harm anyone, alive or dead, for a couple of eons, at least. *The rest of you begone, too!*" he shouted at the retreating footsteps outside. There was a lesser flash of brilliant white light, and the unseen Barrow Wights cried out one more time in panic and fear.

And then complete silence.

"Let's go," said Douglas to the Otter. "It's safe now. I doubt they'll care to return here even if they found the power."

"I don't think my knees will hold me up yet, if you don't mind waiting a minute or so," said Marbleheart. "What a foolish thing I did! Thank you Douglas! I promise I won't wander off again, ever and never."

"I somehow doubt that," chuckled Douglas, stooping to stroke the Otter's back fur soothingly. "Phew! Goblins certainly do stink up a place. Come on!"

He led the Otter quickly from the mound, through the mist to the tiny rill, where the Sea animal rushed to drink from the first tiny pool.

"What kind of a place is this, anyway?" he gasped.

"Come on!" repeated the Wizard, beginning to feel his own exhaustion. "Better to talk about that around a nice, friendly fire."

"What . . . what would have happened, tell me?" insisted Marbleheart. He shook like an aspen.

"They would have made you one of the Undead. They would have bowed down to you and called you 'King' but all the time they would be mocking your spirit because they had bested a Mortal."

"Never to swim again? Never to see the sun again? I would have died."

"That's the worst part," said Douglas grimly. "Once you'd been gowned and crowned as King Underhill, you'd have become a Near Immortal. Unless you were lucky enough to be killed by a Wizard or a Faerie with a magic arrow or a powerful specific like the four-leafed clover, you would have lived a totally miserable non-life for almost ever and ever!"

"Whew!" shuttered the Otter, but his spirit revived as they settled down side by side in front of their campfire. "These adventures of ours can get pretty scary, you know?"

"You can always turn back," Douglas reminded him gravely.

"No, no! I was scared out of my whiskers, at least, and to tell the truth, I still am—but I want to go with you, Douglas. I at least owe that to you—if you still want me."

"Well," warned the Journeyman, "be careful where you walk and when, and look before you leap. Best thing to do is carry one of these."

He searched for a moment in the wet grass, plucked another four-leafed clover, and handed it to the Otter, who sniffed its pleasantly fresh aroma and relaxed for the first time since his wakening.

"I don't have any pockets," he wailed. "Will you carry it for me?"

"Certainly, Marbleheart, good friend! As soon as we get anywhere where they have such things, I'll have a goldsmith make you a locket to wear around your neck, to keep this clover in. In the meantime, stick close and move with care. We're alone in a land where evil is all too common, I fear."

And they sat before the cheery little fire until dawn touched pink to the snowfields atop the distant Tiger's Teeth Mountains.

PART TWO

Wizard in Transit

Chapter Nine

Very Impatient Lady

"NOW in this next syllabus," droned Augurian, "we'll study water as related to living bodies . . ."

"I'm a woman, a sailor, a pearl diver!" snapped Myrn irritably. "Don't you think I know about the bodies and water?"

The Aquamancer slowly lowered the book he had picked up, preparatory to beginning the lesson. He was silent for so long that Myrn glanced up at him and flushed in chagrin.

"I . . . I . . . I'm really very sorry, Magister!" she cried, laying her hand on his arm. "I guess I'm out of sorts today. Please continue."

"It isn't at all like you, Myrn," said Augurian, "to be so short and snappy!"

"I know, but I . . . well, Magister, I'm frustrated and worried and impatient and distracted and—"

"And in love," came Flarman's voice from the door.

"And making absolutely splendid progress in your studies, despite all that," added Augurian. "Really, Myrn! Even Douglas Brightglade grew more slowly in the craft than you have in less than two years of apprenticeship!"

"But . . . ," she began, wringing her hands together.

"I'll leave you two to talk about it, if you wish," apologized the Fire Wizard, still standing in the doorway. "Perhaps this should be a matter between Master and Apprentice."

"No, no, no! Of course not!" cried Myrn, jumping up to throw her arms about the plump Pyromancer. "I need you both! Stay, please!"

"It occurs to me," said Flarman, seating himself on a wide window ledge, "that we are pushing you along much too fast, my dear. Under the circumstances, I mean."

"What would you say," he turned to his colleague, the Water Adept, "to a short hiatus? A vacation for the lass. Give her time to sort out what she's learned and unwind?"

Augurian scowled and didn't reply for so long that Myrn rose and seated herself by his side, taking his hands in hers, looking at him pleadingly but silently.

"I mean," said Flarman.

"Yes, you mean?" asked the other Wizard.

"Well, let's be frank. You and I never married. Never had children of our own."

"True," observed Augurian.

"Well! I at least had some hard experience with the young, bringing up Douglas at Wizard's High."

Augurian nodded silently.

"Well, think of . . . think of my cats. Pert and Party have raised a dozen healthy litters between them. Despite the great differences in their personalities, both are wonderful mothers. Oh, Black Flame is a good father, too. Don't get me wrong, but he isn't really involved in the basic training of the kittens. He teaches them how to hunt and how to take care of themselves in the fields and barns—things kittens must learn before they go out on their own."

"Will you be making a point?" asked Augurian, but he softened his words with a smile.

"The point is," replied Flarman, "that there are things a child must learn from her father, but there are things a child must learn from her mother, too. How to cope with living. How to make certain decisions. I, for one, am not certain those things are any less important than what the father imparts. Or the Wizard Magister."

He paused, pulled his battered old briar pipe from his right sleeve, and took time to light it with a snap of his fingers. He blew a cloud of fragrant tobacco smoke out the tower window. The others watched him and waited.

"My goodness! I'm sounding so trite and stuffy, am I not?" Flarman chuckled. "Dear hearts, what I am trying to say is that perhaps this child needs to spend some time with her own good mother back on Flowring Island!"

Augurians's Apprentice laid her head on his shoulder and hugged him tightly.

"Oh, Magister! It's not that I don't love and admire and respect you of all men, as much as my own father, but . . ."

"But sometimes, I imagine," Augurian said, returning the embrace warmly, "a lassy needs her mother. I am not so old I cannot recall my own mother, bless her! The things I learned at her knee!"

"Do you agree that you need a mother's touch for a while?" Flarman asked Myrn.

"I really hadn't thought of it at all, honestly, before you said that about Pert and Party," said the Apprentice softly. "I'm entirely delighted and enthralled with my studies here, Magisters, and I look forward eagerly to a long time yet of learning and practicing Aquamancy. But there *are* things my mother alone can understand and point out and suggest and recommend to me . . . and comfort me for."

"Then go home, sweet lass! You couldn't be in better hands than those of Tomasina Manstar!" cried the Aquamancer. "Have I been so hard a taskmaster? I am so very sorry, Myrn my dear!"

"No need of that," said Myrn. "No need to feel bad, Magister! I really have loved every moment of it, wet or dry. But Flarman Flowerstalk, bless *his* soul, is right. There comes a time when a girl needs to talk to her mother about . . . *things*."

"Things?" asked Augurian, but she saw the crinkling of the corners of his eyes that meant he was teasing. "Things?"

"Don't be any more dense than you have to be, to be a Water Adept," laughed Flarman. "Weddings and marriage, love and homemaking, career and caring for us poor menfolk. Let the girl go home for a while. It'll give us all the time we need to tackle these blasted spells. And soak up some sun. I came here expecting to get a healthy tan, and here I am, pale as the underside of a Porpoise!"

The quickest way to Flowring was to ask the Asrai, the Cold Fire Being, to carry Myrn with it under the waves. Asrai's way was always exciting and interesting, and the Phosphorescence itself was a good traveling companion for a student Aquamancer. It had wide and deep knowledge of all the depths and shallows of Sea a student of Aquamancy could learn nowhere else.

The journey was pleasantly short between Waterand and Flowring Isle, Myrn's home. She stepped into the Asrai's cool presence late that evening and early the next morning she hopped ashore near Flowring Town Square.

Her mother was sweeping the front stoop with a twig broom, humming cheerfully to herself. When the front gate gave its customary *ker-thump* as its counterbalancing stone pulled it shut, Tomasina Manstar looked up expectantly and at once shouted with surprise, threw aside the broom, and rushed down the flower-bordered path to sweep her daughter into her arms.

"Welcome home!" she cried, and the two of them stood crying for joy, clucking and laughing for several minutes until Mistress Manstar broke away and waved her daughter into her neat cottage.

"You came over by Cold Fire? You'll want a hot cup of tea, I think. Come inside! Tell me everything you've done and thought for the past ten months! Why are you come home? Lord Augurian hasn't thrown you out for being too pert, has he? No? Good!"

"I just needed to see you and Dad, to talk to you, smell your flowers, eat some of your cooking, walk on the beach, and swim among the blue coral heads, once again. Do you understand that, Mama?"

"Of course, child! It's called 'checking to see if your roots are still firmly attached,' or words to that effect. No one understands it better than an islander. It's because our world is rather small and well outlined. We can go far over Sea but we have to know home is still there when we need it."

"Home, and you, Mama! I'm so glad to be home! My only wish is that Douglas were here, too."

"Ah, my future son-in-law, the Fire Wizard! And how is handsome, young Douglas? Burning as only a Fire Wizard fiancé can, I guess. Never have a cold bed with that lad to husband, I say again."

They talked and talked, sitting in the cosy front parlor and later working side by side to prepare dinner for the Manstar men when they returned from their fishing. There was all the news of Waterand and the rest of World to tell, and all the news of Flowring, too—from who had wicked Frigeon enchanted and Flarman and Augurian rescued, to who was newly wed and newly with child, in the island's tiny world.

Myrn explained Douglas's mission to investigate the Witches' Coven in Kingdom.

"You be worried about your man?" asked Tomasina. "He can take care of his own self, I know from experience, but I know what it is to worry about an absent loved one. Haven't been a sailor's wife for close on forty years without knowing loneliness and worries, lass."

"I know in my mind that Douglas will be just fine," Myrn continued, "but what my heart wants most is to be with him. Whether I could help or not."

"It's dangerous, messing about with Witches of any kind. If you were with him, could you be a help? Or would you distract? It's a bit like the old sailors' notions about women aboard ship, I guess. Your father made sure I could pull my full weight, sail and tack and reef and furl before he'd let me sail very far with him when we were young and thinking of marrying."

"I know what you're saying, Mama. Yes, I suppose in a storm I might be a burden to Douglas yet. But still . . ."

"You could be a comfort and a help, and that's what marriage is often all about, for both a women and her man, Myrn."

The menfolk arrived, greeting their daughter and sister with boisterous surprise and evident pleasure, asking many of the same questions Tomasina had already asked. The evening and far into the night was filled with their rapt attention, until Myrn fell into her old, familiar childhood bed and went to sleep with a smile.

Somehow her worries felt smaller here.

"Do you remember how to fish up pearls?" her father Nick teased.

They had sailed just after dawn, out to the oyster beds recently marked by the great Sea Worms as ready to harvest.

"Some things one never forgets," claimed Myrn.

She poised on the gunwale of her father's smack, a vision of grace and beauty in a brief but sensible swim costume. Nick handed her a heavy, oval stone tightly bent to ten fathoms of hempen rope. She cradled it in her arms and, giving him a nod, leaped feet first into the sparkling water.

The stone drew her swiftly down to the bottom at thirty feet. The early sun slanted down, stage-lighting a mountain of coral reaching almost to the surface. Off to the right she caught a glimpse of a deep purple Horniad, a giant Sea Worm, one of those strange, ever-so-slow, immensely patient creatures she and Douglas had first met in these waters some years before.

Once she would have been terrified by the sight of the Worm, but now she knew many of them quite well by name. She settled to the sandy bottom, waved after the Worm—it did not wave back, having no arms or tentacles, but she knew it had seen her—and began expertly to pry oysters from the coral with her sheath knife, ignoring the thousands of tiny, red fishes that swarmed about her, curious about her movements and darting in swiftly to snap up some morsel of food she disturbed as she gathered the bivalves.

"Would you carry a message back to Augurian at Waterand for us?" a small voice sounded in her ear. A school of stippled silver-and-blue wrasse hovered before her as she turned to load her catch in the weighted basket her father had dropped down after her.

She nodded, moving her hands in a universal fish-language signal of greeting and agreement.

"Tell the good Water Adept that we've located the wreck of the ship *Windskipper* not far from Battle Shoals. He asked us to keep an eye out for her, you see."

Myrn wigwagged her understanding and added, carefully, "We'll send a Porpoise to look her over. She was lost at the beginning of the battle, I recall. It's their job to investigate all wrecks, you know."

"We know," said the school of wrasse. They bobbed politely, all in unison, and turned as one, shooting off into deeper water.

A pearl diver with years of experience, Myrn stayed at the bottom for five minutes, unaided by any magic or mechanical device, although she would someday be able to work underwater as her Master did, through magical means. Now, unbuckling her lead-weighted belt from her slim waist and hooking it to the stone's line, she began to ascend to the surface.

The basket, hoisted by her father and brothers, passed her on the way up. When she broke the surface beside the smack, Nick Manstar and his two sons were already shucking oysters.

"It still amazes me!" said the eldest Manstar, when she was in the boat again, drying herself with a rough towel. "You bring up a dozen oysters and ten of them have good pearls in them!"

"The Horniads leave the pearl-bearing shells for us and eat only the others," she explained, although she knew he was as aware of the arrangement between the Flowringers and the Worms as she was.

So as not to overfish the rich beds, the fishermen took only a few of the valuable gems, pink and white, blue and pale yellow, sometimes gray or black, each season. Nick Manstar claimed that this also helped keep the price for pearls high.

"If the Worms can manage to curb their appetites for the oysters, we certainly can curb ours for the pearls," he insisted. While a few local fishermen still distrusted and feared the great Worms, Nick Manstar was their strongest defender whenever the question arose.

Mother and daughter sat atop the cliffs at the north end of Flowring Isle, watching the surf crash against the rocks far below, throwing spray halfway to the summit. This had always been Myrn's place for quiet thinking and talking. She and Douglas had first realized they loved each other here on a windy, rainy day two years ago. It seemed both a long time ago and just yesterday.

"I found the cliff tops a generation before you did," her mother said, reading her mind, as mothers so often do. "Your father and I often walked up here to get away from the crowd in town. When we were courting, that was. Always loved it and still do."

"I'm glad that you had this place to come to, too," said her daughter. It was late afternoon and they had hours before they had to be home for supper. Rich, creamy oyster stew was traditional on oyster-fishing nights, and the whole town, the whole island, would gather in the Square to eat the full bowls with salty soda crackers and drink beer imported from somewhere on the mainland, where barley and hops would grow.

Tomasina sighed contentedly and, turning to Myrn with a smile, said, "Was there something special you wanted to talk to me about, daughter Wizard?"

Myrn took her hand and held it in her lap for a moment, returning the smile.

"No, nothing special, now. Well, you know, Augurian was upset because I was distracted, and Flarman said, under the circumstances, it wasn't surprising, because of the wedding next winter and Douglas halfway about World in a dangerous land and all."

Tomasina nodded. "It still gives me a turn of sorts, hearing you talk about two of the greatest men of this Age as if they were family. I'm used to taking a deep breath before I even think of Flarman Firemaster, he's that far above the likes of me."

"Nonsense! Flarman is an old dear, a really wonderful old uncle, you know."

"I know. I like him very much, and not just because he's been so good to you and us. But he's one of the Great Ones, nevertheless. It daunts me at times."

"He would be the first to scoff at that, however true it might be," Myrn assured her. "He'd also insist that you are an even greater person than a mere Pyromancer."

"What? Me! Now it's you speaking rot, girl! Me? What am I but a fisherman's good wife?"

"He'd say being a good mother is much more important even than being a Wizard," Myrn told her, seriously. Her mother laughed, throwing her head back and slapping her knees in glee. Myrn noticed she wiped a tear from her eye shortly after.

"Six days only?" asked Nick Manstar, the next day but one. "We was hoping you'd stay to help with the blue coral, lassy. You're the best at that of us all."

"You don't need me," laughed his daughter. "Things are going well here at home, even without me."

She stretched her arms above her head and examined the fresh tanning on her forearms and the backs of her capable hands. That was one other thing she'd missed, studying on Waterand Island—the chances to be out in the wind and sun all day, glorying in her health and youth.

There just hadn't been time. She resolved to take more time off from her studies. But it would be hard to do, she loved the lessons that well.

"Well, I won't gainsay your Wizardry is important," admitted Nick. They were seated on the seaward end of the town dock, kicking their bare heels over the running tide and watching her youngest brother walking beside a pretty, dark-haired island lass along the crescent beach in almost-full moonlight.

"Be another wedding in the family, I guess, soon after you and Douglas are spliced," observed her father, lighting his pipe. "She's a good lass. Not as good as you at diving and sailing, but few are, since your mother's time."

"I like my mayhap sister-in-law. How long have they been courting?"

"Since the middle of winter. He sort of discovered her, all of a sudden. He's known her since they were babes on the sand, together, but he never paid any mind to her before midwinter time. Funny!"

"That's the way it goes sometimes," said Myrn. "I've got to go back to Waterand. I feel the pull of my lessons and the work I have to do there. I might otherwise stay here forever. But then there'd be no career as Water Wizard, as I've set my heart upon! Nor any Douglas by my side, either. These are what draw me away from you and Mama, you know."

"I find that not hard to understand or believe," said Nick Manstar, comfortably puffing away. "I believe, myself, that a good pair will find each other, no matter what the rest of World does or says."

"I think you're right, Papa," said Myrn. When he looked at her she gave him a special daughter smile and after a while they strolled down the dock to meet her brother and his best girl, as if by accident.

■ ■ ■

"Back so soon?" asked Bronze Owl. He and Stormy, Augurian's familiar, were sharing a warm spot on the black rocks below Augurian's Water Tower. The Petrel nodded to the girl, who had just then stepped from the waves, perfectly dry.

"I needed a little taste of home," Myrn said. "Now it's good to be back."

"Augurian has been a cross-eyed whirlwind since you left," said Bronze Owl. "Flarman says he would send the Waterman home, if he weren't already there."

"Has he been grumping about so terribly, then, because I was gone off?" Myrn chuckled. The birds accompanied her up the steep path to the Water Gate that would admit them to the Palace. "I don't know whether to be flattered or worried."

"Flattered," declared the metal bird. "I have to say with sorrow, however, there has been no word from our traveler out west, Myrn."

Myrn paused for a moment before she opened the gate.

"I was hoping for, but not really expecting a letter. It's so far away, Owl!"

"Mark my worldly-wise words," said the Owl, following her through into the moonlit Fountain Forecourt. Augurian and Flarman were arguing amiably, seated on a stone bench beside the vast basin. "When word comes from Douglas, it'll be worth the waiting."

"I know!" agreed Myrn, waving to her Wizards. She ran to greet them and bring her parents' admiring regards.

"Probably shake World, too, when it comes," Bronze Owl added aside to Stormy.

The great black-and-white Seabird might have chuckled, deep in his throat, but nobody could be sure. Not even Bronze Owl.

Chapter Ten

Whitewater

AS they entered the foothills of Tiger's Teeth Mountains, Bloody Brook suddenly became a swift-charging flood and then a wildly leaping torrent between high, narrow walls. It went quickly from shallow to deep in a wink and back again, throwing itself recklessly to the right, then to the left.

Its bed here was fretted with jagged rocks, often barely awash, and then shallow, madly foaming rapids. Its sources were the glaciers and snow caps of the Tiger's Teeth, and the water was freezing cold, white as milk with rock-dust carried in turbulent suspension.

It became more and more difficult to control the gondola, designed entirely for smoother and quieter waters. Unexpected cross-currents tossed her sideways and tried to roll her end for end without warning. Douglas fought both with Myrn's magic spell and the long sweep to keep her head-on to the current and inching slowly forward.

The canyon walls rose twenty, fifty, then a hundred feet high. Tributaries plunged into the mainstream as thunderous cataracts, churning the water to foam and threatening to swamp the frail craft if he allowed her to come too close.

At the end of the day Marbleheart, fully recovered from his harrowing barrow fright, swam bravely ahead to investigate an even greater commotion. He soon returned with bad news.

"There's a great wall of water, fully ten times as tall as you," he panted. "Its voice is louder than any storm surf!"

"A waterfall? Any path around it?"

"Not that I could see. The water fills the whole ravine from side to side. To pass, we'll have to climb to the top of the wall and find our way on foot around the fall."

"We'll take a closer look, however," decided the Journeyman Wizard. He'd known from the beginning that at some point the river might become too narrow, shallow, or wild to allow even Myrn's propelling spell to force the boat against the flow, and yet he disliked the thought of abandoning her just yet. She had served them well since Summer Palace.

Around the next sharp curve the waterfall appeared, as awesome as Marbleheart had described, allowing for some exaggeration. It dropped at least fifty feet, smooth as green glass at the top and plunging into a constantly roiling, rolling pool at its foot with a force that shook the very rocks of the canyon walls.

To one side, Douglas spied a narrow beach of coarse sand and rounded pebbles caught between two enormous boulders. A lush stand of drooping willows and water-loving bushes had taken precarious root above the narrow beach. Other than this, the walls of the canyon were almost vertical, dropping straight into the swirling river.

"Not a particularly promising place," Douglas admitted to the Otter. "But, somehow, I think the better choice is to stay here, rather than go back. I can't recall any place within two day's paddle where we could get safely ashore to climb the walls."

"You hate to backtrack, is what it is," guessed the other.

Douglas made a face at his words and drove the slender boat around the edge of the whirlpool into the lee of the two house-sized boulders. Together they hauled it out of the water and tied it securely to keep it from being swept away if the water rose during the night.

They stood on solid ground, looking about. The beach was tiny. The black rocks on either hand cut off not only the worst of the current, but some of the wind and thunder as well.

"Actually, it's not unpleasant if you ignore the grumble," observed Marbleheart. "Not many enemies would bother to get at us here, at any rate. Too tall the cliffs, to climb."

The Journeyman carefully examined the narrow strand and the bit of tanglewood behind it. Here were slender white birch, rowan and beech growing beyond the first screen of willows, and, higher on the slope, a small stand of sturdy maples. The air smelled sweet, well washed, and fresh.

"We'll spend the night here, anyway," decided Douglas. "Do you think you could climb these walls?"

Marbleheart craned his neck so far back he toppled over on his tail.

"Not bloody likely!" he sniffed. "I got webs between my toes, not sticker pads like an octopus."

"You're probably right. Some might be able to climb here, but getting the boat up would call for a Dwarf's skill at engineering. As far as I know, the nearest Dwarf is a long way off. There're levitation spells I could use, I suppose, but it would tire me dreadfully. I'll have to think about it."

"First we'll need a fire," said the Otter, "and then supper."

There was plenty of dried driftwood swept up on the tiny beach by a hundred or a thousand years of spring storms. They gathered a good supply and Douglas touched off a cheery blaze, over which they warmed their weary limbs and shared Faerie Waybread, which filled them comfortably.

The sun disappeared quite suddenly behind the cliffs, but the glow of the evening sky over the deep canyon allowed them to see almost as well as in daylight.

"Why don't you try the Firefly thing again?" suggested Marbleheart. "A local bug might be able to tell us of a way to the top."

"I'd leave the boat but I prefer not to walk the rest of the way to Pfantas, if I can help it. As for the 'firefly thing,' I'll do it when it gets darker, although this place seems remarkably clear of insects. Haven't seen a fly or a mosquito all day."

"Their sort likes only still water," explained the Sea Otter, curling himself into a comfortable ball before the fire. "There're a few birds, however."

Douglas looked up, following his gaze.

"Crows? I don't trust them. Crows are too often Witch friends, Bronze Owl says. They enjoy making mischief. Even if those crows aren't actually someone's lookouts, you can't trust them to keep their beaks shut. Caw and blab everything to anyone who'll listen when they see a free meal or two for their troublemaking."

After full dark he compounded the green-and-white bead again and dropped it into the fire as before, but no insect informant appeared.

"Huh! Nobody home," snorted Marbleheart.

Sleep was much closer. They both were drowsing in their blankets.

"Careful!" Douglas warned Marbleheart, who lay quite near the flames. "You'll toast yourself!"

"Not I!" cried a new voice.

Douglas sat up slowly and saw the tiny speaker in the heart of the campfire, basking in the glowing embers.

"A Salamander!" he cried in surprise.

"Oh, one of those Fire Lizards I've heard about," said the Otter. "How do you do, Sally Ann?"

"I love your fire! We usually have to wait 'til noontime for such warmth, especially in this chilly place."

The three-inch-long lizard ran up a glowing branch and dived into a pool of blue flame, rolling ecstatically over and over.

"There's something different about this fire," he observed, stopping to peer up at the travelers. "It doesn't quite feel like a common, ordinary fire to me, and I'm a sort of expert."

"That's because it was magically kindled," replied Douglas. "How far did you come to answer my call?"

"I live nearby in nice, safe cracks in the cliff face where the sun strikes best and there's no claw-hold for a hungry crow bent on lizard for lunch. Usually I'd be sound asleep by this time of night, but this evening I told my wife that something unusual was happening here on the beach, and I wanted to investigate. She said I was crazy, but I came anyway. Then I felt your calling."

Douglas explained, "I was calling for information."

"I'll be happy to oblige, if I can," said the Fire Lizard, coming so close they could feel his heat radiate on their hands and faces.

"You see the boat there," began Douglas, and he explained their predicament to the hot little lizard.

"Yes, I can see where the boat would be a problem, even if you could climb the cliff. Well, I can't help you much myself, but there are those who might be able to. The Cliff Swallows,

for instance. They travel quite far afield looking for food, you
see. I've never been above the rim, myself, so I don't know
what's beyond."

"In the morning I would love to make the acquaintance
of the Cliff Swallows," said Douglas. "In the meantime, I
suppose we're safe enough here?"

"Safe as sulfur matches—whatever that means," said the
Salamander. "It's something my grandmother always used
to say."

They chatted awhile about families and fires, the Salamander being very interested in a Wizard who specialized in
his own favorite element.

"I had a great-uncle, now long departed, who was a Wizard's pet," he said. "Nobody much believed him, although I
will say he was good at setting fires when the weather got
too chilly to move about."

"It could have been Flarman," said Douglas, yawning. "He
never mentioned having a Salamander as a pet. But then,
there's a lot about Flarman I haven't found out yet."

"I don't recall the name," said the Salamander. "If you
want to sleep, be my guest. I hope you don't mind if I enjoy
your dying embers for a while yet?"

"Not at all! Glad you enjoy them," said the Journeyman,
rolling into his blanket for the air was cold and damp.
"Remember to speak to the Swallows in the morning, please."

"I'll do just that!" promised the Salamander. Douglas fell
at once into a deep sleep, wearied by the hard work of fighting
the swift river's currents.

The waterfall's roar proved a lullaby for them both, and as
the sun didn't reach into the canyon depths until late morning,
they both slept quite late.

Opening his eyes, Douglas found himself being regarded
solemnly by four pairs of wide blue eyes.

They were set under fair brows and fluffy, tumbled, yellow
hair about regular, oval faces atop small, graceful bodies, like
those of deeply tanned young children.

Water Sprites, Douglas decided. They were slight, slim,
completely naked, and had tiny gossamer wings between
their shoulder blades.

"Oh, Wizard!" one of them called softly. "Have we awakened you?"

"Yes, but it's time I was up and about," Douglas replied. "Hello! I'm Douglas Brightglade."

"So the Swallows told us that the Salamander told them," said the speaker, smiling shyly. "We've heard of Wizards from Mother, and the telling was good. We seldom talk to Men, but Mother said we should help Wizards if we can."

"That's most kind of her and of you. I know you Undines are among the shyest of Sprites. I appreciate your coming to visit us."

"Undines? I thought they only lived in Sea waves," said Marbleheart, awake by then.

"Our distant cousins the Sea Undines, you mean? Yes, they live in ocean waves. We, however, prefer to live near waterfalls, the higher the better."

"The wider the better!" said the second Undine.

"The louder the better!" added a third. He was slightly more boyishly bold than the others. "My name is Niagara. This is my sister Victoria, and that is Rainbow. My eldest sister, who bespoke you first, is Angel."

"Pleased to meet you all," said Douglas, nodding politely. "May I present my friend, Marbleheart the Sea Otter? Join us at breakfast."

"We've broken our fast on sunlit spray and rainbow mists," said the Undine named Angel, blushing prettily. "It's all we require. But you must go ahead and eat as we talk," she added, seating herself on a clean, flat stone near Douglas's knee. The tallest of the four, she was no more than ten inches from toe to upswept topknot.

The others came and sat, but not too close to the fire, which Douglas had stoked up to warm water for his morning tea.

"Sally Ann told the Swallows of us, I gather," said Marbleheart, warming to these delicate creatures who lived by the waterfall. He appreciated the environment they chose, being a water creature himself.

"Yes. And the birds stopped by to speak to us. We understand you wish to pass above the falls with your vessel," said Angel. "And we think we know a way . . . if you're able to perform one bit of magic beforehand."

"Tell me about it," urged Douglas. He poured tea into tiny acorn-cap cups that he had picked up on the edge of the Forest of Remembrance. The Sprites were delighted with the bracing brew.

"Sir Wizard, our most favorite sport is riding over the falls from above and diving into the pool below," began Angel.

"I can see that would be fun, yes," said Douglas, although he had doubts about it secretly. Marbleheart, however, nodded with enthusiasm. It sounded to him like a great lark, as long as there were no hidden rocks below.

"You may wonder, then, how we return to the top to do it all over again, dozens of times each day?" asked Niagara, interrupting his older sister.

"Clamber up the cliffs, like Salamanders?" guessed Marbleheart.

"Fly?" asked Douglas. "I notice you have wings."

"No, no, sir! Our wings are just for show, unfortunately," said the boy Sprite.

"We've found a much better and quicker way. One less exposed to the drying wind and hot sun." Angel explained patiently, giving Niagara a big-sister sort of smile to show she didn't mind the interruption. "We slip through the fall itself. Behind the water curtain is a cave, and from that a natural stair takes us up to the top!"

"Simple and elegant!" cried Douglas. "Many falls have such caverns behind them. I learned that from an Apprentice Aquamancer I know."

"But what of the magic required?" the Otter asked.

"Our stair is very narrow. A mere crack. At your size, you couldn't possibly squeeze through. If you could make yourselves much smaller, more like us, you'd fit. Mother says Wizards can do such wonderful things, easily."

"I see!" nodded Douglas. "I can manage a reducing spell, when it comes to that. I wonder, however, if it's worth carrying the boat with us? What is the river like above these falls?"

"Oh, we've been there often!" put in Rainbow, eagerly. "For miles the river runs between sheer walls. It's swift and shallow but there are no reefs nor rocks in its bed. It might be a very hard row, but in time you'll reach a place where the river curves away to the north. A long, very deep lake begins there. On the north shore of the lake is a town called Pfantas."

Little Victoria added, "Beyond the lake the stream narrows and becomes a series of cataracts climbing halfway up between Blueye and Rumbler Mountain."

"Blueye? That's a mountain?" asked Marbleheart.

"Yes, sir! She has a perfectly round, blue lake in a crater in her peak. The Swallows, who told us about her, call her 'Blueye' because that's what it looks like, I guess," Niagara explained.

"I see. Well, Pfantas is our immediate destination. Your cave under the falls may be the solution to our problem. I'll shrink the gondola and carry it along, too. Will you guide us, Undines?"

"Of course!" cried all four at once. "Willingly!"

Although Douglas had long used enlarging spells to provide blankets and tents from handkerchiefs when traveling, this would be the first time he had used one in reverse, and on living creatures.

For practice, first, he reduced the twenty-foot gondola to a mere six inches. The spell worked on the boat without a hitch. Douglas carefully wrapped it in his spare handkerchief and slipped the miniaturized gondola into his left sleeve.

He then took a deep breath and wove the enchantment again, for himself and his companion. It was quickly done, for the spelling was quite simple, designed by Flarman Flowerstalk for everyday use. Douglas—and the Otter—breathed sighs of relief. Douglas was now as small as Angel, although somewhat bulkier, and Marbleheart, even smaller, in a proper proportion.

Douglas shed his clothes, packed them away in his knapsack and joined the water babies and the Otter, who were already joyfully splluttering and splashing in the swirling pool.

Getting to the base of the falls was just a matter of allowing the circular current to carry them around to the far side of the basin. Near the base of the fall, the Undines led their new friends carefully up through a tremendous boil of mist. An up-angled ledge was just wide enough to tread, if they were careful.

Here at the very edge of the curtain, the falling water was only as thick as a windowpane. Ducking through proved easy for them all, even the slightly built Rainbow.

They scrambled over spray-slippery rocks beyond, deafened by the thunder of the falling water. Buffeting winds filled the cavity carved from the solid rock by ages of water splashing back from the impact zone.

In green dimness they clambered up a series of narrow stone ledges. Beyond the ledges, they reached the relatively dry and smoothly polished floor of a high, shallow cave. At the back a wide crack slanted from the floor almost to the ceiling. Into this the Sprites led the travelers.

Wind blew down the crevice from above and soon dried Douglas enough to allow himself to redress, although the naked Undines were not as happy with the drying as he. Marbleheart galumped ahead, happy either wet or dry, up the steep, natural stair within the crack.

"Not far," said Niagara, leading the way. "See? There's light ahead."

They emerged from the crevice some distance to one side of the stream, above where it leaped over the precipice.

The Journeyman quickly undid the shrinking spell and Marbleheart, accompanied by the Sprites, tumbled gleefully into the river again to investigate the riverbed. The young Wizard selected a quiet backwater further upstream to resize and launch the Summer Palace gondola.

"No problems," reported Marbleheart, surfacing from his swim. "Current's fast and very strong, but you drove the boat through much worse and dodged rocks, too, all day yesterday."

"Then we're ready to shove off," agreed Douglas. "Would you Undines care to go along a ways for the ride?"

"We'd be delighted!" cried Victoria and Niagara, and their enthusiasm convinced their shy sisters to agree.

"No farther than the beginning of the lake, however," warned Angel. "Morgen live in the lake. They're much too rough and unfriendly."

"Morgen? Oh, I remember—Merpeople." Douglas recalled Bronze Owl's long-ago lessons on all the kinds and sorts of Little People.

"I bet they can't dive over crashing waterfalls like you do," comforted Marbleheart, but Angel insisted on returning before the gondola entered Pfantas Lake.

"Learn something every day, almost every hour," said Marbleheart, once they were aboard and under way. "I've known Morgen ever since I was a kit in the Briney. Mermaids were our baby-sitters and taught us to sing and swim and catch the finest anchovies. I never knew their race inhabited lakes."

"Only very large and deep freshwater lakes. Hardly ever flowing rivers, though," Douglas told him. "I was taught the Lake Mermen were once the same as Sea Mermen, but they had a falling out, ages ago, and a few left salt to live in fresh water. That probably explains why they're not very friendly. They must still feel like exiles, driven from their homes to be surrounded entirely by unfamiliar dry land."

"Oh, I can see that," said Rainbow. "Some Falls Undines feel that way—sort of second-rated compared to our Sea-living cousins. Personally, I think we, with our exciting, loud-voiced waters and quiet, cool pools are much luckier."

This started a lively discussion between the Undines and the Sea Otter, who argued the benefits of curling surf and storm surges. The voyage on the upper brook was otherwise uneventful—in fact, quite pleasant. The Undine youngsters chatted endlessly, swam happily with Marbleheart when they felt too dry, and twice begged Douglas to stop so they could scramble up and plunge headlong over tributary falls that plummeted a hundred feet from the rimrock into the river.

"Like rain from a downspout," mused Douglas, watching them from the gondola.

Late in the afternoon they reached the widening and slowing of the current, which indicated, Niagara said regretfully, that they were about to enter Pfantas Lake. The Sprites said good-bye, thank you so very much for the boat ride, and please come again, splashed over the side, and disappeared downstream.

"Wonderful little people," sighed Marbleheart. "Almost as good as Otters in the water."

"I'm glad we met them. They may just be the last nice

people we see for some time," said Douglas, pointing the boat out into the lake.

Upon the tallest of a range of steep, cone-shaped hills on the north shore of Pfantas Lake was plastered a glaringly ugly town of narrow, winding, garbage-cluttered streets and chipped-paint, lop-roofed houses. The town and its hill were crowned by broken, tumbledown, gap-toothed ruins of a large building. Everything, everywhere was streaked gray-white, as if drenched with centuries of smelly bird droppings.

"Such a horrid-looking town to be in such beautiful country-side!" exclaimed Douglas. "That, if I am not mistaken and the Summer Palace maps not totally wrong, is Pfantas!"

"Pfantas? Why is it so unnecessarily ugly, I wonder?"

"I can't imagine! According to what I read, Pfantas was very nice, quite famous as a vacation spa, renowned for its matchless setting and clear, clean mountain air, and the lake for fishing and boating."

"*Something* happened to turn it this sour and slovenly," exclaimed the Otter, his nose a-twitch as he caught a whiff of Pfantas's airs.

"I believe this is the work of the Witches—in which case, Cribblon's warning was not sent too soon. Things in Pfantas have gone downhill, and Witches are renowned for such mischief."

"Everything goes downhill, over there," chuckled the irrepressible Otter. "Drop a dried pea atop the town and it'd roll all the way down into the lake!"

"We'll tie up to the dock there and make no secret of our coming," Douglas decided. "I want this man Cribblon to see or hear about our arrival as soon as can be."

"Common sense, I suppose," agreed the Otter, a bit sarcastically. "Tie her up where that nasty-looking old man is waving at us to go away."

"What we do *not* need to say," Douglas cautioned Marbleheart as they climbed a steep stair to the town's first level, "is anything about a Witches' Coven or Cribblon."

"How do we find what's-his-name if we can't ask for him?"

"Carefully," answered Douglas. "We are what we seem—
a Wizard and his Familiar."

"I? A Familiar? I thought Familiars had to know lots and
lots of magical stuff. A Familiar? Like the black cat you've
told me of?"

"Yes, but no, too. Black Flame just . . . *helps,* I suppose.
By being around, you see? Anyway, it won't hurt for these
people to think of you as some kind of magicker. Otherwise
they might well think of you as a potential stew or a warm
fur jacket!"

"Great Greebs! I should have stayed at Sea! No, I'm not
sorry I came along, Douglas. I agree. To seem to have *some*
magic is better than to be seen as a fur coat."

"In exchange," Douglas promised him, "I'll teach you some
quick and easy spells. To impress strangers. I should have
thought of that before."

"I can hardly wait," said the Otter unenthusiastically.

Flarman, dressed in striped red-and-white trunks that left
his torso a vast expanse of pale, pink skin and grizzled white
hair, basked in the afternoon Waterand sun on the terrace
outside the Reception Hall.

A scribe from Augurian's staff sat at a table under a large
canvas parasol, also striped red and white—Wateranders had
sense enough to stay in the shade on sunny days—reading to
the Wizard from a great stack of letters.

"A letter from one Cycleon of Garenth," he intoned.

" '*Dear Sirs: I beg to call to your attention the facts
of my father's enchantment by the late King Frigeon of
Eternal Ice. . . .* ' "

When he had finished reading, Flarman rolled over on his
stomach and nodded without opening his eyes.

"Send him the 'immediate action will be taken' letter."

"I believe his father was among the people the Wizard
Douglas Brightglade and you found frozen alive in Frigeon's
workshop," the scribe said, calmly consulting a notebook near
his hand.

"Ah, yes, I recall him now! His son must have written that letter before Daddy reached home. He should be back in Garenth by now. Better have someone check it out, in case he got lost. Garenth is a long way from Eternal Ice."

"Yes, Sir Wizard!" responded the scribe. He made a note on the letter and laid it aside on a pile separate from those the Wizard had already dealt with.

"The next is directed to you, personally," the scribe continued. "It says: 'Dear Magister: I have arrived in the town called Pfantas . . .' "

"That's from Douglas!" cried Flarman, sitting up quickly. "Go on, please!"

"The letter continues," said the scribe: " 'I am joined in my travels by a Sea Otter of considerable warmth, wit, and intelligence named Marbleheart. We have managed to come this far—200 miles from the coast as the crow flies—all by water, which explains our good speed to date. From here on our progress depends, of course, on finding the ex-Apprentice Cribblon. We will begin that search tomorrow morning. Pfantas may once have been a garden spot, but its present state is a midden on a mountain, as far as we can see.

" 'I append a note to my loved fiancée and fellow Wizard (She *must* have been passed to Journeyman by now if only on her good looks alone!), whom I miss terribly.

" 'To you and Augurian and all, my love and Marbleheart sends his respectful greeting—but then, he doesn't know you yet, does he?

" 'More when we find Cribblon. May it be soon, as we don't enjoy this smelly old place at all! From . . . Douglas Brightglade.' "

"Wonderful!" cried Flarman, jumping up and beginning to pace excitedly back and forth along the terrace. "Take it to your Master at once, please. I'll take the note to Mistress Myrn myself."

"Better don some clothes first," suggested Bronze Owl, clattering over the palace wall. " 'Tis not proper etiquette to enter a palace in such a scanty costume."

"Right! Of course! One must follow one's host's conventions, I suppose, while one is visiting."

"One never knows whom one might meet," Owl pontificated sarcastically. As a solid-metal creature, he saw no reason to remove one's clothing just because it was hot. "Would you care to meet, say, Queen Marget of Faerie, of a sudden, you being all but in the buff, so to speak?"

"Of course not! You're right," agreed the Fire Wizard again. "Besides, it might frighten Marget into too-early childbirth to see me thus!" he muttered as he retired to his apartment to change.

In ten minutes he was knocking at Augurian's laboratory door.

Myrn answered his knock, soaking wet from head to toe and looking as if she could bite the head off a dragon were the dragon foolish enough to comment on her appearance.

"Ah, the joys of Aquamancy!" chuckled Flarman.

"Watch yourself, Firemaster!" the petite Apprentice growled, a dangerous glint in her eye. "Remember, Water can quench Fire!"

Flarman ducked into the room, glancing up to make sure no black thunderclouds were gathering to pour a tropical shower upon his head. "Call it a draw!" he pleaded.

"Aptly punned." The girl from Flowring Isle grinned. "Draw water and draw fire! I'm sorry, Magister! Things haven't gone aright today at all."

"Here's a certain word I guarantee will bring a smile to your lips and lightness to your heart, my dear," said Flarman, presenting the folded note. "It just arrived."

"From Douglas!" the lass exclaimed gleefully. She snatched the fold of parchment and hastily opened it.

"I'll be on my way, then," said Flarman, but Myrn was already engrossed in her letter and didn't even notice him leave.

Chapter Eleven

Cribblon Found

GRIM, glum, and preoccupied Pfantasians showed no curiosity about the unusual pair when they walked about the next morning. Clambered about might be a better description, for most of the streets of Pfantas were actually steep stairways, slippery with scum and malodorous with piles of rotting garbage.

"What this place needs is a solid week of good, hard rain," observed the Journeyman.

"What it needs," Marbleheart sniffed in disgust, "is a good, old-fashioned Briney tidal wave."

"I suppose one gets used to it," said Douglas, trying not to breathe too deeply.

"Easier for you to say," grunted the other. "Your nose is a lot further away from this mess than mine!"

They had spent the night in the town's only inn and resolved before the first hour had passed to find a nice, quiet pine glade somewhere away from the town to camp during the rest of their stay. That was their first order of business this morning, which had dawned hot, humid, windless, noisy, and extremely overripe.

Circling the base of the conical hill, they passed through a postern gate on the side opposite the lake and dipped down into a trash-strewn valley through which rushed a muddy burn. They crossed a rickety two-plank bridge, which swayed and bucked under their weight, and climbed the opposite hill, upwind of the town. The way here was soft and fragrant with pine needles, through dense stands of dark pine accented here and there by white birch.

"This is far better!" exclaimed Marblehead, who had decided not to take a dip in the poor creek's filthy waters. "How about this nice level clearing? It looks just what we need."

Douglas pitched camp. He not only enlarged his best hand-kerchief into a colorful, roomy pavilion, but added a smooth bit of lawn, a small garden filled with the most fragrant flowers he could think of, and decorated the tent poles with cheerful red and orange banners emblazoned with his own "DB" monogram under the ancient flame symbol of Pyromancy.

"It pays to advertise, if you want someone to know who, what, and where you are," said he. Marbleheart shook his head in doubt but said nothing.

"Where does one begin to look for an ex-Apprentice?" he asked instead.

"With any luck, Cribblon will find us," replied Douglas. "It seems best. We don't know where to look for him, nor even what he looks like. If he has eyes or ears, he can learn about us from just about anywhere on this side of Pfantas."

They settled down in front of the comfortable pavilion to await results. To pass the time, Douglas taught the Sea Otter certain simple magic spells, as he had promised.

"First, a very useful spell to warm and dry yourself quickly after a wetting."

"I've never had trouble drying *without* a spell," objected the Otter. "My fur dries in a matter of minutes."

"Hours," corrected the Journeyman. He wrinkled his nose. "Besides, you don't smell too good when you're damp. This'll be handy when you want to be dry in mere seconds because you have to meet important people who might not be used to wet Otter. And, of course, you can use it on other things if you wish them to dry quickly."

Marbleheart grumbled but learned his first spell quick-ly, then tackled a few more difficult spells with growing eagerness.

Douglas avoided spells that called for complicated hand gestures, as these would prove difficult for a Sea Otter of short legs and webbed toes. He included the first Firemaking Spell Flarman had ever taught to his Apprentice so long ago—for lighting campfires, lamps, lanterns, braziers, sconces, flares, pipes, and candles.

"To be used with caution, of course," warned the Journeyman, unconsciously mimicking Flarman's words and best teaching manner. "It's simple but powerful. You could set a whole town on fire if you aren't careful."

"Say, not a bad idea!" exclaimed Marbleheart, nodding his head toward Pfantas. "Well, perhaps not; at least not yet."

The morning passed quickly but nobody approached them. No Pfantasian even looked up from daily tasks on the hillside opposite. The travelers ate a good lunch (pinecones and pine needles transformed into ham and sharp cheese sandwiches on rich, brown rye bread with cold potato salad). They bathed in a small pooling of the burn that ran below their camp—well upstream from Pfantas, where the water was clean, fresh, and cold. Afterward they basked in the warm spring afternoon sun on their square of lush greensward.

Marbleheart had practiced his first learned spell, alternately diving into the burn and coming out to dry himself by uttering the Drying Spell. Repeated soaking and drying made his coat rather too fluffy, and he then had to lick it back into shape.

"I'm going over to look at that castle at the top of town," decided Douglas in midafternoon. "Just out of curiosity."

"Remember what you told me about curiosity," warned Marbleheart. "Better take me along."

"You stay here in case Cribblon comes along while I'm gone. If he does and can't wait for me, tell him to come back at suppertime. Anyone eating Pfantas's food should jump at the chance to dine on pinecones and needles."

Douglas crossed the creek, passed through the unguarded postern gate, and climbed the stair-step streets to the broken-down old structure at the very crown of the hill.

It was neither entirely ruined nor uninhabited. Dozens of ragged, half-clad men and women huddled in the hazy afternoon sun, under broken arches and in blind doorways, sullenly ignoring the young Wizard as he passed.

"Good fellow," Douglas asked a young man with his arm in a dirty sling, "do you know anything of a person named Cribblon?"

"Do ye want to get me beaten or worse, asking me stupid questions?" snapped the young man. "Only Witchservers are allowed to question! Or maybe you *are* a Witchserver, eh? In which case I'm dead already, curse my bad temper!"

"You're still alive," said Douglas, not unkindly. "Does that prove I'm not a Witchserver?"

"It *might*," stressed the other. "No, I've never heard of anyone named Cribblon."

And he would say no more, fear as well as pain showing in his fever-dulled eyes. Douglas silently recited a healing incantation to set and knit the man's bad fracture. It would be a time before the Pfantasian realized that he'd been cured.

The ruins of the small castle were not particularly interesting, but they were at least cleaner—being more lightly populated—than other parts of town. Douglas spent an hour more, exploring and observing, trying to draw the poor derelicts into conversation, and failing completely. As the sun slipped behind the mountains he slithered and slid back down through the sweltering town, crossed the burn, and returned gratefully to the piny peace, fragrance, and neatness of their camp.

"No nibbles from this Cribblon person," reported the Otter. "There are lots of tasty little minnows and crayfish in the upper creek, however, so you won't have to fix supper for me, tonight. How do you like my fire?" He gestured to a neat blaze before the pavilion. "I set it all by myself!"

"Well done!" Douglas praised him, choosing to ignore the five or six patches of scorched grass where the Otter had practiced. He set about getting his own supper.

After darkness fell, they sat talking about the constellations in the cold, clear sky above—Otters had some interesting names for the Big Bear, the Little Bear, and other major arrangements of stars. Douglas learned that Otters were expert celestial navigators and could find their way over great distances by the positions and elevations of the stars alone.

Marbleheart stopped in the middle of a description of his journey from Dukedom across the Broad to Kingdom. He raised his black button nose and sniffed.

"Someone's just crossed the burn—and not by the bridge! He's taking many pains to move unheard and unseen, but I can smell him. I believe it's a him. Smells better than the usual Pfantasian, too."

Douglas said, "I sense him, also. Whoever it is has some small magics about him."

A dark figure appeared below their campsite, lying prone in the deep shadows under low-drooping pine boughs.

"Come on up and join us," Douglas called. "Others have not seen you but we've been watching you since you waded across the stream."

The man rolled out from under the pines, stood, and walked stiffly up to the fire, throwing back a deep hood to show a young-old, deeply tanned face, a mouth drawn taut in apprehension.

He said simply, "I am Cribblon."

"And I am Douglas Brightglade, Journeyman Fire Wizard taught by someone who remembers you of old, Cribblon."

"Yes, good old Flarman Firemaster! Or Flowerstalk, as I now hear he is calling himself. The change in name is why it took me so long to find where he'd settled after Last Battle."

"Aside from Flarman, Augurian, Marget of Faerie, and of course Frigeon, you are one of the few I've met who remember that time."

"Yes, Frigeon," said the other, sourly, accepting a seat by the fire and a plateful of supper leftovers. "The less we say about *that* Wizard gone bad, the better."

"You'll be happy to know he has reformed, or so we believe," Douglas told him. "This is my Familiar, Marbleheart Sea Otter."

The young-old man shook the Otter's paw solemnly.

"Pleased to have you find us," said Marbleheart. "Although I'm still not convinced standing on a hilltop and waving flags is the best way to avoid detection by your enemies."

"It worked," Douglas pointed out with a shrug. "Probably much faster than any other way."

"It poses dangers," agreed Cribblon, nodding to the Otter. "Which is why I chose to wait until deep darkness to leave town. The Witchservers are everywhere in Pfantas. They watch everyone and everything. Including you, Journeyman, when you visited the center this afternoon. Very little goes unnoticed by those Witch-Men. Their punishments for minor infractions are swift and cruel, too."

"Do they watch you?" asked Marbleheart.

"Oh, yes," said Cribblon with a tight smile, "but I try to blend into the scenery. I disguised myself as an itinerant bellows mender. It allows me to move about the countryside and assures me, if not a welcome, at least a reason for being here, close to the Coven."

"Where *is* Coven, then?" asked Douglas.

"Two days' walk to the northwest, on the east-facing slope of Blueye in the Tiger's Teeth. You could see her tip plainly from the other side of this hill if you knew where to look."

"Have some more supper and a mug of good brown Valley ale, transported direct from Blue Teakettle's cellar at Wizards' High," Douglas urged him. "We have the whole night to talk and decide what to do next."

Cribblon proved to be a good-natured, if rather high-strung man who looked younger than his two hundred years. His memory went back to the very beginnings of the war.

"I was apprenticed to . . . an Aeromancer," he said once he'd satisfied a voracious hunger for decent food and slaked his thirst on the Oak 'n' Bucket's best ale.

"Not Frigeon!" exclaimed Douglas.

"As it happens, yes," said the other, nodding. "You who knew him later may find it hard to believe, but he was quite a good Master when we both were a lot younger, before the war. He taught me carefully and treated me fairly. We never actually liked each other, but I certainly respected his skills as a Wizard."

"I've spent some time with him since he was captured and his power destroyed," Douglas assured him. "I've seen the good side of him restored. I, for one, don't think he's trying to fool World with pretended remorse. As Serenit of New Land, he's already doing a splendid job of righting what he did wrong. We keep an eye on him, of course."

"I'm glad to hear that," sighed Cribblon. "I would be relieved to forgive him what he did to me, toward the end."

"Witches first," said Douglas. "Tell us all you know about this Coven."

Cribblon took a deep breath and shook his head.

"There is definitely no safe place to talk of the Coven, especially here."

"I've protected us with some useful spells. You may feel them, if you try."

The former Apprentice Wizard closed his eyes and appeared to be listening. A faint smile quirked his lips, and he relaxed slightly.

"Very powerful, yet very, very subtle! Stronger than anything I could do in the old days, believe me! Worthy of Flarman Flowerstalk, I'd say. It should keep the Witches from detecting our meeting—for a while, at any rate."

He sat back, considering his words very carefully.

"Where to begin? Briefly, when Last Battle was over—nobody really won, you know—chaos descended on us all. The various bands, armies, tribes, nations, troops mustered to fight for—or against—the Dark Forces were widely scattered . . . just as our Fellowship was dispersed to the four winds."

"Yes, Flarman fled east and settled in Dukedom and Augurian went to an island in Warm Seas," Douglas said, to show he knew the broad outlines of their history.

"Yes, well, as they did scatter, so did the Beings and dire Beasts on the other side, the Warlocks and Black Witches as well as the Red Sorcerers and Turned Wizards, Ogres, Goblins, Trolls, evil spirits, banshees and so on.

"Many were hunted down by our allies, destroyed or driven far away. The most powerful and luckiest survived, however, hiding deep in tangled black forests, in the western desert, the northern wastes, or under mountains and under Sea.

"They hoped that, in time, Mortals, and Near Immortals would become so concerned with their own problems and pleasures they'd entirely forget the Wicked who remained out of sight."

"Their waiting might have paid off in the long run, except that Frigeon lost his patience and showed his reviving powers too soon," the Journeyman observed. Cribblon nodded soberly and continued.

"In those days during the Chaos there arose terrible Beings we called Searchers, looking for revenge on Men. To avoid them, I fled west and south and settled in Farflung, as far away as I could get, to the very edge of Emptylands.

"I settled there, under a new face and new name, growing grapes for wine and raising goats. Five years ago a wanderer appeared at my door, emaciated, exhausted, in rags, only half-sane. He'd been horribly burned by magic fire and begged me to put him out of the unending pain.

"I'd not practiced any sort of magic for a century and a half—except a little here and there to earn a scant living among the farmers of that distant place. Cures for diseases among the cattle, broken arms, things like that. Nothing that would give me away.

"I thought I'd forgotten the air-curing spells for dire burns Frigeon taught me. Air is a great curer, you know."

"I remember my lessons well," said Douglas, chuckling to soften the implied rebuke. "Go on!"

"I treated him for almost a year. As his burns healed, his mind cleared and he slowly told me his story. He'd been a royal herald at Bloody Brook, had fled to the Far North when it was over. He hired himself out as a court musician. The proud Yarls of Northmost, not having joined Last Battle on either side, remained prosperous and able to pay well for good things like music and heroic poetry, which they love.

"But the Yarls began to war among themselves . . . great bloody battles with much looting and cruel slayings, he told me. My musician fled south again at the first chance, coming down into what had been Kingdom along the unbroken chain of Tiger's Teeth Mountains.

"His wanderings, filled with mischances, adventures, and narrow escapes enough to make a great saga-song all his own, brought him at last to the barren slopes of Blueye.

"Here he begged shelter from a terrible winter storm at the hut of an ancient woman, sightless and nearly deaf. The crone grudgingly took him in, more to hear his news than any kind of hospitality. He stayed two years slaving for her, cooking her meals, tending her half-wild cattle and cutting her firewood.

"She claimed she was wife of a herdsman who, with their sons, had perished in some obscure skirmish long before the Last Battle of Kingdom. Each night she prepared for the musician a tasty draught. After drinking, he always slept ten dreamless hours before awakening.

"At first the posset was welcome. He'd suffered from insomnia, fearing terrible nightmares ever since Last Battle, as so many did. After a time it began to worry him, however. He'd been a light sleeper all his life. Now he barely put head to pillow at dusk and suddenly it was morning!

"One night he pretended to drink but poured it out in the snow when he went to throw down hay for her three-legged cow. Then he went to his bed in the loft over the byre and lay fully awake.

"Not long before midnight he heard singing, shouting, and wild laughter. Creeping to the hay hatch, he peered through a crack and saw six women and a handful of men, some old, some young, some ugly, some comely, all dancing in wild abandon, completely naked despite the midwinter cold, about a furious fire in the old woman's dooryard.

"He realized at once they were Witches and attendant Warlocks, having seen many such in Grummist's court toward the end of the war. He sensibly remained hidden. Each night, pouring out the sleeping potion, he watched and listened in growing terror.

"Eventually the old woman became suspicious. He was ever tired, fell asleep over any task she gave him that allowed him to sit down. Fearing for his very life—or something much worse—he ran away into a heavy snowfall one night.

"The Warlocks pursued him on foot—disguised as ravening werewolves—and the Witches in the air on their broomsticks until he swam across upper Bloody Brook. Clean, running water they could not easily cross, of course.

"But just as he waded into the torrent, a Witch threw a magic fireball at him that ignited his clothing and terribly burned one side of his face, his left arm, and upper body.

"Fortunately, the fire didn't touch his legs—when it hit him he was already hip deep in the brook. He dived in, smothering the deadly flames before they could kill him. Once across, he was able to run.

"In terrible and continuous pain and with no help offered by anyone he met, he came at last to my most distant neighbor who told him he might find healing help in my house.

"Well, I treated his near-fatal burns, which had never

healed, although it'd been a year or more since his narrow
escape. I kept him in my house. Finally healed, he insisted
upon leaving, as he would only bring down the dreaded
Searchers on us both if he stayed.

"I said I was able to protect him from pursuit as I had
protected myself for over a century. But he didn't believe
me and slipped away one night, and I never saw him
again. His trail led out into Emptylands' desert. At least I
had helped him to become healthy and relatively sane before
he left!"

Cribblon shook his head sadly, remembering.

"He told me he'd heard the Witches speak of the old
woman's hut as 'Coven.' Knowing something of Witches
from Frigeon, who hated them passionately—"

"Which explains something I've always wondered about
Frigeon," interrupted Douglas. "Why did he never seek alli-
ances with Black Witches in his own rise to power?"

Said Cribblon with a nod, "After the musician—his name
was Illycha—left me, I was in a fearsome quandary. I wanted
desperately to remain hidden where I had kept myself safe for
a hundred and fifty summers. I was afraid that these Witches—
this Coven—would, while seeking Illycha, discover me. My
powers had been enough to hide from the Searchers, but
Witchpower? I feared I would be too weak to avoid their
all-seeing.

"On the other hand, I realized they posed a great danger
to World, and especially our much-weakened Fellowship of
Wizards.

"I determined at last to find who remained of my old
Fellows and warn them of this Coven. I had to spy a
bit on Coven so that I would have firsthand and con-
vincing proof of the danger. I hoped I might be able to
assess their strength and purposes from a near distance,
then send report to the most powerful of the remaining
Wizards.

"That's how it came about. I came to Pfantas in disguise
three years ago. I saw clearly the danger Coven presented to
Wizards and World. After much careful inquiry I sent word to
Flarman by way of a Kobold I met in an iron mine under one
of the mountains. He agreed to pass the word through a certain

Dwarf Prince who had befriended some of the Wizards . . ."

"That would be Bryarmote, I'd guess," put in Douglas.

"That was his name. Kobolds, or Knockers as they call them in these parts, are even more secretive than your average Dwarf. I often doubted the message was ever delivered . . . until this afternoon, when I saw your flags, Douglas Brightglade."

"Tell me, what goal do these Witches pursue? If all they do is dance in the snow and throw an occasional fireball at a runaway slave—I know he was not, but they would think of him that way—there are far too many other and much worse things to take up the Wizards' attention these days," said the Journeyman. "Frigeon alone was responsible for a thousand unrecorded major enchantments that must be uncovered and undone. You could be helpful to us in that work, Cribblon, unless you really believe these Witches are a real danger!"

Cribblon thought about this, staring across at the late lights of Pfantas.

"When I came to this country I found that it had been changed drastically by the Witches. Pfantas was once a lovely and prosperous city on its majestic hill. Some of the Old Kingdom's finest families lived here. Everyone in those days hoped to earn enough to buy a home in fair Pfantas.

"The nature of this place was changed when I returned here. It had become filthy, its good people mean-spirited and quarrelsome, whipped to sniveling submission by Witchservers set to govern them by fear alone. Now Pfantasians are powerless to change their garbage-strewn, sewage-washed, stinking-to-the-high-sky existence!

"And that was just my first hint that the Witches had been working evil. I very cautiously wound my way to Coventown itself, following the directions given me by poor Illycha. I climbed between the Teeth of the Tiger, got close to where Illycha's old woman had lived in her mean hut.

"I saw a hut no longer, but a lurid, seething town, half-buried in blasted rocks, with a castle lifting crooked spires and twisted horn towers into choking smokes, fouled with acid fumes and nauseating vapors that could only mean Black

Magic rites. I saw the Witches with my own eyes, stalking on its crooked battlements or flying their broomsticks over its blackened walls.

"Coven has become a center of Black Magic! Great wickedness is being plotted and practiced there. I could see as well as feel it!

"I found out two more things before I fled in great fear. First, that I had neither the training nor the power to confront the Witches of Coven alone. Secondly, they had been brought together by a Witch who styled herself Queen, a regal, tall, dark-haired woman they hail as Emaldar the Beautiful, and World Witch! By instinct alone I recognized her as the old crone, but no longer in disguise. I am convinced that her goal is to rule what once had been Kingdom. That, at the very least!"

"I trust your instincts as I believe your observations," said Douglas gravely.

"I fled in terror, as I say, and sent the message to Flarman. I need help! Can he give it to me?"

For several minutes Douglas was silent, listening to the sounds of drunken cursing coming across the valley from Pfantas.

A star shot across the sky from east to west, followed by a sound like a single great stroke on a bass viol. Marbleheart and the Air Adept's former Apprentice sprang to their feet in startled wonder, but Douglas leaned back to watch the shooting star disappear in the west.

"I was sent to set things right here, if I can," he said at last. "And I believe with your help, friends, I can do it. We'll start in the morning by taking the path to Coventown and then we'll see what must be done."

"Thanks be!" breathed Cribblon. "I feared that I had waited too long."

"It's never too early or late to oppose Evil," said Douglas with a grim smile for his companions. "But a good night's sleep is our first requirement."

"I must return over there," said Cribblon with a shudder of revulsion. "Goodness knows, I don't want to go, but there are things I've left undone and some good people I should try to warn. Whatever we do in Coventown will affect Pfantas, and they must be ready for it. I'll be back by dawn."

He stood and strode down the hillside to the bridge. The last they saw of him he was a shadow climbing the winding path to the postern gate.

Chapter Twelve

Cribblon Lost

DAWN came—but not Cribblon.

"Do you trust him?" asked the Otter, uneasily. "He could have tipped off these Witchservers by now, you know."

"There's every reason to trust Cribblon," Douglas reassured his companion. "If they'd captured him and forced him to tell of us, they would have been here looking for us by now. Such creatures prefer to do their loathsome work by night."

They sat together on their lawn under the awning of the brightly embroidered tent. The morning had come up gloomy and damp, with a drizzle of rain intermittently falling. Uncomfortable, but not hard enough to flush Pfantas's streets, Marbleheart commented. Drops fell noiselessly from the tips of the lowest pine boughs.

They ate a simple breakfast of Waybread and tea. An hour passed, then a second.

"I think I'd better go see what happened to him," the Journeyman said at last.

"Oh, no, I don't think you should! If you start asking questions, these Witchservers will know at once who you are seeking, and they might harm Cribblon," protested the Otter, pushing the other back to a seat on the ground.

"How are we . . . ?"

"Let me go," insisted Marbleheart. "I can move silently and lie hidden and listen for hours, if need be. I'll be as invisible as anyone can be without a spell."

Douglas sat thinking a few moments, and then nodded his head.

"Go, then, and bring me back what news you hear."

The Otter scurried down the slope, staying under the pines. Douglas, even though he knew what to watch for, soon lost sight of him entirely.

It was nearly full dark when the Otter returned. He threw himself prone across from the Journeyman and sighed mightily.

"I'm afraid I've wasted the whole day, Douglas. Not one word about the missing, dead, or arrested bellows mender! I even made it a point to wallow in the filth to listen in on those Witchservers. What vile creatures! Disgusting habits!"

"Tell me what you did hear, even the littlest things," urged Douglas. "Anything at all might help."

"Let's see. I went up to the market and slithered under the fishwives' counters. Smelled better than most of the town. The fishmongers didn't say much of anything at all! They snarled prices, shortchanged everybody, complained about the catch, the weather, and their customers. That's all! No gossip. No banter. No smart remarks behind their customer's backs. Not even a single curse word! Would you believe it? I've tangled with fishwives before, many a time, and you always expect them to use the foulest language."

"Hmmm," said Douglas.

"Then I listened outside the back door of a barber's shop. Men in barbershops are always the best talkers, the bad-news spreaders. 'A little off the bangs,' these said. 'Some of your strongest-smelling toilet water,' they said, and who's to blame them for that? But not one word about the Witchservers' capturing a dangerous spy. Drunks and curfew violators, yes, but no Cribblon the bellows mender. Nary a word!"

He rolled over on his back and stuck his short legs in the air, stretching and arching his back against the short-cut grass.

"These people, even the Witchservers, are just plain petrified. Afraid to speak the least casual word. Cribblon told us Witchservers watch everyone, didn't he? I didn't believe it then, but it's true!"

"I'd better go myself," decided Douglas, rising.

"They'll see you!" cried Marbleheart in alarm. "They came very close to catching sight of me!"

"I can prevent it," said the Journeyman. "I've one man in mind to seek out. He may be willing to break silence enough to help us find what happened to Cribblon."

Under a broken arch in the ruin at the top of the town, he found the young man, his no-longer-broken arm still in its dirty sling, sleeping fitfully with his head barely out of the rain.

"Here!" called Douglas softly, shaking the man's leg. "Waken, sir! I want to speak with you."

"But not I with you," growled the other, turning further away from the rain.

"I might be able to give you something that will make your time worthwhile," said Douglas.

"Oh, a bribe, eh? How long do you think I'd get to keep the smallest coin? The Witchserver smell small change in a man's shoe, let alone his pocket."

"You're really in bad shape," said Douglas, letting his disgust and sarcasm show. "I offer you help and you'll probably run to the Witchservers yourself as soon as my back is turned, to curry favor by setting them onto me."

The man sat up, rain and all, and retorted angrily, "Now, *that* I would never do! Not even for a meal or three meals or a week of meals would I help the slimy, sneaking scum."

"If you really feel that way, why not answer my questions? I am against the Witchservers even more than you are."

The man glanced nervously about, studying the shadows under other arches and the dark places in empty doorways.

"Very well! I'll answer. What've I got to lose? If they take me, I'll at least not die of hunger. They'll fix me so that I won't ever die—of anything, including hunger, hard labor, whippings day and night!"

He struggled to sit up using just his left hand and arm, taking Douglas's proffered hand at last.

"Your right arm is healed. You'll notice if you try it," Douglas pointed out. "It happened since we spoke yesterday."

"By Hecuba! So it is!" whispered the man in surprised awe. "You did that?"

"I did that—for you. I did it out of pity and sorrow at the state you and your townspeople are in, not in payment for anything. Not then, or now," said Douglas, speaking with urgent sincerity. "Now tell me! Have you heard of the man called Cribblon? The bellows mender? You had not heard of him yesterday."

"The bellows mender? You didn't mention his trade before, did you? Yes, I've heard of him. There was soft word in the night about him."

"Where is he?"

"Gone! Someone saw the Witchservers take him at the postern gate last night, very late."

He shivered and gasped as the cold rain suddenly increased. Douglas gave him a strong dose of Flarman's favorite Warming Spell and his quaking subsided.

"The slime eaters held him overnight in the town gaol," the man went on at last. "This morning they put him in a trash cart and hauled him off."

"Where would they take him?"

"Only one place. Coventown!"

Douglas hunched down under the driving rain, thinking swiftly. Why take Cribblon to Coven?

"Did they question him? What happened overnight in the gaol?"

"Being in that foul place is torture enough for most men," sighed his informant. "I don't know what they did to him. I'm sure, from experience, that they made his life miserable."

Douglas was silent again. No one, not even a Witchserver, would see or hear them in this downpour.

"What can I do for you?" he asked.

"Kill them all, the Witchservers and the Witches and the Warlocks! Clear them out of our once-beautiful city! Out of our lives!"

"You'll just have to believe I'm working at that," said Douglas. "But what can I do for you right now?"

"You've healed my arm. Now perhaps I can get some kind of work on the docks or in the fisheries, enough to eat. My father's business is gone, along with my father and my brothers, taken as slaves by the Witches. We were leather merchants. The Witchservers came and just took over everything; the city, the businesses, everything!"

His voice was rising toward hysteria. Douglas laid a calming hand on his arm.

"Tell me more," he said, "but quietly, please."

"You can tell by just looking at Pfantas. They stopped all self-governing. They took all profits, and then they took our capital and our savings. They reduced every merchant, every shop owner, every craftsman to as near despair as the mind can stand. They came one night and carted off every scrap of leather in my father's warehouse. And they took my father and my two brothers, too. I've neither seen nor heard of them since!"

"Took them to Coven, you believe?"

"That's what I've heard the Witchservers say. To be slaves."

He was calmer now but tears of hopeless frustration mingled with the rain on his face.

"Something is about to be done about all this." Douglas said. "I have power to see to it these Witches don't create any more havoc. I promise you the wrongs they've done shall be righted."

"I - I - I almost believe you ! If what you say is true, it's all I want. All I would ask of anyone."

"Well, look at this, anyway," said the Journeyman, and he showed the wretch the four-leafed clover picked on the night of the Barrow Wights' attack on Marbleheart. "Carry it on your person. It's powerful protection against all sorts of enchantments."

The man brightened at the sight and scent of the limp clover leaves. Both could smell the sweet aroma of the tiny green plant, even over the stench of Pfantas in the rain.

"A Witch or any kind of enchanter will have to call on extraordinary powers to harm you if you carry a clover with four leaves, believe me! And it won't call their attention to you, either, as most other amulets would."

"I think I know where to find this growing, although it's been scarce of late," said the man. "Can you tell me your name?"

"I always tell my true name," replied the Journeyman. "I am Douglas Brightglade. I have no other names, but the title Journeyman Wizard."

"And I am called Featherstone," his informant said. "It's been a proud name in Pfantas for at least six generations."

They shook hands formally and Douglas smiled at his new friend.

"What road would the Witchservers take?"

"There is only one road a carter can take to that cursed place," Featherstone said, and spat in the mud. "It runs first north, then west, then northwest up a deep cleft in the side of Blueye Mountain. Midway to the top lies Coventown, I've been told. I've never seen it. Those who do—return as Witchservers, if they return at all."

"I intend to go up that mountain, and I'll come back unchanged. In the meantime, I must do something about the Witchservers. If you've clover growing in these parts, quietly tell your friends and neighbors about its charm. It would help confound these servants of Emaldar."

"I'll begin at once," said Featherstone eagerly.

"In a few days, you'll see them become confused, anyway, when I distract their attention to their stronghold. Watch your chance, then overpower them. Without the constant, close attention of their Queen, the Witchservers will become powerless. Ordinary Men again."

"I see. Yes, I'll pass the word."

"I have to go. I've put a Warming Spell on your clothes, such as they are. That should keep you comfortable until the weather improves. It's a small thing I can do for you, Featherstone."

"You've done more than enough! You've given me some hope!" whispered the leather merchant's son.

Douglas waved good-bye and retreated unseen down the hill to the postern in heavy rain—which hid the sound of his footsteps. He paused within two yards of a pair of slovenly Witchserver guards at the postern and heard them talking.

"What news, brother?" one asked.

His fellow glanced around with care before answering. "The night watch captured a powerful Wizard on this very spot just last night! They've taken him off to Coven Castle."

He blew his running nose noisily between dirty fingers.

"Who? A powerful Wizard? Wish I'd been there!"

"You lie in your teeth," the other sneered. "You and I were lucky to be off watch when the orders came. Wizards like this here Brighteyes are not to be trifled with! I'm just surprised that he didn't tear down half the town fighting them night dogs off."

They moved away. Douglas slipped behind them through the postern gate and escaped over the plank bridge without being challenged.

"They think Cribblon is *you*?" said Marbleheart when Douglas told him of his adventure. "How nice for us but how terrible for Cribblon! I was beginning to like him."

"If Cribblon told them he's me," said Douglas, starting to dismantle the campsite, "and they believed him, he's fairly safe. They'll fear him mightily, I would think. At least until Emaldar examines him more closely. I hope Cribblon will have the wits to remain silent as long as he can. This Witch Queen will want to know what the Fellowship knows of her, so perhaps she won't do anything too drastic until she realizes that she has caught Cribblon, not me."

"Where are we headed, then?"

"For Coven, of course!"

Marbleheart chuckled. "I suspected that would be the case. Well, let's hope the mountain streams are filled with trout. I've heard they're great eating."

"You're not afraid of going near the Witches?" asked Douglas.

"Not yet!" The Sea Otter checked to see if his marble disk was safe in Douglas's pack. "But I undoubtedly will be, very soon."

Stormy Petrel, on midday patrol over Waterand, spied the black speck while it was still miles away to Sea. He beat his long, strong wings to gain altitude, circling the peak of Watch Hill.

The speck slowly resolved itself into a waving black line with a dot in the middle. The Petrel's sharp bird vision soon recognized the stranger as a large Crow, coal black with a wickedly sharp yellow beak and ragged tail feathers. Although his body weight was about the same as the Petrel's, his wingspread was less than half. He flopped, flapped, and labored to stay aloft in the turbulent updrafts and downdrafts along the northwest shore of Waterand.

The Petrel silently glided between the rising sun and the approaching bird. Then, with a hoarse and terrifying battle scream, he shot almost straight down on the intruder as the Crow crossed the line between rocky beach and trees.

"Aaaaa-eeee! Hold off! Hold off!" screamed the Crow, flipping completely over on its back and dropping like a stone to the shingle. "A message! I carry a message!"

At the last possible moment Stormy Petrel veered to the right, his razor-sharp talons just missing the cowering Crow. A few dull, black tail feathers fluttered off as a warning.

"Messenger?" hissed the fierce seabird. "Message to whom, craven Crow?"

"To one called Flarman Flowerstalk," sobbed the bird, flattening himself to the rocks in abject submission, wings spread out on either side of him. "Flarman the Fire Wizard, I was told, was here."

"Stay where you are. Don't wiggle a pinion!" ordered Stormy, still gliding back and forth over the grounded intruder. "I'll speak to someone about this. *Do not move!*"

"I shall remain as one dead," promised the Crow, quaking in terror.

Stormy found Augurian and Flarman in the Water Adept's tower workroom, poring over lists and catalogs just arrived from the former Ice King, his reconstructed accounts of enchanted victims.

"Message from whom?" Flarman asked Stormy.

Stormy merely shook his head.

"Didn't ask? No matter," said Augurian. "We'll have to hear him out, anyway."

"A big, black Crow a year ago would only have been a spy for Frigeon or maybe Eunicet," mused Flarman, taking up his conical Wizard's cap and setting it square on his sunburned, balding head. "But now? Witchery, I would guess."

"A good working theory," agreed Augurian. "I'll have Stormy bring this Crow up here, shall I?"

"Please," agreed Flarman. "It can only be bad news. Send for your Apprentice, also. She should hear it with us, if it concerns a certain young Witch hunter."

Stormy Petrel was back in ten minutes with the sandy, shivering Crow, flopping ungracefully in the Petrel's silent wake.

Myrn had arrived sooner than that and stood beside Augurian, trying not to look worried. She clasped her hands together behind her back so no one would see that she was white knuckled.

"You are?" inquired Flarman sharply, with evident distaste. He had never cared much for Crows.

"Eboneser, Sir Wizard. You are the Firemaster Flarman to whom I am sent?"

"Right you are, Eboneser! And what is your tribe?"

The Crow hesitated for a heartbeat. He was familiar enough with magickers to sense the aura of power these three carried about themselves.

"Of Battlesky," he muttered. "My ancestor was . . ."

"Beakert the Brash," finished Augurian, nodding. "The Black Force standard flyer at Last Battle of Kingdom, you recall, Flarman."

"I recall Beakert. Last time I saw him he was Beakert the Bashed, however. I didn't know any of his tribe survived the carnage."

The Crow, Eboneser, shivered even more and squawked bitterly.

"Our tribal memories are most unpleasant, unkind sirs! Can we get to the business at hand, if you please?"

"Very well, Crow messenger! Our interest is not in you but in those you serve."

"Serve only as messenger!" insisted Eboneser. "None of us has entered into the doings of the Seven Sisters."

"You come, then, from Coven?" asked Augurian.

"Aye, Sir Wizard. With a message for Flarman Firemaster."

"You can speak it aloud in this company," said Flarman. Crows tended to follow evildoers, were often thieves and always braggarts, cruel mischief makers and cowards.

"This is my message, from the lips of Emaldar Queen, as fast as black wings could cover the distance: 'To Flarman the Firemaster, also called Flowerstalk. . . .

" 'We have found a sniveling little pest of a Journeyman Wizard, so young he has hardly yet put razor to beard. We hold him securely so he cannot be hurt in this wild land. If you wish to see him alive and whole after this moon, swear to turn your eyes elsewhere, Wizard of Fire!

" 'Leave us to our own devices or we will recruit him to our Service. I speak with Power, for I am . . . Emaldar, Witch Queen of Coven.' "

The messenger stood uneasily with head bowed, expecting storms to break and punishments to be meted out on an innocent messenger, but the three Wizards before him stood silent for a while before the Fire Wizard spoke.

"You would be well advised to return not to Tiger's Teeth or anywhere in Old Kingdom, Eboneser." His voice was almost kindly now.

"I . . . must return with your answer, Magister!"

"I repeat, you would be wiser to go elsewhere, as fast and far as possible. There is to be retribution and destruction to follow this deed in Old Kay's mountains. Those who adhere to—those who willingly serve—this Emaldar Witch are sure to be consumed in the conflagration I see ahead."

"I may go, then?" said the bird, crouching low, as if expecting a blow.

"Go, and quickly!" cried Augurian angrily. "My islands are not for your likes, carrion eater!"

The window was open to Sea and the black bird wasted no more breath but hurled himself ungracefully through it and was gone.

"See that he goes, and where," ordered Augurian. Stormy Petrel was already following the crow into the warm air over Waterand.

Flarman stepped quickly to a nearby workbench and began fiddling with a spirit lamp under a clay crucible. Flame sprang up and in a moment he gestured over the pot. It began to smoke and sizzle industriously.

"You . . . ," began Myrn, looking very worried.

"Wait!" softly cautioned Augurian, laying his hand on her arm. "He's looking for some answers."

The Pyromancer perched heavily on a stool and the other two magickers stood silently by as he studied the smoke and listened to the crackling of the crucible. After two minutes—it seemed much longer to Myrn—he waved his hand downward and the flame died, the smoke drifting out the window.

"Well, maybe this Emaldar is pulling some sort of a bluff," he told them, dusting his hands together. "It's just possible that she *believes* she had Douglas in her hands, but her prisoner is really someone else."

"Cribblon?" guessed Augurian.

"Not the Sea Otter, certainly," said Myrn.

"I don't think she would dare claim to hold Douglas if she didn't believe it was true," mused Flarman. "It's possible, also, that this is part of Douglas's own plan to confront Emaldar, with her thinking she has him safely under lock and key."

"And Douglas has not said he needs our help, which he should be able to do even if he is captive. No Witch has the power to shut a Wizard up," declared the Water Adept. He sank down onto another stool and waved Myrn to a seat also.

"We're making some large assumptions," said the Apprentice Aquamancer. "It is entirely possible Douglas is not able to communicate with us just now. We could ask Deka to seek Douglas out. . . ."

"Yes, but there's not sufficient evidence to show it's necessary to intervene. Besides, Black Witches are bad medicine for Wraiths like Deka. She would go, of course, but Emaldar might harm her."

Myrn fell silent but listened carefully to the ensuing discussion between the Masters. In the end they agreed to await word from Douglas himself. It was a measure of their confidence in the Journeyman's ability that they refused to take a direct hand at this point.

"But, Magisters," objected Myrn, "I feel in my heart Douglas needs and deserves *some* assistance."

"You're not only a woman but a Wizard in training," said Flarman, nodding his head. "Your intuitions can't be ignored. But please recall, Douglas is *Journeying* as is required by the bylaws and regulations of the Fellowship of Wizards in order to earn his Mastery. Assistance from another Wizard might—would certainly—disqualify him from advancement based on this Journey. He'd have to await another opportunity and it might not come for years, decades!"

Myrn considered his words as they went to lunch in Augurian's private apartments. Her elders spoke of many things, but she was preoccupied and took little part, although she knew much of what they said was part of her own education.

At last, when they were rising to return to their work, she held up her hand for attention and said: "I *will* go to Douglas's assistance."

"We've already discussed that," said Augurian with some impatience. "You've just begun your training, Mistress, and need to devote all your time and attention to your studies. They become more important and more difficult each day, as you know.

"Besides," he added after a pause, "you've heard Flarman. Even if Douglas is in serious trouble and we interfere, we'll have set him back years, maybe decades, professionally."

"I understand that, Magister," insisted Myrn. "But what if the assistance came not from a Master Wizard, but someone of lower rank?"

The Water Adept turned to the Firemaster, raising his eyebrows in question.

"The regulation says simply that 'a *Wizard* may not interfere or assist in any way,' " Flarman quoted. "It obviously means a full Master Wizard, or it did so when I wrote it. These things tend to take on a life of their own, as you know, Augurian."

He drew his bushy brows together in deep thought. "I have known of cases where two or more Journeymen cooperated in fulfilling their requirement to Journey in their art. In addition, there are many cases where a Journeyman was ably assisted by a Familiar."

"Then, honestly," said Myrn, reasonably, "assistance from a mere Apprentice . . . ?"

The older Wizards looked at each other again and eventually Augurian shrugged mightily, deferring to Flarman.

"Yes, I would have to support your contention," said

Flarman. "How about you, Fellow Wizard?"

"I - I - I suppose," sighed Augurian. "Although, I must admit . . . Sweet Fanny Adams! You've got me in a corner, lass!"

"I'm most sorry, Magister, but—"

"I agree that assistance from a 'mere Apprentice,' as you put it, would not constitute intervention under the regulations of the Fellowship. However," he added quickly, before she could comment, "I must ask whether you would be of real help to Douglas?"

"That's for you to estimate, as her Master," pointed out Flarman.

"Myrn is a remarkable young woman. She's learned a great deal in the year since she began her studies with me. She'd be useful to anyone, especially a Journeyman. She is highly useful to me, I must admit . . ."

"Then I may go?" asked Myrn.

"I would rather it were two years hence," sighed the Water Adept, slowly. "But, yes, you have my permission."

"And your good wishes, too?"

"Of course, Flowring lass! You always have those."

Myrn stood straight, managing to look relieved, excited and grateful all at the same time. She rushed to embrace her Master and his best friend, making Flarman grunt with the strength of her hug.

"Thank you! Thank you!" she cried. "I *must* go, you see. Douglas needs me, now. I feel it!"

"Intuitions must not be ignored," repeated Flarman, feeling his ribs carefully, but he found they were well protected by his girth. "He'll certainly be pleased to have you with him, at any rate."

"Take your notes with you," admonished her Master. "I'll give you some handy spells you haven't learned yet that may prove useful. You can study them out as you travel."

"Stop and talk to Bryarmote's Lady Mother, Goldesfine, in Dwelmland," Flarman suggested thoughtfully. "She's the closest to a Lady Wizard I know of in World these days. Perhaps she could give you some sound advice about traveling alone."

Myrn Manstar nodded eagerly.

"My dear, wonderful Magisters! I've a great deal to do, so please excuse me now." She gave them both another quick hug and a kiss each and dashed from the room, nearly upsetting the servant who had come to clear the luncheon dishes.

"Flarman, old friend, have we done aright?" Augurian asked, worriedly watching her go.

"Of course!" cried Flarman. "We never make little mistakes, do we?"

"No, only big ones," said Augurian glumly. Brightening a bit, he turned to lead the way back to his tower workshop.

"I admit to you, now she is gone it will actually be much better training for her than being cooped up here. Young people need to get out of doors in the fresh air and rain and sunshine every now and then."

"That's the spirit!" the Firemaster chuckled. "Remember, you and I were slaying monsters and leading Ogre-killing raids before we were Journeymen ourselves. A little help will be received gratefully by my Journeyman, I know."

Augurian nodded, then chuckled, recalling certain adventures they had shared as independent young Apprentices centuries before. They chatted about the old times until they reached Augurian's tower.

Myrn walked beside her lifelong friend, Sea, just after dark, having already said her good-byes to her friends on Waterand. The farewell supper had been a glad event, but she had chafed at the need to wait for darkness.

"Sea Fire!" she called. "Myrn Manstar has need of you!"

A bright flash of green light lanced through the waves at her feet and in a moment she had stepped boldly into the dark surge, sinking down into the warm, dry protection of Asrai, the Phosphorescence.

"Can you take me, before the Greatest Star rises, to the shore of Dwelmland?" inquired the Apprentice.

Without flashing an answer, the Asrai shot away from the shore, heading at breathtaking speed to the northwest.

Chapter Thirteen

![anchor/wave symbol]

Two More Players

DONATION came about smartly, her head now into the wind. Her movement slowed dramatically until she was virtually dead in the water.

At a shouted command, her best bow anchor roared down into the water of the Choin harbor, which was surrounded on three sides by gentle, wooded hills.

The sound stirred thousands of gray-and-white seabirds into raucous, excited flight. Few ships anchor here, they cried to one another. What fun! A chance to sample foreign food when the ship's cook empties his slop pails over the side after evening mess!

"Secure the stations!" ordered Captain Caspar Marlin. "Set the anchor watch!"

Seamen rushed from task to task, hauling on this line, casting off that. It seemed a scene of total confusion, except that things were quickly and efficiently accomplished. The great Wayness square-rigged ship came to rest with hardly a ripple, tugging only gently on her anchor chain and swinging slowly to the breeze.

Caspar watched from the break in her poop as hatch covers were lifted away, a shade awning was rapidly rigged amidships, a table and chairs set out. Sails were neatly furled about their yards, stoutly lashed yet ready to break out at a moment's notice.

Her sailors were sent below, watch on watch, to change into clean, freshly pressed uniforms, blue-striped open shirts, and dark blue trousers. They returned to fall in by divisions, toeing cracks between deck boards to form perfectly straight ranks. They tried manfully not to grin and caper in their boylike anticipation of new things to see and do in a strange port.

"Junk approaching, sir!" reported the Officer of the Deck, in a loud, carrying voice.

"Very well!" responded Captain Caspar Marlin.

He ran an approving eye over the ship and crew. Even the Emperor of Choin could not help but be impressed by this show and substance, he thought. And the Imperial Governor, now preparing to climb aboard Thornwood Duke's flagship from his smaller vessel, was said to be a nephew of the distant Emperor.

He took the chance afforded by the wait to study the Imperial Governor's junk, now hove to a cable's length off on the mirror-smooth surface of the beautiful but empty harbor. The Choinese were famed around World for their silks, yet the sails of the junk were of poor-quality canvas, ragged, patched, and stitched together. They were patched with lighter, cleaner pieces ranging in size from a few square inches to square yards. They hung untidily from their steep-slanting yards, looking like Monday morning's wash hung out to dry.

"Mustn't judge without information," Caspar said aloud to the Officer of the Deck, a tough young Waynessman named Pride. He, too, had been studying the Imperial Governor's high-sterned ship.

Just as the Imperial Governor's head appeared above the level of the deck, a bo'sun's pipe shrilled and six sideboys snapped to salute.

"Welcome aboard *Donation,* Excellency!" said Caspar, bowing from the waist. Wouldn't do to be *too* subservient, no matter what this Governor expected.

"And most welcome to the Great, Endless Empire of Choin, the Land Most Ancient and Wise, Cradle of All Civilizations, and so on and so on," said the chubby, middle-aged Imperial Governor, puffing from the climb over *Donation*'s tumble home. "A most interesting construct, your *Donation*," he continued, looking about with evident curiosity.

"May I offer the Imperial Governor a cup of a poor imitation of Choin's wonderful *fungwah*?" asked Captain Marlin, standing very straight but smiling warmly. He beckoned to the ship's steward to come forward with a decanter of Dukedom's best brandy.

"Ah, you know of our local customs!" cried the Imperial Governor, reaching eagerly for a cup. He tossed the contents into his throat at one gulp and appreciatively smacked his lips.

"I've had the honor to be a guest of Choin and Choin's Divine Emperor previously," explained Caspar, bowing again, as required at the mere mention of the Emperor.

The visiting dignitary also bowed as did all his attendants, rather perfunctorily, and chose another glass from the steward's silver tray. He waited until Caspar had selected another, also.

"To your own Emperor!" the Governor cried.

"Thank you! You are most courteous," responded Caspar. "But let us drink first to His Heavenly Majesty, the Emperor of Choin."

"If you wish," said the I.G. offhandedly, bowing a second time. He tossed off the new dram of brandy as if it were water. Caspar took a sip of his own, feeling the strong liquor burn toward his stomach. Good stuff, but he'd rather have *fungwah*—the very potent yet tasty liquor of this strange and exotic land.

The Imperial Governor reached for a third glass without being asked and drank it only a bit more slowly. Caspar neglected to match him cup for cup, pretending ignorance of the Choin custom.

Courtesy or not, he thought, I'm not going to deal with this August Person while tipsy.

Lunch was a cautiously pleasant affair. Afterward, the Governor, fortified by the rest of the decanter of brandy, followed Captain Marlin on an inspection of the ship, then into the Main Saloon to discuss matters of trade.

"All shall be as you wish it," he assured the Westongueman. "Choin is eager to reestablish trade and cultural relations with the Duke Thornwood. I understand he only recently came to his ducal seat after much unpleasantness. Something about an evil Wizard?"

"News travels amazingly fast to Choin," Marlin observed dryly. "Yes, we were fortunate enough to nip his plots against us. All's quiet and peaceful now. Dukedom and her neighbors are ready to resume World trading."

"I am interested in timber mostly myself," said the Governor. "Choin lacks forests, as well as the skill to manage and harvest trees."

"Lumber, timber, and fine furniture woods are all available at the other end of my shipping lanes," Caspar assured him. "Only tell me your needs, and when we agree on prices, I can have your first shipments here in less than six months, weather permitting."

Their discussion went on until soft dusk, when the I.G. apologized for breaking off to return to the shore in his junk, which he said was named *Bird of Paradise*.

"We shall continue our discussions in the morning, brave Seacaptain," the I.G. promised, rather unsteadily. By then he was pleasantly buzzed on seven more brandies and considered himself Caspar's closest friend.

The bo'sun's whistle shrieked again, stopping abruptly as the local potentate's head disappeared from view over the side. Caspar stood at the taffrail to watch the sampan row the tipsy I.G. back to his rather tacky-looking ship.

"Well, that takes care of the formalities," he said briskly to his First Mate. "Send the men to supper, Pride, and set the first Dog Watch, please, Mister. Give the men the left-over foodstuffs, if any. The Imperial Governor and his crew ate like they were starved and drank like sailors back from a seven-year voyage! The starboard watch will go ashore first."

"Our business is concluded, then," said the pudgy, slightly hung-over Imperial Governor.

They had met in the splendid, luxuriously furnished Audience Chamber in the gilt-sheathed Governor's Palace just before noon the day following. "You may give orders to have your ship moved to the Imperial Warehouse Pier on the riverfront, at your convenience."

"If it's possible, sir," said Caspar. "Is the water deep enough for her, do you think?"

"The water is deep enough for *Donation*. I so order," said the I.G., glancing significantly at his third secretary.

"Now, Honored Captain Marlin, I am most pleased with our transactions and wish to offer you a gift of personal esteem. What can I give you to show my goodwill and deep gratitude?"

"There's nothing you have denied me," protested Caspar. "But I do have a small personal request."

"If it is in my poor, limited power to grant . . . of course!"

"As you know, I visited Choin once before, years ago."

"I am aware of your former visit, yes."

"At that time the Captain of our ship . . ."

"The . . . er . . . *Sally*?" asked the Governor with a smile.

"Yes, *Sally* Brigantine, she were, of Westongue in Dukedom. Ye're correct, Excellency."

"What, then?"

"Our good Captain became ill and was cared for by a physician of your city, one Wong, I believe."

The Governor frowned but nodded for him to go on.

"After he recovered, so taken was he with your ways and life that he decided to stay behind and become a citizen of Choin . . ."

"A subject of the Emperor," corrected the Governor, frowning still. "But no matter . . ."

"I'd like very much to greet my old Captain before I leave your . . . uh, fair city . . . if he is still alive and well."

"Oh, most alive and most well, I assure you!" cried the Governor. "I think. When you've unloaded your cargo, tomorrow, I will have located him and arranged for him to see you the next day, if that suits you, dear Captain Marlin. See to it at once!" he hissed sharply to his second secretary.

One of the five other secretaries leaned forward to whisper in the Governor's left ear.

"Ah! I am informed that your good Captain Foggery resides in a town not distant. I will send for him."

"If I could," said Caspar, "it would be more proper, rather, that I travel to visit him. In respect to his position and age, you understand."

"We will arrange it, then," agreed the Governor, although it was evidently not fully as he would have liked it. "The day after tomorrow."

Caspar and Pride left the spacious but wildly overdecorated Governor's Palace after much required bowing and scraping.

They were escorted back through the scrupulously clean but run-down city by a squad of twelve fiercely scowling guards in red-lacquered leather body armor, bearing twelve-foot pikes tipped with ominously gleaming, razor-sharp blades.

"Very good of ye to look me up, Caspar!" cried the elderly Foggery, once a Westongue Seacaptain himself. "I thought I'd never miss the old people, places, and ways, but I do, quite often. This is a strange land, although I have never seen a more beautiful one, nor a more friendly and gracious people as a whole."

"I've had some doubts about that," said Caspar, shaking his old captain's hand heartily. "That Imperial Governor—"

"Is a damned fool!" concluded Foggery, softly. "Just between you, me, and this garden wall here. He's dealt well with you, Caspar?"

"Very profitably and cordially, too," said Caspar, nodding. They walked together in a small but immaculately manicured, walled garden under carefully placed willows and lace-leafed maples, amid thick beds of bright yellow and crimson iris. "But I have the strong feeling that he is, perhaps, trying to keep the news of our arrival and the value of our cargo a secret from everyone else."

"Undoubtedly true! He runs some risk of displeasing the Imperial Court if they hear of it. His uncle, the Emperor, is very ancient, however, and never was terribly bright to begin with. Let me tell you a little about Choin, Caspar Marlin. Things not immediately evident to a visitor. I've watched and listened for some years now."

"I'd be happy to know all you can tell me, Foggery."

"This is a truly vast Empire. Peopled by several races of Men, in numbers almost too large to comprehend. I once asked, and was told that there are more than a hundred of millions of souls supposedly under the sway of the Divine Emperor on his Dragon Throne."

"Supposedly?"

"A population that size is as difficult to rule as it is to count, of course. Once, I understand, the Emperors of Choin were masters of public administration and of military control. But over the four centuries of this present dynasty, things have slowly gone to pot, you might say."

If Caspar was disturbed by this news, he didn't show it.

"The Emperor is but a gilded ivory figurehead. A powerful symbol, but still . . . a vast bureaucracy of ministers, governors, judges, generals, and clerks rules in his Celestial Name. Without a strong leader at their head, they've divided into factions, combining and recombining with each other to gain private ends and political advantage. The Empire of Choin is on the verge of crumbling! A pack of playing cards stacked on edge. The slightest breath might bring it crashing down."

Caspar nodded understanding.

"Which, in a way, is a shame, because these are delightful and intelligent people, as I said."

Foggery paused to shake his head sadly.

"I don't regret retiring here but it's easy for me only because I am now quite old . . . oh, yes, I am, Caspar! I passed a hundred summers ages ago. Age is venerated here. I'm respected and loved and happily served by the young, who gain great merit by being kind and useful to one of so many summers.

"Sages and scholars from all over the Empire come to consult with me on this and that, mainly on trade and technical innovations I can tell them about. Progress is extremely slow and quite frustrating. Did you know that they have never figured out how to sail against the wind? I've explained it to them in great detail, and a few of their more adventurous sailors have tried it. Yet when word got out about it, the Emperor's advisers forbade them using the technique, on pain of long imprisonment!"

"Good for us, however," Caspar observed.

"But more and more our young and intelligent are questioning such unreasonable constraints, wishing to explore far lands, earn vast fortunes in trade directly with other nations."

They rested on an intricately carved wooden bench beside the garden pool.

"It is not to be allowed! Captains who have merely speculated aloud too often are severely punished. Celestial navigation is, the Bureaucrats insist, the sole province of the

Celestial Emperor himself. I'm not supposed to know this, but I have friends who tell me the truth in private."

"They fear it might be the breath that brings down the house of cards?" asked Caspar.

The retired Seacaptain nodded but fell silent as serving maids appeared with lunch and spread the repast on a polished jade tabletop under a twisted, ancient cherry tree beside the peaceful pool full of flashing golden fish.

"We should be careful how we tread here in Choin, then?" asked Marlin. "If we want to continue trade, that is."

"Trade will be very profitable, as long as you follow the rules," agreed Foggery. "Try some of these fried noodles with the tiny prawns. It's my favorite dish!"

They ate and talked companionably, remembering mutual friends and recalling ports of call they'd visited, long ago. For the first time Foggery heard the tragic history of *Sally* Brigantine and the finding of the Great Gray Pearl, of Eunicet's usurpation of Thorowood's Dukedom and his ill-advised invasion of Highlandorm—and of the great Battle of Sea and the victory over Frigeon, the Ice King.

"I managed to keep life and body together through it all. In the long run it was the making of me, of course."

"I see it was! Ye've grown in wisdom as well as craft, young Caspar. I never doubted but ye'd command a capital ship one day."

As the visit ended with twilight darkening the sky, the retired captain drew Caspar aside by the garden's delicate moon gate.

"I promised a good friend of mine that ye'd meet with him. He can't be seen talking to ye, for his safety's sake, and yours, too. If ye agree, however, he'll come aboard *Donation* in disguise, shortly before ye sail. I trust this man. He may be the salvation of Choin, my adopted land."

"If it won't harm me ship, crew, or cargo."

"Nothing is certain, but I believe Wong Tscha San is important enough to risk listening to. It's an urgent matter, he tells me, but that's all I can say. Will ye, for my sake, receive him? Give him assistance, if he asks for it?"

"Of course I will, Captain! Ye needn't ask. Will I see ye again before we sail?"

"I . . . I don't think so. The Emperor's jumped-up clerks and palanquin generals are quite suspicious of me, as it is. They see me as disturbing their rigid calm. Perhaps we'll see each other again on your next voyage. They can hardly refuse ye, as long as your trade is so profitable to them."

Donation's departure was set for the last day of that moon. Caspar, caught up in the feverish activity of loading a highly valuable cargo, forgot all about Foggery's request.

The day before, *Donation* had been moved into the open roadstead, fully laden and low in the water. Caspar was trying minor discipline cases and meting out shipboard justice at a Captain's Mast when his cabin boy came to say a ragged fisherman had hooked his fish-reeking sampan onto *Donation*'s chains, asking for an interview with her captain.

"What's he want, I wonder?" asked Caspar. "Doesn't he know it's dangerous for his kind to bespeak us?"

"He would but say you and he had a mutual friend," said the boy. "Shall I warn him off?"

"Of course not!" exclaimed Marlin. "It would at the very least be discourteous. Allow him to board and bring him to me here."

The boy returned leading a small, frail-looking Choinese wearing a musty woven-reed cloak and a broad, downward-spreading hat of the same reeds, looking much like a farmer's haystack and smelling strongly of fish.

"I am Wong Tscha San," he announced with a deep bow. "We have a mutual acquaintance, Captain Foggery."

Caspar bowed to his visitor in return. He had become entirely accustomed to the Choin custom of bowing, rather than shaking hands.

"Let me take your . . . er, cloak and hat," offered Caspar, moving around his desk. "And I'll send for some tea."

"If you would, a cup of your coffee would be even more pleasant," said the little Choinese. "I have only tasted it once or twice, in the home of Foggery. I find it most invigorating. I am in dire need of invigorating, having just rowed all the way from Wing Ting on the far shore of our bay."

Caspar had no idea how far that was but ordered the cabin boy to find some hot coffee and cakes for them to share as they talked.

"I come in this guise," explained Wong Tscha San, "because I am watched constantly by our Imperial Guards. I have, I'm afraid, made myself distrusted, even feared, by our Divine Bureaucrats."

"Why, I'm wondering."

"Because I have been saying aloud what many Choinese have long thought in silence. Our Empire is sweeping toward economic and political mayhap even social ruin. Despite some relatively minor inequities and stupid or malicious practices, Captain Marlin, my people are worth saving from the suffering that will follow collapse."

"I'm a stranger here meself," said Caspar, pouring coffee for them both, "but from what little I've seen, I see ye're right."

Said Wong, lifting his cup to savor the brew, "And that is not the only problem."

"Tell me, if you please. Captain Foggery seemed to think I could be some help."

"So I hope, too. Listen, then! I am a Sage, what you would call a Wizard—although in these clothes I don't suppose I look like one—and for many years I have been seeking a way to ease the imminent fall of Choin.

"We Sages long ago dedicated ourselves not so much to preventing this downfall, but to guiding it, so as not to lose all that is good of Choinese culture, art, and science. And to minimize the bloodshed and suffering that the transition will bring to all my people.

"Oh, a fond hope! We must make the effort and bear the blows to our fortunes. For this, then, we have worked silently—to avoid the kind of Darkness that destroyed Old Kingdom and precipitated the terrible Chaos after the Last Battle of Kingdom."

He sipped his coffee, gathering his thoughts, and set the cup carefully in its saucer.

"Among my humble accomplishments is an ability to *See*. While seeming to sleep, I am in reality propelled from my body to wander World."

"Something like a Wraith?" put in Caspar.

"Very much like a Wraith. Just a few months ago I *saw*—it is very difficult and wearing on one of my years, you understand. I surveyed World, looking for ways to invigorate my country. And, as well, to watch for dangers that might precipitate our collapse."

"Wickedness is ever with us, never completely banished," observed the Seaman.

"I discovered a source of very real wickedness in the western mountains of Old Kingdom. A gathering of Black Witches; a Coven."

"I'd not heard that!" exclaimed Caspar.

"I needed a way to communicate my discovery directly to your Wizards, feeling they could act against this Coven. While trying, I learned that Flarman Flowerstalk is already aware of it and has sent one of their Fellowship to deal with it."

"Who was sent, do you know?"

"His name? It is obscure. Something like, 'Well-lit Clearing in a Forest.' Does that suggest anyone to you, sir?"

Caspar Marlin closed his eyes and repeated the words to himself twice, then snapped his fingers and laughed aloud.

" 'Twas 'Brightglade,' I imagine! A good friend and a good man, Douglas Brightglade."

"Ah-ha! You have said it! That is the sound I *saw*."

"Douglas, I would venture to say, is capable of handling a whole pack of Black Witches in full cry. He'll also have the assistance of the two most powerful magickers in our part of World, plus some pretty impressive Near Immortals, even some Immortals, too."

"Yet the latest news I garnered a few days ago is most disturbing," said Wong, raising his hand. "I *saw* a frightened black bird bearing a message from the self-titled Queen of these Witches—her name is Emaldar. I *saw*—to one of your Wizards, the Firemaster. She says she holds the young Wizard as hostage against interference with her plans to assume the vacant throne of Kingdom!"

"*Great Grumbling Gadzooks!*" gasped Caspar. "Douglas! Captured by a Black Witch?"

"So it *seems*. I could check no further than to confirm the Queen Witch does indeed hold a Wizardly prisoner. Presumably it's your friend Brightglade."

"What's to do?" wondered Caspar, anxiously.

"Sail at once! Get word to Flarman Firemaster that I, Wong Tscha San, will go to Brightglade's assistance."

"I wish I could do more than that," cried Caspar Marlin. "I owe Douglas much more than just to be a messenger!"

"I appreciate your position, Captain, although I don't see how you can help further," protested Wong, rising as if to go. "Personally, I can withstand the Black Witches' power. You, however, would be in considerable danger!"

"Nevertheless," began Caspar, but his words were drowned by a sharp rapping on the transom set in the deck above them.

"Captain," called down the First Mate, "a fleet of Choin junks has appeared at the mouth of the river. They bear down on us at speed!"

"*Ecksraded* Governor!" swore the Sage. "I am undone! Someone has traced me to your ship. I have put you all in danger!"

"You think they're coming for you?"

"I am under penalty of instant death if I bespeak any alien person. It was meant to keep me from contacting our friend Foggery, but recently it was expanded to include any of your crew or officers!"

He ran to the stern windows overlooking the harbor.

"There may yet be time. I will take to my sampan and escape," he decided, regaining his calm. "Good-bye, Captain Marlin. I will try to reach Brightglade, even so."

"I'm afraid it's too late to flee," said Marlin, measuring distances, angles, and wind force with a Seaman's eye. "Look to the north! A storm is coming in from Sea. The high winds will favor them, not you. You'll never outrun even those raggedy boats. We'll make sail at once, and take you with us, Sir Sage!"

"They will impound your ship and cargo and imprison you and your crew for helping me flee," the Choinese Sage protested. "You'll lose all to the Imperial Governor if they catch you up!"

Caspar stood a moment, lost in thought. He smacked his fist into his hand.

"They're after you, eh? Well, we'll give them something to chase while we slip away to Sea across the storm's path. Foggery says they don't yet know how to tack."

He dashed up on deck, giving orders in rapid fire. Sailors dashed about or scrambled up ratlines. The anchor chain was heaved up short, ready for hoisting. Sails were swiftly unfurled. Men braced, ready to haul handsomely at halyard and stay once the order was given.

"Set that sampan's sail to run her downwind," shouted Caspar to his Bo'sun's Mate. "Lash her helm!"

Two experienced sailors were told off to drop into the wallowing fishing boat alongside. In short order they had hoisted her single sail and lashed her tiller oar in place. Shoving her away from *Donation*'s side to catch the freshening wind, they made sure she was on the proper course before they dived into the choppy harbor waters and swam back to the ship.

The tiny sampan scuttled off before the nor'wester. The Governor's junks, much too far off to make out details, saw the sampan fleeing across the roadstead, back in the direction she had come.

"If the wind holds, Sir Sage . . . ," cried Caspar. "*Ah-ha!* They're altering course to intercept your boat."

"Take 'em hours to catch her up," observed Pride, expertly judging the sampan's course, the wind, and the distant shoreline.

"Make all good sail and hoist anchor," ordered Caspar. "Signalman: make 'Regret unable to say farewell in person, Honored Governor, but must claw off windward shore to escape storm!' Good! Send it! Haul 'em all taut! Heave that anchor up! Move, ye sand-dabs!"

Donation shivered like a racehorse eager to run. Her sails ballooned and cracked like nearby lightning, then were hauled flat. Halyards rattled and sheets snapped as if they would part, but held.

She leaped forward, meeting rising, rolling swells at the harbor's mouth and heeling sharply as Caspar ordered her about to skim across the first of the storm's in-rushing combers.

The Imperial Governor's junks paid no attention to *Donation* besides barely acknowledging her parting signal. They chased the tiny sampan over the horizon.

Chapter Fourteen

Myrn on the Move

THE Asrai arrived silently off Dwelmland's coast just before dawn. Racing against the coming sunlight, Sea Fire set her quickly ashore on a sloping beach fronted by a dozen or so sturdy, slate-roofed cottages facing Sea and surrounded by neat squares of flower-and-vegetable gardens.

She had never been there, but Myrn at once recognized Fairstrand, the village Douglas had visited two years before. She'd met and liked its hardworking, friendly fisherfolk at the homecoming party.

She walked somewhat stiffly to the largest of the cottages. As she raised her hand to knock on the weathered door, it flew wide and she was swept into the strong arms of an elderly lady with laughing eyes and a vast, loving smile.

" 'Tis the Lady Myrn herself, come out of Sea!" cried Maryam Beckett. The hallway and dooryard quickly filled with all her sisters, daughters, granddaughters, nieces, and their young children. Almost everyone in Fairstrand had been to Wizards' High and knew Myrn by sight.

"What news? What news?" everyone asked, but Grammar Maryam shooed them back to their work.

"Put breakfast on the table, youngsters, and we'll all hear the news when 'tis time, properly. Come, my Lady, sit ye here at the table's head, where we can all see and hear ye."

"Please just call me Myrn," pleaded the Apprentice Wizard, breathless at their welcome.

They served her steaming oat porridge with rich brown sugar and thick, warm cream, hot toast, fresh-churned butter, and orange marmalade, followed by hot cups of strong, black coffee.

Myrn hadn't eaten much at the dinner Augurian had given to send her off adventuring, and it had been a long night's journey with Asrai under Sea. She ate with gusto, much to the pleasure of her many hostesses.

At last they were sure she was truly filled and asked her for all the news. Myrn sat back in her chair and started at the beginning—the news of the Coven.

"And your Douglas, bless his Wizard's heart, is up against these wicked people, all by hisself?" cried Maryam. Her family and friends echoed her dismay.

"Oh, Douglas can take care of himself," said Myrn to calm their agitation. "And I am going off to help him, right after I pay a short visit to Princess Finesgold at Dwelmland."

Declared Maryam, always the most practical of women, "My grandson George will take you to Bryarmote's door, posty hasty!"

"I could go alone," began Myrn, but Grammar Maryam wouldn't hear of it.

"You'll need an escort. There be still a few wild kinds about in the mountains. Not," she hastily added, "that a Water Wizard couldn't handle such, I suspects. But the sight of big, strong young George will serve to scare 'em off, I imagine, and save you the trouble."

George Beckett proved a good oxcart driver, remarkably informed about such things as the rock formations, canyons, and mountains that surrounded them, so the ride passed quickly and pleasantly for them both. The oxen settled contentedly to their task. A light load was an unexpected pleasure for them, Myrn decided. In good time they arrived at the nearest entrance to the Dwarf Prince's considerable underground domain.

Waiting for them was a smiling Dwarf named Fortoot, Bryarmote's Chief Steward. Lookouts had recognized Myrn from their mountaintop posts hours earlier, and sent word ahead.

"Prince Bryarmote and Princess Crystal are away on their wedding trip, of course," Fortoot told Myrn. "They'll be disappointed that they weren't here to greet you."

Said Myrn, "I was hoping that Lady Finesgold would see me for a few minutes. I cannot stay long, however, as my journey is urgent."

"Her Ladyship knows you are here and has asked that you come straight to her," said the Steward. "I'll guide you myself through the caverns to Great Hall. Young George here didn't bring any full barrels this time, so I'll not be delayed by fishy business."

He invited the Fairstrander to come with them to the Hall of the Dwarf Prince, but the husky lad excused himself, saying the oxen should be back in their stalls before nightfall.

"He doesn't want to miss any of his grandmother's cooking, I suspect," said Myrn to Fortoot. The Steward and three soldiers from Bryarmote's House Guard led her under the mountain along the same twisted and mazed ways that Douglas and Bronze Owl had been led along during their visit.

Eventually, they reached the Great Hall, and Myrn was shown to a large, comfortable guest room, to rest for an hour from her travels, bathe, and replait her waist-length, jet black hair.

She was barely finished before there was a knock at her door and Bryarmote's mother, Finesgold herself, stood beaming on the threshold.

"My dear, dear young Lady Wizard!" she cried happily, embracing the pearl fisher's daughter most warmly. "It's indeed a great pleasure to see you once again! Where is your husband-to-be? Not far off, I hope?"

"I'm afraid he's very far off, indeed, Princess," said the Apprentice Aquamancer with a curtsy. "In fact, I'm on my way to join him in Old Kingdom. He's investigating a Coven of Witches."

Finesgold led the way to her own flower-filled apartments. She called for tea and light sandwiches. "These cucumbers are grown in our very own garden caverns," she said, proudly. "Dwarfs have not been the best of gardeners in the past, but many of us learned to love it from the farmers of Flarman's beautiful Valley during the late unpleasantness."

Her rooms were filled with flowering plants in pots, barrels and stone planters, an amazing assortment of both common and exotic greenery. They filled the air with their fresh, green-growth fragrances.

"Going off on your own, then?" inquired the Princess, pouring tea for them both. "How I envy you! When I was a girl your age, I had trouble getting out of our caverns. My father and mother said, 'It just isn't done, you know.' "

"I have always been allowed to come and go on my own," Myrn told her. "My parents felt that I should learn the ways of Sea and World as early as possible. Pearl diving and coral gathering are not always easy professions."

"My father and brothers tended to protect me over much," sighed Finesgold. "However, after I married Bryarmote's father and moved to this Hall, I made up for it in great part. My late husband loved to travel, you see, and I would not be left behind. I've never been to Kingdom, however. In those days it was considered too dreadful and far too dangerous for casual travel, especially by well-born ladies."

"I think it still may be," said Myrn.

"But as a Wizard, I realize, you have important duties to perform. A Coven in Kingdom, eh? That doesn't sound good to me. How will you go? It's a long, long way."

"I thought to go with the Phosphorescence to Westongue on the Broad," Myrn told her. "There I must find out, if I can, where Douglas landed on the shore of Old Kingdom and follow him as best I can and as quickly."

"But not much in the way of scenery, I imagine, going under the waves that way. Seeing Sea's bottom may be interesting, but . . ." Finesgold shrugged.

"Yes, I tend to agree, ma'am. There'll be an awful lot of empty deeps between here and there, all the way south around Wayness and up the west coast of Dukedom, then across the Broad. But it seems the fastest way, even though the Asrai can only travel by night."

Finesgold paused to nip some withered blooms from a scarlet geranium. She was thoughtful.

"Your training under Augurian goes well?" she asked over her shoulder.

"Very well, thank you," replied the Apprentice. "It's difficult and sometimes very frustrating, but never is it dull."

"I imagine not," laughed the Princess, seating herself again at the tea table. "I'm thinking that Augurian probably hasn't provided as many spells as he might have liked, as you've not been Apprenticed for even a year, at best."

Myrn defended her Master vigorously. "He gave me what he thought I can handle. There are many enchantments and spells that a more experienced Wizard could use, but—"

"I meant no disrespect to your good Master, my dear. I was thinking, however, of at least one bit of magic that I came by many years ago and have used only sparingly since. Would you care to see it?"

"Yes, ma'am," said Myrn, dutifully.

Finesgold clapped her tiny hands and a maidservant appeared from another room in answer to her call.

"Opal, my jewel, please fetch me my Memory Box. Do you know which I mean?"

"Of course, Princess," replied Opal, and in a minute she returned to place in the Dwarf Princess's lap a finely crafted alabaster box carved all over with entwined ivy vines. Looking more closely, Myrn saw that what appeared to be drops of dew on each leaf were actually hundreds of tiny, many-faceted diamonds.

"A gift, this box, from my dear, late husband," said her hostess without affected sadness, but rather proudly. "He was ever so thoughtful and had excellent taste—for a Dwarf."

She opened her Memory Box by pressing a hidden catch somewhere even Myrn couldn't see. Soft chimes played a lively tune and Myrn smelled a delightful, woody odor, like fresh-sawn sandalwood, while the top was ajar. Finesgold rummaged about with a forefinger for a moment and lifted out an inch-long gold pin in the shape of a gracefully curled feather. She held it out to the girl.

"How truly beautiful!" exclaimed Myrn. "Such delicacy! It must be Faerie workmanship, is it not?"

"You are absolutely correct, dear Myrn. It's more than just beautiful, however," went on Finesgold, taking it back and pinning it securely on Myrn's left shoulder. "It's a Token of Power, made by Cloud Faeries hundreds of years ago for a Near Mortal friend so that I—er, she—could fly to visit their magnificent cloud castles. There."

She sat back to view the pin set against Myrn's Sea blue blouse.

"It *feels* magic," said Myrn in surprise. "What does it do, please?"

"If I were Augurian, I would make you figure out its spell for yourself, young Wizard-to-be, as a lesson in spell analysis. But you don't have the luxury of time. There is a Power Word you must say: *Cumulo Nimbus*. Repeat it, please!"

Myrn was accustomed by now to getting magical words right on the first try and uttered it quite perfectly. She felt the pin shift slightly against her blouse and then it seemed to vibrate, as if eager to be going somewhere.

"You've got it!" exclaimed Finesgold. "Look below."

Glancing down, Myrn found that she was seated in air fully six inches above her chair.

"Oh, my!" she cried in delighted surprise. "I'm afloat!"

"Not just floating," said Finesgold with a merry laugh. "If you bend your mind to the other side of the room . . ."

Myrn followed her instruction and found herself flying gently across the sitting room, three feet above the carpet, to the far corner.

"Yes, that's it! That pin will fly you anywhere you want to go following your word or thought, as slow or as fast as you care to go. And by fast, I mean *really* fast!"

"How wonderful!" exclaimed the Apprentice. She flew around the room twice to the Princess's pleased applause. Not everyone mastered a magical device so quickly. When the Apprentice returned primly to her chair she reached calmly for her teacup.

"Would it not be handy for hastening a traveler such as yourself?" asked Bryarmote's wonderful mother.

"Oh, my, yes!" said Myrn. "But I couldn't . . ."

"You really must, though," insisted Finesgold, "for, you see, once given, it can never be returned to the giver. It's yours, my dear, at least until you choose to give it away, yourself."

Myrn shed a tear or three of very pleased gratitude, which the Dwarf Princess said, more than repaid her loss.

"When you wish, then, it'll fly you and you can look down from the sky and see Dukedom and Dwelmland or the Briney and the Broad at ease. It should get you to Douglas's side faster than the good Asrai—and its power won't inconveniently fade with the rising of the sun, either."

"You've hit, of course, on the single shortcoming of faithful old Asrai," said Myrn.

"Nor, if I'm not mistaken, can Asrai carry you into fresh water. The Feather Pin has a few other attributes that might come in handy. Flying in the sky was the Cloud Faeries' idea. Flarman himself added another spell to the pin, designed to assist friends of Dwarfs who might otherwise get lost in our amazing Dwarf tunnels. The wearer of the Feather Pin never gets confused in underground passageways and always comes out safely wherever she wants to emerge."

"It's absolutely marvelous!" cried Myrn.

"Use it well! There are no cautions, except that you should avoid overloading the flying part. I carried two elephants once, but more would sorely tax the pin's powers, I fear."

"That," said Myrn, "sounds like a very interesting story."

"I'll tell it to you over supper," promised Finesgold. And she did, but that is another tale, entirely.

Donation tossed and rolled in the teeth of the gale, slowly winning northing against its force. Her sailors labored to make her beat as close to the wind as possible, to avoid being driven on the low, sandy coast of Choin.

Caspar Marlin used every trick and maneuver of a long life at Sea to work his ship, staying on deck for twenty hours at a stretch, ready to order instant changes in the sails and the ship's course. By dawn of the second day out of Choin the wind at last fell off and slewed about to become a brisk southwest breeze. He fell into his bunk exhausted and slept ten hours away, leaving the handling of the vessel to the capable Waynessman Pride.

It was well after dark when Caspar awoke and called for food.

"Tell Master Wong I'd like to see him when he would care to come," Caspar said to the cabin boy who brought his dinner.

A captain's "when you care to come" usually meant "right away," and so the Sage interpreted Caspar's summons. He appeared at the cabin door as the Captain was tucking into a plum duff.

"Ah, Master Wong," Caspar greeted him, cheerily. "Come in! I trust the little storm we ran through didn't bother you overly much?"

Wong, although he may have looked a bit pale and pinched—what landsman wouldn't after such a first-rate blow?—smiled and took a proffered seat under the cabin's stern windows but refused any of the dinner Caspar devoured so enthusiastically.

"If that was a 'little' storm," said he, "I hope we can avoid anything greater."

"We sailors prefer to avoid any kind of storm at Sea, if possible," chuckled Caspar. "Have some pudding?"

"No, no," declined Wong. "I have had a cup of excellent soup and a stoup of very good bread, thanks to your excellent ship's cook. We spent the stormy hours yesterday comparing notes and exchanging recipes."

"You cook?" asked Caspar, much surprised. It had never occurred to him that a man might cook for pleasure. Next to the ship's boy, the ship's cook was usually the lowest-ranking man aboard a modern ship.

"There is as much to enjoy in preparing food as in eating it," claimed the Choinese. "Recall, please, that without good, sustaining food, your ships could never sail as far as they do, nor the crew arrive as healthy."

"I suppose ye're right," admitted the Seaman. "You managed to keep well, then, despite the turmoil?"

"It would be foolish to deny that I was uncomfortable," said Wong. "There was little I could do, of course, save talk to the cook, who is a man devoted to his craft. He was the only member of the crew who had time, all day long."

"I suppose that's true," said the other.

"And now that the storm has passed?"

Caspar pushed away his dessert plate and reached for his pipe, using the time it took to fill the bowl and get it fired up to think hard about their mutual problem.

"You still feel that you should go directly to Brightglade's aid? Not to Flarman and Augurian?" asked Wong.

"Yes, I do."

"I have decided you are correct," said the Choinese gentleman. "Flarman is with Augurian on his island in Warm Seas—considerably farther from us than Old Kingdom."

"Of course, of course," said Caspar. "In best conditions we are fifteen or twenty days' sail from the southeast Kingdom coast. Longer, unless the wind swings more to south. Who knows how far it is from there to wherever Douglas is being held!"

"I intend to attempt another means of travel," said Wong, carefully.

"What other way is there?"

"A most useful spell, learned in my studies over the years," said Wong. "Properly cast, it would carry us quite near to Douglas Brightglade."

"Hoy!" cried the Seaman. "Why didn't you say so at once? Of course, a spelling is to be preferred in our circumstances . . . if it's reliable."

Wong nodded several times before he replied.

"You must remember, Captain Marlin, that I have lived for several hundred years in a nation where it is a major crime to practice magic, punishable by instant execution."

"I had no idea!" cried Caspar. "Yet you studied it, at danger to your life?"

"In fact, I was a Sage long before that Imperial decree was sent down. To avoid trouble with the misguided Imperial Bureaucracy, I have posed as a lesser scholar, a mere Mage. Magedom was never officially banned—everyone, even Bureaucrats, depend on common Mages for curing loathsome diseases and casting horoscopes, important things like that."

He smiled broadly at Caspar, who grinned back.

"I remember the old spells very well, although I have not used many of them in recent years. I thought seriously of using this one two days ago, when I wished to avoid the Governor's soldiers. There wasn't time then. Fortunately, you had a better solution."

He paused, as if reluctant to recommend his new course of action. At last he shrugged at his inner misgivings.

"If you're willing to chance it, I'll attempt to move the two of us to the last place Brightglade is said to have reached, a town named Pfantas, on the river known as Bloody Brook."

It was Caspar Marlin's turn carefully to consider his options.

"I don't wish to send ye alone into a dangerous situation, even if ye are a Wizard," he said at last. "Besides, I wish to take a hand in this meself, out of duty to Douglas and Flarman. We'll go together to this Pfantas."

Wong merely nodded his acceptance and prepared at once to perform the requisite spell.

Caspar shouted for the ship's boy and, when he had come running, sent his respects to the Mate. Would he please come to the cabin for a moment?

Pride, who had also been catching up on lost sleep after a long, stormy day and night, came to the Captain's cabin as soon as he heard the call.

"Aye, Captain?"

"Pride, Master Wong and I must leave the ship. Ye'll take her home to Westongue."

It was the work of a spare quarter hour to officially turn the command of *Donation* over to the younger man. The ship's log was brought up to the minute with the whole story, so that Thornwood would know why Caspar had left his command at Sea.

"Now, Wizard Wong, what have we to do to fly to help me old friend?"

"It's good to hear my humble self entitled 'Wizard' once more," sighed the Choinese Magician. "A few minutes of thought, a few verses of incantation, and we will be on our way, Captain."

Caspar armed himself with a short, sharp sailor's cutlass and a dirk to balance it on the other side of his wide belt and proclaimed himself rested, ready, and impatient to begin.

Wong sat on the bare deck in the middle of the saloon, cross-legged, in a flowing robe of black silk marked with embroidered symbols: horses' heads and roosters, seven-pointed stars and quarter-full moons, and others no one recognized. He placed before himself a clear, crystal pyramid about the size of a man's fists together, which he had produced from his deepest inside pocket.

He motioned Caspar to sit on the deck opposite him and began to chant a strange, variably pitched tongue. Caspar knew it was neither Common Tongue nor the usual Choinese way of speaking. Some much more ancient language? Shivers coursed down his spine.

The air about them seemed to tingle, as with storm electricity on a bad night at Sea. The crystal pyramid glowed from within and the light seemed to pulse, although that might have been an illusion of the golden light. It shot upward on the faces bent close over it. Acting-Captain Pride and the ship's boy stood in the shadows to one side, watching in fascination and no little awe.

The forms of the sturdy Captain from Westongue and the delicate-seeming, willowy Choinese flickered in time to the changes in light intensity. After a while the bodies of the two men, and the crystal itself, blurred and wavered, then flashed once brightly and disappeared with a solid *carrump* of displaced air.

Pride and the boy let out long-held breaths. They turned as one to go on deck to explain the strange events to the crew, their estimate of Caspar Marlin's grit, always high, increased manyfold.

Chapter Fifteen

Flight of the Feather Pin

"WAIT half a moment," said Marbleheart, in a whisper. "Something . . ."

He leaned forward, his sleek body making a straight line, nose lifted to sniff the morning air, like a bird dog at the point. Douglas stood perfectly still, his own Wizard-sharpened senses detecting nothing out of the ordinary.

They had followed a faint trace north from Pfantas in another dense morning fog the day before, climbing through the pine-forested hills by way of a narrow cart path. There they'd picked up signs of the Witchservers' wagon bearing Cribblon to Coventown.

They followed the uneven track as swiftly as Wizard and Otter could go . . . much faster than a heavy cart and the overconfident Witchservers, it seemed to Marbleheart.

"They stopped here for the night," he declared, sniffing softly. "See? They made no fire but ate cold food. Ugh! It's nothing I'd care to put in my mouth!"

"Poor Cribblon, if they made him dine on *that!*" agreed Douglas, kicking at the remains of the Witchservers' meal. "I hope they starved him, instead."

"Let me see, how far ahead of us are they?" pondered the Otter. He was using a talent for tracking that he never realized he had. He calculated aloud, "It's midmorning and they left here no later than an hour after dawn, I'd guess. We're going so much faster than they . . . I would think they are only two or three hours ahead of us now."

"I'm torn between rescuing Cribblon right away or letting him stay in their clutches until they reach Coventown, showing us the way," said Douglas.

"The latter course will save us time and trouble," said the Sea Otter, turning to follow the trail again. It was plain to read, softened as the ground had been by a day of drizzly mist. "Besides, Douglas, he's the lucky one in at least one way—he doesn't have to walk. They're carrying him in that cart of theirs."

"I suspect Cribblon wouldn't agree, right now. Well, it seems better to allow these Witch's creatures to lead us to their Coven. Without their guide, I suspect we'd never find it. I sense . . . a Hiding Spell of some sort. Probably Emaldar's work. They won't dare to harm Cribblon seriously before they deliver him to her, especially if they believe he's a Wizard."

He followed the low-slung form of the Sea Otter along the rough path, trotting to keep up with Marbleheart's *gallumping* gait.

Myrn arrived at Westongue in the middle of a busy morning. Seven square-rigged ships lay at anchor in the roads, and the waterfront swarmed with stevedores and roustabouts manhandling cargoes, outbound and inbound. The three stone moles were crowded and several ships were unloading their cargoes by lighters, unable to find space to tie up directly to the docks.

Few of the longshoremen glanced up as they worked, and those who happened to see her just as she arrived doubted their eyes and said nothing to anyone, for fear of being teased about the ale they'd tossed off so thirstily the night before.

She made no commotion, therefore, until she confronted a burly young man who seemed to be in charge of work on the longest pier.

"Sir, could I ask you where I can find someone in authority here?" she asked, ignoring his startled look. A very pretty young woman in a place where almost everyone was rough, sweaty, and male!

"I . . . ah, er . . . well, ma'am, that is . . . !"

"What's the matter, sir? Haven't you seen a lady since you left home?" Myrn teased.

"Well, ma'am, to tell the truth . . . never, at least not here! Most respectable ladies keep to the landward side of town, ye see. This be mostly a roughneck's world."

"I must tell you I've sailed with tough Seamen since I was a sprat myself, and had never a fear."

"Oh, no fear, ma'am! Thornwood Duke puts up with no bad acting in a lady's presence. No, ma'am! He's up there, at his new house, I believe."

"That's where I can find my old war comrade, then?" asked Myrn, enjoying herself greatly. "I've urgent Wizard's business with him."

These words so topped the foreman's surprised confusion— a lady *and* a Wizard!—that he simply pointed out to her high-roofed Sea House a short way down the shore.

"On better thought," he said with an embarrassed grin, running to catch up with her, "I'd better just go along with you, just in case."

He said his name was Simon. He'd worked at a counting house in Westongue ever since it was discovered, when he was just a lad, that he had a talent for counting and doing sums and such.

"I like my work," he told the Apprentice earnestly, "but I wish I could go to Sea. So many of my mates've done. I'm going to petition Thornwood Duke one day to appoint me Supercargo on one of these new merchantmen."

"Do it today," advised Myrn. They were mounting the wide steps to the front porch of Sea House when she saw Thornwood coming through the double doors, calling out to her and waving his arms in greeting.

"Do what?" he cried, taking Myrn's hand and squeezing it before he kissed it, gallantly. "Welcome to Westongue, Lady!"

"You know your foreman Simon, Thornwood? He tells me he's good at figures and counting but wants most to go to Sea on one of your new ships."

Simon turned several shades of red deeper than his normal tan, especially when Thornwood threw back his head to laugh.

"Why did you never apply?" cried the Duke to Simon. "I need Supercargoes ever so much more than I need Able-bodied Seamen! There are half a dozen berths begging to be filled. When you are finished with your day's tasks, come see me here. I'll tell you what must be done and where."

Simon thanked both Myrn and the Duke as gracefully as he knew how and ran back to counting bales and checking crates. He looked like a man with a glad song in his heart.

"He was very nice," said Myrn. "Reminded me a bit of our Douglas."

At the mention of Douglas's name Thornwood turned somber.

"You know of the shipwreck? We have no idea—"

"Shipwreck? No, no one mentioned a shipwreck, certainly not Douglas in his letter from Pfantas." She was immediately concerned, and confused.

"If you had a letter from him from somewhere in Old Kingdom," said the young ruler of Dukedom, much relieved, "then he survived the wreck of *Pitchfork*. She went down in a sudden storm near the coast of Old Kay. I sent a report by Seagull to Flarman and Augurian a week or more ago, as soon as I heard report of it."

"It hadn't come before I left Waterand," Myrn told him. "It would have caused some concern, except that, as I say, we have had word from Douglas since he reached Pfantas, and also a nasty blackmail note from a Witch calling herself Emaldar. She claims she holds Douglas prisoner . . ."

"Prisoner!" exclaimed Thornwood.

" . . . but we know that it is not so, either. *Someone* is prisoner, no doubt of that, but not my Douglas. However, we—I—thought it time he got some assistance. Did he tell you of his mission?"

"In detail," said Thornwood. "Wait, let's go in and have some lunch. I was about to sit down to it when I saw you coming."

Over their meal Thornwood described the shipwreck as if he had been there himself, which led Myrn to ask how he knew so well what had happened.

"There was one survivor. Poor Pargeot! He lost his young wife during Dead Winter, and now his first ship, a good crew, and a newfound friend, Douglas. He'll be relieved to hear that Douglas wasn't lost, at least I must tell him at once! He's taken it very, very hard, I'm told."

"Send for him, if you will," suggested the Apprentice Water Wizard. "I should like to talk to him, and certainly to reassure him."

One of Thornwood's staff, sent to fetch the young Seacaptain, returned shortly with a very long face.

"He's been drinking heavily for days, they tell me," he reported to Thornwood and Myrn. "He's a mere shadow of himself, so . . . sick . . . he can hardly stand upright, they say! I could have had him carried here, but I thought—"

"He's that bad off? I've sorely neglected my duty to him!" cried Thornwood. "I should have given more attention to the reports I heard of the poor man! I forgot how young he really is."

He would not hear of having Captain Pargeot brought to Sea House, but decided to go to him, instead. Myrn followed, although for a moment Thornwood doubted it would be a fitting sight for a proper young lady.

"Nonsense!" Myrn exclaimed stoutly. "I'm the daughter of a sailor and a sailor myself. I'm no stranger to this sort of thing, Lord Duke."

Thornwood apologized and with no further demur, led the way down the bustling beach to a three-story, square, brown-shingled building at the far end, the Westongue Seamen's Hostel.

The manager, a retired sailor himself, met the Duke and the Apprentice at the door with a respectful bow and tug at her forelock.

"Captain Pargeot? Yes, he's within. Second floor rear, Lord Duke and Lady! Comes in this morning very much the worse for . . . er, for hard spirits, begging your pardons. I'll have him rousted out, hosed down, and brought to you, I shall, if you but say the word." He looked extremely worried, fearing the Duke might blame him for the Captain's binge.

"Belay that!" said Thornwood, sharply. "Take us to him, immediately."

They found Pargeot in the dim back room, lying on a simple cot among tangled blankets, looking wretched, very ill, and very pale. Recognizing Thornwood through a slowly clearing alcoholic fog, he struggled to rise, but Thornwood pushed him down again with rough gentleness, saying, "Stay where you are, Pargeot! I would have come sooner, had I known you were taking your losses so hard."

"I . . . I . . . I," stammered Pargeot, acutely embarrassed, "I am so ashamed, my Lord Duke. It was just too much, so close after my Marta's passing. I though I could handle it, but I . . . I . . . I just fell to pieces!"

He sank back down on his pallet sobbing, tears running down his unshaven cheeks.

"Self-pity will do none of us any good," said Thornwood, sternly. "And even good grog can't wash away bad memories, for what that's worth. Are you over it now? Or will I see you thus again?"

"Never!" promised the very contrite Seaman. "Who's this? A young lady seeing me in this awful state? Beauty has no place in this miserable, stinking rat's nest!"

"No ordinary young lady," Thornwood told him. "This is the Lady Myrn Manstar, Douglas Brightglade's betrothed. She's Apprentice to the Water Adept, Augurian of Waterand."

"Oh, oh! And I lost him for you, my poor, poor Lady! I'm not worth your forgiving." And he tried to turn his face to the wall.

"Stow it, man!" snapped Myrn, purposely harsh. "Douglas did not die in the wreck of *Pitchfork*, after all, but is far inland in Old Kingdom, doing his duty when last I heard from him."

The news cheered Pargeot considerably, although he was guilt ridden still by the thought of forty crewmen lost at Sea and stout *Pitchfork,* too.

"Ships are living persons to Seamen," Thornwood said sympathetically. "But deaths of Men, ships, or family members are part of the price we living have to pay. As you yet live, you owe it to them to go on living and working and playing and loving, as a tribute to them. Do you see?"

"I never th-th-thought of it that way," said Pargeot, sitting up slowly and very painfully, for his head was about to split down the middle. "I really must stop this . . . this . . . nonsense. I really will!"

"If you let me," said Myrn, more sympathetically, "I can help."

Pargeot made no objection while the Apprentice stood before him, closed her eyes to help concentration, and murmured a certain spell to drive the fumes from his brain and heart.

Watching, Thornwood was amazed to see an immediate improvement in the Captain's appearance. His eyes focused and his head came up. The pallor of his skin was infused with a healthy glow.

Myrn opened her eyes and smiled at Pargeot.

"Now, don't let this happen, ever again! I command it of you!"

They left him feeling well enough to eat for the first time in days and nights and then to bathe, shave, and get a haircut, at Thornwood's strong recommendation.

"Come to me at Sea House when you look, feel, and smell better," he ordered. "Lady Myrn needs to ask you where Douglas would have gone ashore. She goes to join him."

Thornwood was silent as they walked together back up the beach, and Myrn let him go in silence. She knew he had to think, and so did she.

"Will he be right, now?" wondered Thornwood, aloud. "For some men, rum is a sickness, a weakness that can take them unawares and threaten their crewmen's lives and their ships, too."

"I can give no guarantee," said Myrn, "but I do believe Pargeot's is a one-time kind of troubling. He'll haul himself out if it, now he has finished punishing himself. And he'll learn a great deal from this, do not doubt."

Thornwood turned to look at her gravely.

"You have learned a lot in a year yourself," he said. "I would always have said you were a lively and good-natured lass with a strong practical streak. Now I see you have wisdom, also. Aquamancy agrees with you."

"Thank you, sir Duke," she said, and curtsied. "I'll try to live up to your estimate."

A dozen men waited to capture his attention on his return to Sea House, so the girl went off to the room with the brass bed and brass telescope. Once settled in, she wrote a short note to Flarman and Augurian, telling her progress. A local Sea Gull was drafted into carrying it to them when she was finished.

Thornwood had asked her to dine with him that evening, so she spent some time altering her basic wardrobe with a few useful housekeeping spells, starting with her traveling costume of a light blue blouse with long sleeves and pearl buttons, a darker blue, full skirt, and stylish yet sturdy shoes.

When she came down to dinner she was at once the center of all the eyes of Thornwood's masculine staff, gathered in the drawing room. She had swept her lustrous black hair up onto the top of her head and tied it with a blue ribbon sprinkled with tiny Flowring pearls. Her sensible travel dress had become a long, gracefully sweeping gown of white linen with tasteful navy blue piping at the collar, hem, and lapels.

"Westongue has never seen such beauty," Thornwood complimented her, offering his arm at the bottom of the stair. "My Lady Mother hasn't had time to extend her benign influence to this part of Dukedom yet. You should see what she has done for Capital, however."

"Westongue is already a very attractive place," said Myrn. "A woman's touch could make it even more so, and that would bring wives and mothers, sweethearts and families, I believe."

"It's part of my overall plan for the Port," admitted Thornwood. "To that end, Mother is ever gently prodding me to give her an assistant by marriage. I think there's still time for that. I haven't found anyone like you to ask to be my Duchess, as yet."

"I'm highly flattered," said the Apprentice Wizard, blushing more than a little. "I'll keep my eyes open for a suitable Duchess-elect, if you wish."

"I'll find her for myself, thank you anyway. You sound a lot like my mother, however," he added with a boyish grin.

"Most women share a desire to see good men wedded, bedded, and presented with sons and daughters," Myrn told him, softening her words with a fond smile. "Duchess or sailor's daughter, it makes little difference. She will be a very fortunate lady, whomever you choose, Thornwood."

"That is *exactly* what my Lady Mother says," Thornwood exclaimed. "Ah! Here's our young Seacaptain, dried out, shorn, shaved, and smelling much the better for a hot bath."

Pargeot bowed deeply before Thornwood and again gave him his thanks and apologies.

"I vow I will never succumb to self-pity again," he said.

"In which case—and you can be sure life will test your resolve, again and again, Pargeot—I offer you command of my new *Firefly,* when she's delivered up from Perthside. She's smaller than most of my new bottoms, but faster and much handier, Douglas of Perthside assures me. I have some great plans for her."

"I'll earn and accept her when the time comes, Your Grace," said the Captain, bowing deeply again. "Meanwhile, I offer to assist the Lady Myrn in her quest to find her betrothed. I consider him a close friend on even such short acquaintance. I wish to help settle this business of the Witches, and I'm determined to stay by Mistress Manstar's side until it is accomplished, despite all dangers. Old Kay is no place for a woman to travel alone!"

He gazed beseechingly at the beautiful Myrn as she offered him her hand.

"I hope you'll accept me as escort and aide," he begged her. "It will make me whole again, if I can do this good deed for you and for Douglas and for World."

Myrn, somewhat uncomfortably, said she would think about it and let him know on the morrow.

"Quite the romantic sort, he *thinks* he is," exclaimed Myrn to Thornwood, later. "I'm not at all sure he wouldn't be a nuisance on my journey."

"He is, nevertheless, a most capable young man and an undoubtedly brave and skilled mariner," Thornwood pointed out. "I must admit I would feel much better about you going on alone if I knew you had him with you. It's up to you, of course."

Myrn shook her head resignedly.

"Now I have a very unladylike appetite to assuage," she said, merry once again. "What's for dinner?"

"I don't need a ship," Myrn said. "I have other means to reach Old Kay. Much safer, and faster, too."

"Safer!" exclaimed Thornwood. "How can you say that?"

"Safer than enduring a storm at Sea," she said, pointedly. "Safer because there are fewer ways danger can reach me when I fly."

"Except for accidentally falling to earth," Thornwood said with a sour grimace.

"I've more control over my flying," explained Myrn, who had flown with the Feather Pin from Dwelmland, over Parch, the wasteland between the Dwarf Prince's domain and Valley, and then across Dukedom to Westongue—without incident, "than over, say, a murderous troll in a forest, or a desperate goblin deserter from some evil army, bent on stealing . . . whatever I have to steal."

"Well, it's not *my* choice of danger," said Thornwood, shaking his head, "but, I must accept your decision. You're the Wizard, after all."

They were seated in the Duke's busy office at Sea House early the next morning. Myrn announced she was ready to continue her journey. As they talked, Pargeot was announced. He looked much healthier and heartier than he had the evening before, smiling brightly, bowing to them deeply when he stood before them.

"I've come ready to accompany you, mistress, if you'll accept me to share your quest."

Myrn nodded. "I have decided to take you along, Captain Pargeot, both for my sake and for your own. However . . ."

"I sense there are conditions to be met," said Thornwood with a deep chuckle.

"Yes, of course," Myrn exclaimed. "As you've said, I *am* a Wizard and this is a matter more of magic and spells, and possibly wicked Witches, than it is of courage and skill facing natural dangers."

She turned to Pargeot.

"You'll be most welcome, Captain, to come and help me with the latter, if they do arise. But you must understand that in matters concerning magic, Witches, Wizards, and the supernatural, I must practice my craft and art unhindered. In other words—"

"In other words," said Pargeot with a quick nod, "dear Lady, you are to be in command."

"Exactly!" she replied. "Do you not agree, Lord Duke?"

"I long ago learned to leave wizarding to Wizards," said Thornwood. "If you're not completely willing and able to follow this young Lady Wizard as you would any good commander, you'd better not go, Pargeot."

"I'm entirely willing," promised the Seacaptain. "When do we leave?"

"Right now, if you've had a good breaking of fast and have brought your traveling kit," said Myrn, rising. She was this morning again dressed in her traveling outfit. Her personal effects were stowed in the large canvas bag she now slung over her shoulder.

"I have my ditty kit," said Pargeot, hefting a smaller canvas bag tied with a rope long enough to loop over his shoulder. "What ship takes us?"

Said Thornwood, grinning, "Just follow your leader, my boy."

They led the puzzled young Seacaptain out of Sea House and down to the pebbly shore. The sun was bright and warm with early spring. A brisk breeze blew from the Broad, scudding puffy, white clouds away to the east in long north-south ranks.

"I need to know the position *Pitchfork* had reached when the storm hit her," said Myrn to Pargeot, all business.

"We were almost within sight of the Old Kay coast where Bloody Brook flows into Sea. When that blue Sea Light plucked me from the bottom, I believe we were in onshore shallows. Poor *Pitchfork* would have made landfall in a few hours at most if the storm hadn't struck her."

"When we arrive, I'll need you to point out the estuary."

"I've been there several times, but never have landed," explained Pargeot. "There is no trade to be picked up on Kingdom's coast these days. There's much trouble from wild men, bloodthirsty beasts, and evil Beings, my father-in-law tells me. Things like brainless Goblins and malicious Sprites."

"We're ready then," said the Water Wizard's Apprentice. "Thank you, Thornwood Duke, for your help and your hospitality. Give my love to your Lady Mother when you return to Capital. I'm sure we'll see you both when we return from this task, Douglas and I."

She kissed the Duke on the cheek and, without further ado, grasped Pargeot firmly by the arm, twisted her shoulder bag to a more comfortable position, and said, "*Cumulo Nimbus!*"

The two rose smoothly into the clear morning air, Myrn waving to the Duke below, Pargeot clutching his kit bag and looking both amazed and disconcerted.

"Relax, Captain," Myrn advised in the amused voice of an experienced flier. "I'll handle the flying. Your job is to be a good passenger for now and, when we get there, to tell me which way to go. Have you a compass? We'll very shortly pass out of the sight of land."

Wordless, the Seacaptain produced a pocket compass and directed her out to Sea, away from the rising sun. In a very few minutes the coast of Dukedom, the bustle of Westongue, and the green-and-gold offshore shallows slid from sight behind them and they flew in a perfect dome of sky over a perfectly round shield of deep blue Broad.

"We're going quite fast," Myrn said to her passenger. "I judge it'll be perhaps eight hours before we sight Old Kay."

Pargeot swallowed mightily but, to his credit, within a very few minutes he'd accustomed himself to the idea of flying and began to enjoy it. They overtook swift-flying Seabirds as if they were standing still in midair. The surface of Sea far beneath them looked like watered blue silk, strangely and intricately patterned, and constantly changing.

After two hours of flight, the pair saw approaching them from the northwest a towering line of black-bottomed clouds trailing diagonal curtains of rain. The cloud bank reached from horizon to horizon and high up into the sky.

"Pretty strong storm, that," warned Pargeot. "We'll get buffeted about, I'm afraid."

"I've found it's better to avoid passing through such clouds by flying over them," Myrn told him matter-of-factly. "There we have the advantage over sailing ships. The clouds hide very turbulent airs, I've found the hard way, sometimes hail, and of course lightning. Any one of those can make it as dangerous for the flyer as for the Seaman."

She reached her arm upward, directing the Feather Pin to gain altitude. The cloud tops proved too high to overfly— the air at the cloud tops was bitterly cold and difficult to breathe, she said—but she guided their flight smoothly through a gap between two splendid glittering and grumbling thunderheads. They shot safely through to clear air on the western side of the squall line before the gap could close again.

The cloudscape was spectacularly magnificent. The Feather Pin kept them aloft and moving swiftly with no effort on Myrn's part except to indicate the way, right or left, up or down, or straight on.

She'd experimented on her flight from Dwelmland to Westongue and felt entirely comfortable with the dynamics of flying now—although she admitted to herself that a flight of eight hours over open, empty Sea was more than a bit daunting. A daughter of Seafarers, she knew better than any landlubber the sudden surprises Sea often hid behind a calm surface and a bland, blue sky.

They were so busy enjoying the scenery and the sensation of flight that at first there was no conversation between them. When the first exhilaration subsided, however, Myrn asked her new companion to describe everything he remembered about the last hours of *Pitchfork*.

Although it was still painful to recall, Pargeot strove to give her a clear and complete picture of the foundering, especially when he found she knew the most technical Seafaring terms. He neither blamed others nor took too much on himself. He knew, as Myrn did, that Sea can be a harsh and unforgiving mistress. He'd accepted that when he had first decided to become a sailor.

"I was swept overboard," he told her, "so I've no clear idea what happened to the ship after that. When I realized that the Asrai had saved me from a watery grave and that we could speak with each other, I asked it to retrace the path to look for *Pitchfork*, who, when I had left her, was safely breasting the storm waves.

"We searched above and beneath the waves for some hours, saw . . . terrible wreckage everywhere and bodies. . . . we were too late to save anyone!"

He paused to regain his composure. Myrn patted his arm, sympathetically. She found that, as long as she touched him, even very lightly, he remained aloft under the magic of Finesgold pin. They flew, therefore, arm in arm, upright but canting slightly forward, like strollers in a strong gale.

"My ship must have been battered to pieces in a very few minutes. All hands had gone down with her; no boats had been launched. They had no chance to escape.

"In the end the Asrai warned me that it had only a few minutes remaining before the coming of daylight, which would so weaken it that it would no longer be able to carry me. So we gave up the search and it set me ashore on a wild, uninhabited, wooded point to spend the day. I had nothing to eat and no place to go, so I tried to sleep all day. The Phosphorescence came back for me after dark that evening."

The Seaman cleared his throat several more times.

"There was no reason to search further, so I asked it to carry me back to Westongue. We made it before dawn the next morning!"

"So you don't know where Douglas could have gone ashore, then?" asked Myrn.

"There is no way to tell for certain. My best estimate, based on the wind and the condition of Sea at the time, is that he was carried on to shore somewhere in the delta of Bloody Brook. I knew he planned to travel up Bloody Brook to a town called Pfantas.

"At the time, I mourned him as lost with my crew and *Pitchfork*. I was in no shape when I arrived back at Westongue to do anything but mourn. It was only yesterday, just before you and Thornwood came to me, that I at last said to myself, here! You *must* appreciate your luck that you survived this catastrophe!"

"Luck and the Asrai. It was not there by accident," guessed Myrn. "The Asrai only comes when called. I suspect that Douglas called it when you were lost overboard."

"I am sure of it, from what Sea Light said," agreed Pargeot, softly. "I'm positive that Douglas was my savior."

In the late afternoon they sighted the low, sandy coast of Kingdom and approached it more slowly, swinging first north, then south, searching for the river's delta. The landmarks Pargeot knew were hard to identify from aloft. Myrn flew lower and lower until they skimmed over the waves at a much reduced speed.

"See? The color of the water has changed to green. Here ends the outer shelf of Kingdom," decided the sailor. "Ha! There's the headland on which I spent the day after the storm! Head a bit down the coast here. I think I see the river!"

Shortly they located the several mouths of Bloody Brook's delta and, following the largest of them upstream, almost at once sighted a vast but ruined city upon its northern bank.

Myrn at first was inclined to continue without stopping, but Pargeot, with his sharp Seaman's eye, noticed smoke from cooking fires in the ruins and movement on the crumbled pavement between the houses.

"We should go down and speak to them," he advised. "It's possible Douglas stopped here to get directions and assistance from these people."

The Apprentice banked over and down, landing gently near a gang of workmen who were repairing a marble building near the riverfront. They stopped their digging and hoisting fallen blocks of white stone at the fliers' arrival, showing no particular fear or surprise that two people dropped out of the sky.

Myrn waved to them cheerfully and they approached, smiling and bowing. Anyone who flew was worth bowing and scraping to, seemed their attitude.

"Welcome to Summer Palace," called one. "I'm the Major-domo. That is, I was, when this was the summertime residence of King Grummist the Last. Now I'm the elected mayor, instead. My name is Delond."

"This must have been a beautiful city once," said Myrn, by way of greeting.

"Yes, it was, truly," agreed the new mayor. He apologized for the sand and sweat on his hands and face and rough clothing. "We're just beginning to rebuild, after centuries of neglect. We were long enchanted to await the King's return."

"Enchanted?" asked Myrn. "May I ask who broke the spell?"

"Surely!" cried Mayor Delond. "A great and powerful Wizard came this way two weeks ago. He told us the truth at last, and it set us free—that the King was not ever coming back, having been slain in a Last Battle. Suddenly, all was clear to us and we've decided to take charge of our destinies, to be a free and independent people."

"We're rebuilding Summer Palace as a place to live and raise our children and earn our livelihoods," said another worker.

"Wizard?" asked Pargeot. "May we ask his name?"

"Of course," said Delond again. "Our savior was the Fire Wizard Douglas Brightglade!"

Myrn clapped her hands delightedly and Pargeot breathed a great sigh of relief at this final proof that Douglas had survived the shipwreck.

"I am Myrn Manstar of Flowring Isle," the young woman introduced herself. "This is Captain Pargeot of Westongue in Dukedom. Douglas Brightglade is well known to us. He is, in fact, my betrothed."

The Waiters gathered around them applauded with surprise and pleasure. Delond and the men went off to the river to wash off the grimy sand and marble dust of their labors. The ladies of Summer Palace came to greet the visitors.

In short order a delicious supper was prepared and laid out, served in the shade of a neatly patched gold-and-blue awning in the clean-swept Central Plaza.

Myrn told her part in Douglas's adventures, and Delond and his council eagerly consulted with Pargeot about trade with Westongue.

"We haven't given it a lot of thought, yet," the new mayor admitted, "but perhaps we could sell dried and salted fish? We have plenty of both fish and salt. Would there be a market for that?"

"Even fresh fish, nowadays. We can carry them in the cold boxes Thornwood Duke has installed in all his ships," replied Pargeot, enthusiastically. "Your best fish will reach port as fresh as when they were caught!"

This news amazed the Waiters until they were told that the famous cold boxes were inventions of the Fire Wizard, Flarman Flowerstalk, Douglas's Master.

"In the days of the Last King," Delond went on, "many of us in Summer Palace were expert gold and silver workers. The skills are still here, but unfortunately there're no mines nearby and we've no money to buy any metal, so those arts cannot be revived just yet. Sand we have in plenty, and we were considering studying the arts of making glass. Our problem there is finding wood, charcoal, or coal with which to fire glass pots and annealing ovens."

"I can arrange to have coal of the best quality delivered to you in exchange for your blown-glass wares, if they will be of good quality and carefully packed for shipping," said Pargeot. "It would be profitable to us both. Good glassware, even common vessels, are much sought after everywhere."

"But we need the capital first," Delond objected.

"I think I can find an investor or two who would advance you the price of a shipment of coal," said Pargeot, thinking of Thornwood in particular.

"Wizard Brightglade went up the river in one of our gondolas," said one of the Waiters who had seen the Wizard and the Otter leave. "If you've heard from him from Pfantas, he must have made good time, despite the dangers of getting lost . . . or waylaid."

In the morning Delond brought the same atlas of Kingdom that Douglas had consulted during his visit and pointed out to Pargeot the way to Pfantas.

"Just follow the river," he advised. "It runs, as you see, fairly straight from the west. Watch for this crescent-shaped lake and the cone-shaped hill of Pfantas on its north shore."

"We'll be there in a matter of hours," said Pargeot. "This Lady Wizard can really fly!"

They said good-bye and good luck to the Waiters. Myrn uttered the Power Words to the Feather Pin and off they shot, climbing once more to an altitude from which they could see the entire delta. This made it easy to spot the main course of Bloody Brook through Wide Marsh and avoid getting lost in the tangled maze of channels which had so troubled Douglas and Marbleheart.

After finding their bearings, they set out and made good time. Below them passed the savannahs—they caught glimpses of Wild Horses grazing on the riverbank—then the great, green expanse of the Forest of Remembrance. Myrn felt watchful eyes on their progress as they flew high over the forest, but the feeling passed as soon as they entered the rolling meadowland beyond.

In late afternoon they flew over the burial ground of Last Battlefield with their long, evenly spaced mounds, not knowing what it was they saw, and climbed over rugged foothills where the brook became a rumbling, raging torrent squeezed between steep canyon walls.

The sun was beginning to set when they glided down over Pfantas Lake to circle the town on its steep-sided hill.

"Phew!" said Pargeot. "What's that stink? Comes it from that dirty little hill town? Maybe we should land elsewhere!"

"Douglas's letter said Pfantas was a garbage heap," recalled Myrn. "Yes, I think we should avoid it for the moment. We'll camp on that other hillside for the night, I think."

"Good idea," replied the Seaman. "It's upwind of the town, I judge!"

She set them down—or rather the Feather Pin did—on the grassy lawn where Marbleheart and Douglas had pitched their pavilion and raised their pennants just a few days earlier.

Chapter Sixteen

Coventown

DOUGLAS and Marbleheart smelled Coventown long before they saw it. A fitful breeze carried a stench like burning sulfur mixed with the hot, sour reeks of molten lead and wet, rotted wood.

"Woof!" The Otter snorted and sneezed. "First Pfantas, now here! How in World do they stand it, these Witchpeople? I'd think they'd suffocate in no time!"

Douglas climbed to the top of a sharp ridge, screened from the town by thick-leafed, thorny brush. He crawled the last few yards on his stomach, carefully parting the stiff branches to peer into the deep cleft between two barren, out-flung mountain spines.

They'd climbed steadily all day, losing sight of the Witchservers' trail hours before. Nothing short of a mountain goat could climb the sides of the main valley the Witchservers had entered until the Sea Otter found a side gully for them through which to scramble unseen.

In the narrow canyon before them, the travelers saw, at first, thin and twisting columns of sooty smoke rising from red glints of flickering fire. As they looked closer, however, they saw that what they had first thought sharp pinnacles and overbearing tors were in fact crooked, smoke-blackened, too-thin buildings climbing from the valley floor up the opposite mountain ridge.

A dark and dreary castle stood above it all, its topmost towers taller than the edge of the ridge behind it. In its embrasures and from arrow-slit windows, flares blinked malevolently, like wicked watchful eyes.

The castle outline blurred and shimmered in waves of heat, columns of dun-colored smoke, and gray steam. Before its narrow gate a company of Witchservers armed with pikes and long, curved swords stood watching, unmoved as heavily burdened lines of slaves were whipped through into the castle courtyard and back out again. The crack of whips, the rattle of chains, and the groans of the driven came clearly to the Journeyman Wizard across the dim vale.

"Coventown," he said emphatically. "Could be nothing else."

"And that's the abode of this Emaldar the Beautiful," sniffed Marbleheart. "So called."

Douglas pointed down and out from their vantage. On the path approaching the town along a narrow stream at the bottom of the cleft moved the party of Witchservers, surrounding their rickety garbage wagon. Its wheels squealed as it swayed and jerked painfully over stones and ruts.

In its bed knelt a forlorn figure, heavily chained and carefully watched by his captors.

"Cribblon!" cried Douglas softly, although the constant din of Coventown made his care unnecessary. "I should have rescued him before this! Now we'll have to get him out of that . . . that nasty place!"

"Nothing we could have done about it," Marbleheart said to comfort his friend. "There was no other way to find the Witch."

Douglas slid back down the ridge, out of sight of any watchers on the dark castle's battlements. The Otter sniffed twice more in disgust, and followed.

"Let's find a place to hole up," he said. "I assume we'll need to scout about a bit before we move in on this Witchperson. The landscape looks a little cleaner and a bit more hospitable up in that direction."

Douglas nodded and motioned the Sea Otter to lead the way beside a tiny mountain rill that fell by uneven and uncertain stair steps from the treeless mountainside high above.

Marbleheart stopped to taste a mouthful of the water from the creek, spat it out, and made a wry face. "It tastes like the town smells. And it's warm, not cold as you might expect decent mountain water would be. Nothing but slime and scum lives in such water. You see? No trout for dinner tonight!"

"I'll treat it to remove the taste and the slime," decided Douglas. "I don't want to go much farther up than this. Do you see a sheltered spot where we can camp?"

"A little farther up, I think," urged his companion. "See? There's a fairly deep overhang a minute or two farther on."

In fact, it was a cave, low and narrow at its mouth but opening up into a large, low-ceilinged room beyond.

"Clean, quite warm, and nice and dry," Marbleheart decided after peering about with satisfaction. "Who'd have believed I would ever be grateful for a dry spot! It'll do, don't you think?"

"Suit admirably," agreed Douglas. He chose a flat ledge near the cave mouth on which to build a small fire—worth the risk, he decided. Since the cave entrance faced the opposite canyon wall, a seeker could be ten steps away and not glimpse a blaze within. A continuous wind sighed mournfully down the mountain, whisking the thread of smoke away with it.

"Ah, supper!" sighed the Sea Otter, slumping down on the dry sand before the fire. "What will we conjure up this evening, Wizard?"

Douglas suddenly realized he was both very hungry—they hadn't stopped for lunch at all that day—and very weary. Climbing mountains was something to which you had to grow accustomed.

"Pancakes and maple syrup?" he asked, beginning to make the requisite passes in the air. "A few rashers of hickory-smoked bacon? Cold, fresh milk from Blue Kettle's springhouse?"

"If you can't produce 'em, don't torture me," moaned the Otter, although in truth he had no idea what pancakes might be. "If you're not teasing, don't waste time talking about it!"

At the moment he would have eaten almost anything.

Once the meal was prepared—spelled, rather, out of Blue Kettle's kitchen a thousand miles away at Wizards' High—and eaten, the travelers could say they were fairly comfortable. The cave, at first dim and cheerless, took on the feel of home.

"A night's sleep? Then what, Wizard?"

"You're right. Tomorrow morning we'll sniff about some, get the lay of the land. I'd like to catch a glimpse of this Emaldar person, just to make some assessment of her. We'll

have to face her, eventually, but I'd like more information
about her and her people before I jump into the Witchfire."

"I'm not at all sure I like your mentioning fire," complained
the Otter. "Well, take 'em as they come, I say. I'm going to
look about in the dark—make sure there are no Witchservers
snooping up our gully—and then get some sleep."

"Good idea," said Douglas, sleepily. "Don't wake me up
unless you have a good reason."

By the time the Otter had paused to let his eyes adjust to
the darkness of the mountainside beyond the cave, the Journeyman Wizard was sound asleep and dreaming of swimming
in Warm Seas with a very pretty pearl fisher's daughter and a
Giant Sea Tortoise named Oval.

Marbleheart had the right coloration, the low build, the
hunter's instincts, and the very strong desire to move quietly—
silently, in fact—through the wind-tortured brush and over
shadowy, scoured-bare rock. He crossed the crest between
the little creek gully and the deeper, wider one in which had
been built the Castle of Coven and its wretched village.

From a narrow ledge just below the rim of the larger canyon,
he studied the setting. The main valley continued on up the
slopes of Blueye Mountain almost as straight as an arrow can
be shot, until it topped out in a jumbled, torn field of jagged
black stones, which looked as if they had been shoved into
place by a gigantic hand and left for the centuries' rains and
snows to pack down hard.

About the village, the Otter could see no living plant except
an occasional patch of shriveled broom or ground-hugging
heather. There were few thornbushes, still without leaves at
this altitude, although it was well into spring in the lower lands.

Down the sharp cleft past town and castle dashed a foaming
stream. It caught the light of a few stars, reflecting it feebly to
the lone watcher. At Coventown it slipped reluctantly into a
long, narrow pool. Here the water, stilled, reflected the dirty
red and yellow blur of the flambeaux on the battlements and
a few dim sparks of lights in the town. A crude earth-and-
rock dam had been dumped across its course to flood the
narrow lake.

Below the dam the stream waters reappeared as overflow,
now dark and muddy, with no reflections but slimy swirls and

oily stains. From the canyon rim the Sea Otter's sensitive nose caught its stench of sewage, the smells of human sweat and offal, bad teeth, worse breaths, and other foul castings.

Downstream the rivulet seemed to slink in shame among great, tumbled rocks thrown down from the mountainsides in ages past. It completely disappeared, perhaps underground, before the canyon curved away to the southeast toward the pinelands and distant Pfantas.

"Argh!" Marbleheart gagged, willing the wind to change and take the smells away. "Worse by far than Pfantas!"

It was past a normal bedtime in the town's maze of cramped alleys and uneven stairways and there were only guttering torches here and there as people huddled for warmth indoors and spoke in low murmurs not meant to be overheard.

The castle above was black by day and blacker by night. Its glaring window eyes looked over the town, the canyon, and off toward Pfantas and beyond, to Old Kingdom.

"To judge by this Witch's windows," muttered the Sea Otter to himself, "she really does cast greedy eyes on Old Kingdom."

At last he turned about on his narrow ledge and climbed up over the ridge again, dropping quickly down to the cave where Douglas slept. Even in his thick waterproof fur he was glad to be out of the stinging, acrid wind once more. And away from the odors, especially.

Here the air smelled of the stream's hot, sulfurous water and, a pleasant surprise in such a place, tiny, white flowers such as grow on the edges of glaciers.

My dear young Otter, he said softly to himself as he gallumped down the last rockfall to the cave mouth and safety, *you might as well get used to the smells and the eye-watering fumes and the mysterious lights. You're going to have to go much, much closer than this, soon.*

One of the red-shot eyes of Coven Castle was larger than the others, although Marbleheart hadn't noted it particularly. It was the embrasure that lighted and aired, more or less, a large, bare-walled, dank-smelling anteroom of a haughtily beautiful woman. She sat erect and proud in an ebony chair supported by writhing, deeply carved jade-eyed serpents with golden fangs.

The Black Witch called herself Emaldar and was called by her sycophants, servers, and slaves "Emaldar the Beautiful" and "Queen Witch" and, sometimes, "Woman of Bare Mountain," among a number of less happy things not worth remembering now.

She was silently studying the young-old man in the tattered gray robe standing unhooded before her with his head up and, his eyes slitted, bravely waiting.

"You are Douglas Brightglade."

It was a statement, not a question.

"If you say so," murmured Cribblon.

"Eh? Speak up! Louder, so we can hear you, Brightglade Bumbler!"

Cribblon winced at her shrill tone but stood, still silent. A Witchserver guard prodded him with a three-tined pike, none too gently, making him flinch and stumble forward. The former Apprentice Wizard glowered over his shoulder at the soldier.

"They'd love to tear you limb from limb, of course," remarked Emaldar with a throaty chuckle. "Or use your pitiful body for target practice at the archery butts."

"I am sure," agreed Cribblon.

"Not now. Not just yet, however. I want some answers from you, Journeyman. Then a long stay in my sweet dungeon, a remarkably vile place. Even my Witchservers hate it down there."

She stood and paced back and forth before her chair for a moment, looking down at her dainty feet as they moved under her heavily jeweled and crescent-spangled gown.

"Where, now, is Flarman the Freak?"

"I don't know any such person," said her prisoner.

"Flarman Flowerstalk, then, or Firemaster, if you prefer."

"I assume he is at his home at Wizards' High in distant Dukedom," said Cribblon, shrugging. "He doesn't tell me his comings and goings."

"I'm sure of that!" laughed the Black Witch, scornfully. "Were I Flarman, I wouldn't give you the time of day, either. But you must know what he knows about me or you wouldn't be here. That's what I want to hear from your lips, either now—or later, when they are broken by beatings and blistered with thirst and your body is twisted and screaming with remembered pain."

"I forget the question," said Cribblon, seeking to string the moment out, fearing what would follow when the interview ended.

"I want to know what Flarman knows—and Augurian, too, blast him—about Coven and about me."

Cribblon shuffled his feet about, not looking up at the Witch Queen. He was, in fact, struggling to recall a simple spell Frigeon had taught him, ages ago. It was supposed to make one impervious to pain. He had too long forgotten some of the words, and the passes would be impossible with chained wrists.

"They know *who* you are," he said just as the soldier raised his pike to prick his backside once more. "They certainly know *where* you are, and *when* you came here. I'm not sure even you know *why* you came."

"My goals? Well, *someone* has to rule Old Kingdom! It's laying about completely ungoverned, in utter chaos. All sorts of people and things come and go as they please! Or they sit and sneer at you when ordered to leave! There are even some here who are happy and at peace with themselves. That won't do! It just won't do! There are too many things to be done and run and taken to pieces and put back together again the right way—my way!"

She sat abruptly on her chair and leaned back, stroking one of the carved serpents thoughtfully. There was a speculative look in her eyes that gave Cribblon more shivers than her threats of torture.

"Personally, I like things neat, straight laid and perfectly efficient," Emaldar went on more quietly, as if to herself. "I require all my people to know *exactly* where they stand . . . or grovel, if in my presence. I don't like that it's sometimes warm in winter and cold in summer. People must realize World will be much better off when everything is exactly the same everywhere, for everyone, forever!"

Cribblon sagged—he had been standing braced for hours now, and the chains about his arms and legs were very heavy. Wasn't there a spell Frigeon had drummed into him? Something to do with rusting heavy iron?

She thinks I'm Douglas, he thought. *The least I can do is prolong her misconception, for Douglas's sake—and Flarman's, too, and for the people who have a spot here or there to be happy in and content, despite all the wrongness brought about by people like her.*

"So, Flarman knows of me, eh? Who told him?"

"I did," said Cribblon, stoutly.

The Witch leaped to her feet again and threw up her hands in quick fury.

"Sneak! Spy! What business is it of yours or Flarman's or Augurian's what I do?" she shrieked.

"It's a Wizard's business to fight evil and right wrongs," quoted Cribblon from some long-forgotten text. "A Wizard has the duty to—"

"Duty! To be a pest and a nuisance to people who are making things run neatly, on time and straightforward, once again? You've seen Old Kingdom. It's a mess, crying out for a good, severe housecleaning, for a strong-armed ruler!"

"I hadn't noticed that," disagreed Cribblon, wearily. "I suppose you would point to Pfantas as a model of house-keeping?"

"Pfantas? Of course! What's wrong with Pfantas?"

"I never saw a filthier or more disreputable place than Pfantas. It was once a garden spot. People came from all over World to enjoy it; fresh air, warm sunshine, and soft rains in their seasons. . . ."

"Seasons! That's one of the worst excuses for doing something I ever heard," scoffed Emaldar in exasperation. "Put on bright colors because the trees are budding? Nonsense! Go sledding because it's snowed? Nonsense again and it must stop! Pfantas now is well organized, straightened out, a real no-nonsense kind of place, a paradise. I shall soon do the same for all Kingdom. Or Queendom, perhaps I shall call it."

"You intend to rule, then?" asked Cribblon, tiredly.

"None of your blasted business!" the beautiful Witch snarled. "You won't be here to see it, at any rate. You will—"

She stopped in midscream at the entrance of a uniformed and plumed Warlock officer of her Witchserver guard. He bowed deeply and held out a folded parchment.

"A message? From . . . ?"

She cracked the red wax seal with her sharp thumbnail and read the missive aloud: " 'Emaldar Witch: This is from the hand of Flarman Flowerstalk and is carried by the wings of Curfew, a Great White Sea Gull.

" 'You boast of holding one Douglas Brightglade as prisoner. I must warn you that you do this at extreme peril to yourself and those who are misguided enough to belong to your Coven.

" 'Augurian, of whom you may have heard, and I join to send you this good advice. Release your prisoner and set him on his way home. Disband your Coven at once, on pain of swift and fiery retribution for the evil you have perpetrated. Abandon your mountain before it is too late, or you lose all!

" 'Flarman Flowerstalk of Wizards' High (For the Fellowship of Wizards).'

"Nosy, witless busybody! Gossipy old wart-curer!" keened the Witch Queen. She crumpled the letter between hands trembling with fury. Before she could hurl it to the floor it burst into hot, white flame, scorching her fingers so that she cried out in fear and pain. The burning parchment dropped among dry rushes scattered on the stone floor.

Fire instantly caught at the rushes. A Witchserver with quicker wits than most of his kind rushed forward and doused the burning spot with an ewer of water.

Instead of being extinguished, however, the flames floated on the surface of the wash and raced across the uneven floor toward the Witch herself.

"Wizard's Fire?" she screamed in terror. "Put it out! Put it out!"

It looked for a minute as though it might burn the entire castle—and Cribblon, too—but the former Apprentice Aeromancer remembered one of his very earliest lessons. He stooped over the fast-spreading flames and blew on them gently, reciting an air-based specific against fire learned from his Master.

The flames died out with a sullen sizzle. The Wizard's message became a pile of fragile, black ashes among a tangle of half-consumed rushes.

"Guards! Take this sniveling fire dabbler and throw him in the wettest part of my dungeon where he can't do any fire harm!" ground out Emaldar, still shaking with fright. "I'll question him myself later. Get out, all of you! Say nothing of this to anyone on pain of . . . of painful and an extremely slow death!"

The Witchservers and their Warlock officer scuttled out in disorder, not forgetting, however, to drag the chained Cribblon after them, much to his relief.

The Witch Queen retired to her inner bedchamber to recover her wits and self-control.

Chapter Seventeen

Spring Cleaning

THE sun would have risen over Pfantas—if it could have found the town under a dank, brown fog that wrapped itself about the hill. Myrn and Pargeot ate their breakfast before a small campfire and watched the smog swirl and reluctantly begin to lift. On their own hillside, the spring sun shown warmly.

"How do we go about finding Douglas?" wondered the Seacaptain aloud.

"I'll go over to town and ask if they've seen him," said Myrn, rising. "No, you stay here. A lone lass will seem less a threat to Witch-ridden people. They might refuse to talk to a woman accompanied by a big, strapping man with dirk and cutlass in his belt."

"I'll leave 'em behind," Pargeot called after her, but she was already halfway to the plank bridge. He watched her go with an inane look of infatuation mixed with anxiety. "Be ye careful, Mistress!"

She waved her hand at him without turning around and disappeared through the postern gate, which stood unguarded and open, onto the steep stair-streets of Pfantas.

Myrn climbed through several of the poorest, smelliest levels before she reached what seemed to be a main avenue circling the hill. The houses here were in slightly better repair, somewhat larger, and had fewer broken windows.

Pfantasians she met ignored her, walking in a listless, cringing manner to and fro. The few whose eyes lifted to catch a quick glimpse of the attractive young woman at once swiveled them to either side to see if anyone had noticed their interest in the stranger. Nobody answered her cheery "good morning!" but she continued to greet them, anyway.

She walked around the hill on that level, observing and making conjectures, not ready to ask anyone about her Fire Wizard. She sensed a pall of strong Black Magic about the city, but was unable to name it yet.

There must be soldiers or policemen or spies here, she reasoned, *to enforce the Witch Emaldar's commands.*

She had reached the arc of the level that overlooked the waterfront and the narrow, wind-ruffled lake. Three disreputable-looking men in food-stained uniforms and battered tricorn hats rushed at her from a sleazy alehouse as she passed.

"Halt! Halt! Stop right there, girlie!" they shrilled. "In the name of Emaldar the Beautiful! Stop at once!"

They made a great commotion, but stopped short of laying hands on her, encircling her instead. They drew short, rather rusty swords and waved them recklessly at her, as though she were a dangerous criminal.

"Well, good sirs, what can I do for you? Have I broken a law, perhaps?" asked the Aquamancer's Apprentice sweetly.

"Halt! Halt!" one of the Witchservers continued to bawl. The other two silenced him with scathing looks and moved closer to Myrn.

"Ye're a stranger here!" one shouted in her ear.

"I certainly am that," agreed Myrn. "Is that a crime in Pfantas?"

"Yes! Of course! You're required by the laws of Emaldar the Beautiful to ask permission of us, her loyal Witchservers," said the largest of the three. "You must come with us to the Onstabula. At once!"

"Fair enough, I suppose," responded Myrn with a gracious smile. "Which way do we go?"

They fell into step, one on either side, the largest going before, swinging their battered swords to and fro in an impatient manner, trying to look very important and succeeding only in looking extremely silly, at least to Myrn, who tried hard not to giggle aloud.

Pfantasians they met stole startled sidelong glances at them. Some, she noted, looked sympathetic but most showed only sullen resignation. They kept well clear of the Witchservers' swords, parting before them like a bow wave before a ship's prow.

"Make way!" bawled the loudmouthed Witchserver on her left. "Make way for the Mighty and Dreaded Minions of the Witch Queen's law!"

"You certainly are a noisy lad," commented the girl with an easy laugh. "They're doing everything they can *not* to come too close to you, it seems to me."

"Be not impertinent!" shouted the lead Witchserver, spinning about and marching backward. Loudmouth fell back and raised his sword to prod her in the backside with its blunted tip. Myrn cried aloud in anger and stopped suddenly, whipped about to face him, her eyes flashing fire.

"Touch me with yon dirty steel on pain of a very hot bath!" she said, sharply. "I'll *not* be harried by such a mud-wallower as you!"

Loudmouth thought better of prodding but gave her a wicked leer instead.

"You'll soon change your pretty tune, me sweet cuddle, when we reaches the Onstabula," he sneered. But he fell in beside her again, just the same. The lead policeman took out a rumpled notepad and wrote something with the stub of a pencil, snarled out of the side of his mouth at Myrn, and tripped on a loose cobblestone.

"Watch your step," Myrn called, pleasantly.

The policeman regained his balance and turned to face forward, once more, glaring at the watching Pfantasians, daring them even to smile at his near pratfall.

They came to a low, moss-covered stone building with a low-pitched roof half caved-in, and reeking, even from a distance, of stale beer, old tobacco smoke, and long-unwashed bodies, among other unpleasant things. A faded sign over the entrance had originally said Constabulary, in large, gilt letters but now it read ONSTABULA, the C and the RY having long ago lost their grip and fallen away. In its narrow doorway, watching them approach, stood a hollow-cheeked, mean-looking little man wearing a dusty cocked hat sporting a broken and greasy cockade. His rusty black uniform coat was decorated with tarnished brass braid loops and swirls that hung from his epaulets by a few loose threads.

He looked, Myrn thought, like a large, dirty, and starving starling deep in molt.

"What have we here, what have we here, good fellows?" he chortled, strutting down to face the captive. "An out-of-town girl? Well, now, tell me all her crimes."

"I caught her sneaking along Main Level in broad daylight!" exclaimed the lead policeman quickly, so as to get for himself all the credit for the daring arrest. " 'Twas only a matter of minutes before she would've started *talking* to people, I'm certain. About to intentionally and with malicious forethought disturb the peace, you can be sure, Loo-tenant, sir!"

"Oh, yes, I know her kind," snarled the officer. "Drag her inside. I'll examine her very carefully in private."

He turned on his heel to reenter the building, looking out of the corner of his eye to be sure the gathering crowd of Pfantasians saw how evilly important he was.

"In ye go!" shouted Loudmouth. He felt brave enough in front of his officer to shove Myrn from behind.

The Apprentice Aquamancer stood like a rock.

"I warned you, fellow! I don't allow the likes of you to set even a little finger on my person. Ever! Draw back, filthy dog!"

Something in her way with words caused the constable to do just what she demanded. He took several steps backward and was content just to look daggers at her.

"We'll tote you in like a sack of potatoes if you resist," the leading policeman shouted. "Here, you men! Seize her by her hair and haul her before the Loo-tenant!"

The other two constables exchanged doubtful glances—as if to say to each other "Why me?"—but, seeing their leader's black scowl, they moved toward the angry Apprentice.

"Well! No more Mistress Nicelady!" cried Myrn. "*There!*"

Before either of the constables could reach her, the sky above their heads split wide open with a sharp bang. A torrent of very hot, soapy water cascaded over all three of the constables. They yowled in pain and shock and fell to their knees on the road, scrubbing the steaming suds into their eyes and spitting bubbles from their foul mouths.

When they attempted to jump to their feet, now cursing with anger—and their eyes full of stinging soap—their feet slipped out from under them and they flipped over onto their backs. Being close to the edge of the level, they skidded right off the soap-slick pavement and tobogganed down the stair-road, rocketed across the wooden dock, and plunged into the lake.

Somewhere, someone in the watching crowd laughed aloud in delight. It was immediately taken up by the throng, despite their struggles to remain sober faced.

"Loo-tenant!" wailed the lead constable as he shot down the hill, arms flailing. "Help! Help! She's fighting back!"

Myrn made an easy gesture with both hands. The lieutenant, just reemerging from the Onstabula to find out what was the commotion, found himself flying up into the air, borne off atop an enormous soap bubble, its sides iridescent with gay rainbows as a belated sunbeam broke through the overcast.

Myrn and the Pfantasians watched in varying degrees of satisfaction as the spinning bubble carried the little lieutenant out over the lake and, at a flick of the Apprentice Wizard's right index finger, burst with a pleasant musical chime. The screaming Witchserver dropped headfirst into the cold water, making a most pleasing splash.

The Witchserver policeman uttered a terrified gurgle as he popped like a cork to the surface. His three henchmen were trying to clamber ashore, but their hands and arms were coated with a thick, fragrant lather and, unable to get a grip on the wet dock planks, they slid back farther and farther downstream with each try.

"I'll clap you in irons for this, you . . . you . . . !" the lieu-tenant cursed most foully, thrashing his arms to remain afloat and stirring up a good lather all about him in the water.

"Have you learned nothing at all from this?" called Myrn. "Your mouth certainly could use a good soaping, too!"

A strong along-shore current carried the four Witchservers a quarter mile down the shore. In three or four breaths they were mere specks, far out on the lake, moving with the flow toward lower Bloody Brook.

Listeners on Pfantas's Main Level heard all four Witch-servers wasting breath in futile cursing and terrified sobbing. They disappeared around the bend in the shore.

(Where they came ashore, Pfantasians never knew or cared. Four Undines, playing happily in their waterfall, saw them come hurtling over the brink, to be swept around the pool onto a narrow pebble beach between two great rocks, where they managed to scramble ashore. By that time they were much too exhausted to say a word, or even clamber up the canyon wall to freedom.)

"Now," said Myrn, dusting her hands together—a mannerism very similar to one of Augurian's—and smiling at a young man in the forefront of the crowd, "is there anyone else who needs a good scrubbing up around here?"

"All the other Witchservers went off to Coventown with a prisoner, ma'am. All of us could use a good bath, if it comes to that," the young man commented, smiling in return. "Bathing is—has been—forbidden by law as a waste of valuable time and resources here in Pfantas for some years."

"I can see—and smell!" said the pretty Water Adept, wrinkling her nose. "Well, I'll do something about that. But first, I need some information."

"You can ask me, I guess. If I don't know, I'll try to find out for you," said the other. "My name is Featherstone."

"I'm Myrn Manstar, and I'm Apprentice Water Adept to Augurian of Waterand," replied Myrn, proudly. "Very pleased to meet you, Master Featherstone!"

"*Very* adept with soap and water, too, I'd say," chuckled Featherstone. "As it happens, ma'am, you are the second Wizard I've met this week."

"Ah, that would be my Douglas!" cried Myrn, seating herself in relief on a bench in front of the now-empty Onstabula. "Tell me of him! I'm here looking for him."

Featherstone quickly told of his two meetings with the Journeyman Fire Wizard. The Pfantasians about them listened in surprise, for this was news to them, too.

"Since then I've been working odd jobs, enough to put some food in my mouth, at any rate," said the leather merchant's son, "and talking quietly to people, especially my father's friends. We'd give anything to break away from Emaldar's thralldom, but we don't know how to go about it."

"Well, Douglas—and I—will help in that regard, never fear. And I'm about to make a great start by giving this place a thorough cleaning, believe me! Such a stench!"

Featherstone sighed. "It's one of the ways Emaldar keeps us cowed," he told her. "No washing, no cleaning, no dusting, nothing like that! A person's pride is easily smashed when he feels grungy and greasy all the time and can't even put on a clean shirt or shave his beard nor even carry a bit of soap without getting slapped in jail."

"First things first, then," said Myrn, sympathetically. She stood in the middle of Main Level and rolled her sleeves above her elbows. "Pfantas is about to take a bath, top to bottom, round and round!"

The spell she wove was not spectacular, nor did it call for much in the way of incantations or mysterious passes. And yet, in less than a quarter minute the overcasting smog, redolent of rotten fruit, kitty piddling, rancid cooking grease, and all manner of other nasty things, began to boil and roil above the town.

Its color quickly changed from brown-yellow to light blue-gray and then to pure white as the midmorning sun shone on it. It began to snow—but the dainty snow-drops were soap flakes!

When everything—and everyone—was quite dusted white with the lacy flakes, a fresh-smelling mist descended, warm and clinging, swirled by a wind whipping around and around the cone-shaped hill, changing directions after every other circuit to trace back on itself, whirling and swirling the soap flakes into every nook and cranny of the town.

The wind moderated and a hot rain began to fall, pelting straight down, soaking everything, until all Pfantas—including the townspeople who had rushed outside to see what was happening—was soaped and sudsed and scrubbed by the rain, the wind, and the flakes that smelled like your own mother's laundry, long ago at home.

The shower became a downpour. It rinsed the houses and streets, washed the straggly trees and the dispirited, yellow grass—and the filth-laden men, women, and children, as well.

Running rainwater charged through the gardens, the yards and the alleys, flushing away years of garbage, trash, dust and dried mud. It washed through the Pfantasians' tangled, oily hair, through their clothing, leaving everyone sparkling bright and squeaky clean from topknots to toes. Even their boots were shined!

Pfantasians cheered and wept and laughed through it all. A new, warm wind buffeted them in playful fashion, drying their clothing and ruffling their hair as it dried their skin— and shined the few panes of glass left in their windows.

Chimneys, clogged with soot and sour ash, suddenly began to draw easily, and when the wind had stopped, the smoke of breakfast fires rose into the still air, straight as ruled lines, pausing only long enough to scent the whole town with pinewood smoke and the aromas of frying bacon and eggs, toast and coffee.

"It's a beginning," conceded Myrn, wringing the last of the soapy water out of her skirts. She examined her handiwork with satisfaction, especially young Featherstone, who looked entirely different. Now he had clean hair, a clean face, and a clean shirt. "You'll have to keep it clean for yourselves. There's a warehouse full of soap left over from the storm, over there, enough to last until you can get your own again."

"Wonderfully splendid!" Featherstone shouted with glee and relief.

"There're still lots of other problems to be tackled here, although most of them you can solve for yourselves. As for this Witch Emaldar, with your kind help, Douglas will surely see she does no more harm, here or anywhere."

"Yes, well," said Featherstone, "getting back to Douglas . . . he came looking for his friend, Cribblon, but the Witchservers had already captured him. The Wizard set out three days ago to follow them to Coventown, to the Wicked Queen. No one's seen or heard of him since. I'm beginning to fear for him."

"No need," said Myrn, stoutly. "Douglas doesn't really need me to do his work. But perhaps I can make it easier. Besides, you can never have too much help from good friends."

"You've already made it easier for him, I think," said Featherstone. "Hello? Who's this?"

"This is my good friend, Captain Pargeot," introduced Myrn. The Seacaptain, seeing the spring cleaning of Pfantas from the next hillside, had rushed to town to see the results up close. The two men shook hands.

"The look and smell of this place have certainly improved," observed Pargeot in considerable awe. "I saw it all from across the way. People were laughing and singing!"

"So they were," said Myrn, pleased by his words despite her modesty.

"So very wonderful!" cried Pargeot. "Isn't she absolutely marvelous?" he asked Featherstone—and anyone else near enough to hear.

Most of the Pfantasians didn't connect the cleansing of their city and themselves with the slim, black-haired Apprentice. They were too busy laughing and talking freely for the first time in years, and marveling at the conquest of the Witchservers, to ask how it all had happened.

"I'll tell them," declared Featherstone. "They will want to know whom to thank."

"Let them think it was their own doing," said Myrn. "I don't need to be thanked. Just breathing newly fresh, clean air in Pfantas is reward enough, don't you think?"

"So self-effacing! So modest!" raptured Pargeot, shaking his head in wonder. "What a great lady!"

"Pargeot, I wish you'd stow it!" growled Myrn in exasperation.

"If you say so, adorable Apprentice," sighed the Westonguer.

"Back to business now!" interrupted Myrn. "Where do you think Douglas is, Master Featherstone?"

Said Featherstone, "He must be somewhere between here and Coventown. I'm sure he means to rescue the bellows mender, at the very least. He was most concerned about him when he left here."

"And he needed to know where to find the Witch Emaldar, of course," said Pargeot.

"Yes, that certainly is true," replied the Pfantasian. "But I can't tell you much more than that."

"Will you guide us to Coventown?" asked Myrn.

"Well, there's a big problem there. The Witch put a hex on us a long time ago. No one from Pfantas has ever been able to find Coventown, although we have a general idea where it must be. A number have tried, hoping to rescue the men and boys the Coven has enslaved. They never found the way!"

Myrn closed her eyes a moment, studying the strong hex she had already sensed about the town.

"A complex confusion spell, and one, unfortunately, that's beyond easy breaking," sighed Myrn. "I can feel its outlines but to do anything about it may take me days of trial-and-error experimenting. I just don't have that much skill at demagicking."

They sat on the Onstabula bench in thoughtful silence. Pargeot at last snapped his fingers and cried, "The Witch-servers are able to find Coventown. They took the captive Cribblon there, didn't they?"

"That's so," said Myrn. "How does that help us?"

"If we allow ourselves to be captured by them, they'll drag us off to the Witch, just as they did the man Cribblon! It seems to me they would do just that, under the circumstances."

"Good thinking!" approved the Apprentice Wizard. "But we don't have any Witchservers left."

"We'll have some, shortly," said Featherstone. "The Witch will send her Witchservers back, after they've delivered the bellows mender to her. Their departure left the Witchserver constabulary down to just the four you popped in the lake."

"We'll have to await their return, then," decided Myrn. "No use wandering about in the mountains looking for the Coven and mayhap getting lost. While we wait, I'll try to dismantle the Witch's hex. If the Witchservers don't arrive first, perhaps Featherstone can guide us to Coven."

"Wise plan," enthused Pargeot. "We'd waste that much time just getting lost, anyway."

Featherstone said, "You can perhaps give us advice on how to prepare for the Witchservers' return. We must organize a defense against their attempt to recapture Pfantas."

"That's the spirit!" cried Myrn. "You can do it, if you are firm in your purpose. You'll have surprise on your side, it's certain."

"We allowed this to happen to ourselves—through cow-ardice and selfishness—once. Once is more than enough," declared the Pfantasian. "I'm going to call together a town council. Most of the old Council are dead or enslaved, but there must be many here who will take their places."

"I'll stay right here, a pleasant spot now that the sun's come out," declared Myrn. "I need some peace and quiet to work on the hex."

Taking her hint, both men went separate ways. Featherstone dived into the crowd of townspeople who were still happily discussing the morning's events, talking of a town meeting.

Pargeot, with no specific task in mind, walked carefully down the still-soapy stairs to the waterfront, drawn by professional curiosity, to examine the various boats, barges, canoes, rafts, and lake craft moored there.

The lake sailors were already industriously scrubbing years of grime and grease from their vessels, laughing and singing as they worked.

"We've been tied up here for longer than I care to remember," said one to Pargeot. "Emaldar—blast her green eyes!—forbade us going up or down or across the lake without her permission, which she sold very dearly. Few ever got to go, unless it was on her own nasty errands."

"How did you make a living?" wondered the Westonguer.

"Fishing, mostly. That was allowed, but it tends to make any boat dirty and smelly, which pleased the Witchservers. They liked us to be filthy."

"I'll lend you a hand," volunteered Pargeot, and shortly he was swabbing decks and sweeping out cabins, while learning the words to a cheerfully off-color chanty long current among the sailors on Pfantas Lake. Looking up from his work some time later, Pargeot saw a very strange sight.

A puff of pink smoke on the dock swirled about like a tiny tornado, then coalesced into the figures of two men. The rivermen paused in their cleaning, polishing, and scrubbing to stare, startled by the sudden appearance of strangers. They reached for long-hidden knives and cudgels, determined to defend their regained freedom.

"Avast! I know that man!" cried Pargeot. He hopped ashore, telling the men to put up their weapons, and ran to meet Caspar Marlin.

Caspar, an old friend, was accompanied by a yellow-skinned child overdressed in stiffly swishing, carnelian-brocaded silk robes that swept the wooden dock about his tiny feet. The child wore a black, flat-topped hat with a wide, shiny brim all about, tilted down in back and up in front.

"Ahoy!" called Caspar, sighting the Westonguer. "Well met, young Pargeot! How come ye here?"

"I was about to ask the same of you, Caspar," said Pargeot, pumping his hand. Caspar introduced the child as Wong Tscha San, who bowed deeply, and Pargeot realized with something of a shock that Caspar's companion was not a child, after all, but a diminutive, very ancient Choinese gentleman with brightly twinkling eyes and a modest smile.

"I'm here as escort to Lady Myrn Manstar, the Apprentice Water Adept," Pargeot began to explain.

"Ah, the beautiful Myrn!" exclaimed Caspar. "I told you of her, Wong, didn't I? Fiancée of the Wizard Douglas Brightglade?"

"Many times, Caspar," chuckled the Magician from Choin. "I am pleased to meet you, Captain. I look forward to meeting both the Water Wizard's comely Apprentice and her intended bridegroom, also."

"Wong is a Wizard, too," explained Caspar. "We also came to help Douglas put down this Witch, Emaldar . . . if he needs any help."

"I can't tell yet whether Douglas is being successful or not," Pargeot told them, and as they climbed the stairs to Main Level he related their adventures and what he knew of Douglas's Journeying.

They found Myrn still seated on the bench in front of the building marked Onstabula, speaking to a very scruffy teenaged boy in torn, dirty, and ill-fitting clothes. He looked very much out of place in newly scrubbed Pfantas.

When she saw Caspar she excused herself and flung herself into the old Seaman's arms, shouting his name joyfully.

"I can't think of anyone short of Flarman and Augurian I'd rather have with us at this juncture," she told him after the kissing and hugging was satisfactorily completed. "We've all sorts of problems and troubles."

"Of course," said Caspar. "Where Wizards are, there is almost always trouble for someone. I've brought more assistance, too. Meet Magician Wong Tscha San of Choin, my dear."

Caspar began to tell how they came to be there, but Myrn held up her hand in apology. Turning to the waiting youth, she said, "Now, Willow, run back and keep a close eye on the Witchservers, please. Let us know where they are and how fast they approach."

The ragamuffin saluted jauntily, gave the others a broad grin and a wink, and dashed off around the level.

"There's a small band of young Pfantas rebels hiding in the pine forests," explained Myrn. "Willow is their leader and he came to warn Featherstone of the approach of a party of Witchservers—they are the willing servants of Emaldar, you must understand—a half-day's march off, coming toward us from Coventown where the witches have their stronghold."

"What's to be done?" asked Pargeot.

"Coming straight on, marching all night, they can't be here until tomorrow morning at the earliest, Willow says. We shall wait for them and persuade them to take us to Coventown. The way is hidden by a Witch's hex of confusing. Unless, Sir Magician," she turned to Wong, "*you* can wipe out the spell. It's beyond me."

"I understand," said Wong, thoughtfully. "Let me see. . . ."

He sat upright on the Onstabula bench with his eyes closed, humming softly to himself for a long moment. Then he frowned and looked once more at Myrn.

He said, "It is not a terribly difficult spell to weave, nor to unravel, even for my poor skill. However, I must warn that when one tampers with such a spelling, the magicker responsible will at once become aware of it. Would you wish to warn this Witch of our presence before it is absolutely necessary?"

"I hadn't even thought of that!" exclaimed Myrn, making a wry face. "We'd be better advised to wait for the Witchservers to come to us and capture them. They can be made to show us the way, I should think."

"I see no problem with that plan," agreed the Choinese. "It will be no great problem to secure the cooperation of these poor, deluded men. Their allegiance surely cannot be overly strong."

"Nor their intelligence, if those I've met are any measure," agreed the Apprentice. "Thank you, Magister. I feel much more confident, having you here to advise me. You will have to be careful of what you do, however, or it may hamper my Douglas's efforts to achieve his Mastery."

"I shall keep that in mind," said Wong, nodding his understanding.

"I'm not particularly worried about Douglas's handling of this problem," said Pargeot, expansively, "especially with Mistress Myrn and myself to assist."

Featherstone arrived to ask Myrn to address the town meeting, which had convened outside their city hall, the ruin at the top of the hill.

"Ten good and true men and women have agreed to serve as interim town council," he explained, proudly. "There's a new spirit in Pfantas, already. A week ago, none would even have spoken to me about such a move!"

"I'll be happy to consult with them," said Myrn. "Master Wong Tscha San, will you add your wisdom to an Apprentice's advice? And, Featherstone, perhaps you'd better hear what young Willow just told me of the approaching Witchservers."

Myrn and Wong went off, talking earnestly with Featherstone, while Pargeot and Caspar went to the town's inn to arrange accommodation for the night. Pargeot asked a boy who had followed them to retrieve their kits from across the burn. The lad rushed off, eager to oblige.

"It seems a small thing," Pargeot said with an apologetic laugh, "but as it happens, I am now the only man in Pfantas who badly needs a shave!"

When they were settled at the inn, Pargeot and Caspar sat down to await the return of Myrn and the Choinese Wizard. They were approached by a messenger from the youth Willow, who sent news of the Witchserver band.

"The scum have stopped three hours' march away. Camped for the night," the scout reported. "We'll watch them still, but it seems they'll not enter the town until tomorrow sometime."

"Hmmmm!" said Pargeot. "I'm a fifth wheel here at the moment. Perhaps I'll return with this man to help his people on their watch."

"A good idea," agreed Caspar, who understood the impatience of youth, even when that youth was a full-ranked Seacaptain. "I'll stay and tell the others."

Willow's messenger looked skeptical until he noticed Pargeot's heavy cutlass and wicked-looking sailor's dirk.

"Come and welcome, sir," he said. "We might need your help, if they get an idea to move in dark of night, after all."

Myrn and the Choinese Sage came to the inn after dark, tired and hungry.

"Good for him!" Myrn sighed when she learned of Pargeot's departure. "He's been able to give only small help so far, and I feel sorry for him. Such matters as these are outside his experience."

"A good man, however," noted Caspar. "He has the reputation of being an excellent Seacaptain with a cool head in emergencies."

"The trouble is, we haven't had any real emergency, yet," said Myrn. "I'm afraid he believes he owes me some sort of knightly service."

"There is more to it than that," put in Wong, softly.

"Yes, I'm aware of his feelings toward me. He's hopelessly infatuated, I fear. Does it give him some sort of pleasure to beat his head against my devotion to Douglas, and to my profession?"

"He will grow out of it," promised the Sage, "if it is truly just an infatuation."

"I may have a stern word with him," said Caspar. "I know his father and served under his grandfather as well. Perhaps he'll listen to me."

"And what would you tell him? To forsake the lady's presence, forever and forever?" asked Wong, shaking his white head. "No, my good friend! Such opposition, however well intended and sensible, would only serve to harden his resolve to suffer in a hopeless cause."

"A misty-minded romantic!" snorted Caspar. Then he sighed. "Well and well-a-day! I was that way meself once.

Being at Sea gave young Caspar Marlin a dose of common sense and reality that's cured him of such foolishness, I guess."

"It's not too late," chuckled Wong, laying a sympathetic hand on his friend's arm. "Love has a way of striking when least expected—even the most mature of us."

"Personally, I think we should be planning about tomorrow. It's full night, already," said Caspar. "How's the table in this inn?"

When they had dined—quite well, as it turned out—they retired to the inn's common room and after three hours of discussion around the coal grate they all went off to their beds.

There had been no further word from the scouts or Pargeot.

Douglas and the Sea Otter had spent the whole of that day clambering about on the rugged mountainside, taking as many close looks at Coventown and its castle as the barren rock landscape allowed. They returned to their cave at dark, tired but little satisfied with their small gains in information.

"Cribblon is well and unhurt, as yet. He's uncomfortable, cold, and wet," declared Douglas after studying the embers of the fire for a while. "He's in a rock cavern beneath the castle. A dungeon, rather. I feel locked doors, heavy chains, and bars. But at least until this moment Emaldar hasn't harmed him. Maybe . . ."

"She's softening him up for later?" yawned Marbleheart. "Sorry, I didn't mean to sound flippant. Do you foresee any action in the next four hours or so, Wizard?"

"No, none. Even Emaldar is asleep just now."

"Then I'll bathe my poor, rock-ravaged paw pads in the stream for a while, then get some sleep."

"I'll be before you," said Douglas, yawning in turn. "However, I'll sleep with an ear to the ground, in case the Witch takes it into her head to question Cribblon under cover of night."

He awoke to listen with Wizard-sharp senses several times during the chill night but it was not until false dawn that he sensed a commotion in the castle in the deep canyon.

"Something's afoot," he said to himself and, so as not to disturb the sleeping Otter, crept silently from the cave and made his way to the top of the ridge, where he might have line-of-sight contact with Emaldar's stronghold.

"We've captured *another* man who says he's Brightglade!" reported the breathless Warlock officer to Emaldar. He'd ridden a rawboned nightmare since before midnight to bring the news. "He came to us out of the night, demanding that we bring him to you, Your Magnificence!"

"Describe this man who claims to be Douglas the Fire Wizard," demanded Emaldar, pulling her thin dressing gown closer about her.

"My Queen, he is not yet in his middle years . . . I'd say, maybe twenty and eight or so. He carries himself easily and with grave authority. He is sandy of hair and blue of eye. He stands just under six feet tall."

"That could be a third of all Men in World," snapped the Witch Queen. "Now, why should he say he is Douglas Brightglade, in the circumstances, if he is not? In which case . . . where is this newly taken prisoner now?"

"My men bring him to you as fast as they can, Most Foul, Most Wise Witch. They will be here later today."

Emaldar sent her breathless and painfully saddle-sore minion away and hurriedly dressed, not neglecting to arm herself with certain Witches' amulets and dire charms. She went down by secret, dim, and winding stairways, below the cellars of her castle to the deepest and wettest of her dungeons.

"Waken the prisoner!" she barked at Cribblon's guards. They hastened to do her bidding, cruelly yanking on his chains to disturb the first slumber Cribblon had gained in more than three days.

"Waken, lowest of the low!" She herself prodded him with a sharp heel until he groaned in his misery and turned his head to look up at her, eyes still muzzy with exhaustion.

"Who in the name of Lady Beelzebub herself are you, really?" she asked at once.

"Why . . . why . . . you said I was Douglas Brightglade," answered the other.

Witches school themselves in reading the outer signs of men's inner thoughts, of course. A look of surprised concern had crossed Cribblon's sleep-loosened face for just a second. It told her the truth more surely than any words he might utter.

"No, *you're* not Brightglade!" she shrilled at the top of her voice. "The *real* Brightglade has now been captured. You're only a stinking flunky of some sort, even if you do know a smidgen of magic. He's being brought to me, even now. And you, my lad, are in deep, deep trouble!"

She turned abruptly and stalked off down the wet dungeon corridor almost at a run, forgetting, in her anger, to order the prisoner slain at once, as she had intended.

Cribblon was grateful for small blessings.

"Oh my, Douglas!" he murmured almost silently in the blackness of his cell, "I trust you know just what you're doing. What *was* that spell for rusting chains? I almost had it when I fell asleep."

Emaldar, returning to her quarters, sent for the weary Warlock officer and ordered him to ride back at once to his Witchserver constables. They were to keep their prisoner very carefully and rush him to Coven Castle as fast as possible, stopping neither to rest nor eat on the road.

"Not too gently, this time," she snapped at him. "I'm tired of these people playing games with me! When he gets here, it's the Chamber of Pain for him, at once! What are you standing around for, vile varlet! Be off with you at once. Fetch me my enemy!"

On his ridgetop Douglas couldn't hear or see these events, but he sensed them in ways learned from Flarman after long, hard study and practice. Emaldar now knew her first prisoner was not Douglas Brightglade. Someone else, unknown, had been taken by the Witchservers.

"Who can this one be, I wonder?"

He slid down the gravelly grade to the hidden cave mouth. "Certainly not Flarman. I would be able to sense his nearness. I've given him no reason to come to my aid, and he knows I must do this on my own."

"What'll we do?" asked Marbleheart when Douglas awakened him and told him of his discoveries.

"Emaldar's attention is diverted from Cribblon to this new captive," said the Journeyman. "We've got to get inside the castle and get Cribblon out, first of all. We'll rescue the other when he gets here. Only then can I confront Emaldar, when she has no hostage to hold against me."

He sat staring into the fire, reading what the flames had to say.

"Could it be . . ." He hesitated, examining this new intuition again. "Could it be Myrn? I sense her presence at a distance and in that direction, too."

"I wouldn't be at all surprised," said Marbleheart calmly. "She would seem, from all you've said, the kind to come to your side in trouble."

"Not too hard to believe she would come after me," agreed Douglas. "And I can believe she would allow herself to be captured, just to reach Coven, as Cribblon did, intentionally or otherwise."

He continued to gaze into the embers and the Otter watched in silence.

"It can't make any difference in our plans. If we go off to rescue this new prisoner, whoever he or she is, the Witch will be warned of us, making it extremely difficult to rescue Cribblon."

"Nice lady, that!" snorted the Otter. He rolled over on his back and stuck his short legs in the air. "Are we going to go or not?"

"Not, although it galls me to say 'stay put.'" Douglas sighed, reaching for his blanket. "Try to get some more sleep. It's still too dark and the castle people are astir now with the bringing of news. While Emaldar's distracted, perhaps I *could* use a spell of invisibility. . . ."

He pondered and prepared himself while the Otter slept again, quite soundly. Eventually Douglas, too, rolled over to face away from the ember's glow and willed himself go to sleep.

He dreamed of Myrn in a rocking manure cart, chained and unable to stand, on the rough pinelands path, rolling toward Coventown.

Chapter Eighteen

Road to Coventown

WILLOW, as dirty and disheveled as Pfantas itself had been two days earlier, slipped into town by the postern gate in the smallest hours of morning. He made his way up scrubbed-clean streets and past levels so spotless and neat he hardly recognized them.

He supplemented loud pounding on the inn door with a handful of gravel thrown against the innkeeper's bedroom shutters, finally rousing the sleeping host.

"I just *can't* wake the lady," the innkeeper sputtered indignantly when he at last opened the door to admit the rebel. "Can't it wait 'til morning?"

"It's urgent, man! *Urgent!*" Willow shouted. "The Lady Wizard *knows* me! She awaits my news."

Grumbling testily but prodded on by the ragamuffin, the innkeeper at last climbed the stairs and rapped gently on Myrn's door.

"Here, old gaffer!" hissed Willow in exasperation, pushing the innkeeper aside. He beat so loud a tattoo on the door panel it made the host wince in pain.

"You just *don't* rouse important guests in such a manner!"

He remembered that much from the good old days, when his inn was always full of rich and cultured patrons.

Myrn opened her door, greeted the boy and the man sleepily, and said she'd be right down. The messenger and innkeeper retreated to the public room, where they sat glaring at each other in hostile silence from opposite settles before the banked fire.

Five minutes later the Apprentice Aquamancer appeared, looking fresh, rested, and anxious.

"Good morning, innkeeper! What is it, Willow? Good news or bad?"

"I . . . I . . . I'm not sure, Mistress. That there Seacaptain . . ."

"Pargeot? Yes?"

"He's went and turned hisself over to the Witchservers!"

Myrn gasped, "I don't understand . . ."

"And he said to run fast and tell you what he done," continued the lad. "So, I did. He said he'd pretend to be the other Wizard, the one you seek, and leave a trail you can follow when they hauled him off to Coventown, too!"

"He didn't! Well! You did wonderfully well, Willow," Myrn assured him as understanding dawned. She sent the innkeeper to wake the older Seacaptain and the Choinese gentleman, too, at once.

"Our Pargeot is bound and determined to be a tragic hero as in the old romances," Myrn told them when they came down. "When he was shown the Witchserver's camp, he simply walked up to them and told them *he* was Douglas Brightglade!"

"I assume," said Wong, "that our young Seacaptain hopes the enemy will dash off to their Witch mistress with him."

"That's as how I sees it," agreed Caspar, nodding vigorously.

"He says we should follow him, as Douglas followed Cribblon's captives. Well, it *may be* a quick way to find the Witch without taking the time to untangle that hex," Myrn conceded.

She turned away with decision. "I'll go at once. Willow will guide me."

"I'll go with you," said Caspar, and he wouldn't hear otherwise. "A sailor always comes in handy, be it fight, flight, or finding safe harbor."

Wong said he would stay behind in Pfantas.

"A great Choin general once told me, 'Always have something in reserve,'" he said.

Myrn finished dressing while the innkeeper went to rouse his good wife to make them a hearty breakfast. In less than an hour, with just a hint of dawn in the sky, the Apprentice Wizard and the sun-grizzled Captain followed Willow through the postern, across the creek, and up the path toward Coventown, to Cribblon, to Pargeot, to Douglas and Marbleheart.

Shortly after the sun cleared the eastern horizon, Marbleheart and Douglas were again lying on their stomachs under the thornbushes, peering down into Coventown's vale through the morning's steams and mists.

"Your invisibility thing seems to me our best bet," advised Marbleheart. "Although you sounded doubtful of it."

"Not so much doubtful of the spell," explained Douglas, "but whether it will work on a watchful Witch. On the rest of Emaldar's people, I have no doubt it'll work. But Witches can see the unseen, you know."

"No, I don't know much about such creatures," said the Otter, giving his sleek, brown head a sharp shake. "How about this, then? We go right through town, being invisible, and examine the castle as closely as is safe. A Witch would have to be looking right in our direction to see us, would she not?"

Douglas nodded. "Recall, however, that there's more than the one Witch over there. 'Coven' implies at least two other Witches in addition to Emaldar, banded together. There could be a dozen or even a score!"

"In my considerable experience stealing the wary tern's eggs or sneaking up on squid in deep water—they're delicious!—I've found you can get amazingly close to anyone who is looking another way. I would guess Emaldar and her sister Witches will be very busy this morning with their new prisoner, wouldn't you?"

"It's quite possible. A chance we'll have to take, I see."

"A little caution?" Marbleheart waved a casual paw. "Pick our cover before each move?"

"It's our best idea, anyway," agreed the Journeyman. "Let's do it, before I change my mind!"

He drew the Otter close to his side, and invoked Flarman's Invisibility Incantation Number 7, a series of slow hand passes to a monotone chant in Faerie, followed by certain Power Words merely whispered in their proper order with just the right emphasis.

"Not working," sniffed the Otter in disappointment. He stared at his right forepaw and left hindpaw in turn. "I can still see me."

"It's working," Douglas reassured him. "The spell doesn't affect you and me, just everyone else—I hope! Go quietly, though, and speak low, for the spell doesn't keep us from being heard."

"There's the easiest part, then," said Marbleheart. "The Man hasn't been born who can hear an Otter being quiet. Well, if it's working as you say, what are we waiting for? Into the heart of Coventown, I say! Crossing that rather dangerous-looking dam might prove risky, however. Let's look at it more closely."

They reached the stream bank at the near end of the rough earth dam that backed the mountain stream to form Coventown Pool. The water was high, spilling through widening cracks and between boulders. A treacherous-looking footpath crossed on the top of the dam.

"Something's shaken the dam up. Close to collapsing, I should think," Marbleheart said, stroking his whiskers nervously. "Others crossed here, as late as yesterday evening. Watchmen, I would guess. But . . ."

"We won't take the chance," Douglas decided. Taking the Otter's paw firmly in hand, he sailed them over the stream with a short-hop Levitation Spell.

"Hoo! Whee!" squealed the startled Marbleheart. He clapped a paw over his mouth and whispered, "You didn't tell me we were going by air."

"Shush!" warned Douglas. "There are washerwomen ahead."

A silent crowd of women knelt on flat rocks at the lake's edge, dousing their laundry in the scummy, opaque waters and beating each piece listlessly on the stones with sticks. They worked without joy—no gossip, no laughter, nor even bickering—as you might expect of folk doing a common household chore together.

"Did you notice what they were washing?" asked Marbleheart once they had passed out of earshot. "Black gowns! Dead black, all of them, from top to toe, even the underneath things! Not a shred of pink or white or . . ."

"Witches wear black," Douglas observed with a shrug. "It's part of their mystique. What's this?"

They had come to where the town's sewers emptied, by way of a large open ditch, into the lake. All the stenches of Coventown were concentrated in the sludgy ooze. The travelers held their noses and tried not to breathe too deeply through their mouths until they were well past.

"Depressing as a dying whimper," muttered the Sea Otter, looking about with curiosity after they'd passed through the town gates. Although the sun shone brightly high above the mountain peaks, the very air here at street level was a gray-brown, eye-watering haze that filtered out most of the sunlight and gave a winter's-dusk appearance to the scene.

Lanterns flickered feebly at a few street corners, although it was midmorning. The people they saw in this dimness walked like old, blind men, canes tapping, slowly shuffling, eyes ever focused at their feet.

These, Douglas guessed, were the ordinary folk Emaldar had enslaved, stolen from places like Pfantas, to do the hard, dirty work of her Coven. They were terrorized hewers of wood, carriers of water, washers of clothes, the servants who scrubbed the Witches' floors and prepared their meals.

The weirdest thing about Coventown, Marbleheart noted, was that no one spoke louder than the merest whimper. Not even the pinch-faced little children they saw spoke out loud. Nor did they smile or even play, but stood about, leaning on grimy walls, in the deepest shadows, staring away with haunted eyes at nothing at all.

The travelers climbed the steep streets to the castle—it seemed to Douglas he had spent an inordinate amount of energy lately climbing up and down. When they reached the uneven stone paving of the castle foregate, they sheltered under a blind archway, away from a hot, sulfurous wind that whipped about them from the mountain heights.

Marbleheart gazed with grave interest at the castle. He'd never seen a structure so large and lofty.

"Carved right out of solid rock, it is! Not cut pieces of stone, like Summer Palace or Westongue Quay," whispered the Otter. "Take some of your best fireworks to break them down."

"The place is big," Douglas whispered back. "We can go in and explore as long as we avoid the Witches!"

"How do I tell Witch from Witchpeople?"

"That's easy. Witches'll be dressed all in black and they'll wear tall, pointed hats. A Black Witch stores part of her witching powers in her hat."

"Well, let's go in and see," sighed the Otter. "Here comes a pack train. Supplies for the castle, I'd guess. If we walk along right behind them the clatter they make on the drawbridge will cover our own."

"You're the expert stalker," agreed the Journeyman, gesturing for him to lead the way.

They hurriedly crossed the sagging, swaying draw-span over a noxious-smelling moat, in the wake of a gang of almost-naked men carrying huge bundles and heavy boxes.

The slaves were driven by a brace of most villainous-looking Witchservers, as twisted and cruel as the long black-snake whips they flourished and cracked, applying them with wicked glee to the slaves' backs, bottoms, and legs.

Once out of the dark gate tunnel through the thick outer wall, the invisible companions emerged into a cramped, crowded, flagged courtyard surrounded by twenty-foot walls. The interior was broken only by the heavy doors and tiny arrow-slit windows in the gray stone inner keep itself. The keep seemed to lean backward and merged into the cliff behind. Cornices under frowning, overhanging eaves were evilly decorated with ugly, wicked-looking serpents, scowling demons, and long-fanged gargoyles.

Douglas stopped to study these and saw that they weren't stone at all, but living monsters the same dark color of the surrounding stone. They clung, perfectly still, to the edges of the castle's roofs, their tiny, dull eyes alone moving, restlessly scanning the courtyard and everything in it in slow, sweeping glances.

"'Ware the Griffins," he breathed in the Otter's ear. "They're Watchworms."

"Can they see us?"

"No, I think. They're stone deaf, fortunately. But let's get under cover somewhere. That small door—there, next to the stable archway."

They slipped quickly but quietly across the rough and stained flags, until they could edge through the half-ajar door and plunge into the welcome darkness of the passage on the other side.

"So far, so good!" breathed the Journeyman Wizard. "Look for a way leading down."

After several minutes of exploring, they found a stairway at the far end of a side corridor, blocked by a massive fence of tarnished brass bars.

"Why brass?" wondered Marbleheart.

"Witches fear the touch of iron," the Journeyman murmured back.

As Douglas started a subtle unlocking spell that would spring the lock without calling the magic to anyone's attention, the heavily burdened slaves and their whip-cracking overseers burst noisily into the corridor. Stepping right past the invisible pair, one of the Witchservers coiled his whip about his forearm and fumbled a large key from his belt. He unlocked the brass gate, flung it wide, and growled to the panting slaves to carry their heavy burdens down the steep, uneven stairs.

The Wizard and the Otter followed, again letting the sounds of the shuffling and groaning captives cover their own footsteps.

"Move it along, damn you!" growled both guards in bored monotones. They were as thick as they were tall, which wasn't very tall, and wore wide, spiked collars like those given hunting dogs to protect them from wild bears' bites. "No talking, there! Faster, faster, faster!"

Urged by the whips and the words, the slaves rushed headlong down the steps. One stumbled and fell. Several tripped over his sprawled body before they could stop, their burdens tumbling ahead of them down the stairs.

The guards roared in anger and raged impatiently, lashing out at bare backs, until the poor bearers sorted themselves painfully out, gathered their burdens once more, and fled on.

"Good thing for you there's naught breakable in these bales," screamed one of the Witchservers. He cracked his twelve-foot whip viciously after the last of them.

The train descended into a vast, low-arched cellar at the very bottom of the castle. Here were stacked, binned, hung, and piled all sizes of boxes, barrels, and bales, some spilling over with half-rotten carrots, spoiled, reeking cabbages, and limp, blackened greens. The cellar had the heavy stench of a rotting compost heap.

Bales were loosely wrapped in dirty sacking, banded with rusty metal strips and stamped with lead seals. Great bunches of garlic hung in braids from the rafters. In a separate, barred enclosure were stored enormous casks and kegs of wine, beer, and brandy.

Guttering torches lit the cavern just enough to show the slaves where to lay down their loads. Without allowing their panting charges any rest, the overseers drove them back up the stairs at a run.

"Radishes!" exclaimed Marbleheart softly as he examined the newly arrived stores. "Fresh, too! I didn't realize that Witches ate good stuff like this!"

He nibbled hungrily at the peppery red roots, offering several to Douglas. Fresh produce was welcome after weeks of camp fare, even with the occasional meals magically imported from Wizards' High.

"What did you think Witches ate?" Douglas asked, taking a bite out of a radish. It burned his tongue pleasantly.

"Don't have the slightest idea," sniffed the Sea Otter. "Nasty, slimy things, I suppose, like roasted lizards and toasted toads. Have some new cabbage."

Douglas ate a quarter head of raw cabbage while he carefully roved back and forth across the storeroom floor. Was the stair the only access to the room? Behind a stack of barrels oozing sticky black-strap molasses he discovered a trapdoor.

"Stand back," he warned, and shook his fist at the hatch. Slowly it rose, making horrible creaking sounds. It wasn't opened very often, he was certain.

"Whew!" gagged Marbleheart, jumping backward. A rush of stale, damp air almost knocked them over, but after a moment it blew away, to be replaced by the dank odors of rotted wood and stagnant water. The sound of dripping echoed from far below. A wooden ladder allowed them to clamber slowly down, after Douglas had gestured the trap closed again, to a landing along the course of a narrow winding stairway.

"At least we're going in the right direction," growled Marbleheart. "Down! Give us a light, Wizard!"

Douglas floated a tiny, bright flame over their heads and by its light they could see the steps going down, down, to a wetly gleaming stone floor. As they neared the bottom, a swarm of large, black Rats with bare, pink tails rushed by.

"On their way up to check out the fresh food," guessed the Otter, watching them with distaste. The Rats paid them no heed at all, except the very last and least, who stopped long enough to peer up at them for a moment.

"Follow our example and get out of this place, too," it said, not unkindly. "It's not food we run for. There's great danger here!"

It dropped to all fours and dashed off up the stair.

"Hey," called Marbleheart after it. "Wait up! We need some directions here."

"They won't help you much," said a squeaky voice near Douglas's ear. "Rats are single-minded when it comes to desertion."

Looking up, the travelers saw a number of Bats hanging upside down from the ceiling.

"I'm a Wizard," Douglas told them. "Can you give us some information?"

"Wizards . . . explains why we can't see you, just hear you," said the largest Bat. He blinked solemnly. "Name's Tuckett, young Wizard. What's yours?"

"Douglas Brightglade," Douglas answered, switching off the invisibility spell. "Pyromancer."

"Ah, yes. I've heard about your kind. A long time ago a friend of mine spent his days in a Fire Wizard's cave."

"How'd you come to raise your family in this frightful place?" asked Marbleheart.

"It seemed like the ideal place to hang out at first," explained the Bat. "Damp and dark enough to be comfortable. Quick access to the outside. Swarms of tasty bugs everywhere. Witches' castles are usually good places for bats, as they generally leave us alone. However . . ."

"You regret moving here?" asked Douglas

"We're beginning to," said the Bat's wife, joining the conversation. "Hush, children! We're talking, the nice Wizard and your mama and papa!"

The Batlings peeped softly among themselves and stared, fascinated and horrified, at the huge, ugly Man and his terrifying companion-beast.

"Better nor Hollowe'en," one whispered to his sisters.

"This Witch's castle is so noisy! Grumblings and rumblings and groans and rocks shattering all of a sudden," confided the Bat wife with a shiver. "But worst of all, they shut a prisoner in the wettest part of the basement without even fixing the bad leaks. The poor man is knee deep in hot water and can hardly sit himself down."

"Wouldn't be so bad, were he to hang by his toes like normal folk," put in one of the Batlings with a sniff.

"A prisoner, here?" asked Douglas. "I'm looking for a friend who is Emaldar's prisoner."

"Pssssh! Don't speak *her* name," warned Tuckett, glancing about with sudden caution. "She comes down here much too often for our liking. Three or four times yestereve alone."

"But nonsense, my dear," said his wife, nudging him affectionately, "this here's a Wizard, and a Wizard can best a Witch any day—or night!"

"All very true," said Douglas, "but right now I want to rescue my friend. Have you seen him?"

"Oh, most surely," said Tuckett, nodding—a bit disconcerting as a Bat's nod goes in the wrong direction, up and down, instead of down and up. "Last evening—"

"We were going to bespeak him. Sort of buck up his spirits, that would be," his wife interrupted again. "But we didn't want to call ourselves to *her* attention. He's there now, a-setting in water and trying not to fall over in his sleep and drown."

"He's whipped up a bit of magic, I believe," said Tuckett in admiration. "He's managed to stay above water for a long spell. The problem—"

"Is that the air in there is falling too fast. First it was at his ankles, then it fell to his shins, and now it's down to his waist, as was said before. By tonight he'll be setting in it down to his chin!"

"Is Em—er, the Witch drowning him on purpose?" asked Marbleheart. The thought of deep water didn't bother him all that much, but he could see how it might bother Cribblon.

"Oh, no! It's springtime on the high slopes, you see," explained the Bat wife. "The snows are a-melting and the river is a-rising quite fast. We always have some flooding around about now—although, come to admit it, this year it seems greater than usual."

Douglas smacked his fist in the palm of his other hand. "We'd better go get him out!"

The Bat family obligingly led them to the far end of the right-hand corridor, past a row of empty cells hacked roughly out of solid bedrock, each less than six feet cubed and all heavily barred.

The floor here was six inches underwater. The Witchserver guards had earlier been playing cards on an empty barrel's head and shouting vile-sounding insults at their prisoner, said Mistress Bat. They'd abandoned this corridor for a higher level when the hot water reached over their boot tops.

As they neared the end cell they heard a voice softly singing in a pleasant tenor:

> "O Castle Doom!
> Thy towers glower o'er me.
> And from afar
> I hear the roar of raging fires!
> When will he come,
> My bonny, bravest warrior?
> His lonely friend of so few su-uh-mers
> To Save?"

"The poor man!" choked the little Batlings. "He's suffering great pain!"

Douglas put his face near the cell door grille and called out, "Is that a folksong of your western country, Cribblon, or are you making it up as you go along?"

The song stopped in midverse and the Journeyman heard a frantic splashing approaching the door.

"Is that you, Douglas, old Journeyman? Are you a prisoner like me or are you 'my bonny, bravest warrior'?"

"Just your friendly neighborhood Pyromancer," chuckled Douglas. "Stand to one side, old air blower. There isn't time to pick the lock. I'm going to blast the door open."

He stood tall and suddenly severe—or so Marbleheart described it to his grandchildren under a gravel bank on the Briney, years later—and, rolling up his wide, Wizardly sleeves, he threw a solid, right-handed blow at the door, shouting a single powerful word.

"*Champianawirl!*"

His fist hardly touched wood when, it seemed to Marbleheart and the Bat family, a great blue bolt of lightning cracked. When the smoke cleared, the door lay in splinters too small even for kindling, floating on the surface of the slowly rising seep water.

"So *that's* how it's pronounced!" cried Cribblon. "I've been sitting here for hours trying to remember how to say that dratted word. I did manage to talk the chains into rusting through, hours ago."

He waded quickly through the smoldering wood chips and joined them in the higher, if not much drier, corridor. Douglas shook his hand and Marbleheart thumped him gleefully on the back, proudly performing his warming and drying spell on the bedraggled former Apprentice. The Bats twittered excitedly about their heads.

"I managed to dredge up a few helpful old spells," said Cribblon, proudly. "I was trying to remember something that would float me on the water when it got too high. Not much success on that, however. Thank you all! You arrived just in time."

"Thank the Bats," said Douglas. "Right now, I'd better get us elsewhere. That blast must have been heard all over the place."

In fact, sounds of shouts and thuds of running boots came from above them as the Witchserver guards pounded toward the stair to see what had happened.

"Where does the corridor go in the other direction?" Marbleheart asked Tuckett.

"Under the mountain, a long, hot way," answered Tuckett. "Calm down, children! The fireworks are over. There are ways to the outside, however, that we use."

"Now, we should let them make all the noise they can and we should help," said the practical Mama Bat. "To cover the sound of our friends' retreat, you see."

And they did so, acting just like Bats disturbed by all the racket. Waving a hurried good-bye to them, Douglas lead the ex-Apprentice and the Otter past the foot of the stair and down the narrow dungeon passageway in the opposite direction.

They ducked around the first bend. The floor was suddenly dry underfoot. They heard the dungeon guards hit the bottom of the stair and start cursing the Bats, who flew in frantic circles about their heads, screeching at the bottom of their Bat voices. One of the little Batlings flew boldly against their torch, plunging the corridor into sudden darkness.

Following his example, the other Bats streamed away, pausing to snuff out all the other torches in the vicinity, laughing gleefully as they went.

This left the Witchservers running wildly about, bumping into each other and the hard rock walls, long enough for Douglas to lead his friends to the far end of the other corridor. They were stopped by a heavy bronze grill.

"There's time for lock picking," Douglas decided. He brought his floating headlight close and, taking a thin, hooked instrument from his right sleeve, began to tease the tumblers back and forth as the Dwarf Bryamote had long ago taught him. After two very long minutes the old bolt rasped back and Douglas swung the heavy grille open.

"In! In!" he urged. Once they were all through, he swung the gate closed and relocked it.

The air here was considerably warmer and dry. The walls themselves felt warm to the touch.

Cribblon nodded. "Blueye is, after all, a volcano."

"Volcano!" exclaimed Douglas. "I should have seen it! The blue lake that gives her the name—a crater lake, eh?"

"I was thinking, while I was sitting in the water listening to the guards tell dirty stories," said Cribblon, "that somewhere I read volcanoes are often riddled with—"

"Of course, tunnels and passages. To carry off molten lava during an eruption, and steam and hot gases at other times," said Douglas. "What kind of a Pyromancer am I to have forgotten that!"

Marbleheart was bewildered by their elation. "Dangerous, isn't it? There is a mud volcano north of the Briney. It blew a lot of smelly steam and spewed out lots of boiling-hot goo. Nasty thing, I thought and still think."

"But if there are passages within *this* volcano," explained Cribblon, "we should be able to follow them to the outside and make our escape."

"That explains what the Bats meant, that there were ways to the outside," Marbleheart said with a quick nod of understanding. "Let's be on our way, then!"

They trotted along, following the rough-cut tunnel on a slightly upward trend. After five minutes they came to a great, domed room from which several vents led in different directions.

Marbleheart walked a dozen Otter paces into each, sniffing the air carefully. Of five, two smelled faintly of fresh air. He chose the larger, mostly because it tended upward at a right angle to the course of the Coventown vale.

"This way," he said, and the others followed. Marbleheart hesitated only once, glancing back down the way they had come. Sounds carried far in these enclosed spaces. He heard distant running steps and then frustrated curses.

"They've reached the gate," Douglas guessed. "They must not have the key to that one. That'll slow them down considerably."

"Plus," said Cribblon, beginning to pant a bit from their fast trot. "I gather they're all terrified of the mountain; the Fiery Furnace, as they call it."

"Be that as it may, we're all running out of steam in this heat," panted Douglas, pausing to wipe his face and neck with his handkerchief. "I'd better whip up a Levitation Spell to carry us out of here soon. It'll be a long, hard climb otherwise."

The tunnel shortly took a right-angle turn upward. The shaft had smoothly polished walls offering hardly any handholds. They could hear no sounds from behind except a whisper of hot air moving rapidly past them, up the chimney.

The Journeyman Wizard drew a wide circle on the cave floor with a piece of red chalk he plucked from his left sleeve.

At his command, they all sat down within the circle. Douglas replaced the chalk in his sleeve, produced his magic kit from the other sleeve, and mixed two quarter pinches of tiny white crystals and a drop of viscous amber liquid—it reminded Marbleheart of pancake syrup—on the smooth stone floor between them.

A cool blue flame consumed the mixture and its residue coalesced into a round pool of milky liquid. It spread under them, right to the circle's edge, where it suddenly congealed into a pearly, hard-surfaced disk.

Douglas spoke a short word of command, and the disk at once detached itself from the rock floor with a ripping sound and rose into the air, carrying them all upon it. Douglas directed its flight with hand signals.

"Elevator Spell," he explained.

"That's one I never learned from Frigeon," said Cribblon in admiration.

"Beats climbing the walls," said Marbleheart, grinning. As the other two discussed professional details of the spell, he watched the shaft roll down toward them and pass out of sight beneath the rising disk.

There were great clumps of pinkish crystal flowers growing from cracks in the shaft walls. As they passed one large bunch, the Otter stretched out his neck and sniffed at it. It smelled the same as the air and water of Coven. He wrinkled his nose in disgust.

Their flight lasted perhaps ten minutes, until Douglas estimated they were considerably higher than outside ground level, although perhaps not so high as the tallest tower of the castle. He stopped the pearly disk when they reached a promising horizontal tunnel leading off to the left. When they stepped off, the disk crumbled to powder and floated slowly up the shaft, sparkling like snow.

"Air's fresh," announced Marbleheart, greatly encouraged by the fact. "We must be near an outlet."

They emerged suddenly upon a rock ledge high on the Coventown canyon's north rim, surprised to see that night had already fallen. Douglas and Marbleheart had been inside the castle and its dungeon since just before noon.

"From here we'd better walk—or climb," said Marbleheart, not at all sorry to say it. "We'd be like a bandaged ear, flying over the canyon on another bit of milk glass."

"We'll stay here for tonight, rather," decided Douglas. "Too easy to miss our step without enough light for the way. And I want to see what happens next, if I can, in the castle. There's the other prisoner to consider, you recall."

"When Emaldar came to me after midnight," Cribblon told him, "she spoke of *another* Douglas Brightglade who had been captured."

"I suspected it was something like that," said Douglas, thoughtfully. "Someone else has taken a hand in the game, I can see. Who it is, I haven't the slightest idea. Unless it's Myrn? But I would sense her close presence, if it were, I believe. I know she is not far away, but not as close as the castle."

Finding a sheltering bit of overhang at the far end of their ledge, they crowded under. Douglas built a tiny but comfortably hot fire against the night's chill, and sent out to Wizards' High for supper—roast beef and mashed potatoes, savory brown gravy, and a greens salad, all downed with cups of Precious's best cider.

"It's been a long, long time since I ate this well," sighed Cribblon. "A mightily long time! Old Frigeon's housekeeper had trouble boiling water, let alone an egg! I often thought if Frigeon had had a decent cook, he might have turned out differently."

"He's luckier now. He has a very good cook in New Land," said Douglas, pausing with his fork half-raised. "His steward at Ice Palace, as it turns out. A frustrated chef. A couple of marvelous cooks taught him all about cooking, after the Fall."

Marbleheart ate until his tummy was a round, furry ball, then, excusing himself, curled happily about himself and fell asleep at once. Douglas and Cribblon talked Wizardry and nibbled at the remains of the meal until nearly midnight, and tried in vain to penetrate the spells that now surrounded the castle. Belatedly, Emaldar was taking precautions.

Then they, too, fell asleep.

■   ■   ■

Myrn, Willow, and Caspar dined on pinecones and fresh birch flowers—converted into roasted, spicy redfish and a crisp lettuce-and-pine nut salad. For dessert Myrn created a delicious mousse from the froth of a tiny waterfall nearby. Then the three gathered up their stout walking sticks and struck out once more on the trail of the Witchservers carrying Pargeot to Coventown.

"An hour since midnight," Myrn said wearily, "and perhaps we'd better try to get some rest."

"I can make it," said Caspar, puffing up a steeper-than-usual rise. "It would be nice if ye'd learned a Flying Spell, however."

Myrn stopped in her tracks and threw up her hands.

"What am I thinking of! Of course we can fly! What am I thinking of?"

She gathered them near her and, touching Finesgold's Feather Pin, spoke the words *"Cumulo Nimbus!"*

She spread her arms and led them into the air like a trio of gray doves.

"Beats walking," said Caspar, in unknowing imitation of Marbleheart. After a few jerky minutes getting the feel of flying, he and Willow settled down to enjoying the flight.

"By a pinelands mile!" enthused Willow. "Look sharp, mistress. I see the Witchservers ahead, crossing that ridge!"

"Keep 'em in sight," advised Caspar, "and fly as high as ye can without losing 'em. Men hardly ever look up, even when keeping the most careful watch."

"Those people are in a real hurry!" observed Myrn after a few minutes of trailing the Witchservers. They were close enough now to see Pargeot, who was being led on a heavy chain, not carted as Cribblon had been. "How long will it be before they reach Coventown, Willow, can you guess?"

"By all accounts," said the lad, trying a gentle up-and-down swoop for himself, "they're just now coming into Coventown Vale. See there, mistress? The valley runs between those two great ridges looking like a wolf's outspread claws!"

"We'll stay with them until they're in sight of Coventown itself," decided Myrn. "It may take a while to find Douglas after that. I don't think Emaldar will harm Pargeot until she realizes that he is not, after all, Douglas. He will be a mystery to her."

The flyers ranged back and forth so as not to get ahead of the slower-moving Witchserver band. Within two hours they first sighted the red gloaming and black smokes of Coven Castle and then the town beneath it.

"We'll look for my Douglas, now," cried Myrn in growing excitement. "Hang on, fellows!"

She increased their speed to that of a swift, darting forward through the stinking smokes, reciting a Finding Spell under her breath as she led the way.

Chapter Nineteen

The Six Sisters

EMALDAR, scowling impatiently from her sitting-room window on the path up the vale, spotted her Witchserver band when it came around a last curve.

She shouted orders for the captive to be brought at once to her apartment. The sight of the approaching band restored—more or less—her temper to merely bad. It had been particularly foul since she had been told that the first prisoner had somehow managed to blow the door off his cell and escape.

Perhaps, she thought, *the first one really is Brightglade, the Fire Wizard. It smells like Fire Magic to me.*

"No word, yet?" she snarled at the Warlock officer who entered just then.

"N-n-no, Most Graciously Gentle, Bounteously Beautiful Queen," he stammered, falling to his knees. "He . . . he . . . we think he escaped into the fiery heart of the mountain somehow. Those tunnels are . . . well . . . an endless maze, you might say."

"You've got plenty of men to follow him right into the Furnace, if need be," snarled the Witch. "See to it! Either *he* is Brightglade, or this new prisoner is. I want them both under lock, key, and Binding Spell until I discover which is which."

"Yes, O Great Black Witch, Queen of Dreadful Darkness!" whined the officer. He crawled on hands and knees backward, out the chamber door.

"Sisters!" called the Witch Queen. "Attend me! I require your expert assistance and advice. Now!"

The air before her chair warped, as if suddenly overheated, turned dark gray and coalesced into the figures of six black-clad women wearing peaked Witches' hats.

They all appeared elderly and much uglier than necessary, even for Witches—and thus posed no competition for Emaldar—being haggard, deeply lined, wrinkled, warted, and generally looking like death reheated. Which, in a sense, was what they wished to look like.

The other Witches of the Coven greeted Emaldar respectfully but with none of the groveling subservience of the Witchservers and the other Coven slaves.

Emaldar kept the six near her and content because at least five-sixths of her enhanced Witchly Powers were borrowed from them. They allowed her to tap them in exchange for luxurious castle living, no onerous duties required, a share of all loot taken, and frequent opportunities to watch innocents suffer horribly at the Coven's black rites.

"Stay by me now," invited the Witch Queen, after she made sure they understood all that had happened. "We must find out which prisoner is Douglas Brightglade and when we do, ensorcel him, so that his goody-goody Wizard Master and his friends cannot recover him or bother us. This is most important."

The oldest and ugliest of the Six Sisters sat in Emaldar's chair and whined, "I was sound asleep, Sister Witch! Need you call us at this hour? Dawn is no more than an hour away, I see."

"When I call, it's because I *need* you, Sister," said Emaldar, firmly but gently. "This is the sort of thing you promised to help me with."

"Oh, right! Sure," murmured all the Sisters, nodding. They found places to sit about the room.

"Where are the Warlocks?" the youngest Witch asked, leering about, nearsightedly. "Not much of a party without menfolk, is it?"

"This is *not* a party, Grayelder!" ground out Emaldar, striving to keep her temper.

The Warlock officer returned. He flinched at the sight of all seven Witches where he expected only one. Swallowing mightily, he announced that the new prisoner was without.

"Without what?" chortled Eldest Sister. "Without his trousers?"

"Now, Eldest," began Emaldar, but her admonition was cut off by the appearance of Pargeot, dusty, dead tired, and draped in heavy bronze chains.

"Comely youngster, that!" crooned Eldest Sister, leaning forward. "If you don't want him, Emaldar, when you're finished with his body, I'd like it for a while."

Emaldar ignored her comment and stood stock still, looking at Pargeot for a very long time, her eyes locked with those of the Westongue Captain. She quickly sat down on a stool, not breaking eye contact.

"I do *not* believe you are Douglas Brightglade," she said at last, with a slight sigh.

"I'm not," admitted Pargeot. "I'm a friend of his, however, and a Seafarer of some repute in the service of Thornwood Duke of Dukedom."

The gathered Sisters expected Emaldar to detonate in one of her famous furies, but she sat calmly studying the young man. "Your name? It isn't important, really. I'll destroy you shortly, anyway, but it's convenient to call you something other than 'prisoner.' "

"You are too kind," murmured Pargeot, and with a weary smile he gave his name and rank.

"I've always been partial to sailor boys," cackled Grayelder, rubbing her arthritic knees.

"We don't need comedy, Sister!" Emaldar snarled. "Our other prisoner is Douglas, obviously."

"Not necessarily," said Pargeot. "I don't know where the real Douglas is, but I don't think he's ever been anyone's prisoner."

His directness disconcerted the Witch Queen. It was a moment before she understood what he had said.

"Brightglade is free and somewhere about!"

"I imagine so," replied the Seacaptain. "Do you mind if I collapse on the floor? I've just walked the better part of a day and two nights at top speed, and I'm a bit pooped, as we sailors say."

"Sit," commanded Emaldar, surprising even herself. "Tell me who my first prisoner is—or was."

"I can't really say for sure," said Pargeot with an enormous sigh of relief as he sank to the floor. "I don't remember hearing his name. Some other friend of the Journeyman Wizard's, I should imagine."

With that his head fell forward on his chest and he began to snore softly.

"The silly little man is exhausted, I see," observed one of the Witches. "You won't get much more out of him tonight, dear Emaldar. A little excruciating pain, judiciously administered, later . . ."

"I need no more from him," agreed Emaldar. "Guards! Take him and drop him in the dungeon. Keep a *close* eye on him this time! He may not be a Wizard but he is strong, resourceful, and dangerous."

The Sisters turned to each other, exchanging bemused comments. Their murmurs reminded the Witch Queen of their presence and she frowned.

"I'm *most* sorry to have inconvenienced you, Sisters all. You may go about your own pleasures. I will call you if I need you again."

"Yes, do let us know before our pretty Coven is overthrown," sneered Eldest Sister. "We'd like to pick the bones of your Queendom, after you're done botching it."

Emaldar wasn't listening, it seemed, so the Six snuffed themselves out, leaving a smell like burned wool after them.

The Warlock officer looked up in fear as storm clouds gathered about the Witch's brow.

"I'll go myself to find the escaped Brightglade," she declared coldly, reaching for her black cloak and peaked hat. "You incompetents probably fear to go where he has fled!"

The first rays of the rising sun struck through the rank smog blanketing Coventown and its castle. The clear light showed how really worn and dirty the furnishings of the Queen's apartments were, the dusty taffeta and the badly scuffed velvet. But there was no one to see, except a large black tom sleepily licking his paws in the warming sun on a window seat.

But then, Coven was filled with cats, most of them black.

■   ■   ■

"Ho! Something's coming," whispered Marbleheart. "Make us invisible again!"

Douglas rolled out of his handkerchief-blanket, rubbing his eyes sleepily.

"Come on! Hurry!" urged the Otter. "They're circling around to get a whack at us and knock us off the mountain!"

With a gust of fresh wind in the blush of dawn Myrn Manstar landed lightly before them, her flying companions beside her. The narrow ledge was getting crowded.

"Douglas, my love!" she cried. "You certainly find the strangest places to camp!"

The two young people flung themselves into each other's arms and seemed to be calling each other's names over and over. Marbleheart turned to Cribblon.

"Now I get it! She's the sweet, innocent, plain-looking, stay-at-home fisherman's lass Douglas has been mooning over since I first met him."

"Highly likely," Cribblon said, grinning broadly. "Highly likely she is not some of those things, however."

"This is Marblehead, then, of whom you wrote?" asked Myrn. "How cuddly and cute!"

"Marble*heart*," retorted the Otter. "Heart! Heart! Have a heart, lady!"

"Now, children," chided Douglas, stifling his laughter. "Don't fight over me."

"You?" exclaimed Marbleheart with a puzzled frown. "Who are you? A bumbling, bumptious, second-rated rabbit puller from some Briney sand spit snake-bite-tonic show? You, however," he said to Myrn, "are pretty cute, too. You don't, mayhap, need an experienced Familiar, do you? I can start fires with the snap of a claw."

"You are much too familiar already," said Douglas. "Besides, I saw you first."

"Does that mean I am really your Familiar?" asked the Otter in surprise.

"Of course, fish chaser!"

"You never exactly said so! Does he treat you like this, Mistress?"

"Call me Myrn, darling," said the girl, bending to scratch behind the Otter's ears. Marbleheart purred like a kitten. "No, I must admit he's usually very thoughtful."

"Well, Myrn darling, if you can put up with him, I guess I can, too."

Cribblon was looking on, first amazed, then shocked, slowly realizing his new friends were teasing each other—and him. He burst out laughing so hard he almost rolled off the ledge. Caspar Marlin deftly snagged his gown tail and dragged him back onto the ledge.

"Let's get off this frightful mountain," said Myrn, "before someone does fall off by accident. And I must hear your tale! We've had some adventures, too."

The three escapees joined hands with the three fliers and, avoiding a line of sight from Coventown circled far up the vale, and then down to Douglas's cave. By the time they arrived, each party knew what the other had been up to. Douglas was surprised about Pargeot's willing surrender to the Witchservers, commenting that the sailor must not have known what they were like.

Myrn set about exploring the cave hideout while Douglas called for breakfast for them all.

"There is a sort of uneasy feeling here," Myrn commented as they finished. "Don't you feel it, Douglas?"

"Yes," said Douglas, pausing to listen. "I felt it even more strongly in the dungeons and in the caverns under Blueye. It's . . . sort of . . . a tension, a trembling. Do you think it's Witchcraft? Is Emaldar aware of us?"

"No . . . ," said the Apprentice Aquamancer, hesitantly. "It seems to be in the air and in the ground, also. Something is about to happen, I think, but I don't know what."

"Blueye is, remember, volcanic," said Willow. The party exchanged uneasy glances. "It trembles often."

"It can't make any difference," decided Douglas. "We still have to rescue Captain Pargeot from the Witch and see what can be done about the Coven. And very soon!"

"None of us has had enough sleep," said Myrn.

"We'll have some more coffee. It'll help us stay on our feet and on our toes," Douglas agreed, yawning mightily. "Well, you know what I mean. Now that we know a way in and out of the Coven's castle, we can rescue Pargeot at least."

"Let's get that hussy Witch Queen, too," urged Myrn with surprising ferocity.

"We should try to capture her, if at all possible," admonished Douglas. The question of actually *destroying* the Black Witch hung between the two Wizards, Apprentice and Journeyman, for a long moment.

"If possible," Myrn agreed at last, nodding. "From all I hear, Emaldar is a real . . ."

"That she is, I can attest!" exclaimed Cribblon. "Whatever word you thought to use would not be strong enough, mistress."

"Call me Myrn, please," said the young lady. "You're saying, my Douglas, that we should shove off at once?"

"Finish your coffee, sweet bird of Waterand," Douglas said, half teasing. "I think I'd like to take a quick bath, after all that slithering around in dusty tunnels and sulfurous shafts. We'll leave in an hour, folks. Be ready!"

Breakfast, bathing, shaving, and some attention to hard-used clothing—Myrn wielded a quick, clever needle on Willow's trousers and Douglas's shirt—and they were ready to go.

"We'll split up. Smaller groups will be harder to spot if any of the Coven take it into their heads to be watchful," decided the Journeyman. "Myrn, Willow, and I will go after Pargeot. The Bats will know where he is in Emaldar's dungeon. Cribblon, you know the Spell of Invisibility now. Lead the rest unseen into Coventown. Watch Emaldar's movements as closely as you can. We'll join you here as soon as we get Pargeot out. When we can catch The Witch alone, we'll pounce. Any questions?"

"I've a change to suggest," said Myrn. "I don't think I should be one of Pargeot's rescuers."

Douglas looked at her for a moment, then nodded. "There's a reason for your words I don't quite understand, sweetheart. Should I know it?"

"Take her word," advised Caspar. "Pargeot's already much too smitten with Myrn for her comfort and his well-being, too. If she rescues him from a deep, wet durance—"

"You see, my dear," said Myrn, "Pargeot thinks he must

make amends by serving me for his lost crew and ship and putting you in danger at Sea. That's why he sacrificed himself to the Witchservers. He hoped they'd bring him here, and that I would follow."

"I suppose I understand that. I can understand a man being smitten with you, Mistress Manstar. Wasn't I bitten that way long since?"

"You are one of World's most sensible, sweet, caring, understanding, forbearing . . . ," said Myrn with a bright blush. "Pargeot is a very good, brave man, but he has this weird streak of romance that makes him a danger to himself—and to us all."

"Let's go before it gets too sticky in here to fly," growled Marbleheart, winking at Caspar and Willow.

"Right, then!" agreed Douglas. "It's me and Caspar and my faithful Familiar to the rescue! Myrn, you take Cribblon and Willow into town. If we need it, you can create a diversion for us."

"Hand in hand, then," cried Myrn to her team after the invisibility spell had been re-cast. "*Cumulo Nimbus!*"

The Feather Pin worked instantly, and her invisible flight left the cave mouth, circled a moment, then flew off toward Coventown's gate. Douglas led his own assistants to the ledge, where they spied on Emaldar. They watched while Myrn, Willow, and Cribblon landed just outside the gate.

Then he carefully crafted Flarman's Levitation Spell and his team followed, flying directly to the ledge.

"Quietly, now," said Myrn, leading the way up into the town. "Back out of the road! Look who comes!"

Six old women dressed entirely in black, each carrying a well-worn broom in one hand and a dusty, black leather suitcase in the other, approached, heading down to the gate.

"Witches!" whispered Myrn. "Here, duck into this doorway. They might pierce our invisibility if they look our way!"

The six Coven Sisters bustled past. One or two glanced about, as if they sensed a strange spell nearby, but Eldest Sister impatiently waved them on.

"Why cannot we fly now?" whined Grayelder, the youngest.

"My poor feet aren't made for walking, you know."

"Fool of a Beldam," snapped Eldest Sister, swinging at her with her broom. She missed by a wide margin when the other ducked away. "Fly here and Emaldar'll know at once we're leaving her, for sure. Hurry up! If I read the signs a-right, Sisters, there are at least six powerful Wizards arrayed against us, and Emaldar's gone off her nut right amidst it all! I don't like those odds!"

They disappeared down the path toward distant Pfantas, bickering loudly among themselves but moving fast.

"Now, that's interesting," whispered Cribblon. "Deserting Emaldar, are they? I wonder why . . ."

"Six powerful Wizards, I heard," said Willow, mentally counting on his fingers. "I only think of three."

"Bad news tends to exaggerate itself," replied Myrn. "Here we go again. Ooops!"

The ground shook, as if an explosion had been set off deep underground. Stones fell from poorly mortared walls nearby and heavy cobbles heaved themselves out of the street beneath their feet.

"Come on!" cried Myrn. "Time would seem to be getting even shorter than we thought!"

"No need to panic, perhaps," said Cribblon. "Tremors like that can go on for days or months and die away to nothing, I've heard."

They walked up the middle of the steep and winding street, avoiding the walls of rickety buildings on either hand, in case any more stones worked their way loose. The town that had appeared deserted when they entered now began to fill with frightened residents. They stood staring in fear up at the castle.

Douglas, Marbleheart, and Caspar wafted down the shaft, much more quickly than they had escaped up it, and arrived at the bottom in a very few minutes.

"Down this way," said Marbleheart, taking the lead once Douglas had spelled his headlight on. Douglas followed, then Caspar, who looked about in great interest but with secret misgivings, keeping his hand close to his cutlass's hilt, just in case. A man of the open air, he was unused to being hemmed in by hot, quivering stone.

The Bat family slept hanging by their feet from the dungeon ceiling, swaying gently to and fro with each tremor from within Blueye. At the other end of the passage Douglas saw a bright light and heard a murmur of uneasy conversation.

As Douglas paused to awaken Tuckett, Marbleheart slipped silently toward the edge of the guards' light.

"Yes, yes," muttered Tuckett, shaking off his daytime sleep. "Oh, Wizard Douglas Brightglade! I thought you'd be coming along, seeing as how the Witch has put another poor victim in her awful wet cell."

"He's there, then?" asked Douglas softly, for sounds carried far in the rock corridor. "Heavily guarded, it seems."

"Twelve Witchservers under a Warlock officer," said Mistress Bat, also awakened. Her Batlings stirred but kept silent.

Marbleheart, returning just then, confirmed the Bat's report. "I can't see who's in the cell, but whoever it is is thrashing about in chest-deep water and actually singing some sad sailor's lament. Something about 'Sweet Fanny Adams' or some such."

"That'll be Pargeot, all right," chuckled Caspar. "That song is one Westongue sailors sing when they want to feel sorry for themselves."

"Sing it for me, sometime," snorted the Otter. "But now, what's to do, Fire Wizard?"

"We need a few moments to snatch Pargeot. How to get rid of the guards? If they're sensible, a distraction wouldn't draw all of them off, I think. Has Emaldar been down?" he asked Tuckett.

"Yes, an hour or more since. She yelled at the prisoner, then screamed at the guards, and left the Warlock behind to keep them alert. She went off in the other direction, letting herself through the grille at the far end, there," Tuckett answered. "By my ears I could tell she went deeper into the mountain than you, however. Very angry and looking for you, Master Cribblon, I would guess."

"I would so guess, also," agreed the Journeyman Wizard, thoughtfully. "We didn't meet her coming in, so she must have taken one of the other passageways back into the mountain, there."

"Shall we follow her?" asked Caspar, gripping his cutlass.

"No, Pargeot comes first," declared Douglas. "There's a Sleeping Spell I could cast over them. Trouble is, it loses full effect if used on more than a half dozen people at a time."

"Only Emaldar could call them away," said Mistress Bat.

"There's that," said Douglas with a pleased nod. "All right! Everybody but the Bats, up the stair a short way."

When the Otter and the captain had retreated out of sight up the staircase, the young Wizard stood in the deepest shadow he could find, quietly cleared his throat twice, and called aloud . . . in a strident woman's voice, hoping it sounded a bit like Emaldar's.

"To me! To me! Leave half your number, Warlock, and bring the rest this way—straight into the mountain! Hurry, you lazy layabouts!"

Douglas hoped the echoes and mufflings of the stony passages would serve to cover the deception. That, and the habit of instant, unthinking obedience he had noticed in the Witchservers.

Heavily armed and wild-eyed, a squad of soldiers pounded by the invisible Wizard and the hanging Bats, past the stairwell, and through the open grating at the far end.

Caspar and Marbleheart came back down the stairs.

"Never hesitated one second!" said Caspar, shaking his head. "She has them trained, I'd say."

"What we do now is nip in, put the rest of them to sleep, fish Pargeot out of his hole, and run back the way we came, exactly," ordered Douglas.

He sent his Sleep Spell before them and when they arrived at the end of the corridor, the guards were all soundly asleep, snoring and mumbling, lying on wooden benches. The floor was covered with almost a foot of dirty water.

"Pargeot, it's Douglas!" called the Journeyman Wizard at the door grating. The door he had splintered the night before had already been replaced by a new, tougher panel.

There was no response. Putting his ear to the door, Douglas listened.

"Someone is in there," he said. "And whoever it is, is snoring with the worst of these."

"Of course," said Caspar, vastly amused. "Your own spell . . ."

"This should help him awaken," cried Douglas, and he again sent a terrific jolt of electric fire against the new door's lock, enough to shatter the mechanism and swing the heavy door open on its hinges.

"Hey, Pargeot!" he shouted. "Wake up, man."

"Let me," said Caspar, squeezing past Douglas in the doorway. He cupped his hands to form a megaphone and yelled at the top of his voice, which was considerable, thanks to years of shouting orders above the sounds of storms and sails.

"All hands on deck! All hands on deck! Man your battle stations! Captain Pargeot to the quarterdeck!"

The dimly seen Pargeot, propped up to sleep against the far wall, sprang immediately to his feet, fully awake. He plowed across the cell, creating a respectable bow wave by his passage, and leaped up the three steps to the doorway, almost bowling Caspar over.

"Now, now!" soothed Douglas remembering to dispel the invisibility charm. "It's Douglas Brightglade and Caspar Marlin and this is my friend, Marbleheart Sea Otter."

Pargeot shook his head to clear the last of sleep and scrubbed his eyes with battered knuckles.

"What's to do?" he asked at once.

"Run!" cried Marbleheart. "This way!"

He swam off down the corridor, pausing under the Bat family to say, "You Bats had better evacuate. No telling what might happen next."

"We're on our way, although it's middle of day outside," said Tuckett. "The whole mountain trembles. It bodes no good, I fear. Up and away, Missus! Come, girls, lad! Follow Mama and me!"

Marbleheart led his own companions past the stairway, through the open grille, and on into the passage.

They paused a moment in the domed room with the five exits, listening for sounds from the fiery interior of Blueye. Shouts and the scrambling of boots. Faintly came a woman's voice, raised in shrill fury.

"Time to go," said the Otter, urgently. They followed him once more to the spot where the passage became a shaft.

"Go to the ledge, above," said Douglas to the others. "You'll be out of harm's way, there. I'm going after the Witch!"

"I don't . . . ," began Marbleheart, but his feet were scrabbling in thin air. He, Caspar, and an amazed Pargeot shot up the shaft.

" . . . want to fly without you around!" came the Otter's voice, fading into the distance.

Douglas returned to the domed chamber, arriving just as a band of Witchservers followed their panic stricken Warlock out of one of the other passageways, on their way back to the dungeon proper. They didn't notice Douglas as they passed.

Douglas followed them as far as the grille, closed and relocked it after them, using a minor Freezing Spell to jam the lock mechanism, in case the officer had a key.

Then he dusted his hands together and walked calmly into the heart of the volcano.

On Waterand Flarman leafed through a thick, gilt-edged book chained to a heavy marble stand in Augurian's tower workroom. He felt something rub against his calf and looked down.

"Back so soon, Black Flame? How goes the Journeyman's journeying?"

The big, very black tom sat down, curled his tail around himself, licked his nose, and grinned at his Master. He swished his magnificent tail twice and blinked thrice, slowly, glancing to the right.

"Augurian!" called Flarman, closing the huge book with a bang. "Augurian?"

"I am here, Fire-eater," said the Water Adept, coming in from the next room. He was holding two glass vials of smoky liquid, which he had been pouring back and forth to mix. "What is it?"

"Black Flame says Douglas's adventure is drawing to a climax. Do you wish to be in at the end of it all? Purely as observers, of course."

"I could use a break," sighed the Aquamancer.

"Right as rain! I'll just toss a couple of singlets and a change of drawers in my kit and meet you in fifteen minutes on the west battlements."

"Give me a few minutes more," said Augurian. "I'll have to leave some orders for my absence."

"Oh, the place will run very well without you while we're gone," scoffed Flarman Flowerstalk cheerfully, but the Water Adept had already disappeared down the stair.

Myrn, Cribblon, and Willow stood unseen near the front gate of Coven Castle for almost an hour when a flock of blue-and-white ducks landed with a splash in the castle's green-scummed moat. A large and brilliantly colorful teal mallard swam to the near bank and, picking his way through the trash on the margin along the bank, waddled past them, pretending to peck at some imaginary bit of food between the cobbles. From the side he regarded Myrn with a steady, round eye.

"You'd be the Water Adept's Apprentice?" he asked in a low quack.

"I am Myrn Manstar, Apprentice to Augurian of Waterand," Myrn replied.

"Stopped to have a word with a couple of sailors and a Sea Otter perched on a ledge up there," said the Drake, as if it were an everyday occurrence. "They say they are safe out of the Witch's dungeon, and to tell you not to worry."

"Just two sailors and an Otter?" asked Myrn, a worried frown clouding her pretty face.

"Only the three of them. That's all, mistress."

"Where is Douglas?" she wondered aloud. "But thank you for the message, Sir Drake . . ."

"Just call me Francis," said the bird, turning to rejoin his flock in the moat. "We're on our way north but we'll visit Waterand next winter, for sure. Nice place, I understand, to spend a winter vacation. Come, ladies, let's get out of this sickly mess of a moat. How can anyone let water become so fouled?"

And they were off in a sudden flurry, not attracting any attention at all. Before they turned to fly over the nearest ridge, Francis returned for a last word.

"I thought you ought to know," he said hurriedly. "Blueye

Lake boils and fumes threateningly, up there at the top!" And he was off.

"Now what do you make of that?" Myrn asked the others.

"What would make a tarn boil and fume but the fire beneath?" echoed Willow. "But, then, Blueye often acts that way."

Cribblon looked rather worried, too. "Blueye is a volcano."

"Go on."

"I climbed all over this mountain when I was spying on Coven. She's been dormant for centuries, but she is by no means dead! There are steam vents and gas fumaroles all over her. I suspect this castle is built over some of them. Hence the foul-smelling smokes all about it."

"Ah, I see," said Myrn, remembering past lessons. "The ducks believe Blueye is about to erupt!"

"I would guess rather sooner than later," said Willow. "Birds and small animals seem to know well in advance of Men."

"And we're right on—*and in*—her at a very bad time!" Myrn gasped.

They all craned their necks to gaze up at the truncated peak of Blueye Mountain. Did they see a plume of steam rising, or was it only a rain cloud clinging there? In answer, the ground heaved under their feet.

"We can't take the chance," said Myrn, decisively. "Cribblon, we'll fly up and take Pargeot, Marbleheart, and Caspar off to safety—as far away from the mountain as we can get! Willow, I'm going to make you visible. Run all over Coventown. Spread the warning! Create panic if you must! Tell everyone to run for their lives, that the volcano is about to erupt!"

"Will they listen to me?" the boy wondered.

"There'll be plenty of evidence to back you up. The earth is starting to quake and the mountain to roar. Start as many off as will listen, but don't hang about waiting for those who won't. Don't wait! Run with them, down to the pinelands!"

Cribblon said, "I can speak Flarman's Levitation Spell, having heard Douglas use it. You must find him!"

"I'm going in to help Douglas then," she agreed quickly.

Cribblon shot into the air without further ado. The first really strong tremors shook the ground. The lines of slaves carrying sacks of potatoes into the castle stopped dead in their tracks and dropped their burdens. With their Witchserver guards they stood frozen in fear, peering upward.

Willow, suddenly visible, stumbled on the first heave of the ground, dodged a stone that fell from the battlements above, and began to scream at the top of his considerable voice.

"Earthquake! Earthquake! The mountain is falling on us! Everybody run! Run! Run!"

The slaves and the guards in the foregate square immediately picked up the fearsome cry and took to their heels. A Witchserver guard at the gate, pelted with sharp chunks of granite fallen from the walls, let out a short, terrified scream and fell to the ground unconscious.

The nearby streets of Coventown immediately filled with scrambling and screaming slaves, shaken from their lethargy by a fear greater than they felt for Emaldar and her Coven.

Following the shouting ragamuffin they headed as one for the town gate and the path down the vale, away from the mountain.

"Best I can do for them," decided Myrn. "Now, Douglas, where are you?"

She ran through the unguarded castle gate into the courtyard, dodging falling blocks of stone as she went. A stone-colored Griffin shrieked at her and flapped its heavy wings, but the building to which it clung slumped wearily into the courtyard with an awesome grumble and groan and a great cloud of acrid dust. The Griffin screamed once more as it disappeared into the rubble.

Seeing the fate of their fellow Watch Worm, the other Gargoyles and Stone Demons abandoned their dangerous perches. Some flew, others dropped to the ground and fled from the courtyard on awkward, clawed feet.

Myrn muttered an Umbrella Spell as she ran, and hoped it would work. She paid no further attention to rolling and flying stones, hurtling beams of oak and sheets of gray slate that slid from the roofs with a slithering shriek to smash into wickedly flying shrapnel on the cobbles.

She stopped coolly to look about for a path to follow. Where the castle workshop had collapsed she spotted an arched entrance into the rock of the cliff itself, exposed by the complete disintegration of the structure.

"Looks promising," she said to herself and, whispering the Power Words to the Feather Pin, she flew swiftly to the opening and through it, into a blackness filled with choking dust and ear splitting roaring.

The air rushing out at her almost slammed her to the ground but she righted herself and flew on, more slowly now to keep from braining herself on the uneven ceiling.

Now the Feather Pin's added virtue—guiding its owner underground—helped her along. Where there was a choice of passageways, she unerringly chose the best, and flew on without slowing. The heat of the air and the walls on either side was intense. The rumbling from inside the mountain grew louder by the minute.

"Douglas?" she called, but the twisting and breaking of solid stone drowned out her small voice, even in her own ears.

The first strong movement of the earth beneath him startled Douglas. He fell to his knees and stayed there until the quake subsided. It seemed like an hour, but was only a scant minute.

When he stood again, he was hit by a fiery blast of air from ahead. The Witch Queen had gone this way, searching for her escaped prisoner.

Rising, he walked steadily forward, entering another, low-ceilinged cavern. As he stepped out onto its floor it jerked wildly sideways and split across its middle, just in front of him.

The sudden chasm filled quickly with eye-searing molten rock, popping and bubbling up like white-hot oatmeal. The heat was unbearable. His eyebrows sizzled and his gown smoldered.

"Need a spell," he gasped, falling back into the relative safety of the tunnel behind him. "Which one?"

He settled for a standard Fireproofing Spell, one of the earliest he had learned at Flarman's knee.

"People who deal with fire must protect themselves from it, for it can turn savage when aroused," the Fire Wizard had warned. "We Pyromancers command fire, but first you have to get its attention, and that isn't always easy, my boy!"

With the coolness of the spell wrapped about him like a cloak, Douglas stepped again into the room before him. He thought of turning back but, Witch or not, Emaldar was somewhere within this quaking, fiery mountain. She would need help to escape.

Or she might prove powerful enough to use the quakes to cover her escape.

He leaped carefully across the wide crack. The lava was no longer boiling, cooling rapidly on contact with the air. Beyond, he paused to decide which way to go.

Far ahead he heard a sudden shriek of alarm; a woman's voice. Emaldar no longer screaming in fury but in fear. Emaldar had at last realized that there were things other than an escaped victim to concern her.

"Emaldar!" shouted Douglas, magnifying his voice as loud as he could. "Stay where you are! I'm coming to help you get out of here!"

And I am, he realized as he dashed forward. *Doesn't a wicked Witch deserve to die in her own caldron?*

"No," he said aloud. "I'll help her . . . if I can."

The passageway twisted and turned but ran on, fairly level, except for blocks of stone shaken from the walls and ripped from overhead by the force of another series of tremendous shocks. The heat increased, but Douglas's spell held.

Then there were no more quakes, but a continuous, rolling rumble and a mighty, brain-rattling groan as rock moved against rock along ancient faults, slowly but inexorably at first, then in violent jerks. The mountain shivered as if it were cold, and cried out in a sort of insane fear of its own.

"Emaldar! Hang on!" shouted Douglas, dodging a rain of half-molten boulders from above. "I'm almost there."

A faint cry came from behind him. "Don't give your life for Emaldar, my love! She deserves to die!"

Myrn!

"I have to try," shouted Douglas, plunging through a screen of hot steam.

Then he saw the Witch.

That she was Emaldar, the Black Witch of Coven, the Beautiful Queen of Witches, he never doubted. Her cloak was aflame from the heat of a rapidly advancing wall of white-hot lava beyond her, and as he watched, her tall, black hat was swept from her smoking hair and whipped into the approaching molten river of stone. It simply exploded like a firecracker, sending its large metal buckle flying to embed itself in the wall beside Douglas's head.

And between the Witch and the Wizard had opened a much wider crack. It plunged down, down as far as the eye could see, and at its bottom was a molten lake. Falling into its abyss were chunks of the mountain as large as Emaldar's whole castle!

Without conscious thought the Journeyman Wizard turned to the relatively cool stone wall beside the passage from which he had just emerged. He made a scooping and hurling gesture with both hands and muttered a chain of powerful words.

As if a giant hand had plucked it out of the cavern wall, a great mass of solid, unmelted stone hurled itself into the abyss, half filling it with debris. The mountain roared in fury but before it could tear away the cooler stone, Douglas flung a second and a third handful after the first.

The last filled the burning abyss to the level of the floor on which he—and Emaldar—stood.

"Come this way!" he shouted. "Hurry, Emaldar!"

She couldn't see or hear! He dashed across the bridge he had made, protected by the Fireproofing Spell from the blast-furnace heat of the volcano's interior. Reaching her side, he flung part of his spell about her, quenching the flames that were about to destroy her beautiful face.

Grasping her firmly, he shouted in her ear to follow him back across the temporary bridge, but she shook her head.

"I cannot see!" she screamed in agony. "I am blinded!"

"Come, anyway," insisted Douglas. He set their feet on the bridge just as the whole chasm filled with an intense and gleeful flash—the volcano sensing victory.

"Oh, no you don't," cried the Wizard. "I am a Pyromancer and you must serve me! Down, down and back to your place, Mountain Fire!"

He added a few choice, desperate magical words of the strongest sort he knew, and for a brief moment the fire halted and retreated into the abyss as if in startled dismay. No one told Fire what to do, and yet . . .

In that moment promising safety for them both, the Witch Emaldar wrenched herself free of Douglas's grasp and dashed ahead of him onto the crumbling bridge.

Out of the Journeyman's protecting spell, she screamed with her last breath, burst entirely into flame, and turned to black ash, which was swept away by the volcano's blasts of burning gases into the abyss, gone forever!

PART THREE

Coven Destroyed

Chapter Twenty

The Eruption of Blueye!

MYRN, moving in a cloud of steam from her own spell of protection, would have missed her way had she not heard his dismayed shout. Turning swiftly toward the sound, she dashed down the wildly tossing tunnel, calling his name aloud. She stopped only in time to avoid crashing into Douglas, who had sprung from his temporary bridge before it collapsed, its thunder drowned in the greater shriek of the mountain in agony.

"Come! I know the way," Myrn screamed at the top of her voice, clutching Douglas's arm.

"She's gone! Dead!" cried Douglas into a sudden and frightening silence.

"You're burned! You can't do more than you have," said Myrn, holding him tightly in her own arms, letting her protective magic flow over them both as Douglas's spell threatened to weaken. "Let's get out of here, Douglas!"

"Which way?" asked Douglas, regaining his common senses. "The way I came is blocked."

"Follow me," said Myrn firmly, pulling him along by the hand. "The Feather Pin will lead us out."

Twist and turn, climb up and slide down, the pin would not let them take a wrong step. The two Wizards trotted as fast as the rolling, bucking floor allowed them to go. Behind them, the mountain renewed its self-destructive fury, but they managed to outrush the swelling inferno until, at last, they caught a breath of intensely cold outside air.

They burst from a crack in the mountain wall onto a broad, flat shoulder of rock overlooking the entire Coven Vale.

"Take a breather," panted Douglas, either a command or a request, or both. "The Witch is burned. I tried to save her, but she ran away from me!"

"Let me take a look at your hurts," said Myrn. But first she kissed him. Their lips were badly scorched, blistered, and in great pain, but neither minded at all.

With the Water Adept's assistance he stripped the burned and smoldering tatters of his clothing from his shaking, pain-wracked body. The cold air of the mountaintop burned like new flame, making him cry aloud for a moment. His Wizard's gown was a total loss, but his inner clothing was unburned and had protected his skin. It steamed with his body's escaping moisture in the cold air.

Myrn made a rapid pass with her hands. A cool, sweet shower fell from the sky, quenching the last of the fires in their clothing and hair, moistening their lips and eyes. Douglas moaned in relief, but arched in renewed pain as his poor body realized it was terribly hurt.

"I've got to get us off this mountain," cried Myrn. "Oh, if I only had one good healing spell! Can you remember one?"

Douglas, clear headed despite his burns, held up his hand.

"Wait a minute. I think . . ."

Remembering, he reached for the sodden ruin of his gown and found what was left of the left sleeve. Fumbling within its depths, he produced a tiny swirl of green leaves.

"A four-leafed clover!" cried Myrn, clapping her hands. "How marvelous! Just what we need!"

Douglas, drained by the effort, slumped to the hard ground. The sound of his breathing grew ragged and rapid.

"Hurry, or you'll lose him!" Myrn cried to herself.

She fell at once to massaging gently the Journeyman's ravaged face and neck, then his arms and feet and above his heart with the tiny but powerful plant. He cried out, then groaned and tried to pull away, but Myrn held him tightly with one arm, continuing to apply the healing herb.

Finally, the young man on the ground heaved a tremulous sigh and relaxed, appearing to fall into a deep slumber, breathing steadily and easily.

Myrn then touched the clover to her own eyebrows and other crisped parts of her body, hands, ears, and ankles. She finished and looked carefully at her fiancé to see if she had missed any burns.

They were all completely healed and disappeared without scars. Douglas awakened with a start and reached out for her.

"Let me have the clover. I'll treat you," he said, in a strong although hoarse voice.

"I'm fine," said Myrn, holding out her arms to show him. "You got the worst of it."

"I'm afraid the worst is yet to come," coughed Douglas. The mountain was now swaying like a flagpole in a hurricane, threatening to shake them off their high perch. "Let's fly for Pfantas. We'll be safe there."

Myrn nodded and, taking Douglas firmly by one hand, she whispered the Feather Pin's Power Words once more. They rocketed into the air just as the whole mountain peak beneath them gave a tremendous lurch and slid into Coven Vale, falling in slow motion to block the course of the stream above the town itself.

Above it all they then heard a high, earsplitting shriek, as if Blue Teakettle were boiling over, magnified a thousand times.

"The lake," gasped Myrn, glancing back. "Its rim has burst!"

The boiling waters of the crater lake cascaded down the volcano's side, exploding into live steam as it overtook streams of molten rock from side fissures.

"Come on!" shouted Douglas, tugging at her sleeve.

"But it will destroy the road below Coventown," said Myrn. "All those people fleeing down the mountainside before it. . . ."

She stopped still in midair, screaming a spell at the top of her voice. At first the rushing, falling, boiling waters of Blueye Lake didn't seem to hear. Then suddenly they seemed to back up and turned in their course, flowing as swiftly to the north as it had a moment before flowed toward Coven Vale.

A great rift opened and the lake waters plunged into the new chasm. The sides of the rift directed a jet of superhot steam straight upward—a thousand feet, two thousand, a mile or more, where it cooled rapidly and began to rain down as a fine, still-warm mist, washing dust and mud before it.

Luckily, the mud flowed infinitely slower than the waters had. By the time the great avalanche had reached Coventown and its castle, the refugees had topped a far ridge and reached relative safety. Myrn's magic had done the trick.

Douglas and Myrn watched in horrified fascination as the steaming mud flow delivered a tremendous blow to the yards-thick castle walls, and carried them away as if they were made of sand. The tallest tower toppled into the vale, the sound of its collapse lost in the overall din.

"Will it quiet down now?" asked Myrn, smiling tremulously at Douglas. "The mountain has spent its pressure for the while, I hope."

"No way to tell. Let's get to safety," said Douglas. He allowed himself to be carried swiftly through the air, heading east and a bit south, toward Pfantas.

The ground below them jumped and twisted as lesser earthquakes spread from an epicenter within the mountain.

The feeling of dire tension and pressure was finally lessening and they flew on through warm rain toward the darkened horizon. At last they passed over untouched forests and sighted Pfantas's steep cone ahead.

Douglas pointed to the hillside clearing he and the Sea Otter had selected as a campsite when they first came to Pfantas. As they touched down on the bit of smooth, green lawn he had planted—it seemed a great, long time before—there came an unimaginably loud explosion from Blueye.

Treetops above them were whipped in demonic fury by gusts of gale winds. Looking back, they saw a rocketing, spreading plume of black and red smoke, coruscated with white-hot flashes of lightning.

"She blows!" shouted Douglas above the infernal racket. He swept Myrn into his arms and they clung together, watching in awe as the cloud rose and rose, higher and higher, straight up into the clear afternoon air.

At last it slowed and began to spread westward with the high-level Sea winds from the east. In the wake of the streaming cloud, back-lit by the lowering sun in the west, torrential rain fell on the barren Emptylands beyond the Tiger's Teeth.

"Well, it may do the least damage in that direction, I guess," said Myrn, expertly calculating wind, altitude, and direction. "The watershed in that direction slopes toward Emptylands and the Great Steppes, according to Augurian's old maps."

"Always the Aquamancer," said Douglas in mock surprise. "Water, water, everywhere!"

"As for me," snorted the pearl fisher's daughter, "I've had my fill of fire for today—and tomorrow and tomorrow, also."

"But not of Fire Wizards," said Douglas, "I hope."

"Of course not!" She grinned at her betrothed.

The pair walked hand in hand to the very top of their hill to view the scene of destruction.

Where the rising badlands beyond the pine forests had been was now a vast steaming, barren, bleached plain. Of the mountain itself nothing remained but a low, smoldering, still-quivering stump. In the far distance, several other mountains spouted flames and gases, hurling vast chunks of glowing rock into the air, higher than the strongest birds could fly.

"What of the others?" asked Myrn. "Did they get out in time?"

"I don't know," answered her husband-to-be. "If they are far back there, there is little anyone can do for them. But if they had time . . ."

They flew back along the road to Coven as far as the edge of the pinelands, looking for survivors. There came at last a shout and, dipping down in that direction, they found a crowd of people, led by a tattered young man with a tall staff bearing a makeshift pennant of white and red.

"There's Willow!" cried Myrn, "and the Coventown people, I think. If Cribblon reached Pargeot, Marbleheart, and Caspar in time, and I'm almost sure he did, they'll be waiting for us in Pfantas!"

They hailed young Willow, who left his exhausted band of ex-slaves to rest on soft, fragrant pine needles under the restlessly tossing conifers, and came to meet them. They embraced each other and all three cried tears of relief and joy to find each other safe once more.

"I've no idea," began the boy, wiping his nose on his sleeve. "I think most of 'em left when I called to them to get out."

"I'm sure some poor people got caught in the steam and the mud," said Douglas, soberly. "It was so awfully quick."

"Set your people to camp in the hills by that stream there. There's good water in the creek and shelter under the trees. We'll send them food and clothing from town," said Myrn.

"If there are enough handkerchiefs among them, I can make them into tents," said Douglas.

"And Wong Tscha San will help, I'm sure. You haven't met him, but he is a much more powerful Wizard than are either of us, yet," said the Apprentice Water Adept.

They said farewell to Willow and flew as swiftly as the pin could take them—which, as Finesgold had said, was really fast!—across the pinelands, over the creek with its two-plank bridge, and to the back gate of Pfantas, landing on Main Level.

Crowds of citizens who had been watching the eruption of Blueye and the destruction of Coven in mixed horror and gratification rushed to greet them and get the latest news.

At Pfantas Inn they were greeted with immense relief by Caspar, Pargeot, Marbleheart, all looking none the worse for their escape from the volcano, Cribblon and Wong.

Said he, pulling a comic face, "I stayed behind and enjoyed this pleasant village on its hill as much as the fireworks you provided. Most fitting!"

"You mustn't believe him," said Featherstone. "He has worked very hard to help us!"

"It was the least I could do, after the kind hospitality you have shown me," said the Choinese gentleman. "Besides, it has been so long since I worked my little spells, I vastly enjoyed it. Mostly, we planted flower beds and arbors of new trees."

"When the eruptions began, he told us we would have victims to feed and injured to heal, so we've set up hospitals and kitchens," added Featherstone.

Pargeot greeted Myrn a bit sheepishly.

"I could think of no other way to help you than to give myself up to the Witchservers," he confessed.

"Dear Pargeot!" Myrn laughed fondly. "Do you realize that if you had not, I might have taken two or three days to annul Emaldar's hex? The mountain would have blown up long before I got there and hundreds would have died horribly, including Douglas, Cribblon, and Marbleheart."

"I . . . I really hadn't thought of it that way," admitted the Seacaptain. "I thought I might have made a perfect ass of myself."

"Well," chuckled Myrn, "nobody's perfect."

"The Witch? The Coven?" asked Pargeot, blushing red at her teasing.

"Emaldar's dead, burned in the fires of Blueye, I'm afraid," said Douglas. "We tried to save her, but—"

"*Douglas* tried to save her. I arrived after she was gone, but just in time to save *him*," Myrn insisted, and the whole story had to be told right then and there, with as many Pfantasians listening as could crowd into the inn's common room or lean in at its open windows.

"This day we've seen mindless and inhuman power beyond our wildest imaginings," said Wong, nodding to the crowd and especially to Douglas and Myrn, "and also goodness and courage so completely unreserved that it fills me with wonder to remember it."

The onlookers shouted their agreement and applauded while the young Wizards blushed deeper and deeper crimson.

A new-old voice spoke from the door to the common room.

"The Witch is destroyed, and her Witchery annulled by two of Wizardry's finest," said Flarman Flowerstalk.

Chapter Twenty-one

Pfantas Reborn

"MAGISTER!" Myrn and Douglas shouted together. They pulled the Pyromancer into the center of the room and Augurian after him. "How wonderful to see you here!"

"Welcome to Pfantas, Wizardly sirs!" said Featherstone, bowing and shaking their hands by turns. "We are greatly honored!"

"Here is Wong Tscha San," said Caspar to the elder Wizards. "I'm sure you know him or know of him."

"So we do!" cried Flarman, beaming at the Choinese Magician. "By reputation, at least. My very great pleasure, sir!"

"No less than mine, estimable Pyromancer!" said Wong, bowing deeply. "I was able to follow your recent adventures in the matter of the Ice King. I regret deeply that I was unable to render you any assistance at the time."

"Think nothing of it! We understand perfectly," Flarman reassured him. "Hello! You must be Marbleheart, the famous Sea Otter. Well met!"

Marbleheart offered his right front paw and explained his origins in a large, subarctic bay called the Briney.

"Well, Apprentice," said Augurian quietly to Myrn. "You were more than just moral support to Journeyman Douglas, were you?"

"I was of some assistance, I think," said Myrn. "You'll have to ask Douglas. I confess, Magister, that I would have come, at any rate, just to share this adventure with him."

"No one will blame you for that," said Augurian, flashing one of his rare smiles.

"Now, my friends," Flarman was saying, having shaken hands with the entire town council and a quarter of the population of Pfantas, it seemed, "we have come, not just to meet new friends and greet old ones, but also to assess the damages done by the Witches of Coven, and to see them set right as much as magic and goodwill can do."

"Let's begin at once," suggested Augurian.

The three elder Wizards and the Journeyman Pyromancer sat down at the large library table in the center of the common room and the whole story was begun, all over again, from the very first.

The proceedings began with Cribblon, who was the first to call the Coven to the Wizards' attention. Douglas then described his Journeying and Myrn spoke of Finesgold's gift and her flight to Westongue and to Old Kingdom with Pargeot.

Marbleheart was asked a number of questions about what he had done and seen, especially the episode of the barrows on the edge of Last Battlefield.

The Choinese Magician told them of his discovery of Coven and how he had enlisted the assistance of Caspar Marlin to rescue Douglas when he thought he had been made captive by the Witch Queen.

"We were not needed, after all, but it was worth the trip to meet my fellows in Wizardry," Wong ended with another bow.

When all had finished reporting to the hushed crowd and the deeply interested Wizards, Augurian turned to the Journeyman by his side.

"You realize, I am sure, that with Emaldar's destruction beyond recall, all her spells and enchantments are rendered null and void. We'll have no trouble with them, as we do with Frigeon's enchantments."

"I should have been aware of it," murmured Douglas. "It was not a consideration when I went into the mountain to help her. I simply thought she deserved better than to die in those terrible fires. But she would not be saved. I must admit I have no regrets about the outcome. At the same time it doesn't give me any pleasure."

Marbleheart had mentioned the four-leafed clover and Featherstone said that almost everyone in Pfantas now wore one or carried one in a pocket.

"It was the clover that saved your life," Flarman said to Douglas. "As so often happens, the good you did for others provided you your own salvation, when things got too hot."

Douglas shook his head. "I just happened to have the clover up my sleeve, is all."

"Thanks to the Barrow Wights business," put in Marbleheart. "A Man, or an Otter, makes his own luck, as my mama once said to me when I was a kit."

"And all Emaldar's spells were reversed, then?" asked Featherstone. "The enslaved are now free of her spells? And the Witchservers no longer have power?"

"You understand it perfectly. Nor can much evil befall you hereafter, while you have the quadruple clover close to hand. Very quick thinking on your part, young Douglas, I must say," said Wong, nodding his approval.

"Well . . . I used the clover for its powers against all kinds of evil. I admit, I forgot it was great for curing burns and wounds, also, until I needed it sorely."

"So great problems are many times solved," said Augurian.

"Nevertheless," interrupted an older citizen in the crowd, "without a trial and conviction, it will be difficult to settle many of Pfantas's financial and business problems. Where two people claim a single business, because Emaldar enslaved the father, for example, and the son took over . . ."

"That is for the state to determine, I would say," said Flarman.

"I hasten to point out," said Wong, "that there has existed no state in Kingdom for over two hundred years."

"Yes, that's very true," agreed the Pyromancer. "Augurian, what say you?"

"If the people of Pfantas were to form a government, including courts of law, who could say they didn't have jurisdiction to find in such matters. It was similar in the case of the Ice King, you recall."

"Not quite," objected Douglas. "When Frigeon was tried it was before the regularly constituted court of a sovereign state, Waterand Island. Both state and court pre-existed long before Frigeon became a criminal."

"You argue, then," said Wong, leaning forward, "that a

crime committed where there is no state nor a state court, is not a crime?"

Douglas rubbed his chin worriedly, glancing sideways at his Master. Flarman sat back and reached for his pipe.

"You got yourself into this, son," he chuckled, "and you'll have to argue yourself out of it."

"We want to be fair to those Emaldar harmed—many very painfully, even to death," said the Journeyman Wizard. "But . . ."

"But," finished Augurian, "we Wizards have no brief to do more than examine her deeds from a professional standpoint and make our recommendations to the court, whatever it is, and no matter how recently formed. I should think Pfantas's new government, especially as it is based on a previous, wrongfully overthrown government, would suit quite well."

There followed a lengthy and extremely wordy discussion until Flarman threw up his hands and said, "We Wizards have determined the facts of the matter and will make recommendations to the Pfantas Town Council, which in fact pre-existed Emaldar's misdeeds by many centuries, for their future safety and consideration of claims and adjustments."

"You would place the burden on us, then, Sir Wizard," said Featherstone.

"My good, young man," said Flarman, blowing three smoke rings in the manner of Bryarmote the Dwarf, each within the one previous, "that is exactly where it belongs! If you wish to govern yourselves, you must take the responsibilities of governing—and justice is a major responsibility."

"Will you at least recommend how we should proceed?" asked another Pfantasian.

"To a certain small degree. We'll certainly tell you what *can* be done; never what *must* be done. You've already made a good beginning, I see. Emaldar is gone for good and her enchantments are nullified, as far as is historically possible. What remains is your task, citizens. You are, after all, the ones who suffered."

Featherstone and the newly reconstituted town council went into session even though it was very late, in the inn's taproom and didn't reappear until several hours after dawn the next morning.

■   ■   ■

"Now, I have some professional questions," said Douglas, raising his hand. The Wizards and their party gathered about the fire. Nobody yet thought of bed.

"The floor is yours," said Augurian, leaning back to listen.

Said Douglas, "Myrn tells me that she saw six Black Witches fleeing Coventown just before the eruption. They were, she surmises, the other members of the Coven, deserting Emaldar. Where do you think they went?"

"As for why they left," Myrn stated, "I think they sensed the coming explosion of the volcano. Also, perhaps they recognized that Emaldar was about to lose to the combined Wizardry against her. They spoke to that effect as they fled."

"They knew in advance of our success?" asked Marbleheart in surprise. "They foresaw the future?"

"No, not exactly," said the Apprentice Aquamancer. "They suspected that Emaldar had overextended her powers. Am I not right, Magister?"

"Witches are never comfortable sharing their powers, and thus are never willing to accept risk," Augurian affirmed. "When things went smoothly, the Six Sisters allowed Emaldar to use them. When opposition rose, however, they fled. It's as simple as that."

"Captain Pargeot has told us of his one interview with the Witch Queen in the presence of the Six Sisters. They believed they saw uncertainty and confusion on Emaldar's part toward a prisoner who normally would have been slain out of hand," added the Pyromancer. "Emaldar never before had suffered anyone to deceive her as Pargeot and Cribblon had. It foreshadowed the end of their alliance."

Augurian nodded. "Witches are solitary creatures, which is why Covens are so rare. They agreed to lend Emaldar their power, so when she appeared about to lose her own, they merely took theirs back and left at once. I can hardly blame them, speaking from a purely professional standpoint."

"And where do you think they'll go?" repeated Douglas.

"Scatter all over World, most likely. As I say, Witches are lone creatures and prefer to live by themselves, using their magicks for their own benefit, in selfish pleasure and creature comfort. When Men threaten them, often hoping to gain some of their imagined wealth or powers for themselves, any Witch can be dangerous. If everyone left every Witch strictly to herself, each in her hidden place, there would be much less Witch trouble."

"I suggest, however," Douglas pressed on, "that we have these Six Sisters watched. They've seen the multiplication of powers through organization. One or more of them might be tempted to try it again."

"Your suggestion is noted. If all agree, I'll make certain arrangements," said Flarman, making a note on a pad of yellow paper he took from his left sleeve. All agreed at once to Douglas's satisfaction.

"May I address my concerns to you?" asked Pargeot.

"Speak, of course, Captain Pargeot," said Augurian.

"I am the unfortunate man saved from death only by Witch Emaldar's confusion. I have been a total nincompoop throughout this adventure. I beg your pardon, and especially that of the Lady Myrn. She was most kind to me when I was most foolish and, yes, most selfish."

"You are truly forgiven," said Myrn, earnestly. "Despite all, you've been a faithful friend and a useful companion, Pargeot. You have nothing of which to be ashamed."

Pargeot smiled his gratitude and relief.

Chapter Twenty-two

Ending and Beginning

THE Pfantas council returned from the taproom in mid-morning.

"Speaking for Pfantas," said Featherstone, "we know the freed slaves of Coven wait in a cold camp on the edge of the new desolation. A few are strangers to us, but most are friends and families. They all must be helped, housed and fed, restored to their loved ones and to healthy minds and hearts."

"Beyond that," another councillor said, "we have to get to work at once to reestablish trade and business connections with each other and with the rest of Kingdom, in order to put food on our tables."

"And won't the poor ex-slaves need care or medicine?" a woman asked.

"Probably," answered Willow, who had led the slaves out of danger and now spoke for them, young as he was. "Some are quite weak from lack of decent food, but they say a few good meals will bring them back to strength. A few are very ill and they'll need medicines and nursing, I fear, but they're not many."

"In other words," said a housewife who served on the new council, "it's time we stop talking and get to work!"

Pfantas wildly applauded her blunt words.

Said Flarman, late the following afternoon, "The Witch-servers were self-enslaved. I suspect they're scattering, like the Six Sisters, to avoid being punished for their petty and some major crimes."

"As they have no powers of their own, they are relatively harmless," Douglas pointed out. "On their own, they're merely bad eggs. Can we protect all World from all bad characters?"

"Still, they're wretched beings, even without evil magic to incite them," disagreed Augurian. "If the town council will prepare a list of their names and crimes, I'll undertake to publish it to any interested governments."

"Freed slaves will not have an altogether easy time adjusting to freedom," thought Myrn aloud. "In that work, perhaps Pargeot would be the best adviser they could have. He is a trained leader and they'll respect him."

Observed Featherstone, who had remained with his new friends, "I can imagine from my own experience how utterly crushed a slave feels, even after he is freed. The Seacaptain could do a great deal of good if he recognizes how hard it is to rebuild one's sense of worth."

"That's why I suggest him," said Myrn. "He's been down that road himself."

There was so very much to do.

Pargeot found his role after some fits and starts. He bought a ramshackle old brick building on the lowest skirts of Pfantas and opened it as a school. Into it he took Willow and Willow's forlorn scouts, come in from the pinelands after years of dangerous resistance to the Witches.

They were runaway sons and daughters of Pfantas families, rebelled against the cruel Witchservers. They ranged in age between eight and eighteen. Months wandering in the pie forests, eating pine nuts and half-burned squirrel meat, had given them all an insatiable appetite for learning.

The Seacaptain challenged them with firm but fair discipline, set them high standards, and assigned to them hard lessons, both practical and theoretical. When they were not in the classroom, his boys and girls were apt to be found along the riverfront, rebuilding tumbledown docks and piers, or helping the river men patch and clean their long-unused vessels. When the riverboats sailed again at last, Pargeot's students (and Pargeot, himself) went along enthusiastically as crewmen.

"Our goal is to open the river to trade again," said Pargeot one day.

"I've had converse with the Morgen of Long Lake," Augurian told him. "They plead that Pfantas help them stop the filth and wastes of Pfantas and Coventown from pouring into their waters. I urged them to patience. The pollution is fast clearing, now that Coventown is destroyed and Pfantas clean once more. If Pfantas is careful of its wastes, they will help open the lake to shipping from abroad."

"It'll help make Pfantas prosperous once more!" cried Pargeot.

"How will you get cargoes through the rapids and over the falls," inquired Marbleheart, always interested in matters of ships, Seamen, and Sea.

"I don't know, yet" said Augurian. "The Morgen say there are ways and they're far more expert in such matters than even I. A system of locks, perhaps? We'll just have to wait and see."

Chapter Twenty-three

Homeward Bound

THEY were all seated upon the newly painted benches before Onstabula one noontime after lunch when Flarman said, "I think it's time to leave these good people to solve their own problems. We have problems of our own waiting at Wizards' High and on Waterand Island."

"Yes, vacation is over," agreed Augurian, straightening up from a comfortable, uncharacteristic slump. "There are all those unbroken enchantments of Frigeon's to undo. And I have an Apprentice who has been sadly neglecting her studies these past weeks."

"I think I've learned a great deal out here in the field," protested Myrn.

"Much and much more, no doubt," said her Master, "but there are still things that you have to learn from your books and my fascinating lectures."

"I'll be happy to see the High again," thought Douglas aloud. "I've some serious studying to do myself."

"Yes, there is the matter of the Examination," agreed Flarman. "Wong, by the way, has agreed to be the third auditor for your orals, as is required by the Fellowship regulations. You're lucky, m'lad! Without him, it might take considerable time to find a third Master qualified to sit in on your examining board."

"I'm very lucky and grateful, too," replied Douglas, bowing to Wong, who returned the salute gracefully. "And there are other matters . . ."

"Such as a wedding next Midwinter's Day? I think Autumn Equinox might be a good time for your test, Douglas. I don't have any doubt about your passing to Master," said Flarman. "If, that is, you hit the books yourself for a few weeks now."

"Finesgold's Feather Pin is still working well," put in Myrn. "We can use it to return to Dukedom, don't you think?"

"My way is much quicker," said Flarman.

"But I have some people I'd like you to meet on the way," Douglas told him. "And flying by Feather Pin is really very pleasant and will be less wearing on you, Magisters."

"You make it sound as if I am getting old," sighed Flarman. "I won't be two hundred and eighty until next decade. Oh, well, I do enjoy free-flying. The scenery is so much more interesting that way."

They left quietly, without prolonged good-byes to any of their friends in Pfantas, all of whom were working very hard from first light to dusk. The once-dingy and filthy houses now sparkled with new paint, scrubbed bricks, and retiled roofs. The several levels were being recobbled and the connecting stairs leveled and provided with railings, so that no one would stumble and fall when climbing up or down.

At the top of the town the old town hall had been roofed over again. Local artists were busy decorating its interior walls with murals of the events of Douglas's journeying—the centerpiece was a fanciful depiction of the eruption of Blueye.

Everywhere there could be heard sawing, pounding, the squeal of cranes, shouts, singing, and laughter. Gardens, long abandoned to rank weeds, were bringing forth green spearlets of new growth: onions and carrots, tomatoes, radishes, cabbage and lettuce, four kinds of beans, and six kinds of peppers. The afternoon air smelled of late-blooming jasmine and baking bread.

"It must have been one of the loveliest towns in World," sighed Myrn. "It certainly is well on its way to that again."

"Everyone join hands, or you might get left behind," she added, and when Douglas, Marbleheart, Flarman, Caspar, Augurian, and Wong all said they were ready, she said, in a matter-of-fact tone, *"Cumulo Nimbus!"*

The good folk of Pfantas who happened to glance up saw what seemed a strange flock of birds circling their sun-washed, conical hill.

"I must be working too hard," said a middle-aged leather merchant to his son, Featherstone, as they worked side by side resetting stones in a wall. "I could have sworn one of those birds looked just like that Sea Otter friend of the Wizards'!"

"Just your imagination, Papa," grunted Featherstone. "Pry up this corner while I line this stone up."

The Falls Undines were playing jacks on a flat, wet rock beneath Bloody Brook Falls and didn't notice the flock of strange birds when it flew over. Some weeks before they had watched in relief when three former Pfantas constables had finally managed to scale the canyon wall and escape. The Undines were heartily tired of their constant whining and bickering.

"Someone must drive the Goblins from the Great Barrows," said Marbleheart as they flew over Battlefield. "They have no business haunting the burial places of the Last Battle dead of either side."

"You're quite right," said Flarman. "I spoke to Cribblon about it. He should have a new task to do, since he's decided to seek Journeyman Wizardry under my auspices. You and Douglas can give him a hand, but he'll have to do most it on his own."

"Cribblon has the guts and the grit to do even a nasty job like barrow clearing," said Douglas. "Do you realize he crawled up and down that volcano for three years before he'd gathered enough information about Coven to send us that message?"

The Nixie singers saw the flock of Wizards coming from afar and raised a cheerful shout and a glad song as they flew overhead. Douglas and Marbleheart waved and called out greetings.

"Cribblon will be a welcome addition to the Fellowship of Wizards," said Augurian. "What's that ahead?"

"The Forest of Forgetfulness—or Remembrance, if you're a Faerie Friend," answered Marbleheart, proud to be able to tell the mighty Wizards something they didn't already know.

"Oh, good! Augurian, Douglas, Myrn, and I are Faerie friends in good standing. Let's fly right over, to see if we can catch a glimpse of the Great Gateways," said Flarman. "They say it's a truly marvelous sight."

"Not a good idea, without permission!" warned the Otter, but Flarman led them directly over the great forest at a low level. They were immediately intercepted by a squadron of Faerie soldiers mounted on their great, emerald green and ruby red hummingbirds.

"Uh-oh!" squeaked Marbleheart. "Now you've gotten us into trouble, Magister!"

"Hail Master Pyromancer, Marget's foster father!" the leader of the Faeries called out as the troop approached within hearing. "Hail, Wizards all, and Seacaptain and Apprentice and Familiar Otter! Welcome to the Forest of Remembrance!"

"How do they *do* that?" exclaimed Marbleheart. "They knew all our names and about my new position, too!"

"They're Faeries, after all," explained Myrn. "Aren't they handsome, and so magnificently dressed!"

The Riders led them to a landing in a green glade before the splendid, shimmering Great Gateway to Faerie, and invited them to stay the night and be entertained at a changing of the guard before dinner in their Faerie Hall under a low, rounded hill nearby.

"I'll set a Counterclockwise Spell so we won't be here more than this single night," Flarman told the worried Otter. "Enjoy yourself!"

"I intend to!" cried Marbleheart. "What do Faeries eat?"

But Flarman was already deep in conversation with the Rade Captain. News had just come that Queen Marget's time had arrived and she had been delivered of a beautiful Faerie Princeling. She had named him Justin Flowerbender, for he was large as Faerie babes go, the Captain laughed, delighted at the news.

"Heartiest congratulations!" cried the Wizards and their company.

"We're expecting Prince Aedh himself any minute" said the Captain. "You can congratulate him in person. Look! They're emerging from the Gateway just now."

To a soaring fanfare of long golden trumpets and the heart-stirring throb of eight huge, tuned kettledrums, Prince Aedh appeared in the glow of the Gateway, riding a magnificent white charger in baby blue trappings, in honor of his firstborn son, Justin.

The guards at parade shouted in loud, happy voices, "Hail the Prince! Hail the war leader of his people! Hail the father of our next King, Justin Flowerbender!"

"They do like to make a fuss when I come this way," was Aedh's modest but pleased comment as he reined up before the officers and their guests. He dismounted from his snow white destrier and handed his sword and lance to a young squire before he pummeled everyone, except Myrn, on their backs in soldierly greeting. Myrn, he kissed soundly, making her blush brightly.

"How are the Queen and the Princeling?" Douglas asked for them all.

"Very well! Extremely well, both! He'll grow taller even than I, we think, which is very tall for a fairy."

"When can we see him and his royal mother?" asked Myrn, eagerly.

"It's custom for the Queen and her new babe to remain in seclusion for a few weeks after birthing," Aedh told her solemnly. Then he smiled. "We'll come to Wizards' High with Justin on Midwinter for your wedding, you can be sure. Men will first greet Prince Justin Flowerbender then and there. My wife is eager to show him, and to see you all!"

"What an honor!" cried Douglas. Myrn beamed as brightly as the sun, beside herself with pride.

"What are friends for, except to pay honor when honor is due?" asked Aedh. "Unfortunately, I've got to ride on now, dear friends. We go to investigate the damage done by Emaldar and Blueye Mountain. I understand the destruction was widespread and quite awesome!"

"Ah, so it was you who Flarman asked to keep an eye on Pfantas and search out the runaway Six Sisters?" asked Douglas.

"Right you are, Pyromancer! We'll have a report for you by Equinox, be assured. Good-bye for now!"

And he leaped lightly into his saddle and led his Royal Ride into the gathering forest dusk. The jingling and

sparkling of their harness faded quickly in the coming
night.

Finnerty the Savannah Stallion called to his Mares, who
had wandered half a mile off down the grassy banks of Bloody
Brook while he napped under a grandfather willowtree.

"Do come back, ladies and children! You know we've seen
some fearsome creatures fleeing downriver recently, by day
and by night! Something's happened, far upstream, I tell you.
You shouldn't wander too far afield!"

The graceful mares and their frisky foals trotted quickly
back to his side just in time to see the Wizards' party
arrive.

"We just dropped in to say hello and then good-bye,"
explained Douglas after he had introduced the party to the
Savannah Horses and given each Colt a sugar cube he'd
brought from the inn at Pfantas. "We're on our way home
at last."

He told the Horses the outcome of his journeying westward, ending with a lively description of the eruption of the
volcano.

"We were aware of the explosions," said Finnerty with a
nod. "They happen every third or fourth century, according
to our family traditions. From what you say, the people
of Coventown would have been wiped out had you not
come along to save them. They should be grateful to you
for that."

"I hadn't thought of it that way, but you're quite right," said
Myrn. "A lot of people are alive today because of Cribblon,
Marbleheart, and Douglas."

"And a host of others, including the Savannah Horses,"
said Douglas, modestly. He quickly changed the subject.
"Tell us if all has been quiet on your beautiful savannahs."

Finnerty mentioned seeing dark strangers fleeing downriver
in the past weeks.

"Hard to pinpoint, but I know I smelled Witch reek when
they passed," he said, wrinkling his nose distastefully. "Good
riddance, if that's so! We want our sons and daughters to
move safely out into World now. Living here on our
savannahs is peaceful and quiet, but it lacks a sense of

useful purpose, of service, of accomplishment. When you need stout, strong, and intelligent mounts, I hope you all will call upon us."

"Wouldn't they pine for this bright place?" asked Wong. Horses were rare in Choin, and he hoped, he said, to import some one day soon, where they could do great things for his people, especially the artists, who hadn't had anything nearly as beautiful to paint or draw for many a century.

"They'll always return here to rest or recover from injuries," said proud Finnerty. "We don't want them to think our sweet savannahs are all of World there is, you see, although we want them to think of it as home."

"What noble beasts!" exclaimed Wong as they flew east again.

"We'll stop to say hello to the people of Summer Palace," decided Douglas, "and then leave in the morning to reach Westongue by tomorrow's dusk."

"A feast with Delond and dinner with Thornwood!" exclaimed Marbleheart to Flarman. "I call that excellent planning."

"We should be safe at Wizards' High tomorrow before supper," added Douglas to Myrn. "Your Feather Pin is certainly a wonderful way to travel!"

Delond, the former Majordomo of Summer Palace and now Mayor of the slowly reviving city, greeted them with great warmth and a touch of the old formality, too. He eagerly described the renewal projects the Waiters had undertaken—among them, to renovate the huge, rambling, ornate seaside palace itself. They planned to reopen it as a resort hotel.

"Live like a King, dine like royalty, enjoy the service Kings and Queens once enjoyed, and have Sea breezes, clean sand beaches, clear waters, the wildlife of the river and the delta wetlands, too!" Delond was lyric. "I believe we'll attract more guests than we can handle."

"Don't clear away all these magnificent ruins," Myrn urged. "They're ever so romantic! Perhaps you and I can come this way on our wedding trip," she added aside to her husband-to-be.

"What's for lunch?" asked Marbleheart. "To pay for it, we've returned your gondola that we borrowed. Douglas shrunk it to pocket size and carried it along in his knapsack!"

Thornwood was working on papers, alone on the porch of Sea House at dusk, when a V-shaped flight of very odd-looking birds flashed overhead with shouts and cries of "Hello! Hello! Ahoy!" and landed on the strand in front of the house.

"I say!" he exclaimed. "You pick strange ways to come a-calling!"

"Thornwood, old Sea urchin!" shouted Flarman. "I have to admit that flying like a bird has its advantages. One of your ships is just over the horizon. She'll be here by dawn, I would say."

" 'Twas *Donation*!" exclaimed Caspar, who was not all that enthusiastic about flying, himself. "We left her, Wong and I, off the coast of Choin and we've beat her home! Won't my crew be amazed!"

Thornwood ordered a dinner to be prepared and they sat on the porch, enjoying the cool Broad breezes until well after midnight, telling their stories all over again.

"Pargeot worked out a-right?" Thornwood asked Myrn, privately.

"Oh, simply wonderfully!" the Apprentice said. "He'll stay in Old Kay for a long while, to help them put things back together, now that the Coven is destroyed."

"I'll send him word that I approve, although he is a free and independent man, not sworn to me in any way except his personal loyalty," said the Duke of Dukedom. "Knowing his sort, however, he will eventually return to Sea. It is in his blood."

"We understand that," Myrn said. "We Seafaring people."

In early morning Douglas and Myrn walked with Marbleheart down to see the ships in busy Westongue harbor. Stevedores were already hard at work loading and unloading interesting cargoes from all over World. The place was as busy and cheerful as any place Douglas had seen. When a number of Seamen recognized them and asked Myrn what had become of their old shipmate Pargeot, much of their story had to be told once more.

"Pargeot has found a way to atone for losing *Pitchfork* and her crew," Myrn told them with a happy laugh. "He's become a schoolmaster, at least for a while."

"Do you think he'll come back and sail with us again?" asked the young sailors.

"Of course he will," replied Douglas. "Once a Westongue sailor, never happy as anything else."

Flarman rescued them for breakfast, and shortly thereafter they were aloft again, bound for Valley, and home.

Chapter Twenty-four

▰

Home Again

PARTY and Pert led their latest litters across the cobbled courtyard from the cottage to the Wizard's vast, cool underground workshop, enjoying the first really hot morning of summer.

Bronze Owl might have been dozing, if he were made ever to sleep, on his favorite nail in the middle of one of the leaves of the big, double front door to Wizards' High.

The Ladies of the Byre were already contentedly chewing their morning's cud in the shade of one of the very old and twisted willows beside Crooked Brook.

The family of Thatch Mice in the golden reeds over the southwest corner—above Douglas's own room—paused to listen to Blue Teakettle's cheery whistling in her big and sunny kitchen. Easy Chair, in the front parlor, dozed away peacefully, facing the fireplace, cold now that it was summertime.

Brown-and-red hens led a platoon of new chicks in a wide circle to avoid the kittens, just in case, and showed their fluffy, yellow sons and daughters how to prize tiny bugs and bits of flower seeds from between the cobbles.

"I know something nobody else knows!" Blue Teakettle sang. "Move it, you loafers! We'll need five of your best, tastiest white breads before nightfall, believe you me! Grater! Grater! Where have you got to? There's cheese to be grated so I can make a rare feast this evening."

"Huh!" sniffed Bronze Owl, grumpily. "That Teakettle thinks she knows when the Wizards are coming back. Well, she's wrong, I say! I would know first if they approached."

He noisily flipped himself off his nail and flopped with disapproving clatter of his metal wings to the cottage's roof-tree—just in case. He saw nobody coming by the brook or

by the road from either direction. To the north he surveyed
the low hills that separated Valley from the rest of Dukedom,
now a haze of blue-green marked with the time-worn paths
of the upland flocks.

Southward, he peered for a long moment toward the rocky
hills between Valley and pleasant, seaside Wayness.

"Teakettle's wrong," he said aloud to himself.

"Teakettle is seldom if ever wrong," said Flarman Flowerstalk.

Spinning about like a weathercock, Owl confronted the
plump, grinning Fire Wizard, who was floating in midair
not five feet away.

"Blue Teakettle! He's here!" cried the metal bird, all but
falling off the rooftree in surprise. "And Douglas and Myrn
and Augurian and Caspar and a stranger in a gold robe and a
red hat, carrying a lacquered fan. You were right! How *does*
she do it?"

"Old Blue?" asked Flarman, allowing himself to sink slowly
out of sight beneath the eaves. "No telling how she does her
things, is there?"

Owl threw himself over the edge of the roof and dived to
greet the travelers at the door, as was his duty.

"Here is Wong Tscha San, a Choinese Magician from far
south over Sea," said Douglas. "And this is Marbleheart Sea
Otter, my Familiar."

"Familiar? He's not at all familiar to me," said Bronze
Owl, cocking his head to one side with a loud clang.

"That's *Familiar*—with a capital *F*," retorted the Otter.

"Oh!" cried Owl. "*That* kind of Familiar. Well, come on
in. Come in! Come in! I'll introduce you to Black Flame,
Flarman's own Familiar. He can teach you things about
Familiarity that you'll never find in the old Familiar text
books."

Myrn and Douglas drew Wong into the bright kitchen
and sat him at the enormous kitchen table to watch. Blue
Teakettle's lively utensils hustled about to prepare an early,
hearty dinner—and what a show it was!

Slicer and Grater got into a good-natured duel over
counter space, while all the Knives and Cleaver fell in
line to slide, one by one, down Whetstone's hard, smooth

surface, until their edges were sharp enough to cut silk thread.

Sugar Caster bobbed politely to the distinguished visitor and rushed off to sprinkle the tops of a pan of scones that had just popped out of the big Oven, steaming fragrantly and singing prettily in harmony, led by a tall, thin cinnamon stick.

The Silverware proudly trooped out of their drawers and stood at attention in serried ranks, waiting while the snow white, starched Napery performed amazing gymnastics to fold themselves to look like wide-winged doves at each place setting. When they were finished, the Silverware marched triumphantly around the table, setting place after place in a series of precise and highly polished maneuvers.

Laughing and applauding until there were tears in his bright eyes, Wong himself produced a pair of delicately carved ivory Chopsticks. They performed a series of breathtaking aerobatics over the table at his bidding before nestling down next to the forks by the linen Napkins at his place.

Blue Teakettle, clearly intrigued by this strange, new kind of tableware, stood on the edge of the stovetop spouting pinkish steam in awe while the Chopsticks flashed about overhead. When they were settled, she led her kitchen crew in cries of "Bravo! Bravo!" and everything that could, clapped, snapped, or clashed together loudly, making quite a happy din.

Blue Teakettle ordered the dinner bell beside the back door to ring out, and the Wizards and their guests trooped in to take their seats.

"I've heard all manner of men say that there's no place like home," chuckled Wong as Soup Ladle carefully spooned from Tureen a hot, savory ham-and-beans soup. "No one can say it more honestly than you, Flarman."

"Wait 'til you've tried the main course," challenged Flarman, reaching for the Shakers. "Oh, and Blue Teakettle wishes you would teach her the cuisine of Choin, as she is not familiar with it at all."

Wong, delighted, promised to spend lots of time in the kitchen with the plump little housekeeper.

"I've got twelve weeks to cram for my orals," said Douglas that evening. He and Myrn sat on the curb of the Old Well in the lower lawn, overlooking Crooked Brook. Fireflies came to say "welcome home!" and the stars blinked down at them merrily. Somewhere a bullfrog was singing in a deep, bass voice a song about calm waters and clear skies.

"Lucky!" murmured Myrn, very content just to sit leaning against him and watching the stars spin sedately around the tail of the Small Bear. A waning half moon was rising. "I'll be very surprised if I pass to Journeyman before midwinter myself."

Douglas sat up in alarm.

"It won't delay the wedding, I hope?"

"Oh, of course not!" She laughed at his worry. "If I don't pass before then, I'll have to pass *after* and that may delay our housewarming party, love."

"Oh, well, if that's all it will delay." Douglas sighed in relief.

"And I'll have to do my cramming at Waterand, in that case."

Douglas considered that news in silence. There was plenty to do about the Frigeon spells there on Waterand. He would follow his bride to Warm Seas.

Flarman and Black Flame, accompanied by Marbleheart, strolled down the lawn toward them.

"My! I do love this place," exclaimed Flarman. "Every time I come back I always wonder why I ever leave."

"As do I," agreed Douglas, and Myrn nodded, saying, "Waterand is beautiful and most comfortable and I love it, and Flowring Isle is my home and hearth, but of all places in World I've yet been, I like Wizards' High the best."

"You've seen very little of World, my dear girl, to make so sweeping a statement," Douglas snorted.

"Is there so much, really, left to discover?" she teased innocently.

"Yes, there is," the Fire Wizard stated flatly, to her delighted laughter.

"Did you come to speak to Douglas alone?" Myrn asked "If so, too bad, because I'm much too comfortable to move, just now."

"No, stay where you are," said Flarman, taking a seat on the well curbing also. "You should hear what I have to say, also, seeing as you are a member of the Fellowship as well as our family."

"Uh-oh!" Myrn said, sitting up straight. "This sounds ominous!"

"Not really," said the Pyromancer. "I just want to ask that Douglas prepare to go to Serenit in New Land on a small problem our former foe has detected."

"I was planning to do some studying," began Douglas, gathering some heat.

"A Wizard is a terrible thing to waste," quoted Flarman, ignoring the outburst. "There's three months between now and your examination. We must use Douglas well in that time, my dear. You can understand, I'm certain."

He patted Myrn's hand consolingly when she pulled a long face.

"It shouldn't take him long. Just something that Serenit has found that he can't explain, under the melting glacier. He draws on the experience of some centuries as a Wizard himself, and says it should be looked at by someone with full Wizardly powers. His very words, I swear to you."

"I wouldn't mind seeing how Serenit and Clangeon are doing, now that the glacier has melted back some miles," mused the Journeyman. "It shouldn't take long, Apprentice."

"I'll tell you this," said Myrn, firmly, punching her husband-to-be in the ribs. "If you delay our wedding because someone has enchanted a ton of ice cubes in Far North, I'll . . . I'll . . . I'll . . ."

"What?" asked Douglas, innocently.

"I'll take your Familiar away from you!" cried she in mock dudgeon.

"I think I'll take a midnight swim in the brook," said Marbleheart, hastily. "Maybe it's a good time to look up my cousins, the River Otters."

He slid down the grassy bank and splashed happily into the dark water. He was watched with lofty, feline disapproval by the ever-dignified Black Flame, who never got himself wet unless it couldn't be avoided. Black Flame wasn't convinced yet that an Otter, with that species' bubbly sense of fun and love of food, was altogether suitable to be a Wizard's Familiar.

Oh well, Black Flame thought, exchanging a quick glance with his own good Wizard. *Marbleheart'll do just fine. It's the quality of the Wizard that counts, after all . . . not the Familiar.*

"I agree with you," chuckled Flarman Flowerstalk, Pyromancer, and the two young Wizards thought he was agreeing with Myrn's last words.

Actually he was speaking to the big, black tom.

Don Callander, the author of *Pyromancer* and *Aquamancer*, is a native of Minnesota, longtime resident of northern Virginia and Washington, D.C., and now lives with his wife Margaret in Longwood, Florida. Their children, grandchildren, and great-grandchildren live in Virginia, Connecticut and Arkansas.